Bruce Fergusson

"Fergusson is a master . . . In each chapter he gives us more life than most writers can put in a whole book."

Orson Scott Card,
author of *Ender's Game*

"Adds new depth to the adult fantasy scene . . . Fergusson's deftness and creativity override the conventions of the genre. An extraordinary and highly entertaining read"

Booklist

"Bruce Fergusson's *THE MACE OF SOULS* stands with the best of high fantasy."

Robert Adams,
author of the Horseclans series

"Fergusson is an unusually honest fantasist . . . Most fantasy writers explore the higher aspirations of men, glory, honor and truth. Fergusson explores what is shameful and petty as well, and uses the contrast to show how rare those heights can be . . . I'll be watching for more of Fergusson's work."

Megan Lindholm,
author of *Wizard of the Pigeons*

Other Avon Books by
Bruce Fergusson

THE SHADOW OF HIS WINGS

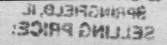

THE MACE OF SOULS

Bruce Fergusson

AVON BOOKS ◆ NEW YORK

AVON BOOKS
A division of
The Hearst Corporation
105 Madison Avenue
New York, New York 10016

FOR PATRICE

BOOK ONE

DRAICA

Chapter One

Fisting the Limbs

As usual the Timberlimb didn't want to pay up. His female stood next to him, holding two babies slightly larger than the rats Falca Breks once kept as pets when he was a boy.

The female keened as Falca walked slowly across the littered room that used to be a wheelwright's shop.

Saphrax stood behind Falca, breathing heavily through his misshapen nose, eyeing a score of Limbs clustered against the far wall. Venar was at the door to the street, just in case. Only last week Falca watched a fister named Tanckar get jumped by a gang of Limb youths when he tried to get money from a scrapemonger, as Falca was now. Whether whole or in the five pieces Falca later dumped into the nearest canal, Tanckar had been a careless ditch-licker, who probably deserved having the head of an eloe stuffed in the mouth of his severed head. But the precedent of his murder was in the back of Falca's mind. The Timberlimbs were getting feisty.

This one cringed, backing away from Falca and the gray light of the empty windows. The Limb shook his mottled green and brown head, his large, dark eyes blinking rapidly at the level of Falca's stomach. He'd been one of Tanckar's marks—Falca was quick to move into new territory. Venar said his name was Teko. Falca didn't care. He'd come up with his own name soon enough.

It was always the same when he fisted money from them. The male had to appear stubborn, defiant, in front of his female, even though it meant getting beaten. The harder you hit them, the easier it was for the male to live with the dishonor of losing scrape money. So said Venar, who had fought against them with the King's Wardens—before he was shoved home from the eastern campaign minus an ear for cowardice. Venar was a worm at best, but still of some value to Falca because he knew a little Limb-tongue.

Falca was only too happy to oblige this Teko with a smattering of respect. He'd done it hundreds of times in the past few years. He slapped Teko with the back of his gloved hand. The Limb went sprawling into a corner of the room, past yipping eloes tied to a post. A rat skittered along the wall, its flimsy refuge of rotting crates and spokes demolished by the Limb's tumble. Saphrax pushed the wailing female away. She stumbled but held fast to her babies, who added their whistlelike crying.

Falca frowned when Teko shook his head again, holding his money-skin to his chest with long, thick fingers. Usually Falca only had to hit once and a mark would surrender the scrape money. His rule: Whatever it took, and no more.

"Hit'm again, Falca," Venar shouted from the door.

"Let me squeeze the maggot. Please?" Saphrax whispered.

"No," Falca said. "You keep your eye on the others."

He strode over to the cowering Teko and lifted him off his feet by grabbing his tattered gamby. With his other hand Falca slapped him again, and not only for his stubbornness. Limbs stunk worse than canal water. He slapped him a third time, and Teko finally dropped the skin pouch. Falca tossed him back and picked up the pouch and emptied it. He threw it at the eloes, who stopped their yapping momentarily to sniff. He put the coins in the safe-keep tied to his belt as he backed away, not taking any chances. Teko never took his dark eyes off Falca, even when his female moved next to him, her babies squealing.

"Let's grab some of his scrape for our trouble," Saphrax urged, in his nasaly voice.

Falca shook his head. "The more we take, the less he has to sell."

"You're just getting soft," Venar cackled.

Falca smacked him in the stomach, doubling him over. "You use too much scrape as it is," he said. "You tell the Limb that if he cooperates better next time, I won't take all of his profits."

Venar did so, after he caught his breath, and hurried after Falca and Saphrax.

"We have one more to go before quitting for the day," Falca said, scanning the street for any sign of trouble.

"Sorelip?" Saphrax asked.

Falca nodded. "Your favorite."

Venar stumbled after them, rubbing his stomach, silently cursing not only Falca's broad back but the rain that had begun to fall.

Sorelip lived—and sold his scrape—from a cracked, tilted landing alongside one of the old, narrow canals that had been forsaken for the newer ones built closer to Cross Keys Island, the royal gut of Draica. The canal was so filled with debris one could almost cross without getting wet. Limbs were collecting vegetation from the other side, hanging from ropes tied to the rusted rings that once secured merchant ships from four of the Six Kingdoms.

The wide promenade paralleling the canal was called Kansvar's Walk, named after a King of Lucidor, but locally known as Twisthead, from the time when a hundred criminals were hung from convenient branches of the copperleaf trees bordering the thoroughfare.

Though the promenade was wide, Falca and the others were almost run over by a carriage that stopped at the stone stairs that led down to Sorelip's landing. A gillie dressed in plum breeches and brown tunic hurried out, rocking the carriage with his bulk, and went down the stairs. Falca leaned against the low wall bordering the street, his annoyance at the arrogance of the carriage driver dissipating at the prospect of a fatter purse to take from Sorelip. The rain had eased off, and that, too, bettered his mood. Someday he'd turn his back on the foul Draican weather, just as his father had done. But for now, there was business to attend to.

While he waited for the buy to conclude, Falca watched Limb children surround the carriage. They were scarcely as tall as the wheel axles. The driver leaned around to jab his whip at them ineffectually, annoyed at their persistence and stink.

The gillie rose on the stairs, glancing at the three men. Saphrax looked hopefully at Falca. "You know he's kept some money his master gave him for the scrape."

Falca nodded.

"It wouldn't be too hard to relieve him of that," Venar added. "Likely the driver would just take off."

"Not this time," Falca said. "Much as I'd like to repay them for almost running us down."

"The odds are good. You always talk about odds. These're good," Saphrax persisted.

"Not good enough. The driver would see us, maybe Sorelip too. He'd be only too glad to inform some constable we haven't paid off. And there's someone else in the carriage, or didn't you two notice the hand parting the window curtain?"

Falca watched the gillie walk past the roan horses, envying the man not his well-fed plumpness but rather the simple pleasure of stepping up into such a handsome carriage and enjoying the ride to some fine town house in Heart Hill or Falconwrist. And having the gates swing wide for you, as if you were the lord. For a moment Falca would have traded all the coins in his safe-keep for half an hour between the wheels of the carriage, savoring its springy ride like he would a woman's. Somewhere, someday, the gates would swing wide for him. . . .

He laughed when a tawny eloe, a hand tall and thrice as long, darted underneath the swell of the carriage's underbelly and nipped the gillie in the ankle.

"That's it, bite the bastard," Venar said, humming his delight. The animal held on to the servant's pant leg with its out-sized arms and scrabbled wildly on the cobblestones with the claws of its four legs. The gillie shrieked and kicked the eloe away. A Limb child called to his pet while others shrilled in squeaky voices at the spectacle of the horse lifting its tail and dropping a glistening pile to the street.

The driver jerked the reins even as the gillie was closing the door to the carriage, which clattered away, pursued by children and more eloes.

Falca grinned as a few of the eloes came back to sniff at the horse's leavings. He wondered if the gillie—or his lord—knew that the scrape they had just bought was little more than the excrement of eloes, cured in a special way known only to Timberlimbs. Even if they did, it probably wouldn't matter. Few people were fastidious about something that made them feel so good. When Venar told him about where the scrape came from, he had the best laugh of his life. It was a few years after the Limbs had begun being herded to Draica from their eastern forests to sweat out the new canal and clear the rubble of the Myrcian siege. The joke was all too perfect, exquisite revenge by the Limbs on those who were driving them from their wilderness homeland so that the King's Regents would have more timber to export and more farmland eventually to tax. The disastrous war with Myrcia had gutted the Treasury. Of course the Timberlimbs ate the scrape, too, though it didn't seem to affect them as much as humans.

Falca didn't care where it came from. It was money in his pocket, enough to keep Solvie and Sincta—his two women—under a roof that didn't leak in the winter rains. So long as he was careful about how much of the scrape he used, he could live comfortably enough until he found *the* Mark. The *one* Mark that every ditch-licker like himself dreamed about, the One that would open gold-flaked gates to the black-on-black livery of *his* gillies, to the carriage on which he'd paint a gloved fist for a crest, to the matched mares he'd stroke every night.

Sorelip was putting out more strips of the dark-red scrape on a low table when Falca and his companions came down the landing steps. Saphrax huffed behind Falca. Venar eyed the scrape. Falca didn't know why Saphrax hated Sorelip so much, though he speculated it was because the brute resented a Limb—a mere Timberlimb—who had managed to cut himself a larger slice of the city's pie than Saphrax ever would.

If Sorelip had a mate, Falca had never seen her. Maybe no female would have him, for Sorelip was as ugly for a Limb as Saphrax was for a human. If Sorelip had a mate, perhaps he kept her in the nearby settlement house that was home to a hundred Limbs and as many eloes. Not having a mate at his place of business spared Sorelip the necessity of appearing resolute when Falca fisted him. Falca liked to save the easiest Limbs for last. It put him in a better mood for Solvie and Sincta later.

Small even for a Limb, Sorelip walked hurriedly to the back of his ramshackle dwelling and returned with an eloe-skin pouch. He held it up almost proudly, chattering something that even Venar couldn't understand. He jangled it like bait. Saphrax grabbed the pouch, and Sorelip nodded vigorously at the brute's belt buckle. Saphrax tossed the pouch to Falca, who poured out the contents into his gloved hand. The Timberlimb backed away toward the canal-side edge of the landing, smiling, pleased with his offering.

Perhaps if Falca hadn't seen the carriage, he might have been satisfied with the silvers and left. But Sorelip undoubtedly had more, and Falca suddenly wanted it, wanted every last coin of the carriage lord. He shook his head as he put the scrape money into his pouch, and gestured with his fingers.

Saphrax and Venar grinned.

Sorelip's smile vanished, and he protested to Venar, whom he knew understood Tongue. "What's he saying?" Falca asked the little man. "Not that I care."

"Something about that being all he made this week. That you're asking for more than what was agreed on in the beginning."

"Tell him he's correct, but that I know his business has been better and I'm raising my cut."

"I can't say all that," Venar whined. "I don't know Tongue *that* good."

"Maybe you'd better learn a few more words if you want to stay with me, Venar," Falca said. "Saphrax, search around that pile of sticks."

As Sorelip continued his squealy protests, Saphrax rummaged through the hovel, overturning a lit brazier whose coals hissed in the canal, flinging aside a few blankets, kicking away three or four pairs of little boots that were obviously Sorelip's vanity. Falca kept his eyes on the Limb, who had his back to the canal, something he'd never done before when being fisted. There was something curious about the way he stood, flapping his long, thick arms wildly but keeping his legs together.

"Nothin'," Saphrax reported with disgust. Sorelip glared at the ruins of his miserable dwelling, then at Saphrax when the brute couldn't see him. Falca shoved the Limb into Saphrax, who pushed him back so hard he almost tumbled into the canal. A thin rope, tied to the rusting dock-ring, trailed over the chipped edge of the landing.

Falca smiled. "Now, Sorelip, you know it's useless to fish this canal. What few there are, not even a Limb would want to eat. Venar, give the rope a pull."

Sorelip had no idea what Falca had said, but his dismay was apparent enough. He stared toward Venar as the runt began hauling on the rope, but Saphrax jerked him back, off his feet, and slapped him hard on his large ear. The Limb yelped.

Venar plopped the fish bucket onto the landing. Brownish water streamed out from tiny holes in the sides. "It's heavy, Falca," Venar said.

"Of course it is. Dump it."

Venar hummed as the coins, mostly silver but a few gold roaks, poured out. Falca walked over and with his foot slid the bucket over the landing. "My, my, what a fish we've caught."

"Let me punish him," Saphrax pleaded, still holding the trembling Limb.

"No, you fixed his hovel, that's enough. That and the fact he knows now he isn't cleverer than I am. Let him go. You and Venar, fill your pouches, mine's full. Leave him something. We can't wipe him out. He's a merchant, after all, with important buyers." Falca laughed.

As Saphrax and Venar kneeled and began putting the coins in their safe-keeps, Falca watched them, making a rough estimate of the haul. Two-thirds of everything they made went to him, which the pair didn't much like of course. But their share was still more than they'd make by themselves, and they also knew that Falca was more generous than other fisters. Falca figured it was worth it. Someday that little extra might buy him a few moments of hesitation, if and when they decided to turn on him. A few moments would be all he'd need.

As the pair finished with the coins, Falca glanced up to the street. Tanckar's mutilation was still on his mind. Sorelip was a loner, unlike most Limbs, but even loners had friends—like Falca himself, if you could count Saphrax and Venar. You could never be too careful with those you thought you knew. Falca's uncle had taught him that lesson early.

Falca let his companions lead the way up the cracked steps, just in case there were Limbs hiding behind the canal wall, ready to jab with a sliver-heart or fling one of those skinny knives they used to cut up eloes for food and hides when they were too old for scrape.

Falca looked back once, expecting to see a forlorn Sorelip wringing his hands over the loss of scrape money. Instead Sorelip was gesturing at the three in a rude manner, which caused Falca to laugh. The little Limb had spunk, like most of his kind. Falca could appreciate that. He didn't care, he had his money and would be back in two weeks for more. Venar, who like a puppy had one eye and his only ear cocked in Falca's direction, saw the gesture when Falca laughed.

"Uh-oh," he drawled.

"What?" Saphrax said, turning. Sorelip dropped his hands.

"The Limb said something about you, Saphrax."

"Yah, what?"

"I didn't get it all, but it was something about fucking with your nose."

Venar glanced at Falca, hoping for a conspirator. Instead, Falca cuffed him. "Never mind," he said to Saphrax. "Let's go count the load."

But Saphrax shouldered past him and broke free of Falca's restraining arm. As he took the steps two at a time, Falca glared at the runt.

"You worm. We don't need this."

"Aww, it's only a little fun. We ain't had none today."

Sorelip was terrified and had no place to run, except the canal, which he was about to jump into when Saphrax caught him. Falca reluctantly decided to let Saphrax have his few blows. The brute was a walking knife, and it was always prudent to dull the edge every now and then. And let Venar watch the beating. Keep the children happy and they'll be more obedient. Sorelip could probably use the lesson too.

But Saphrax didn't stop punching, not even after Sorelip's body hung limply in his grasp.

"That's enough, Saphrax!" Falca shouted.

Saphrax kept pounding the Limb's face.

Falca cursed and ran down the steps and hit the brute in the kidney, hard enough to make him drop the Limb like a doll. Saphrax whirled and gripped Falca's throat, hissing, breathing like a bull, choking off Falca's words. Falca kneed him in the groin and Saphrax loosened his grip, though his fingernails raked Falca's jaw, drawing blood. Falca kneed him again, but the brute only bent over with a groan, then sprang from the crouch with a blow to Falca's temple that momentarily stunned him. Saphrax began kicking the prostrate Limb. Falca reached out to yank him away but grabbed only the safe-keep, which snapped loose from its thong and fell.

Closer now, Falca hit him with all his strength in the ear, and Saphrax grunted in pain, stumbled, kicked the money pouch inadvertently over the landing edge. The coins streamed out. Still reeling from Falca's blow, he tripped over Sorelip and tumbled into the canal.

Above, sitting on the steps, Venar whooped his delight at the fighting. Saphrax thrashed in the murky, rubble-filled water. "Falca!" he sputtered. "I can't swim. Don't leave me! Please!"

Falca stared at the sinking pouch and coins. "You'd kill my best mark, choke me? You stupid ditch-licker! Drown!"

He turned his back on the screaming, sputtering brute and checked Sorelip as he massaged his own throat. The Limb wasn't dead, though his face was a pulpy mess and he'd lost all of his teeth. Falca picked him up like a sack of potatoes and laid him on his pallet. If this Limb died, he'd have to find another mark. And a good one. With the loss of that money, his day of leaving Draica was that much further away. An extra hour, a day, was all it took to walk around a corner, into a knife. . . .

Still tingling with anger and dizzy from Saphrax's blow, Falca walked up the steps to the street, slowly, so that Venar wouldn't bolt like the cur he was. The little man could run faster than a Limb, certainly faster than Falca. He'd done it before. Falca even managed a smile, which he instantly dropped as soon as he snared Venar's arm. "I ought to take your other ear off," he shouted into the runt's face, twisting the good ear. "I lost the pouch to the muck because of you and that idiot down there. You'll get none of this!"

He yanked Venar's safe-keep from his belt, dropped it to the street, grabbed him by breech and tunic, and flung him over the promenade wall. Venar screamed as he twisted in the air and fell into the water with a loud slap.

It made Falca feel only a little better. He was angry at himself for letting Saphrax attack Sorelip. He should have known better. Saphrax was crazy—obedient as a dog on a leash, and then the next minute he might break a man's neck for spilling his ale.

Falca ignored the Limbs—mostly children—who stared from a safe distance across the street, but he kicked at an eloe that came too close. He stuffed Venar's pouch into his belt, walked to the steps, and disgustedly watched Saphrax and Venar struggle toward the landing, using half-sunken timbers and rotting ropes.

He thought, not for the first time, that he might be better off without his lackeys. He resented the fact that he probably needed them, now that the Limbs were asserting themselves more. They came in handy when he needed muscle or stealth—Venar was clever and useful for small places, a quick reiver for Heart Hill thefts. But the pair were becoming harder to control. It had been easy at first, when they had nothing of their own but stories of the prison hulks. Now that they had money in their pockets and a woman to share, they were beginning to forget just who had made that possible. Venar was becoming a nuisance, and Saphrax was unstable, resentful of the authority of a man who was his equal in strength if not size.

Falca hated a man who lost control. He could understand anger and rage. He had enough of that in him. "I could smoke a flank of meat on your skin, Falca," his eldest brother, Ferrex, used to tell him. That made it all the more important to keep in control, else you were so much fish-bait. Like Ferrex was now, a beggar on Furrow Street, the last of the family, who had been careless about his affections for a woman and even more careless about the man she preferred. Every week Falca visited him, putting money in the bowl he held with the stumps of his wrists. Falca had killed the man who'd cut off Ferrex's hands, but he couldn't redeem the ruin of his brother. Nor would he bring him to his lodging. He couldn't abide that. Ferrex was what Falca would become if he stayed one day too long in Draica.

He kept his hand on his hook-hilted dagger as Saphrax and Venar emerged, dripping dirty water and strands of slime from the canal. He wasn't too worried about them. They were coughing and wobbly-legged. But he held the dagger nonetheless, because he could never be sure of Saphrax. It was so tiring to always have to keep things in front of you.

Venar gave him a wide berth as he passed. Saphrax stopped on the steps, wiping mucus from his gruesome nose. His right ear, the one with the earring, was bloody.

"You a Limb-lover or somethin'?" Saphrax said hoarsely.

"It's a business, Saphrax. Yours and mine, especially mine."

"You should've thrown me something. I almost drowned. You should've helped me."

"Shut up with your whining. You would have killed that Limb. That means money out of my pocket—and yours. You should have stopped when I told you to. Next time you do. Understand?"

Saphrax looked away. "I'm sorry, Falca. But I don't like that Limb."

"Do you understand?" Falca repeated.

The brute nodded. "I'm sorry. I won't do it again." He began hitting himself, slowly at first, then harder. It was something he did when Falca was displeased with him, and it annoyed Falca no end. He needed their subservience, but there were limits.

"Stop it, Saphrax."

Saphrax hit himself in the face. And Falca slapped his fist away. "Stop it now. What use are you to me if you pound yourself into a stupor?"

Saphrax stopped and brightened a bit at Falca's words.

"Go on," Falca said, sighing.

They all walked in silence down Twisthead, through puddles

strewn with a few fallen leaves. As usual Falca stayed behind the two, farther behind than usual because they stank to the High Sorrows.

There was a time, after Falca took him from the prison hulks, when the brute would have drowned himself if Falca told him to. Falca loved that feeling: the control, the manipulation, Saphrax's dependence on him. But he would have to give it up. The man was bad for business.

The sun came out momentarily as they turned onto the narrow Skullsroll Street, the unofficial border between the Limb ghetto and Slidetown, where Falca lived with his two women in the loft of an old spice warehouse. The casks of spice were long gone, moved to a newer building farther up the Tears Canal. But the residue of Gebroanan spices—sweet elixith, tart sinnot and ringroot—still permeated the old place, pleasing the sisters and making it a haven from smells of the Limb ghetto. The scent of spices from faraway Gebroan gave easy purchase to Falca's dreams of the time when he'd find the One Mark. Then he would winter in the sun of Gebroan, away from the rain and squalls of Draica, the stink of Limbs, the clumsiness and stupidity of men like Saphrax and Venar, and his own need for such. And maybe he'd run into his father there, who had abandoned his sons so long ago.

Saphrax and Venar lived below him, in a sectioned-off part of the warehouse where the floor timbers weren't rotten. A ladder led up to the loft, and Solvie and Sincta complained often of its loud creaking and the fact that Falca did nothing to fix it. They complained, too, about the two daggers Falca insisted on keeping under the hard pillows. More than once they'd cut themselves on the blades while he made love to them. He would lick the blood from their dark skin and put the daggers back when they threw them from the bed in anger. The sisters were experienced and understood precaution—they carried their own weapons—but they couldn't possibly fathom Falca's determination to survive until he found the One Mark.

Falca and the others kept on along the crowded Skullsroll. It was late enough in the day for tenement cooking vats to add their smoke to the foul reek of curing scrape that filled the neighborhood. On the street the Limb scrapmongers were still selling—to soldiers on leave from the Wardens, to sailors from galleys berthed at the nearby docks, to gillies of Heart Hill nobles and rakes from Falconwrist, to merchants and youths buying persuasion for reluctant girls.

Scrape was officially illegal, but the city's constabulary did nothing to buyers, sellers, or fisters, unless a nobleman was harmed. With an eleven-year-old King more concerned with his toys than his kingdom, little was done to enforce the law. The Regents, who effectively ruled Lucidor in the King's stead, were themselves too busy maneuvering for political power to care.

Falca had already fisted some of the mongers. They nodded at him stiffly and eyed Saphrax and Venar, but if they took pleasure at seeing the men sodden wet, with flecks of muck all over their clothing, they wisely showed nothing.

Within a short while they came to the side street that led to the Tears Canal. Saphrax hurried along, anticipating the evening meal. Venar slowed to observe a stray eloe toying with a cornered rat. Then he noticed a boy and girl coupling in an alley off the side street and came to a full stop. Saphrax, too, looked at the undulating bodies but shook his head and plodded on underneath the flapping laundry strung between tenement walls.

Falca noticed a woman approaching through the crowd on the Skullsroll. Her height—and her golden hair—caught his eye. Instinctively, as if avoiding the glare of a brighter sun, he shifted closer to the shadowy side street, where Venar was still humming at the couple in the alley.

She had a huge split-tail dog on a leash. Half a dozen eloes began yipping at the animal, as if envious of the dog's magnificence. And it was superb. Black, with golden tails, paws, and muzzle. Wherever the woman had gotten it, it wasn't anywhere that Falca had ever lived. Though he'd know sure enough where to sell it. The dog was a fighting dog. Falca had seen a few in the pits of Ditchbank.

The woman walked confidently, not hurriedly or fearfully as one might expect in such a place. Clearly she didn't belong here. Perhaps she seemed so confident because of the dog, obviously her protection. But Falca didn't think that covered it all. Anyway, it was almost too good to be true that she had no armed escort.

Two soldiers, drunk or scraped, hooted at her and tried to block her way. One fished out a handful of coins from a pocket of his blue and green surcoat and offered them to her, leering. The split-tail dog lunged, his teeth snapping at the Warden's hand. The coins scattered to the street as the dog kept straining, snapping, the leash taut, straightening out the woman's arm. For a moment Falca thought she was going to let it loose. By the time she spoke to it, relaxing the animal, the soldiers had fled. The woman shrugged and went on after pointing out the scattered coins to the watching Limbs. They picked them up quickly as birds to seed.

She was close enough to Falca now for him to assess her wide, large eyes. When he saw the necklace of jewels around her throat— she was otherwise dressed quite plainly—he sucked in his breath. He had an urge to dart from cover and rip them off, then run for all he was worth. Here was a year's worth of fisting around the woman's lovely neck.

But though Falca Breks had killed and maimed and stolen, he'd never defaced anything or vandalized. That had always seemed cowardly to him, something Venar would do. Either you killed or hurt someone or stole. Or you didn't. To merely mess something up was just that to Falca—messy. He couldn't abide that. And to take that necklace off such a beauty seemed to him more like vandalism than robbery.

But she was a mark, the most promising mark to come his way that day. He knew instantly he wouldn't be satisfied with merely stealing her dog, profitable as that would be. Any canal-side woman wouldn't have such a necklace, much less disdain picking up the coins from the street. This beauty had more, much more where that necklace came from. She was a fool, a poppy-head. Whatever she was doing here without a bodyguard, Falca was determined to profit from her foolishness. He watched her walk by. He smiled and whistled to Venar.

"Bring Saphrax back here," he said. "Quickly! We have work to do before we eat."

Venar took off at a run.

As Falca watched the woman, noting with satisfaction the length of her bright hair, he removed a glove, wet his fingertips with his tongue, and wiped the blood from his jaw where Saphrax had cut it.

Chapter Two

Amala Damarr

While Venar was getting Saphrax, Falca walked a few steps into the side street, past the twisting alley where the boy and girl were coming out, their clothes mussed and damp. Falca waited until they'd entered the 'Roll, then looked quickly around and stashed his safe-keep behind some rotting timbers and masonry that had slid off the back end of a house, exposing the second-story floor. Not the best of hiding places, Falca thought, but it would have to do for a few hours. He couldn't very well fist the woman in the way he planned with a pouch full of coins jangling at his waist. And he certainly didn't want to give the pouch to Saphrax or especially Venar. The runt wouldn't run off with it, but he'd nick a krael or two, knowing Falca hadn't counted the scrape money yet.

Falca waited impatiently, tonguing the scrape sore in his mouth. It had gotten bigger and more painful in recent weeks, evidence he'd been using too much. He reminded himself to back off.

When he saw Saphrax and Venar coming, splashing through the puddles, he waved them on impatiently. Venar was so excited—perhaps because he felt himself back in Falca's good graces—that he performed a front flip.

Saphrax flicked his earring with a finger. "What've you got for us, Falca?"

Falca was already walking. "I'll tell you on the way. We can't let her get too far ahead."

Venar followed, humming. "Her? No wonder you're in a hurry. She's not as skinny as Sincta, is she?"

"Shut up and listen," Falca said without turning.

The plan was simple enough. Saphrax would accost and distract the woman, Venar would grab the dog. Both would flee, and Falca would suddenly appear, as the outraged bystander, recapture the dog, and give it back to the grateful woman.

"If the reward's not enough," Falca said as they threaded through the crowd along the street, "or if she refuses to give me one, we'll steal the dog farther down the 'Roll. Perhaps we'll steal it anyway. I'll decide later. Then, I'll follow her to her home and see how easy a reive it would be."

"How big's the dog?" Venar asked.

"Big enough. A split-tail."

"Why doesn't Saphrax get the dog if it's so big?"

"Because you're not enough of a distraction, you worm. Don't worry, we'll get some powdered scrape to throw at its snout. It'll be licking your nuggets, if it can find them."

They had to stop at three scrapemongers before they found one who had it in powder. Venar did the asking; Falca took the bag without paying and tossed it to Saphrax.

Falca led the way at a run now, shoving aside people who got in the way. He caught sight of the woman on the hump of Rushes Bridge, not far away at all.

He led the way over the bridge, which spanned Wolf's End Canal, and hurried closer still toward the woman.

"Oh, she's a beauty all right," Venar whispered. "And so's the dog. Too much of a beauty."

"Look, Falca," Saphrax said, huffing his breaths. " She's going to buy scrape."

Falca slowed, watching her stop by two mongers at the corner of the 'Roll and Gullhead Lane. She shook her head at their hawking and the proffered scrape and even talked to them for a few moments after they had resigned themselves to the fact she wasn't going to buy any.

"So she knows Tongue, Venar," Falca said. "Maybe you saw her among the camp-followers in the Rough Bounds?" He added a thought to himself: She could be the wife of a nobleman serving in the Wardens who passed the time learning to speak Tongue from captured Limbs.

Venar shook his head. "I wish I *had* seen her there."

Falca felt more confident about the coming fist. A scrape user would know the streets, could smell a scheme. Still, the woman knew Tongue, which was certainly not a fashion among young women in the wealthier parts of the city. So she had to have some familiarity with the world canal-side. Falca cautioned himself not to underestimate the woman. What *was* she doing here?

"Go on with you both," Falca said to Saphrax and Venar. "I'll be trailing behind. One more thing: She's wearing a necklace. Don't touch that. Just get the dog."

Saphrax nodded. "Maybe some scrape tonight, Falca?"

"Only if you do well."

"I will," Saphrax said. "You can count on me, Falca."

"Of course he'll do well," Venar said, opening up the pouch of powdered scrape to get it ready. "He's got the easy part."

Falca pushed him after Saphrax.

The pair caught up to her just beyond Gullhead Lane. Saphrax bumped into her on the left, away from the leashed split-tail. At the same time Venar threw a handful of scrape at the dog's snout and his snarling jaws. Immediately the animal began to sneeze and hack, shaking his head violently as if he was choking on a bone.

The woman cried out in anger, and Saphrax pushed her to the street, a little too hard, Falca thought, but effective. The dog made a halfhearted lunge at Saphrax, but his hind legs had little spring. The brute slapped the side of his jaw, the dog yelped and landed in a sprawl on the woman.

Venar wrenched the leash loose on a second try from the woman's hand. A dozen people hurried by, ignoring her cries for help. Falca grinned: the better to color his gallant arrival. Venar pulled on the leash, cursing the animal. The dog wanted to stay and defend the woman, but his legs had no strength and he could scarcely bare his teeth at the struggling Venar. The easiest course was to go with the one who was pulling—and he did. The woman screamed out his name—"Shindy" something or other. Falca didn't get the rest because she screamed again as Saphrax pushed her down once more with his boot and her head hit the cobblestones, momentarily dazing her. But she recovered with a quickness that impressed Falca. She whipped out a sliver-heart from a sleeve catch and jabbed it into Saphrax's arm with a ferocious howl. She would have stabbed him again, but he hit her first, enraged. He hesitated, then ripped the necklace from her and fled. Within a few strides he was past Venar.

Falca cursed. He was going to have to be more gallant than he wanted: get the necklace back *and* the dog. He cursed again. The brute and the woman were making this difficult.

She got to her knees, shouting for someone to stop the thieves, when Falca collided with Saphrax, who held up the necklace defiantly. The jewels smeared the streaming blood on his forearm. His stupidity angered Falca even more. A thief wouldn't be showing off his prize to the one who was trying to stop him.

"Give it to me," Falca whispered, seething.

"What? You crazy? Look what the quiver done to me. She hurt me, so I took it."

"Give it! I told you not to take the necklace."

"But Falca, she cut me! And it's worth more than the damned dog."

He didn't have time to argue. The woman was on her feet now, and Venar was already ahead, pulling on the leash but staring at Falca and Saphrax with a mixture of worry and delight that the two big men were at it again.

Falca punched Saphrax hard in the stomach. The brute wasn't expecting it, so the blow was all the more effective. He grunted, almost losing his breath, and dropped the necklace as his hands clutched his belly.

"GO!" Falca hissed into his ear as he bent down to pick up the necklace.

"You should've let me keep it," Saphrax said, turning away to leave. Then he suddenly whirled and kicked Falca in the eye, sending him sprawling on his back. But Falca held on to the necklace.

Saphrax fled, lumbering past Venar, pushing angrily at people who got in his way. Falca staggered to his feet. The street, the gaping pedestrians, Venar, all tilted to one side then the other. Falca, remembering what this had all been about, ran after Venar like a drunken man, the necklace swaying in his fist, and caught up to him near Rushes Bridge. He yanked the leash from Venar's hands.

"Pretty eye you got," Venar cackled. He pointed to the necklace "You want me to take that?"

"Get out of here."

"Don't trust me, eh?" Venar said smiling. "Pretty eye. No fraud there."

Falca shoved him away. At the top of the bridge Venar looked back and laughed as he lifted his leg like a dog, then spun away through the crowd.

Falca yanked the leash in disgust. He was as crazy as they were —for putting up with them. The sooner he got rid of them, the better. First Saphrax, then the runt. He felt around his eye for broken bones with necklace-draped fingers and winced in pain. The only soothing thing was the sweet scent of the woman on the necklace and the fact that his booted eye would be all the proof she'd need of his "heroism," if she had any doubts.

He saw her weaving through the crowd, searching. One good eye was enough for Falca to appraise her beauty, though her face was bruised, her golden hair tangled. She still held the sliver-heart. When she saw Falca with the dog, she hurried on, smiling broadly, though her smile lessened when she noticed Falca's eye.

"These are yours," he said, breathing heavily. Before she took the leash and necklace, she wiped off the sliver-heart on the inside of her sleeve and fastened the catch. First things first, Falca thought. Her fingers trembled only slightly. That impressed him almost as much as her two rings, with jewels the size of a fingernail.

"Thank you," she said, accepting the leash and necklace. "Thank you so very much. I didn't think anyone would help. The necklace could be replaced, but my dog, Shindyvarrek... well, thank you again. Are you all right? Your eye..."

Falca shrugged away her concern. "What about you," he said. "I saw that man give you a hard tumble."

"He gave me two, the bastard. I'm still a little dizzy. I almost got him, though. By Roak's beard he smelled awful!"

Falca had to suppress a laugh. If you only knew, woman. "You were quick with that thing."

"I've practiced with a friend. My dog was a gift from my brother, who worries about my safety. The sliver-heart was a gift to myself, and probably better protection than a dog. Shindyvarrek is really more a companion."

He nodded. So she had some sense behind those green eyes and strong jaw. Her face was generous enough to carry that wide smile. She sucked on a cut lip. And Falca noticed then that she also wore a leechstone on her neck, near the V of her collarbone, only the second one he'd ever seen in his life.

This could be better than I hoped, he thought.

People were pushing by them, some annoyed at the obstacle they were creating. "Let's get out of the way," Falca suggested, "before we get trampled." Having seen enough of her for the moment, he covered his eye with a hand, as much for effect as for the pain, and let her guide him to the side of the 'Roll. It could have been a mistake, because not far away was a Limb scrape monger who had seen him with Saphrax and Venar. The Limb looked a little perplexed, but Falca gave him a stern glance, dropping his hand. He stood between the Limb and the woman, in case the monger wanted to make eye contact with her and forward his suspicions. It wasn't likely, but the woman knew Tongue and Falca didn't, and he had no intention of losing this fist.

The woman knelt down to stroke the dog, who stared glassily at her. He trembled as he licked her face somewhat distractedly.

"A beauty," Falca said softly, staring at the woman's long hair, which almost touched the cobblestones. Her back was straight. Even kneeling and roughed up, she had a gracefulness about her.

"Yes," she said. "Do you suppose he'll be all right?"

"I think so. What did you call him?"

She got up. "Shindyvarrek. *Shindy* for 'storm.' *Varrek* means 'friend' in Timberlimbs' language. I call him Shindy for short."

He was about to ask her where she learned Limb Tongue, but she asked first, "What *did* that little man do to him, to make him so . . . docile?"

Falca hesitated. "Oh, he probably threw some powdered . . . scrape. Do you know what that is?"

She smiled, nodding. "I come this way every day. The mongers should know better by now, but they still offer it to me. Limbs are persistent, but then they have to survive here, don't they, now that we've brought them."

"I suppose they do. Anyway, it's a common enough trick around here, I'm told." Falca winced and gingerly touched his eye.

She looked at him steadily, as if assessing what he'd said. "I'm afraid that eye will completely close soon," she said. "I'm sorry for the trouble."

"I can get an eye patch," Falca said. "I'm just pleased I could help you. . . . I'm sorry, I didn't get your name."

"I didn't tell you. It's Damarr. Amala Damarr. And yours?"

"Falca Breks." He almost gave her another.

"Well . . . Falca. I hope I won't offend you if I give you something for what you did. You could have walked on like all the rest. You might have lost your eye."

"I don't take offense that easily," he said, smiling. There was nothing like a little coin-hunger to make a man seem more honest and straightforward than he was. And he had to let her know he expected something.

"Good," she said. "I'd feel better."

So would I, Falca thought.

"Unfortunately, I don't carry around much money when I'm in this part of the city."

What do you call the necklace and rings? Falca almost asked her.

"But I do have a silver."

She fished for the krael. Falca keened his ears for the sound of more coins. He heard nothing. She was telling the truth, easy enough when the reward was a pittance.

She handed it to him, and he thanked her, graciously enough because he planned to steal her precious Shindy-whatever within fifteen minutes of leaving her.

"Now, that's not nearly enough," she said. "What I'd like you to do is come to my house tomorrow at this time so that I can treat you more fairly. It's the fourth house on the right, just passed Raven's Gate. In front of the fountain and green."

Not Heart Hill, Falca thought, but close enough to smell the perfume in the gutters. You can keep your dog, then. . . .

He shrugged. "If you insist."

"I do. Now, I'd best be off before my brother starts to worry."

He nodded and stroked the dog. "Be careful, citizen Damarr. Sliver-heart or no, in the future you should consider a different way as you go about your business."

"I appreciate your concern, but that can't be helped. I work at a settlement house on Furrow Street, helping the Timberlimbs. I'm afraid this street is the most convenient for me. Usually a friend accompanies me, but he was sick today."

Helping the Limbs! Falca thought. Solvie and Sincta would have a laugh over that.

"Might I suggest one more thing?" he said.

"And what is that?" she replied, a little amused with his concern.

Actually it was nothing of the sort. Falca felt proprietary toward her, as he would any mark he planned to fist more than once. Sooner or later someone else would hit her, and that could only work against his interests.

"Sell your dog," Falca said. "Purchase a cut-ear or mongrel that no one would want to steal."

"I think not. I could never sell Shindy. He's a dear, if not the brightest thing. And my brother would never forgive me if I sold him. He thinks Shindy my sole protection. He can't imagine his twin sister using a sliver-heart." She laughed. "Until tomorrow, then. Tend to that eye, citizen Breks. It's a pity you must enjoy the King's birthday tomorrow with but one to watch the ladies and revelry. Thank you again for your help."

She held out her hand, and Falca took it. "Do you ever take them off?" she asked.

"What was that?"

"Your gloves," she said.

"They keep my hands clean," Falca said, too quickly. "Draica's a dirty place." Inwardly he rebuked himself for his defensiveness. But her boldness surprised him.

"Some parts of the city, yes. I'm sorry, I just have never seen a man wearing gloves in this part, only in Beckon and Falconwrist. I thought it might be that your work requires them."

Falca forced a laugh as he turned away. "Catching reivers, yes."

"Perhaps I might try a pair sometime, then," she said, matching his laugh, and left.

He walked a ways, then stopped to watch her. She was talking solicitously to her wobbly-legged dog. She'd already put the necklace back on.

He decided not to follow her. No need. She wasn't lying to him about her name or address. Falca believed little of what people told him, least of all those who were closest to him. But for some reason he believed this woman. His instincts told him she wasn't lying. She'd been too open, bold, almost welcoming the chance acquaintance.

One eye for the ladies, indeed! When she disappeared in the crowd, he laughed. Here was a mark, a beautiful mark. Not the One, he decided. But still excellent. Her boldness did make him momentarily suspicious, and the comment about his gloves was odd, he had to admit. Falca had never been set up before in his life, but there was always a first time. But no, not her. At worst she thought him an opportunist and, even then, not one offensive enough to deny a reward. Besides, he had nothing she might possibly want. She was the one with jewelry and rings, and an obviously wealthy brother. Could she want something else? Fine, he smiled, feeling a stirring below. He could take a little of that along with the money. That was the easiest way to gain entrance to a house. He'd done it before.

The leechstone she wore told him much. It was actually a parasite, whose carapace was as brilliant and colored as a jewel. The blood of the host was what made the carapace jewellike and no two leechstones were exactly the same, hence their value. They were rare, and only a rich woman could afford one. Once put on, they were hard to remove until the parasite died. The mark that was left eventually healed, but until it did, the redness was considered something of a status symbol.

Solvie claimed to have worn one once, supposedly a gift from a matron in Beckon for whom Solvie had done a "woman's favor." She was probably lying, Falca judged, for he couldn't see even the slightest scar on her neck where the leechstone would have been. Whatever, Solvie loved to be kissed there, and hard, with teeth.

He might enjoy scrape occasionally, but he couldn't imagine attaching a thing like that to his throat, no matter what the vogue. To him—and Solvie was proof enough—it hinted at a private appetite, a willingness to suffer a bit for pleasure.

That would probably be too much to hope for from Amala Damarr, Falca thought, grinning. But he could be like a leechstone himself, using the blood of her obvious pedigree to brighten the sheen of the strongbox of gold roaks and silver kraels he kept under a floorboard in the loft.

As he walked slowly back toward the bridge, he felt like celebrating the success of the day with some scrape, and Roak take his damn mouth sore. He stopped at the monger from whom he'd taken the powdered scrape. The Limb stared at his eye and, perhaps assuming that Falca would be in a foul mood because of it, offered him a small pouch of scrape.

He took it, noting that it would be enough to make Solvie and Sincta happy. The Timberlimb nodded nervously. Falca began walking away, then stopped and tossed the silver krael at the Limb, who was so surprised that he dropped it.

"My first and last charity for you," Falca said. "Compliments of one Amala Damarr."

He took the 'Roll at a leisurely pace, wondering if Saphrax would be at home. Probably. And pouting. He'd apologize to Falca after they had a little talk. As usual. Falca felt in a good enough mood to forgive the brute his mistakes today. After all, the eye had been quite a useful—if painful—prop. So he'd give Saphrax some scrape—no hard feelings. Scrape from a special cache Falca saved for certain occasions.

He smiled. The brute would be dead by morning.

Depending on how it went with the woman, Falca might not need Saphrax's muscle for fisting anymore. He could pick and choose only the best marks. Together with what he could reive from the woman . . . he might be able to leave Draica sooner than he planned.

It would be a favor to put Saphrax out of his misery—before the brute made a mistake more dangerous to Falca than a black eye. Sooner or later it would happen. Anyway, Falca could replace him if he had to. The streets were full of ditch-lickers only too eager to do what you told them, in exchange for easy scrape, maybe a woman, and a dry place to sleep in winter.

He turned onto the sidestreet off the 'Roll and recovered his safekeep. Despite the fiasco with Sorelip and the kick to the eye, it had been a good day and promised to be an even better one tomorrow. As he walked through the shadows, deep with twilight's end, he began to whistle a nonsense ditty: "Rat's Tail, Bang a Nail." He'd learned it from Ferrex, when he was eight years old, the year everything happened, the year his mother died, the year his father left for Gebroan, the year his uncle tried to sell him to the Consort's Guild, where castrated boys were trained for the bloodsnare dens. His uncle made the mistake of telling Falca the price he wanted: two gold roaks and five silver kraels. At the time, Falca didn't know what happened to boys who were sold to the Guild and figured anything was better than having to live with his uncle, whose sobriety was more menacing than his father's drunkeness. Whatever his faults and temper, Barla Breks never beat his sons, but the uncle was violent and cruel.

So at the time, Falca was angered not so much at the attempt to sell him to the Guild but at the price. He was worth at least five roaks, he told his uncle, and then ran away, to the streets.

Chapter Three

The Empty

Rain began to fall more heavily as Falca approached Rushes Bridge, heading for Raven's Gate and Amala Damarr. Anticipating the fouler weather, Falca wore a thick blue wool cape and wide-brimmed caravaner's hat that concealed a small, very thin dagger in the band.

Sincta and Solvie had left the loft before Falca woke up around noon. Their early departure was a remarkable feat considering the night before. Falca had nips on his thigh, chest, and shoulder, but because of the scrape they'd all taken he remembered little of their lovemaking. He still had the typical "cotton-ears" from the scrape and kept seeing a bright glare at the corner of his good eye, which was certainly not the sun. The scrape sore in his mouth hurt even worse.

The sisters were probably making the rounds of the King's Day festivals at Cumber, Cross Keys, and Ringwater Squares, working the drunker nobles and merchants for extra income. Falca didn't care, just so long as they were home by night, available to him if he wanted. Though after last night, all he'd probably want to do is sleep. It wasn't the first time he thought he might be getting a little too old to keep so lively a pair as Solvie and Sincta contented. He definitely had to forgo scrape for a while.

Venar and Vessa had been gone, too, when he got up. They were working the squares in their own way, a pocket here, a purse there. Vessa could also roll her eyes back to their whites, a handy trick for begging. Venar's departure saved Falca the necessity of telling him to disappear. He didn't want the runt along, in case Amala Damarr was on the streets or reveling in Sanksome Square up ahead. Likely she'd be in costume—she could afford one. Falca couldn't have her seeing him with Venar before he recognized her.

Saphrax, of course, wouldn't be enjoying the King's eleventh birthday. He was still on his pallet, stiff as lumber by now, ready to be dumped into the canal when Falca had the vigor to haul away his heavy carcass. He'd apologized and groveled and fussed in his clumsy way over Falca's eye, grateful for Falca's leniency. He had accepted Falca's special scrape like a dog would a bone. Within the hour he rolled off a startled Vessa, groaning in agony.

No one much cared he was dead. Certainly not Vessa—or Venar, who expected to get Saphrax's share of Falca's business. Falca himself felt relieved. His eye was closed now and hurt to the High Sorrows. But he knew very well that it could have been worse. Ditch-lickers like Saphrax, volatile and unstable, were never entirely salvageable, and their usefulness was limited.

Falca came to Rushes Bridge. Below, along the canal, boatmen joked or hawked for customers crossing the bridge. Boats plied the canals, filled with costumed, drunken passengers oblivious to the rain. One man swung around and around a raised bow figurehead, rocking the boat until the boatman pushed him off with his pole, to the merriment of the other passengers.

A few people on the bridge pointed to the south. Falca stopped to watch the fire come alive in the cupped hand of the Colossus that straddled the estuary leading to the harbor. Always the fire was lit for celebrations, and the flames would burn through the night. Everyone on the bridge began to cheer but Falca. What did these sheep suppose they were cheering for? he wondered. They probably expected that the boy King would live a long and prosperous life, helped by wise and selfless Regents, who would guide him to benevolent maturity. No, it was a wonder the boy hadn't already been assassinated by some rival four times his age.

The Colossus represented Roak, who had sent his only daughter Cerere to found the kingdom that later became Lucidor, just as he'd sent his four squabbling sons to begin others, keeping only Myrcia for himself after leading the Sixteen Ships across the Farther Water over eight hundred years before. Roak was huge, given a proud posture, naked except for a scabbard baldric. One hand held aloft a shield, as if to protect the city, and the lower hand cupped the fire, seemingly the only warmth for this rainy, chilly day.

It had taken ninety-six years to build the thing, though it would have been completed earlier if not for the wars with Myrcia and Helveylyn. Falca's grandfather Vlare was a water-carrier during the latter phases of its construction. Or at least that was the explanation he gave for his crippled knees. He had been a mean-spirited, demanding man who'd kept Falca running to and fro with nary a thanks and who spent his last days in a chair on the roof of the Valor Canal tenement, staring at the Colossus, yelling orders like an overseer to the demons of his past.

The day of his grandfather's burial, Falca and his brothers watched his father and Uncle Phalen argue over the last of the money Grandfather Vlare supposedly made working on the Bullhead Canal up north. Barla claimed the money didn't exist; Phalen maintained it did, that Barla was hiding it from him. In the ensuing fight Phalen fell on the lid of the cheap casket, cracking it.

In Falca's view, they built the Colossus too tall. Half the time—today for instance—low clouds obscured Roak's head and shield, making the stone giant seem more a gruesomely wounded apparition than a monument to the mighty progenitor of the Six Kingdoms.

The most vivid memory Falca had of his mother was her contempt for the Colossus. "Don't you be eating that rot about the stone giant coming alive when this flowing gutter of a city is cuffed again by the Myrcians or Helyns. Let the other boys fill their heads with such nonsense. You'll get little help in life, so ask for it only when you've done all you can yourself. It's up to you, Falca; it always will be."

Falca's mother had been a girl from the Isles of Sleat, who Barla had brought to the city. She had black hair, which she never braided or put up. If she was quick to dismiss others' superstitions, she preserved her own. If she was fierce with Falca and her other sons, she was also fierce in her optimism. "You were born in the caul, Falca, and where I come from, that's the best of signs. Your father used a falcata to break it and bring you out, so he named you Falca for the Gebroanan sword that is the best in all the kingdoms. You'll do great things, Falca, wonderful things."

When she explained to him what she meant by being born in the caul, he was too young to understand. And when he was older and understood, his circumstances were such that he didn't believe what she'd said. He'd never seen any Gebroanan sword in their tenement rooms, and when he asked his father, Barla would only say, "It's around somewhere." Falca never found the falcata and assumed Barla had sold it for ale money. He wanted to believe what his mother had said, but he came to think it was a lie. Maybe there had never been a falcata. His brothers never mentioned one. Falca's mother had died before he could ask her what greatness was, and over the years he came to define it himself as surviving long enough to get out of the city that—like her and Barla—he had used but hated.

Of course the Colossus of Roak hadn't come alive during the war. Myrcian catapult barges had knocked off Roak's genitals and sword scabbard. Falca had always been amused by the loss and lack of repair. It seemed indicative of the status of the kingdom, ruled by the boy king. The King's father, Extarr, was killed the day the Gebroanan fleet arrived to break the siege. Falca remembered the day not only for the three orange suns on each of the yellow galley sails. The arrival of the fleet seemed like a gift from Barla, who had left for Gebroan after Falca's mother died. What other son could boast, as he could in a brief and soon discarded moment of fancy, that his father had sent a fleet to save him.

When he finally got to Gebroan himself, the first thing he would do would be to buy a gift, to the memory of his mother: a falcata, the sword some said had made the difference in the vicious fighting that went on for days in Manger Bay and along the isthmus, at the very feet of Roak himself.

Up ahead, at the end of the 'Roll, lay Raven's Gate. The top third of the gate towers had been demolished for stone to build the newer wall on the heights of Falconwrist and Heart Hill. To the left of the gate, Sanksome Square teemed with revelry, despite the rain. Falca walked slowly along the street, savoring the smell of lamb and robie sizzling on scores of braziers under parti-colored tents. The piercing wail and droning of bloodsnares cut the air, dominating the softer melodies of harpists and flina minstrels.

Hundreds of costumed revelers crowded before covered stages, cheering and hooting at acrobats and jugglers. The noise was particularly loud at a wrestling pit ringed by smoking oil cressets. Four men, possibly Gebroanan or Attallissian by the color of their skin, grappled within.

Hawkers shouted everywhere, touting everything from goose wine to a power claimed to be derived from the carapace shed by the fabled Erseiyr. A stoneskin sharpened knives and swords on his arms, charging an ecue a blade.

Children darted down the alleys of the fair, undaunted by the rain, which smeared their facial paint or caused it to run like colored tears. Bigger children pushed away smaller ones for better viewing of the covered exhibits.

There were several new ones, Falca noticed. A man and woman stood frozen in straw-covered ice. A chorus of Attallissian singing snakes slithered around the flimsily covered bodies of three bored-looking women who seemed deaf to their screeching monotone. There were two Skarrian stalkers this year, chained to posts in temporary wooden pits, and a handsome tender sold dead rats—live ones cost extra—to those who wanted to feed the beasts. He used his spear to prompt the stalkers to lift their hairy legs in a parody of dance.

Children scampered through a mushroom castle that rose high above adjacent cages of albino flenx with pink eyes and white horns. Taunting the snarling predators was a midget riding a giant land-moth from the Skarrian rain forests. Around and around the midget went, hawking rides to children, who begged their parents for the half-krael.

Nearer to Raven's Gate, drivers chatted under makeshift awnings stretched between their parked carriages, waiting for their patrons to weary of merriment in the rain, which dripped from the manes of the horses.

Rain streamed over the brow of Falca's hat. One celebrant in particular caught his eye, because he wore only a tunic and nothing else. Whatever he'd been taking—wine, scorchbelly, or scrape—must have fortified him against the wet chill off the bay. He walked listlessly ahead of Falca on the 'Roll, causing a few heads to turn. He left the street walking as if in a daze, like a sleepwalker. Falca paused, curious, and watched the man weave a few yards down one of the lanes between the festival vendor tents.

As people passed him by, laughing, gripping the necks of wine flagons, he squatted and defecated, to the disgust of the nearest vendor. No sooner had the man stood, than someone in an Erseiyr costume shoved him angrily. The man fell, cut his face. He got up again, smeared the blood on his hand and licked it. He kneeled down and swept his other hand over the wet stone of the square and licked his fingers. He stood, dissatisfied. He wandered a few yards, knocking into someone in a boar's-head mask who was drinking from a flagon.

The half-naked man grabbed the flagon and began drinking himself, the liquid spilling down his sodden tunic. The angry reveler yanked it from his lips and shoved hard enough to make him fall. Then he kicked at the thirsty thief until pulled away by companions.

The man got up and wandered back to the 'Roll, ahead of Falca, away from the sound and smells and merriment that had so obviously lured him and abandoned him, like a memory of something he couldn't quite recall. The man rubbed his forehead, and Falca saw the mark.

Now Falca had no doubt the thirsty man was an empty, as they were called, whose cache of life had been stolen by one of the Spirit-Lifters. Falca had never seen a Lifter acolyte and didn't know how the cult performed their abomination, but he was seeing more and more empties every day. Three days before, he'd watched one walk right into a canal. He knew it was an empty because when the body was fished out, it had the mark on its forehead, just as this one did.

It was the ultimate fist, for what purpose Falca didn't care to know. But it was an abomination. You might rob or hurt a man to get something you wanted, or kill to rid yourself of a problem, as he had done with Saphrax. But to . . . drain someone like that, leaving him with only the need to sleep, eat, drink, and defecate, angered Falca and frightened him. When his time came, it would probably be a knife in the back. And though Falca was determined to get out before that happened, he knew the knife could come any moment. He wanted his killer to be good, to be quick, and he wanted the knife keen and deep. He despised and feared hesitation, a dull edge, a bungled attempt. Yet to have your spirit bled away was a walking death and chilled him.

The Spirit-Lifters, whoever they were, had stabbed that empty a thousand times, and still the poor scut was walking under the rain-slick stone of Raven's Gate.

Falca went on, slowly, because he and the man were heading toward Raven's Gate, and the word canal-side was that if you passed an empty, he would take from you what had been stolen from him. It was probably the stupidest of superstitions, Falca admitted, like the Colossus coming to life, but the empties were a new enough phenomenon in Draica to make him cautious anyway.

Falca was glad to lose sight of him as the 'Roll narrowed through the congested gate, where people sheltered themselves from the weather and drank from crocks of ale. Beyond the archway, he breathed deeply of a cleaner air. Even the rain seemed to fall more softly.

Two-story houses surrounded an irregular square, whose center-piece was a patch of brick-edged green, wardened by three copperleaf trees that had shed their summer bounty. At the edge of the green a circular pool boasted a statue of a girl, who held up the hem of her long skirt with one hand. In the crook of her other arm she held a jug, whose spout poured water into the pool.

The 'Roll curved up the hill, Heart Hill. Carriages, pairs, and a few swaying phaetons rattled up and down the avenue, past evenly spaced lampposts and decorative iron railings of town houses. Each was separate now, unlike below, and the distance between them increased, as did the greenery and trees around them. At the top of Heart Hill the brow of the city wall stretched from the escarpment nearest the harbor to the Beckon heights and Falconwrist, where it dipped again to the northern marshes, the last vestige of what the city once had been.

Falca counted the houses from the Gate. He couldn't read a lick and wouldn't recognize his name on piece of paper, but he could count. The facade of Amala Damarr's house was white brick, with light blue trim around diamond-paned windows. A balcony of delicate iron filigree fronted two second-story windows.

He walked quickly to the brick steps leading up to the dark blue door—and immediately thought he must have the wrong house. The door knocker was a bronze phallus, the last thing he expected to see gracing the portal of someone like Amala Damarr. Then again, what did he know of her? She could be a courtesan, for all he knew, her story a plaything. If not, he had to tip his hat at her sense of humor. It was also a little foolish. The knocker was obviously Gebroanan—the three balls underneath gave that away, the legendary symbol of Custennin's fertility. Such door-dogs might be the common fashion in Gebroan. In Draica they were still enough of an oddity to raise eyebrows.

He smiled. Whoever this woman was, she put herself out there, didn't she? He rapped the knocker three times. As he waited, he heard a sound behind him, turned to see the empty drinking from the pool. One hand gripped the bare stone leg of the girl.

The door opened with a gush of warmth. Falca half-expected a servant to answer. It was the woman. "Come inside . . ." she began, wanting to say his name. But she'd forgotten it. "Let's get you out of the rain."

Falca nodded as she closed the door behind him. The oak-paneled antechamber smelled of woodsmoke, wet fur, and Amala Damarr.

"How is your eye—no," she winced, "I can see how it is."

"You?"

"I woke up stiff this morning, but that's to be expected. The cuts and bruises will take a few days."

"I'm sure the cut you gave your attacker will take a while longer," Falca said, thinking: She looks uncomfortable.

"Perhaps. Did you enjoy the festivals anyway?"

"There were enough people without me."

"I stayed away too," Amala Damarr said. "My brother didn't. Will you wait here? I'll get you what I promised."

Falca watched her walk the dozen steps to a larger room, in which he could see a painting: a pastoral of a frozen lake with skaters on it and mountains in the backround.

He heard her talking to a man. When their voices rose to an argument, he went far enough to see them standing before the hearth fire. The woman had her back to Falca. An animal costume lay on a gold velvet divan. The tail draped down over the edge, almost touching the forepaws of the woman's dog. For some reason the discarded costume made Falca think of the empty outside.

So heatedly were the pair arguing that they didn't notice Falca, but the dog growled from under the divan.

"Shindy, hush," the woman said. "Two's enough."

"He's only doing his watch. It's why I got him for you," the man said. Then he noticed Falca standing in the room. "I believe my sister asked you to remain by the door."

Amala turned. Falca apologized only because she seemed a trifle annoyed. "This is my brother, Alatheus," she said.

He was more than her brother. As handsome as Amala was beautiful, he looked like her twin, with the same golden hair, though darker eyes. Falca nodded at Alatheus, assessing his shoulders. He was a large, powerful-looking man who filled out the black tunic and brown breeches. His large hands held a leather pouch of coins. He had a huge ring on one of his fingers. He wasn't smiling.

"So this is the reiver who wants a reward? What's his name, Amala?"

When she looked away, annoyed with both herself for not remembering and her brother for asking, Falca quickly told them. Alatheus shook his head in disgust. "You want to give the man money and you don't even know his name."

"Alatheus, that's beside the point."

"I'm sorry to have caused you both trouble," Falca said. "But it's really a simple matter only of your sister, citizen, offering me a reward and me accepting."

"My sister doesn't know canal-side as well as you," Alatheus said, glancing at his gloves, his scar, with distaste.

"Perhaps not," Falca said. "Though she did well enough to defend herself."

"Alatheus," Amala Damarr said, "I'll not argue with you anymore. The man didn't come to hear a family squabble. Give him the money I promised him."

"It's not *your* money to give, Amala. It's our money, and I say the man set you up."

"Oh, twist it off, Alatheus!" Amala said, suddenly angry. "I've not hid under a blanket while you were playing soldier in the Rough Bounds."

Falca coughed, covering surprise at the woman. He bowed just enough toward Alatheus so that water from his hat dripped. "Well now," he said. "I probably do know canal-side better than your sister, citizen, which is why your dog—her dog—is now lying under the divan growling at me. If I'd wanted to rob your sister, I could have found ways to do it without almost losing my eye."

He took off his hat, so Alatheus could better view the purple, puffy slit.

"There are men who would suffer greater indignities for a glove full of coins," Alatheus said.

"Maybe so, but this indignity hurts to the High Sorrows."

Alatheus snorted and tossed the pouch onto the divan, hitting the head of the costume animal. Keeping an eye on Amala and not Falca, he reached to the burlbright mantel, where scabbard and baldric hung on a peg near the end. It was a Warden's sword. Falca recognized the oak-tree quillons from one he stole off a drunk Warden once. Brandishing the sword, Alatheus knocked one of the colored wooden jars and carved figurines off the mantelpiece.

"Alatheus!" Amala said. "Put that away! You're going too far with this."

The throwing knife in Falca's right boot tempted him for a moment. But all was not yet lost, and he calmed the urge. Beyond that, he felt a curiously strong desire not to show his true colors to Amala Damarr, not to prove her wrong and her pigheaded brother right. And he couldn't very well wound or kill the man and rob the house without dealing roughly with her. Which he was reluctant to do quite yet. He couldn't remember ever being in so strange but amusing a position.

He sighed in resignation and even bowed stiffly to Amala. "I could be a fool as well," he said, "but one is enough for the moment. I'll be going."

"Get out of here," Alatheus said.

Falca flushed. Really, the brother should be taught a lesson one of these days. He hesitated, betting that Alatheus wouldn't stop his sister if she tried to storm past him and get the pouch. He was right about Amala and wrong about Alatheus.

Amala stopped at the edge of the sword blocking her way past the table. She stared in disbelief.

The man, Falca thought, had the anger to survive on the streets, though he was acting more like a jealous lover than a brother—someone who saw rivals in winking errand boys. More was going on here than a dispute over a pouch of coins. With any luck, Falca figured, he would be able to exploit it. The key was staying on terms with the woman.

"Amala," he said, using her name for the first time, "I think your brother *has* been in the Rough Bounds too long, killing Limbs." The last was a deft stroke, he thought as he turned and walked away. He'd remembered she said she worked at the Timberlimb settlement house. At the door he heard her say, furious, "You're crazy, do you know that? Crazy. What's come over you? You're an embarrassment. The man . . . Falca Breks, did me a turn and wanted a little money for his trouble. So what? He *could* have lost his eye."

"Amala," Alatheus said wearily. "I'm sorry. It's my leg and I'm tired. But the man was a fraud. He oozed it. I wouldn't have cared if he was blind and without arms. I'm only protecting you, you know that."

"Yes, and it's enough to choke on sometimes," Falca heard her say. "You never change, Alatheus. When will you understand I don't need yours or father's or anyone else's protection. Why do you think I moved down here while you were away?"

"So you could tend the poor Limbs and get paid nothing for it? I pay your bills, and for Sippio, and make your charity possible, and don't you forget it. I allow you to indulge your little mercies, now that father has cut you off. If he found out, he would have my commission. And don't talk to me about embarrassment. If you keep this up with the Limbs, who are no better than animals, father and mother are bound to find out. I don't care what they think, but *their* embarrassment would be such that they would send some ditch-lickers very much like this Breks to haul you away, send you to a school to force the finish and sheen on you that you so very much want to avoid. So why don't you quit this nonsense, and we can find a place in a better part of town."

Better? Falca thought, raising an eyebrow. It's not bad at all. The last thing he heard as he opened the door was Amala saying, in a voice as chilly as the weather, "I won't give it up. *You* give it up. They're not animals, Alatheus. And tending them is better than killing them."

Falca closed the door and walked down the steps, full of this family if not reward money. He put on his hat and gathered in his cloak. He turned to look at the house, his eyes moving up to the balcony and windows. No, he thought, better to go through the front door while she was tending to the poor Limbs during the day. The lock was nothing. He or Venar could pick it in moments. He really should have given her another name. They'd come looking for him, perhaps, but Draica was a large city, and they would probably weary of the search. Rich people usually did. If they didn't, he could pay off the few constables who knew where to look for him. And maybe Amala Damarr would prefer merely to replace what was stolen or would be too embarrassed to enlist her brother or father in the search. She seemed strong-minded enough to not like being proved wrong.

He bent into the slanting rain, heading for Raven's Gate. It was a pity—almost—that she'd have to lose the dog, too, and whatever jewelry she was wearing when he fisted her on the 'Roll. But he had come for his money and had left empty. She'd have an escort—this Sippio?—but he could be dealt with. Falca could hire a replacement for Saphrax for the day.

It was more a pity he'd never find out which window behind the balcony was her bedchamber. The Gebroanan door-dog was a lick to his ear. Amala Damarr hinted at sunlight after a storm. A shame.

He heard her running steps before she called out to him. She wore nothing else for the rain besides the red sark. Her golden hair darkened with the wet.

"Here," she said, defiantly, handing Falca the pouch of money, wiping rain from her chin. "I keep my promises. I apologize for my behavior and my brother's. The wound he suffered in the Rough Bounds was acting up—or at least the ignominy of the circumstances anyway. He was annoyed I wouldn't dress for the festival as we did before he went away. He can't understand yet that I don't care to celebrate the birthday of a King who's letting the killing of Timberlimbs—never mind, it's not your problem."

Falca shrugged. "I suppose your brother has a right to his suspicions."

"Not to the point of drawing a sword in my home. Again, I'm sorry. I'm surprised I caught you. You walk slowly and act quickly."

Falca smiled, thinking, I walked slowly because I was thinking of what to take from you and how. "Thank you," he said. "I'll remember that." He felt foolish because the remark did please him.

"I'd better get back before I'm chilled to the bone." She started to go, but Falca said, "Wait."

He unclasped his cloak and handed it to her. "Protection," he said. "If you want it."

"You heard."

"You were talking loudly."

"Do you always leave strange houses so slowly?"

"That depends on the house."

"Well," she said, "It's not that far back. Thank you anyway."

"That's not why I gave it to you. May I come to pick it up in two days?"

She decided quickly. Falca preferred to think it not because of the rain and chill. "Yes," she said. "Not here. Furrow Street. The settlement house. Remember?"

He nodded, and she left with his cloak.

It was worth a good soaking, he decided as he walked away. It would probably annoy the brother—not a little revenge for drawing a sword on him. He turned to watch her. He wasn't much surprised to see she hadn't put on the cloak. He hefted the money she gave him. . . .

She neared the steps to her home when she noticed something in the trees or fountain of the green. She flung the cloak over her shoulder and dashed over to see. Under the shelter of Raven's Gate,

Falca watched her struggle to lift the body of the empty from the fountain. He sidled to the gate wall, knowing she would look in his direction for help, he being the nearest. She did. For a moment he thought of helping her. No, he didn't want to spend the next few hours taking the corpse of an empty to the crematorium. No profit in that. She might not be superstitious about handling an empty, but he was. Of course, she wouldn't know the poor bastard was one, now that he thought about it, unless she knew about the forehead mark.

He was also curious to see what Amala Damarr would do, alone in the rain.

She doubled her efforts, got into the fountain, and lifted, pushed the empty over the side. Quickly she got out, streaming water. Falca shivered. It must be so cold. She turned him over, bent down, and put her face to his chest. Then she draped Falca's cloak over the empty, as useless a gesture as Falca had seen in a long while. She was a strong woman, though; the empty had been a big man.

She ran to the house, and when Alatheus appeared—no doubt concerned about her tardy return in the foul weather—she pointed to the fountain. Together, followed by the dog, they went over.

Falca left, wondering what it was like having a thirst so great it could kill you. Wondering, too, about the brother and sister, a curious pair. Arguing so, yet together now in the rain.

The cloak was a pity. Falca had been fond of it, one of the few things he had bought and not stolen. He couldn't wear it again, of course, not after it had been used to shroud an empty. After he got it back from Amala Damarr, he might give it to his brother. Better yet, Venar. As a blanket, since it wouldn't fit the runt. Already he was complaining about the cold, even though the full misery of a Draican winter hadn't arrived yet.

Chapter Four

Saphrax

He was supposed to be dead, but he heard them talking, behind his back, there by the canal's edge. He opened his eyes for a moment, all he could manage. His face was so close to the bronze ship stanchion, he could have stuck his tongue out and licked its pitted metal.

It had taken three of them to drag him from the lodgings in the warehouse across Gangers Street. That had roused Saphrax, finally, from the fool's death.

"You finally done me the favor," Vessa was saying. "I told you more than once—and you could hear it plain enough at nights over the sisters' squealing—that the brute had more fist than prick. You never done nothing about him hitting me until now."

"And I told *you* more than once that you could leave if it got bad." Falca's voice.

"She was waiting for you to bring her loftside for a little touch, Falca," Venar cackled, humming. "Hoping you'd tire of the sisters."

"Shut up, runt," Vessa snapped. "You better not expect to get more now that the bastard's gone."

"Can I push him in now, Falca?" Venar asked.

"Are you sure dead is safe enough for you? Go ahead, do it if you can."

Saphrax wanted to scream a protest, but he seemed encased in stone, hot stone that burned him, every part of his body, even as it

45

smothered him. He couldn't have opened his eyes again even if he wanted. He almost yearned for the fetid water below, to quench the fire that should have consumed him by now.

He felt ineffectual proddings. "Here, runt, you need help, like you always do." Vessa.

"Hurry up, you two. He's not worth the bribe I'd have to pay if we were caught feeding the canal."

"You're so impatient, Falca, put your boot to his back," Vessa said. "Or did Solvie and Sincta wring you out too much on King's Day? They should be here anyway. You let'm run too loose, Falca."

"Just push, Vessa."

Then Saphrax was falling. He felt the impact, then the sinking. He felt so heavy, he should have kept sinking, but he rose, almost against his will, for he liked this cold, suffocating smothering. When his head broke the surface, he opened his stinging eyes.

They were gone, or at least out of sight over the edge of the high canal wall. They hadn't even stayed to make sure. It was just like before, Falca abandoning him. Saphrax's sudden anger saved his life. If he had been on land, he would have torn the warehouse apart to get to Falca. He thrashed wildly in the water, attacking it, in an effort to reach the nearest landing. He slipped under three times and swallowed mouthfuls. His fist finally smashed the gunnel of a boat left to rot at the landing. By the time he pulled himself over the stone slab, he had expended his rage in coughing seizures that threatened to burst his head. He could crawl only a few yards toward the steps to the street above before blacking out.

He woke sometime at night, in a pool of water. The night was clear. The moons lay twin paths across the canal. The lights in the houses and tenements on the other side were stars, swollen with sounds of merriment painful for Saphrax to hear. His head throbbed. His face was as tight as a drum skin. He crawled up the steps and halfway across the rough bricks of Gangers Street. On his feet, wobbly-legged, he staggered over to the warehouse and leaned against the wide, barred doors. Braced, he listened to the passing of men fresh from a drunk at the Baling Hook down the street. They were singing a song, but he couldn't hear the words, no matter how hard he tried.

The entrance to the warehouse was on the north side, off an alley. Saphrax stumbled to the south end, where no one ever went. He knew he was too weak to confront Falca. He tried a fist and could keep his hand clenched for only a few seconds. Not enough. An easy mark for Falca—who was so strong, his muscles so smooth, they seemed almost polished. Saphrax had stared at them in the hot summers, comparing them to his own massive, but lumpy ones. His envy was assuaged only by the fact that Falca sweated and he didn't. Which didn't seem right because Falca was always in control. Of everything. Everybody.

And he was quick, too quick for a big man. No, Saphrax couldn't face Falca now. He thought of hiding somewhere else. But where to go? He was prey here, but also anyplace else he might fall. At least here he would be close to Falca when the time came. The time for what? Killing. Yes. When he had the strength.

In the darkness he stumbled among crates and rotting coils of rope, making noise as he fashioned a nest. Even if they heard, they would think it the noise of prowling canal cats. He tripped over a low stack of discarded timber, slick with decay, and fell hard. He stayed there, on his back, staring up at the light from Falca's loft.

Falca hadn't seen Vessa take away half the special scrape, fully half of what Falca had given him, and drop it down a crack in the floorboards. Infuriated, Saphrax had tried to hit her, but the bad scrape already had him. Vessa hadn't done it out of mercy. She simply knew that when he took too much, he beat her. The slut saved my life, Saphrax thought, though if she'd known the scrape was bad, she'd have stuffed every shred of it down my throat.

Lucky for him that Falca didn't check back to make sure of the thing. Then, too, he was eager to get on with that woman, probably, the one who had jabbed the sliver-heart into his arm. It still hurt. Saphrax promised himself he'd take care of Falca, Vessa, and the worm too. He was thinking of just what he'd do to them when he lapsed into unconsciousness.

He woke up the next morning, cold and stiff but well enough to do something about the hunger gnawing in his belly. He took off to the south, ranging as far as the Gallow's Market, close by the turreted quays of Catch-All. He took advantage of the distraction of a fight to steal a loaf of black bread and a fistful of soft carrots.

He came back at night to his place at the rag-end of the warehouse. He needed to be close, he told himself, in order to sieze the best opportunity for killing them. He'd wait till later, then grab a length of wood for his weapon. They had to be asleep.

He waited. The light went out in Falca's loft with a giggle. Solvie. He knew the sound. He listened to him make love first to her, then Sincta, who got impatient with the lack of attention. She was the more demanding, and Falca usually saved her for last. Saphrax knew their sounds all right, if not Falca's, who didn't make much noise when he rutted. Saphrax loved to listen. If Falca's best sense was his seeing, his eyes, he had the hearing. More than once his ears had saved Falca's life when they worked at night. Saphrax flicked his earing with a finger.

After a while it was quiet in the loft, and Saphrax heard Venar's whining coming through the warehouse wall. A begging, then anger at Vessa's shrill refusals, her contempt.

He was so close, with only the thickness of rotting timbers between himself and what he'd known—the best years, all in all, of his life. Falca had taken care of him, and he had taken care of Falca. They had their bad moments, sure, but so did everyone.

He felt like a Murkman. One of the prisoners on the hulk had claimed to be one and told him what it felt like, and never mind the Murkmen had all been killed years ago. "Oh, no," the man told him once. "I ain't held by any hulk walls, 'cause I ain't alive, an' I could get up right now and walk past the turnkeys anytime I damn well please, without so much as causin' them to itch. They can't see me. I'm a Murkman."

"Then how come *I* can see you?" Saphrax had asked.

"Well, maybe yer one of us, too," the wretch said.

And he tried to escape not long after, only to be bludgeoned to death by the guards, tossed overboard, to drift into the reeds as food for the marshfangs.

Saphrax wondered how long *he* would last after he killed Falca. He had nothing now. Falca had taken him in after he spent his five years in the hulk, given him everything, then taken it away. And for what? A lost purse of coins, a boot to the eye. He was tough all right. If he'd been on the hulk, he'd have wound up sailing it away, to Gebroan, where he said he wanted to go. He'd been drunk when he'd confided in Saphrax, the only time ever. Saphrax hadn't forgotten, and when he mentioned it after, Falca got furious, cuffed him good.

The line between having it, and not, was as thick as your fingernail, Saphrax decided. Thick as the width of the warehouse walls.

Saphrax could hear them all talking and rutting, could smell what they'd left in the cooking pot.

He thought, What am I trying to hear? Falca to say something about me, that I wasn't such a bad ditchie, that he wished he hadn't killed me? And what would I do then, show my face? With my luck, he wouldn't see me. I'd stand in front of Falca's face, like that fool's Murkman, with the stink of the canal on me, and Falca wouldn't see nothing, smell nothing. And why? Because I am nothing. I deserve what he did to me. I messed him up, and Falca can't stand that. He shouldn't have done what he did, but I asked for it, didn't I?

He wondered if Falca would take him back, maybe amused or awed—no, Falca was never awed at nothing—that he came back from the dead. Vessa wouldn't tell about the scrape for fear of what Falca might do to her. Maybe if he promised not to mess up again, he'd do it, Saphrax thought, suddenly excited. Just as quickly he got angry. Why should he go back and grovel like a dog? It was Falca who deserted him, tried to kill him.

Saphrax flicked his earring furiously. While on the hulk, he'd made it for himself, out of wire and nails he pried loose from the bulkhead. It was supposed to be a bird, an iron bird, and it dangled three inches or so from the earlobe Saphrax had pierced himself with a nail. The lobe had gotten infected, and he'd lanced it so many times, it never did heal right. He was proud of the earring, his best and only possession now, and he believed it was a talisman that helped him survive where others died, until Falca got him. His habit of flicking it annoyed Falca no end. Saphrax knew it made him appear stupid, but sometimes it was useful to appear stupid, and he did it deliberately as much as habitually. He reasoned that people would be all the more surprised when you showed a spark of something.

He grabbed a piece of wood so suddenly he jammed splinters into his palm. He lurched up, cursing, hefting the blunt, thick cudgel in his other hand, trying to whip up a frenzy.

He knew he wouldn't do it.

He'd known all along. He hadn't stayed by the warehouse so that he'd be close for the kill. He'd come back, like a baby to the tit, hoping it wasn't dry. He had anger, all right, but not the guts. A bad combination. He hit his leg with the wood and tossed the useless weapon as far as the canal. He heart the distant splash and imagined it to be his own body, dumped again.

From somewhere nearby a couple of mating cats squalled. Saphrax smiled and stared up at the loft window in the dark. I'll be your shadow, Falca, he promised. You don't know you need me, but you do, more than anything else in the world. You took me from the gutter once, and I'll do the same for you. Just wait, Falca, you'll see, you'll be proud to walk beside me.

Chapter Five

The Settlement House

Furrow Street was the straightest in the Stone Reed district of Draica, following the cut of the Tears Canal through the heart of the city. The canal used to be filled with swans, but they had long since been poached by the Timberlimbs for food.

The press of Limbs was annoying enough to Falca, worse than that of the 'Roll and harder to tolerate because he had no fists here; it wasn't his territory. But the beggar children were like swarms of summer bluebites. Furrow Street was lucrative, though shabby, being the main thoroughfare to Rhysselia's Garden, where the wealthy who lived across the canal often went. Falca saw gangs of children risk being trampled by carriages or whipped by drivers, all for a few coppers tossed out the phaeton windows. Falca had to cuff a few of the older, more aggressive beggars to make his way.

The once fashionable neighborhood had been hit hard during the Myrcian siege, and many of the two- and three-story houses hadn't been rebuilt. The Limbs lived in the worst of the rubble. They had carved out crude caves or fashioned three-sided shelters from chunks of masonry.

Some of the debris along Furrow Street had been cleared, however, and one lot in particular caught Falca's eye as he walked, his right hand hooked in his belt, near to the dagger hilt.

In the midst of the ruined shell of a bluestone building, Limbs had cleared away masonry and planted a garden. Where they got the soil,

Falca could only guess. Perhaps they stole it from Rhysselia's Garden at night, enhancing their scrapings from the sides of the Tears Canal just beyond the building ruins. It seemed so typical to Falca that the mottles had chosen as their garden the gut of that building and disdained to cultivate the surrounding area. Maybe the enclosure reminded them of patches of forest land wrested for growing crops in the wilderness homeland, but it still seemed stupid to Falca.

Limb children played on an intricate lattice of crude dock rope and scrap planking built twenty feet above the garden, between the shorn, blackened chimneys and the jagged edges of the walls. Directly below, bareheaded in the light rain of the afternoon, a pair of wizened Limb females were pulling up the last of some execrable tubers or shriveled roots. The ends of their faded red shawls dragged on the ground as they worked, hunched over.

If the children were imitating the stories their elders told of the Snake Road built near treetop level through the core of the Rough Bounds, perhaps they were also pretending that the women were boars or prowling flenx, or maybe even soldiers of the hated Wardens.

Falca paused, mildly curious that the children had suddenly stopped playing. They were oddly subdued, standing side by side, like saltswallows on a laundry line.

He walked ahead and saw a man, previously obscured by part of the ruins. He stood on the canal towpath.

Falca froze.

The hulking man looked like Saphrax, even at this distance. He walked quickly away, as if caught at designs he might have had on the children.

Falca ran toward him, but when he got to the towpath, a gang of Limbs, straining at the ropes of a narrow barge, blocked his view and path.

The man was gone. Falca rubbed at his good eye. It couldn't have been Saphrax. The brute was dead, canal sludge by now. He blinked his eye. The good one must have tricked him, he decided.

Falca sighed and walked back to the street. The Limb children above were chasing each other again in play, the danger of a predator gone now. The old women below still bent to the task.

It bothered Falca. The man had run like Saphrax, had the same shambling gait. Bad eye or no, Falca prided himself on his eyesight. He missed very little; he couldn't afford not to. Perhaps it was the aftereffect of the scrape, though he hadn't experienced anything like this before.

He gave it a smile finally. Maybe the waters of the Tears Canal had some strange recuperative powers. No matter. He had no intention of tracking a wraith.

The settlement house rose two stories higher than those to either side. They were dilapidated, the once vivid blues and reds of trim and shutter faded now, drained away by the Draican rains, eroded by the pall of chimney smoke that hung over the city in winter. The settlement house had fared little better, and the opulence it once boasted made its decline all the more marked.

It had once been a Guild Hall—one of the maritimes. Carvings of full-sailed windwhippers, sturdy galliots, and formidible tresremes protruded over the large, diagonally paned windows that dated it to a style two hundred years old. Many of these windows were broken, and those on the street level were boarded up. Mock turrets, patterned after the octagonal ones of the royal bastion on Cross Keys Island, crowned the corners of the stone building, though one had collapsed onto the slate of the roof. A bartizan in the shape of a tresreme prow and ram surged through a cresting sea of stone over the recessed doorway. Fanned oars framed the entryway.

The hall was now the property of the New Order of the Carapace, one of the few charities that had managed to seed itself in the hard soil of Draica. It was not a popular one. If the women—the Salvatresses—of the order did not exactly worship the winged Erseiyr, as did the Myrcians, that immortal creature was at least the inspiration of the charity. Falca could see some use in Lucidoreans worshiping a creature who annually fisted tribute from the too-fat Myrcian treasury at Castlecliff, but clearly the beast wasn't too interested in increasing his flock. He rarely flew west of the Rough Bounds. Falca knew little else of the order, but it was a fair guess it served mainly as a social outlet for old women and young ones—like Amala Damarr—who were afflicted with a smattering of conscience. The Limbs the order helped were probably the very old and young, orphans and misfits. The Limbs usually took care of their own.

He walked up the steps to the oaken doors, and rapped one of the two curled eel knockers.

Two Limbs pulled open the door to let him in and closed it after.

The smell of the hall hit Falca like a foul rag thrown in his face. He put a gloved hand over his nose and mouth, preferring the ripe smell of leather and sweat to the other for a moment.

The place seemed more like the vast belly of a ship, crammed with the few hundred Limbs who were responsible for the sweetish, musky stink. He looked around for Amala Damarr, expecting to see the beacon of her bright hair in the gloom of the hall. Gray light filtered in from the higher windows that had not been boarded up. Wrist-thick candles added some illumination. Stuck in mounts on oak columns, they flickered with the languid currents of the hall, their droppings mounded on the tessellated floor.

Heavy wooden beams, cracked with age, arched over the entry-way, the higher ones framing an actual ram's-head prow of a tresreme jutting out from the far wall. Draped with icons of the Erseiyr, and Shadow Mountain where he lived, the prow must have once presided splendidly over a dais for the Guildmasters. Now there were only pallets for the Limbs, arranged in an orderly manner on the dais and much of the floor of the hall.

Long tables with benches filled one side, near two smoky hearths. The other side of the hall was curtained off, presumably an area for the sick and dying. Only half the pallets were occupied. The rest of the Timberlimbs milled around, the young ones playing some games with sticks. An old Limb sat cross-legged on the dais, reciting something loudly to no one in particular.

Falca took off his hat and walked ahead, ignoring the stares of a few Limbs, one of whom gently rocked a stuffed eloe in her arms. Falca was gazing up at the balcony that encircled half the hall, looking for Amala Damarr among still more Limbs up there, when he felt something poke him in the back. He whirled, knocking a long-handled ladle from an iron pot a Salvatress carried. The woman's narrow eyes tightened with annoyance as she stooped to pick up the ladle.

"You should announce your presence," Falca said. He smelled fish in the small pot.

"If you've come to court Amala," the 'tressa said, "you're early. Her work is not done yet for the day. The least you can do is make yourself useful while you wait, like the others do." She wiped the ladle on her skirt and speared it back into the pot, as if after fish. "Tressa Kavellia, over by the sick-shrouds, needs help. To your right. She will direct you to our modest crematorium."

Falca smiled. "I'm not yet ready for the coal-belly, thank you. My invitation was with Amala Damarr."

"One of our Limbs has died, citizen, the third one today, and needs to be taken there. You're a much better size than otherwise occupied Salvatresses."

"I'll wait."

"It won't make her come any quicker," the 'tressa said and walked, bowlegged, toward the crowded hearths, formless in her habit. She jabbed a young Limb who was nuzzling a female and sent him off with harsh words.

Falca leaned against an oak column, thick around as his waist. Nearby, two Limbs were squatting by a soft mound of wax underneath a candle abutment. One was an old Limb male, whose wrinkled skin had a dull, silver coloring, unlike the glossy sheen of the youngling next to him. The elder poked at the wax mound, talking to the child, as if passing on some secret or ritual, delighting his charge. Falca shook his head with detached scorn.

He got to thinking of how many other men Alatheus Damarr had chased from his sister's home, when he saw her walking not twenty feet away. She carried a Limb baby, unless, he thought, she was talking to a swaddled flagon. On a whim, Falca let her pass without calling out. It would be amusing to watch her work for a few minutes, though a year wouldn't be enough to explain why she was in this dismal, smelly hall and not in a glassed phaeton at Rhysselia's Garden, nuzzling the perfumed cheek of a Heart Hill dandy.

She took the Limb baby over to a corner opposite the woolen sick-shrouds, where it promptly threw up on her shoulder. She laid the thing in a crib—one of a score—no bigger than a kindling box. She brushed off her shoulder with a cloth from a pocket and checked on more of the cribs, bending over now and again to pick up a baby, saying things he couldn't hear. From the cribs she went through an archway and came back with ewers and proceeded to visit the sick-shrouds, conferring briefly with another 'tressa, who pointed to one shroud in particular, shaking her head. Kavellia went away, and Amala took water to the shrouds, the time varying with each Limb.

She began then to make what soon proved to be interminable rounds of the pallets, kneeling down to talk to the occupants. Falca was about to venture forth to announce his presence, when the old Limb sent off the youngling in Amala's direction. The little mottle sidled shyly up to Amala and tugged on her black dress and pointed. As Amala walked briskly in Falca's direction, followed by the Limb child, the old one turned to Falca and grinned toothlessly as he kneaded a ball of wax in his fingers.

"So you've chased a few in your time, old one," Falca whispered. He might have even nodded his acknowledgment at him had not the old one looked away toward Amala's approach. The youngling dropped down beside him, pleased as he patted her on the head. Both became absorbed again in the mysteries of the fallen wax, seemingly uninterested in the meeting they had hastened.

Amala Damarr's forehead glistened with sweat. Strands of her golden hair had escaped a red linen kerchief. It was slightly askew, and when she straightened it, Falca saw the clipped nails, the reddened hands. A Heart Hill beauty with practical nails and the reek of Limbs, by now used to drawing her own bath water following a day in this place. Her black dress was stained. The glaze of the baby's vomit shone on her shoulder. Her brother had his insignias, she had hers.

"That's Keeva," Amala said, gesturing back at the child and old Limb. "She's a favorite of mine. I helped deliver her sister, the one I was holding for a while. Their mother sickened and died not long ago. Not even Gurrus could help."

"The old one's her grandfather?" Falca asked, not caring a bit.

"Not by blood. It's different with them. I won't bore you with explanations. His name is Juhu. They also call him All-Eye. He doesn't miss a thing around here, nor does his friend Gurrus, one of the newer arrivals. Both are Patient Ones, the Timberlimbs' kings, spiritual leaders, healers all rolled into one. Each Limb village has one. We're lucky to have two here. I'm learning more of the Limb Tongue from Gurrus."

"The king plays with wax," Falca murmured.

"I'll forgive your condescension since you don't know the Limbs. Juhu saw a lesson in the wax, no doubt, and he's telling Keeva about it. Anyway, I'm glad you came."

"My pleasure. We were a little rushed for talk before."

Amala nodded.

"Are you finished for the day?" he asked. "I thought I'd walk you home."

"I'm not quite done. I have to help prepare the evening meal after I take a Limb male to the crematorium. If you don't mind, though, you could do that for me to speed matters. You don't seem the type, either, to idly stand by and wait."

"I've already been asked."

"That would be Beara. She's always the first to put men to work.

She resents visitors, especially my brother, who refuses to help when he comes to see me here. Beara's still suspicious of my priorities, no matter how hard I work. And I've been here for eight months, well, since Cassena's Week anyway."

Falca felt not in the least like carrying a dead Limb to a furnace. Still, she'd asked him, and having come this far, he couldn't refuse a request from a woman he wanted to lull before the fist. Besides, it wouldn't hurt to be excluded from the same category as her brother.

He nodded.

"Good," she said. "The Limb died only half an hour ago. He's in the third sick-shroud from the wall. Take him to that door behind the shrouds. Valnor will carry him from there. He's a strange one, Valnor. Doesn't mind sliding the poor Limbs into the coal-belly, but he refuses to come in here. I'm usually the one who has to do it, since I'm younger than the other 'tressas."

Valnor's prejudice didn't seem so strange to Falca, considering the stink in here. He was trying hard to be affable to the woman, setting her up. He had a fancy, for a moment, to tell her that it was his habit and business to knock her poor Limbs about the head to make them pay up. He wanted to shock her from this maudlin foolishness of caring for the little kings who played with wax. But he was into a disguise, one he hoped would prove profitable—and pleasurable. He sensed she liked him, and why not? He'd done her a gallant turn. Never mind her brother; she had an appetite, he could tell.

"I'll meet you here when I'm done," Amala Damarr was saying. "Thank you for the help."

He nodded and glanced at the leechstone as she left. It was barely hidden by the high collar of her dress. Such a lovely, graceful neck for so barbarous an adornment. Only a rich man could have afforded to give her that.

Falca made his way through the pallets of Limbs, breathing through his mouth to minimize the stench. He hurried, eager to get this gesture to the woman over with. It was the first request he'd granted anyone in a long time. He'd have to watch it around this woman, he thought with a smile.

He reached the sick-shroud Amala had indicated and parted the woolen curtain. And stopped right there.

"Well, well," he whispered. "So you didn't make it after all, did you Sorelip?"

The Limb monger lay on the straw pallet, on his back, his eyes

closed to the timbered arches of the ceiling. The face Saphrax had
pummeled was swollen, distended, but recognizable. Sorelip's long,
spindly arms lay over the edges of his bed, one almost touching the
empty trencher and mug of water. He seemed like a grotesque parody
of a doll, with his tiny, pointed boots, baggy, dirty red trews, and a
belt buckle no bigger than one of the coins he tried to hide in the
canal. A large fly settled on Sorelip's chin, then flew into his open
mouth before Falca chased it away with his hat. He sighed. He'd have
to find a new fist to replace the Limb. He dropped his hat, kneeled
down, wanting to salvage something from the loss. He patted Sorelip's ripped trews, curious as to whether the scrapemonger might have
hidden a coin or two in some inside pouch.

Indeed he had. Falca clicked his tongue to congratulate himself for
thoroughness. It didn't feel like much, but a coin was a coin. "No
sense in wasting money in the coal-belly, Sorelip," he whispered as
the fly buzzed around the Limb's head. As Falca was rolling up the
pant leg to get at what felt like three kraels, Sorelip's hand suddenly
jerked, startling Falca to a quick grunt.

Two tiny black eyes flicked open, then wider in recognition.

Falca stood slowly, inexplicably fearful for a moment. Amala had
said he was dead, hadn't she? Maybe he'd gotten the wrong sick-
shroud. No, third from the end. He decided she'd just made a mistake. Some quirk of the Limb's, perhaps, their dog-sized hearts. His
uneasiness was assuaged by the fear in Sorelip's eyes, fear as familiar
as favorite brogans or a pipe.

Falca laughed, nervously. "All right, I won't take them. If three
kraels is all it takes to get you back in business in Twisthead, it's
worth the money. Persistence like that should be rewarded, you ugly
mottle."

The Limb stared at him, his mouth slackly open. One eye listlessly followed the fly; the other stared at Falca. Limbs could do that.

Falca picked up his hat and left. He met Beara near the entryway.

"The Limb you wanted me to take to the furnace . . . ?"

"Yes?"

"He was in the third shroud from the end?"

She looked, then nodded.

"He isn't dead," Falca said.

"Of course he is. Both Amala and I checked him not long ago,
and he'd died. He was beaten badly, poor thing. Since you troubled

yourself after all to go to him, you may as well go back and take him to Valnor."

Falca fitted his hat on his head. "Check him again, Salvatress."

She did so, and when she came back, she said, "His heart's as quiet as it was an hour ago. Go see for yourself, citizen."

At the sick-shroud Falca placed a hand on Sorelip's chest.

Nothing.

He pulled back the eyelids. No life there either. For some reason he checked the trews again, as if the presence of the hidden coins was an indicator of life. They were still there. As Falca backed away, he realized that Sorelip's hand, the one that had moved from the trencher, was back where he'd first seen it. The fly crawled out from Sorelip's open mouth.

Falca almost ran into the Salvatress Beara, who stood, arms folded, outside the sick-shroud. "Well?" she said.

"He's just died, then," Falca said, his voice clipped, angry. He was not at all sure that was the case. "Is this some amusement of yours and perhaps the 'tressa Damarr?" he asked Beara.

"We don't have time for amusement here," she said.

"Tell the 'tressa Damarr I'll be waiting outside for her," Falca whispered.

"That would be best," Beara said. "I think you need the air, citizen."

Chapter Six

A Walk to
the Garden

Falca stood in the portal of the settlement house, his back to the stone oars that were blackened by years of Draican chimney soot. The rain had stopped. The bustle of the street, the fresher air, was a relief to Falca from the stink and puzzle of the hall.

So far the day was enough to make a man itch where it didn't.

First the sighting of someone who looked enough like Saphrax to make him wonder if the bad scrape and the canal had done their job after all. Now this. Did Sorelip, or did he not, open his eyes and look terrified that Falca was going to fist the last of a eager hoard?

He did, by Roak's beard, and damn the Salvatresses of the New Order of the Carapace.

Was it possible, Falca wondered, that Amala Damarr and that broomhead Beara were trying to pry him from reality by telling him the Limb was dead when he wasn't? If so, it was the most unusual fist Falca had ever encountered. The very preposterousness of the idea was preferable to him than the possibility that he was losing his grip, that his sharp eyes were deceiving him.

He thought briefly of simply taking off and never mind the licking cloak. It was only an excuse to further his designs on the woman, and he wasn't going to wear it anyway, not after she covered the empty with it.

He stayed by the portal, watching the business of the street. No, he decided, it was too early to abandon the potential of Amala Damarr, the curve of her figure, the heft of her obvious station. At the very least he could bed her. At the most he might be able to get what he called boot money from the brother or family, a bribe to leave her alone should she take a liking to him.

A burly man in brown leathers drifted out of the flow of Furrow Street. A crone nodded at him, and he acknowledged her by raising a hand that held a leash. Nearby, Amala Damarr's dog sniffed at the warped wheels of an eel vendor's cart. The man snapped his fingers at the animal, but the dog didn't obey. He sighed, as if used to the disobedience, and went over to leash Shindy. When he got back to the steps, he kneeled down and buffed his boots with a cloth from his pocket. Standing again, he combed his black hair and checked his clothing for spatters of mud. Occasionally he jerked the leash to curb the dog's restlessness.

She has her lackeys, Falca thought, as I have mine.

The dog sensed her arrival before Falca heard the settlement house doors open. She walked right by Falca, since he was off to one side, and clapped her hands for Shindy, who strained at the leash. The man let him go, and the animal raced up the steps. She kneeled to scratch his ears, his split-tail sweeping the stone like a broom. When Falca walked up to her from behind, she turned, as if she'd known he was there all along, surprising him a little.

"Beara said you left angry," she said, stroking Shindy's coat.

"It's been a difficult day, citizen."

Shindy growled at him, and Amala snapped her fingers. The dog quieted immediately. "So I heard. We never should have asked you to take a dead one to the coal-belly. Your reluctance was understandable."

"I would have done it, but he wasn't dead. He opened his eyes."

"Perhaps your bad eye tricked you. Whatever the mystery, the Limb is now with the Cloud Hands, their spirit-deliverer. And Valnor is happy, for once, because I let him keep some money we found on the Timberlimb."

At least I wasn't imagining that, Falca thought.

"I'm afraid I left your cloak at home. I was drying it out by the fire and forgot it," Amala said.

"No matter. I'll get it later."

"Can you spare the time for a detour to Rhysselia's Garden? When there's sun, I enjoy the view from the bridges at dusk."

"That's far. A carriage to get there, perhaps?" Her escort could take the dog, leaving him alone with her. And besides, that route would take them past Ferrex, who might queer his pitch.

"With Shindy?" she replied. Amala patted the dog's head affectionately and let him lick her wrist. She walked down the steps. Falca was a trifle annoyed, but didn't show it, as he followed her.

She introduced him to the burly man as they walked: Sippio, a servant to the Damarrs. Amala gave him the leashed Shindy, and he fell in behind. Falca looked back once, to see his frown.

They headed east along Furrow Street. Falca glanced over to the ruins of the stone house, chancing another sighting of the Saphrax look-alike. The lot was empty. Whatever else he'd seen, there was no mistaking the blue sky, the reef of clouds beyond. Nor the smell of the settlement house on Amala Damarr, who walked beside him at a pace a little faster than his usual. From behind a gable of the settlement house, smoke rose, the last trace of Sorelip rising to the Cloud Hands. Falca thought of going by the landing tomorrow, but by then whatever the little monger had left would be all gone.

The woman knew how to handle conversation with a strange man, Falca had to give her that. She seemed incapable of an awkward move or question, and if anyone had bothered to observe the pair, they would have guessed they had known each other for some time. Falca felt comfortable with her, at one point even laughing loudly— causing Shindy to growl—when Amala described Beara's younger lover, who had come once to visit her at the hall. The Limbs had told her he smelled like "mold that grows on the tickle tree," a reference that mortified Beara.

"In case you're wondering," Amala concluded, "I received no such complaints about you. Then again, the Limbs' sense of smell seems more acute in the morning. Don't ask me why."

"They should be the last ones to complain about someone's stink," Falca said.

"It all depends on who's doing the sniffing," Amala replied, and they changed the subject.

He didn't have to lie as much to her as he'd thought. Mostly he worked a story about his job as an overseer of gangers on the south quays of Catch-All. He'd been ready with a cautiously more respectable line of work, in case he needed it. But he hadn't put too much thought into that fabrication. After all, if the woman was a true child of Heart Hill, she wouldn't be here with him now, nor would she be allowing Limb babies to vomit on her shoulder. It was obvious she wanted something other than the usual fare of Beckon dandies she might otherwise enjoy.

He made his family more respectable, though, turning his father into a canalmaster and having his mother die in childbirth, instead of in the fall from Cross Keys Bridge—the accident Falca would never know to be a suicide or not. He gave himself a sister and kept the number of his brothers the same, if not their fates. He had his two eldest brothers die in the Myrcian war, but that didn't elicit from Amala any patriotic condemnation of Lucidor's rival to the south. Falca was surprised, since she told him her father had been an officer in the Wardens along the Myrcian border, before the first campaign in the Rough Bounds. Evidently she didn't get along too well with the old man, whose best campaign, she hinted, was in wooing the daughter of a patriarch of one of Draica's Twelve Families. No wonder they disapproved of her independence, Falca thought. He'd give his arm to see the likes of the house she grew up in.

The current patriarch of the Damarrs, whose home, Falca learned with pleasure, was located in the Nape of Heart Hill, was hard on Alatheus evidently. Amala's brother had the misfortune of getting burned on the right leg with a Timberlimb stingvine and was still recovering. It wasn't the noblest of wounds, in the elder Damarr's estimation, and only reinforced his low opinion of his son's soldierly ability, Amala told him.

"He drew a sword well enough," Falca observed.

Amala didn't share Falca's amusement. "I understand my brother's frustration with our father, but there was no excuse for him to do that, not in my house."

"Why do you let him stay, then?"

"It's complicated. Perhaps he heals better around me. We're close."

"Well, I'm sure he does heal better around you. Do you around him?"

"And what, citizen Breks, might *my* affliction be?"

"Telling visitors to your settlement house that Limbs are dead when they're not."

"That's your affliction. You're the one who needs healing, your eyes anyway. Stay close. I'll see what I can do to help you."

Falca smiled, and said nothing.

* * *

They came to Stemon's Canal, the central north-south waterway of Draica. Furrow Street widened for the bridge which was encrusted with dwellings and bartizans on either side. In the middle of the bridge rose Gavial's Stele. The bluestone monument commemorated or lamented—there were two schools of thought—that early king's selling of Roak's second gift—the Staff of Strength to a one-armed magist. In return the monarch received a potion that would allow him to bring back his wife and children, who died of the Walking Plague.

Ferrex sat where he always did, with his back to the stele. There was no way Falca could avoid being seen by his brother. He inwardly cursed when Ferrex spotted him and called out, lifting his stumps in greeting.

"Bad eye, brother. Who's the pretty quiver?"

Behind them, Sippio took offense at the word on behalf of his mistress and was about to cuff Ferrex when Falca intervened.

"Easy, friend," he said. "He doesn't mean anything."

Sippio glared at Falca. "Should be taught a lesson. He's only a beggar."

"It's all right, Sippio. I've heard worse," Amala said.

Falca plunked a reive into his brother's bowl and, unseen by Amala and her servant, put a finger to his lips, to tell Ferrex to keep his mouth shut. He walked on, feeling his brother's eyes at his back. The laughter from Ferrex seemed to say, You're fooling yourself, Falca. Whatever you want from her you'll never get. I chased a woman and wound up here. . . .

"Did you know that beggar?" Amala said.

"I've come to know him. I always give him something when I pass."

"Strange, he even looked a little like you."

Falca shrugged. "It's why he calls me brother."

"At least you gave him something."

"I usually don't on the streets. Most beggars are charlatans. But you can't fake the loss of your hands. You seem surprised I give beggars money. You have your own charity."

"It's not charity. It's my work," Amala said.

"Timberlimbs? There are those who think tending dispossessed Limbs is a waste of time."

"I get enough of that elsewhere, citizen Breks," Amala said coldly. "Perhaps you, too, were a soldier in the Rough Bounds before your promotion to the quays of Catch-All. I'll tell you this, and only one time: I won't banter about them. They didn't ask to be here, nor did they ask for our soldiers in their home forests. In most cases their company is preferable to humans'."

"Fair enough," Falca said. "I wish I could say I prefer the company of my gangers. Unlike your Timberlimbs, they are a means to an end, and a lazy means at that."

She said nothing for a while as they walked. Falca listened to the click-clicking of the dogs nails on the cobblestones, and Sippio's breathing, wondering how long it would take her anger to diminish. She certainly seemed serious about the Limbs. But then so was he, if for different reasons.

"And what end is that?" she asked finally. Falca had to think a moment, for he'd forgotten what he'd said.

"If I work my gangers hard enough through enough winters, I expect to spend my remaining years under the Gebroanan sun."

"You sound like a tough but hopeful lizard."

Falca had to laugh. "I've been called many things but never a lizard." The woman had a way of getting things out of him. He hadn't even told the sisters about Gebroan, or anyone, except Saphrax. And he'd been drunk then.

"You merely want a little more warmth in your face than our Draica provides?" Amala said. "Most people hunger for wealth or glory or power."

"Getting to Gebroan could take more ambition than you think, citizen Damarr."

"Yet you throw silver at beggars without hands. Not that I object to generosity. But you seem of two minds."

Before Falca could say anything, Sippio snorted behind. Falca turned to see the servant sneering at him, and closer than he liked. The dog was close enough to take a chunk out of his leg if he so much as brushed one of Amala's arms.

"You have an opinion, friend?"

"I was there for two years," Sippio said. His eyes flicked to Amala to judge how far he could go. Evidently he saw nothing to discourage him. "You'd wilt like day-old cabbage in the Gebroanan sun."

"You might be right . . . Sippio," Falca said. "It depends on what I'll be doing. Whose dogs were you walking there?"

Sippio reddened with anger and let out the leash. Falca leaped back as Shindy began growling, not a foot away from him, his snout wrinkling, his teeth bared. Falca drew his dagger.

Amala calmly snapped her fingers, and the dog quieted. "Pull him back, Sippio," she said, glancing at Falca's dagger.

Falca wondered if the dog still smelled Saphrax and Venar on him. He'd taken a bath for this meeting, but even so. . . . He wouldn't have been surprised if Amala said goodbye right here and now for pulling a dagger on her dog, even though she'd let her fool of a man provoke him. Besides, the walk had deteriorated after a decent start. But she went on with him, if anything, closer at his side.

"Sippio has his grievances," Amala said. "He was a slave ganger on the Gebroanan Aqueduct, one of Rekèlever's Thousand who were sent to Gerim the Grim as a birthday present. Impressed into the Thousand when he was sixteen. At my insistence, Alatheus eventually bought out his contract and got him back."

Falca shrugged. The man was an even greater fool for letting himself get snatched to Gebroan. At least he'd had sense enough to stay off the streets when the King's men swept through Slidetown and Catch-All.

"You work your gangers hard, citizen Breks, and you might just get your Gebroanan sun," Amala went on. "Whether you'll wilt underneath it, as Sippio suggests, depends on how much of the Draican climate you take with you."

"Only what I can't wring from my clothes," Falca replied.

As they walked on, Amala pointed to the green hill of Rhysselia's Garden, which rose beyond the bridge ahead. He glanced at her leechstone while she talked, long enough for her to sense his gaze. Whether it was the shadows on the street or the play of her long golden hair, the leechstone seemed darker than before, when Falca saw it as she walked out of the settlement house. Some trick of her blood, a changing current, or his own eyes?

"Did your brother give you that?" he asked, pointing.

"Yes, before father sent him to the military school at Skene. To become a man." Amala laughed. "So dear of Alatheus, really. The money he spent on it could have helped him become a man rather sooner and with more style than he managed in the whorehouses around Skene."

"How do you know?"

"He told me," she said, surprised.

"Of course."

"Well, didn't you share secrets with your brothers and sisters?"

"Some," Falca replied. He couldn't very well tell her of the secrets he *kept* from them. Such as the fat merchant who tried to buy him for a night when he was seven years old and then wouldn't take no for an answer when Falca refused. He could still remember how the man's jowls jiggled when he stared at the knife Falca had plunged into his thigh.

Falca had a feeling there weren't too many things Amala and her brother didn't share. Still, even for twins, the sharing of sexual exploits between brother and sister struck him as odd, though odder things had happened. He wondered what Amala would think if she knew about the sisters' sharing of him. She'd probably laugh, he decided, thinking of her door-dog phallus.

"From what I understand," Amala was saying, "the leechstone should have fallen off some time ago."

"It's one gift you wouldn't want to give away."

"No, I wouldn't. I'll wear it till it dies. One morning I'll wake up, and there it will be, on my pillow. The Limbs at the house call it my Rogue Tear. Or at least that's the best I can make of my poor translation." She said it in Tongue. "It's a beautiful language, really. Expressive. Do you know what their name for us is?"

"I can imagine a few possibilities," Falca said, thinking of his fists.

"They call us shit-catchers."

Falca laughed. "Something the soldiers do in the Bounds?"

"I'm impressed," Amala said, grinning. "Would you care to learn a few more words?"

"I'll stay with my own, thank you anyway." Though he thought that it might help business, eliminating the last shred of Venar's usefulness. Perhaps later.

As they went on, Falca was aware of the stares that Amala Damarr got from men along the way, well-dressed men of property, for this was a more fashionable neighborhood bordering the Garden and Ringwater. A gentleman in a black and tan phaeton poked his head out as his carriage rattled by, heading for the bridge.

Falca shook his head at her beauty. Suddenly he felt a kinship with Sippio, plodding stolidly behind them, felt a little understanding of his jealousy. The servant was not an unattractive man, certainly solid as a dock bollard. For an uncomfortable moment, Falca saw himself, vividly, with the dog, glaring at the broad back of a man who wore gloves, who had a scar on his face that grew whiter, bigger with the chill of a Draican winter, a scar that Amala Damarr was quite possibly curious about. A man he'd come to dislike in the space of an afternoon's walk.

The feeling passed quickly, and Falca was relieved when it did. He'd had enough imaginings for one day.

At the gateway arch to the Limping Bridge, Amala told Sippio to take the dog back to her home. The servant was reluctant to leave her. "What does Alatheus pay me for, then?" he protested.

"Don't worry," Amala said with a grin, "citizen Breks will be safe with me."

Falca laughed.

"It's not a matter to take lightly," Sippio said. "Alatheus held me responsible the other day when I was sick and couldn't take you home. Roak help me if I'd had any less of an excuse. He almost hit me as it was, the bastard."

Amala scratched Shindy underneath his huge jaw. His tongue snaked out and licked her wrist. "Take him, Sippio. I'll deal with Alatheus if he gives you trouble."

Sippio leaned close to her, but Falca heard him anyway: "What he would do to me is nothing compared to what I would do to myself if something happened to you, Amala."

"Go on with you," she said softly.

She might as well have snapped her fingers, for Sippio left, glaring at Falca with a warning. Falca touched his hat pleasantly enough.

"My gangers should have such devotion," he said.

"Not too lightly here, citizen," Amala said. "He's a friend and a good man."

He shrugged, respecting her loyalty. Still, he wondered which she would choose to save, her dog or Sippio, if he threw both into the canal. She'd gone on about her brother, but it seemed to Falca she wore his collar and leash. One of these days she would have to choose between the soft velvet of devotion and the gritty feel of independence. Well, it wasn't his problem. With any luck he'd get what he wanted from her and get out.

"I'd like to finish with music, flina music while the sun goes down," she said.

"If you'd like."

"I would. Whatever else his virtues, Sippio feels it necessary to talk while music is being played. I've never understood it. A cruel malady, and crueler on me because I can't abide it. Be warned."

"I can thank Roak I'm not similarly afflicted, for my protection has just left," Falca said. "Shall we cover the bridge?"

She nodded.

He'd drawn a knife on her precious dog, and the sight of a blade would have frightened most anyone of Heart Hill. But here was Amala Damarr, pressing closer to him, allowing him to take her elbow. He felt the sharp tip of the sliver-heart move against his hand as they walked under the marshfang crest of Rhysselia, after whose lame first son the bridge was named. Falca thought about the reward she'd given him, and wondered how much of it was in gratitude for services rendered and how much of it might be for services yet to be performed, ones not of his choosing. He dismissed the thought as foolish, more conjuring in a day nettled with imaginings. He dropped his hand from her elbow anyway.

Chapter Seven

The Flina Player

Limping Bridge was one of four that spanned the oval of Ringwater surrounding the Garden. It was a favorite excursion for lovers, given the greenery and paths, the harp and flina music that drifted over the waterside promenade to the canal. Summer was the season for the music and boats that plied Ringwater, but the sun had brought out more people than Falca expected.

Rhysselia's Garden encompassed the hill that rose to the height of the bridges. Queen Rhysselia was one of the last to occupy the site. During her reign Draica was still harried by raiders from the Isles, fierce descendents of those separated by a storm from Roak's fleet.

Though hard-pressed, Rhysselia didn't build a castle. She preferred to trust in her people, she proclaimed, and to the marshes and maze of waterways filled with marshfangs. Later monarchs deemed walls necessary as the city expanded, as Lucidor's enemies grew in strength. Much of the vast marsh was drained. Ringwater was given over to the grazing of animals as the royal seat moved to firmer, more ambitious ground to the north.

The gardens that came later spread over the lower slopes of the gentle hill, with dawnstone pergolas and gazebos dotting the junctures of pathways lined with yellowtongue and cat's-paw. Nearer the top, stands of shiver-not trees surrounded the monument patterned after Roak's Staff of Strength.

As Falca and Amala finished the bridge, she pointed to a pair of children racing up the steps spiraling around the sheaf of staves. Several people leaned on the railing of the vantage point.

"Did you ever go up there?" Amala asked, looking at the children, who were almost at the top now. The low sun caught them as golden flashes each time they reappeared around the breadth of the monument.

"A few times," Falca lied.

"I raced Alatheus up to the top more times than I can remember."

"Who won?"

"I could have, more times than I did. I always had the strong legs. It depended on whether father was watching. If he was, I'd let Alatheus win."

"Why let someone else win if you know you can beat them?"

"It seemed more important to him," Amala said. "Especially with father watching. I didn't much care; I knew what I could do. I had the dancer's legs, as Alatheus called them."

"And now?"

Amala laughed. "Now, neither of us could make it to the top going as fast as those children. Still, it might be entertaining to try. Perhaps after the music?"

"In the dark?"

"The dawnstone provides enough light. I thought you'd been up there?"

"Not at night."

"The city's quite beautiful from up there at night. Well?"

"No one has ever accused me of having dancer's legs, but I accept the challenge. If you win, I give two kraels to the settlement house. If I win, I get your company for another evening."

"You have a bet, citizen Breks. And a foolish one on your part. You might have gotten that company anyway."

"I prefer to make sure of things," Falca said, grinning.

They walked through the Garden arch. Falca gestured to Sciàmachon's Fountain to their right. "You have your music," he said.

A minstrel, coming from the direction of Fiarra's Bridge, had stopped by the low wall of the fountain and unslung his flina.

"I haven't seen that one before," Amala said, "and I know most of the regular flinarra who play in the Garden. His flina is splendid."

They headed toward the fountain, where several people had already gathered to hear the music. Nearby, a mother watched her son play with a toy boat in the now golden waters of the fountain.

It had been a gift from the Attallissian king, Sciàmachon, to the king of Lucidor, for granting him residence after his exile from his homeland. He died several years after it was completed. Falca had quenched his thirst in its waters one hot summer's day several years ago, the day he killed the man who maimed Ferrex.

Six concentric circles of young, smiling men and women—each a perfection of the sculptor's art—descended toward the center of the fountain. In the outer ring, they waded to their ankles and by the sixth and last ring, only their arms showed above water level. From the upturned wrists of each figure, water spurted, like the blood of slashed veins. There was no spray at the fountain's center, like others in Draica. Only an empty circle, said to represent Sciàmachon's heart, or the kraken's lair.

Like the Walking Plague that had once devastated the cities of Lucidor, Myrcia and Gebroan, so the lure of the exotic Summers—the sea folk who lived in the myriad Shelter Isles west of Attallissia—had emptied the towns of that kingdom. Even if Sciàmachon had been a tyrant, he could not have prevented the exodus. The Summer's kraken god would have destroyed any fleet he could have sent, just as it had destroyed that of Gallinuir, who sought to recapture Lanlen his queen, after she eloped with a Summer prince a hundred years before.

Falca watched the boy wading in the fountain, playing beyond the fourth ring of stone figures. He pushed his tiny galley further and further along, nudging it past the sculpted headlands, through the storm of falling water. His mother called him back. "That's far enough, Crellin!" The flina player turned around on the wall he shared with the mother and said something that made her smile in spite of her worry for her son. She called to him again.

"She's being overly protective of the boy," Falca said. "The water couldn't be that deep."

"Not overly. Didn't you see one of those statues turn around and grab for him?"

"What are you talking about?" A moment later Falca knew, and reddened with anger.

"Not amusing, eh?" Amala said.

"No." He was certain now, if he hadn't been before, that she hadn't played some trick on him back at the settlement house with Sorelip. Nor had Beara. He found the certainty in Amala's apologetic eyes and voice. It made him almost sick to realize he *had* imagined Sorelip's eyes opening, his arms moving. He had no idea why, or how, nor did he want to dwell on guesses. He felt a drip of sweat leave his armpit, a trickle of fear, special fear he'd never felt before, not even when cornered in a fight.

He was still angry at Amala, not for her teasing him, but for being in that place of hers, where he'd lost himself, his control, for a brief time by Sorelip's body. Whatever he gleaned from Amala Damarra—money, pleasure, or both—wouldn't cover the cost of those few minutes. It was too late, he couldn't get them back.

"When is that man going to play?" Falca said testily.

To hasten matters, or soothe Falca's impatience, Amala took a few coins from a purse pouch and walked over to the flinarra to drop them in the customary hat of street minstrels. There was none, and the musician didn't hastily produce one to collect the offerings, which annoyed Falca. What was he out here for, then? Was he playing for free? The man had to eat like the rest, didn't he?

The flinarra just sat on the fountain wall, polishing his instrument. Finally Amala put the coins near his feet. He didn't even acknowledge the gesture with a nod. Falca was disgusted. There were other flinarra—he could hear two at least somewhere nearby in the Garden—who would be more grateful. The minstrel did smile, but in a listless sort of way. The coins could have been spit for all he seemed to care.

As Amala turned away, Falca saw a scruffy reiver break from the half dozen people near the musician. "Amala," Falca called out sharply. "Behind you."

She put her shoe on the coins just as the reiver was bending down to scoop them up. The flinarra was within arm's reach of the thief but did nothing.

"Hey, he don't want them," the reiver said.

"And I don't want you to have them," Amala said. "Get away."

The thief hesitated, glancing at Falca.

"Don't look at him," Amala said more sharply. "*I'm* telling you to leave."

The reiver slunk back to where he'd been, a scrawny wolf chased from a kill.

Back with Falca, Amala said, "Thanks for alerting me."

"The scut was right, though. The flinarra doesn't want the money."

"Yes, it's odd. Maybe he'll pick them up later. If he is so unconcerned about his profit, it's a wonder where he got so beautiful and expensive a flina." She shook her head, watching him polish the instrument with a yellow cloth. "A beautiful thing it is," she said in a whisper. "The wings are layered, do you see? Not solid like you find in inferior flinas. The cross-spars to the neck are scrolled and etched —you don't find that very often anymore."

"It also has a crack," Falca said.

"Where? I don't see it."

"Beneath the mouseholes. He keeps polishing it there."

"You have good eyes."

"A lot of good they've done me today," Falca said.

"Whatever your problem, citizen, it's not your eyes," Amala said softly. "That crack's a hairline, I see, now that you pointed it out. It won't effect the texture of the sound, though. If anything it shows the age of the instrument, and its sound improves with age. See that discoloration near the base? That's actually mold that has spread from the inside of the flina. It's called Golden Rot. Improves the sound. Don't ask me how."

"You know much about flinas."

Amala smiled ruefully. "Enough to know I would never have made a good player, or even an average one. My mother gave Alatheus and me a flina when we were children. It was too soon for us, but other families had them, so we had to have one too. I'm sure Mother had visions of afternoon teas where her little darlings would impress all her friends with their precociousness.

"Alatheus was bored with it soon enough, probably because father thought a boy's time better spent doing active things. I stayed with it longer, until Alatheus hid the flina from me one day—and saved me from realizing then what little talent I had, though at the time I was furious."

"I'd be furious, too," Falca said. "I suspect you played the thing better than you think."

"That's gallant of you to say so, but incorrect."

"Did you find the flina?"

"No, Alatheus wouldn't tell, Mother couldn't make him, and Father was just glad to get the prissy thing out of the house. I remember a thundering argument they had about it."

"Perhaps that's the one," Falca said. "Maybe your brother sold it to the musician for a song. He has to have gotten it somewhere cheaply if he's so casual about his livelihood."

"No," Amala said. "I'm afraid not. Not unless flinas also get bigger with age, like bloodsnares."

Falca raised an eyebrow. "Don't tell me you've also played the 'snares too."

She laughed. "Hardly! Do I look like a consort? My complexion is pale, but not that pale. No, I've just heard a few in den."

Falca hadn't seen many people from the high ridges of Draica in the dens. If they came, they didn't show it. The dens were dangerous places. He glanced at Amala's leechstone. Maybe it wasn't so surprising after all. "Did Alatheus take you to them?"

"You must be joking! Twice I went by myself, twice with Sippio, and a few times with others. Never with Alatheus. If he even knew, he'd have a fit. He has a certain idea of who I . . . look, I do believe the man is going to play. Finally!"

"He's a strange one," Falca said, thinking as much of Alatheus as the flinarra. "Did you see him drop his polishing cloth in the fountain?"

They watched it float away behind him, a restless water lily, to lodge against the leg of a stone youth.

"Now there's an odd finality," Amala said. "You would think he'd want to use the cloth again, or clean it if it was dirty."

Most of the people gathered to hear the music had moved on, shaking their heads at the minstrel's eccentricity. Besides Amala and Falca, only three others remained, and the reiver. Falca kept an eye on him as the musician wrapped long arms around the dark-hued flina. As the flinarra began to pluck the three sets of strings, he wondered just how beautifully a little golden-haired girl must have played for her brother to steal away her music. Falca had once smashed an ax into a locked door, behind which Ferrex had fled with a brass-bound cane Falca treasured, pretending it was a falcata. If it had *been* the falcata, he'd have beaten his larger brother to a pulp.

He hadn't heard many flinarra play, the last one with Saphrax at a Slidetown street fair. Surprisingly, the brute loved music, and was so entranced that an impatient Falca had left him to his rapture. For weeks afterward, Saphrax had begged for Falca to steal him a flina. But there was no profit in Saphrax's amusement, and he undoubtedly would have gotten so frustrated trying to play it, he would have smashed the thing.

Falca didn't much care for the flina's sound. It was too subtle, too soothing. He preferred "shiver-music," like that produced by the drone and melody of consort and bloodsnare, music that got so deep within him that he wanted to shake himself to get rid of it. Flina music relaxed him, but Falca couldn't afford too much of that. Too much could happen to a man whose guard was down. It had been fine for the likes of Saphrax, because Falca was the one who had looked after him, the one who always had to be alert, ready to counter those quick moments that could end your life. No one looked after Falca.

He lost himself in the dens, of course, but a den was a safer place to be than most people thought, if you knew canal-side, knew which ones to pick. If you succumbed to the rhythm of the music, so did everyone else. The music was that powerful; some said addictive. Flina or harp music was different. Falca always felt, when he was tempted to drift away for a moment, that someone was watching him, ready to take advantage of his lapse.

Someone *was* watching him now—Amala. He felt her stare.

"You don't like the flina, do you?" she asked, without any disappointment in her whisper.

"I thought you didn't like people talking while you listened?"

"I don't, but he's playing 'Tide's Away,' not one of my favorites, though he's playing it very well. The man's good. His deep strings are the best I've heard in a long time."

The sun fell, the flinarra played on. A dozen people had stopped to listen, mostly couples holding hands. The pile of coins at the minstrel's feet grew. After each song Falca heard the chink-chink of reives, ecues, and even one gold roak. He glanced at the reiver every now and then and determined that the ditch-licker wasn't going to snatch up the pile that Amala had started, even if the flinarra didn't want the money. Normally Falca wouldn't have cared—all's fair canal-side. But he felt a little possessive of it, because part of the money was Amala's.

She stood next to him with her arms crossed, to gather more warmth in the chill of the twilight. She'd moved closer to the flinarra with each song, while Falca stayed where he was. When the musician stopped playing for good, Falca was relieved. There was still the matter of the race up the monument and Amala Damarr's dancer's legs.

That monument hoarded the last light of the day. On Ringwater, lanterns dangled from the sterntails of canal boats, rocking with the polemen's labor.

Falca walked to Amala, just as the flinarra spoke, surprising Falca. He hadn't said a word until now. "One song remains," he said. "Someone choose it for me. You there," he pointed at Amala. "Choose my last." The voice was oddly assertive, Falca thought. Given his silence, the sad songs, Falca had expected timidity or softness.

"Play 'Larks on the Bough,'" Amala said.

"A rousing choice to end with," the flinarra said.

As he fiddled with tuning pegs, Amala whispered to Falca, "That's the song I was trying to learn when Alatheus, damn him, hid my flina. I've asked other flinarra to play it. We'll see how this one does with that beautiful flina of his. It's a difficult song to do well."

The musician began slowly, and it wasn't long before Falca saw the smile on Amala's face widen as she silently mouthed, "One," then "two," all the way up to eight. Falca assumed that was for each lark as they settled on the song boughs, each with the same song yet different. It wasn't so dark that Falca couldn't see the man's fingers humbling the strings with a precision and speed that impressed even Falca. Amala was in rapture when he finished.

"Wondrous," she said softly, before everyone started clapping.

When the approval died down, the flinarra shook his head. "It could have been better."

Amala laughed. "Citizen, if you play better than that, you must tell me where and when! What is your name, so I can remember it for the pleasure you've given me."

"What has my name to do with it?" the flinarra said, standing now. "The music is all."

"Well," Amala said, shrugging off his surly tone. "Everything and nothing, I suppose."

The flinarra gripped the delicate curving wings of the flina and raised it over his head, as if hawking a prize.

"What is he doing?" Amala said to Falca. And before he could answer, the flinarra brought his instrument down, smashing it on the wall of the fountain. Pieces flew off into the fountain water.

Amala's hand instantly covered her mouth, her eyes wide. She and the rest of the audience stared as the flinarra left the wreckage without another word. Falca stared at the pieces in the fountain, the remnants of a tiny fleet, Gallinuir's fleet destroyed by the Kraken.

He had the urge to laugh. Was this a joke?

People began to drift away, whispering, shaking their heads in amazement. When Falca put his hand against the small of Amala's back, he felt the trembling.

"What in the name of the High Sorrows happened?" she whispered.

"I wish I could tell you."

"It doesn't make any sense. He just . . . destroyed it, left it, walked away. . . . Maybe I shouldn't have asked him to play it, the song."

"That makes even less sense, Amala."

"Oh, I know, but still . . ."

"He had it all planned, didn't he? Throwing away the cloth, polishing that thing, like a hangman fussing over his knot."

"Take me home, will you? I'd like a carriage. It's near dark, and I don't feel like walking."

He nodded, then saw the reiver hurrying away. "In a minute. That scut's taking the coins."

"Falca, I don't care . . ."

"I do."

He ran toward the thief, chasing him halfway around the fountain until he caught him. They were still within Amala's sight when Falca hit him twice to loosen the grip of his fist full of coins.

"I'm taking them all," Falca whispered. "Mostly because you were stupid not to wait until we'd gone. We'd forgotten about them."

"Bastard," the man said as Falca backed away from him.

"I don't want them," Amala said when Falca returned. "You keep them."

Falca didn't want them either, now that he had them. The day was making him more superstitious than he cared to be. He didn't want to have anything to do with someone crazy like that flinarra. He never thought he'd be one to refuse money, but then he'd never thought he'd see a dead man open his eyes. This day had been one of the strangest in his life, and Amala Damarr was its centerpiece. Was she a jinx?

He threw one of the coins into the fountain. "That's for the flinarra and what we'll never know about the fool," Falca said. "You keep the rest, for the settlement house."

"Another mystery for the day. All right," Amala said wearily and took the coins. It was all the consolation Falca could manage for her, all he could do to salvage the day. It wasn't nearly enough. He might be the fool, but he immediately felt better without the coins.

They walked in silence toward the bridge, where they'd passed carriages for hire. Perhaps there would be a few left.

"He played so beautifully," Amala murmured as they neared the square lanterns of a phaeton. Falca heard the horses, the driver whistling some tune off-key.

"It doesn't make a damn bit of difference now," Falca said.

"It does to me," Amala said.

He said nothing more. Her thoughts, he sensed, could have lidded a casket. Whatever chance he might have had with her this evening was destroyed as well by the flinarra. Whatever else might have happened, he'd wanted to get a better look at her home, what he might take later, perhaps even surreptitiously unlock a window latch for ease of entry. Ideally he would have slipped down from her bedchamber after she was asleep, a jewelry box under his arm. . . .

He felt a surge of anger: You were always paying the price for the stupid and incomprehensible things people did, people you had no control over. . . . He could have slapped the flinarra, not only for the botched evening with Amala but for what he'd done to himself. The man would probably wake up in the morning, pitying himself and lamenting what had seemed like such an inevitable decision or solution the day before. He'd given up, abandoned the flina, beautiful crack and all, and by extension, himself. Falca despised the man.

The carriage was the first Falca had ever been in, and it smelled like his gloves. He couldn't find the door latch immediately, and Amala leaned over to close it. "You don't take them often, do you?"

"No," he admitted, thinking of the one that came to Sorelip's landing and how he would have given anything to be in it. Now he had one. Amala again.

The carriage lurched ahead as the driver cracked his whip. The clatter of the wheels on the cobblestones didn't quite drown out the driver's whistling. He did it loudly, perhaps because the fare would be a good one. Falca realized then that the driver must have known Amala, and her address, because she hadn't told him where to go. So she went to the Garden often. She'd said that. With her brother?

She wasn't in a talkative mood. Her reaction to the flinarra seemed to Falca to be excessive, despite the puzzle of it all. The incident had cut her deeply. Why?

All that mattered to him was that he would see her again. Despite the strangeness, foreboding even, of the day, he hoped that could be salvaged.

He stared out the window, as Amala was doing. The moons—

Suaila and Cassena—were yellow-orange in the night sky. Suaila was half-hidden by clouds. Cassena shone fully, cupped in the dawnstone hand of Roak. The Colossus had been built with that in mind, of course. The King and Queen who had seeded the Six Kingdoms, together again. Falca had heard somewhere that more babies were conceived when Cassena was full and in Roak's hand than on any other night.

He wondered what would have happened if he and Amala had gone up to the top of the monument, with the darkness, the Garden empty save for lovers, with Cassena full and round in Roak's hand. It would have been an amusing enough brag, to tell—when he was sipping sweet Gebroanan wine in a Sandsend café open to the sun— of the time he creased a golden-haired woman on the monument in Rhysselia's Garden, with Cassena's fullness the only light.

Falca smiled at a further thought as he stole a glance at Amala Damarr. She would have her own brags. A woman who adorned her home with a brass phallus from Gebroan would have her brags. In his mind he saw her lean over to some shocked Heart Hill matron years hence, while rain swept hard against the leaded panes of a drawing room window. "I had a man once," Amala would say, "atop the monument in Rhysselia's Garden. A crude, scarred but handsome overseer of dock gangers." She'd wink, adding a few more wrinkles to her face as teacups rattled in the hands of her guests. "He was so rushed by my beauty then he didn't even take off his gloves."

Falca stared at her leechstone, the brightest thing in the carriage compartment. Amala felt his gaze momentarily and met it. "I would have beaten you up to the top of the monument, you know. The wager is still on."

She resumed her staring out the window. Falca stroked the felt of his hat and smiled at the other window.

Chapter Eight

An Errand for Sippio

After Amala paid the carriage driver, she stood by the steps to her home, her back to the light in the window. Alatheus was in, having used the key she'd given him before he went away to the Rough Bounds.

Sippio approached with Shindy, even as Falca Breks walked away toward Raven's Gate. Sippio had been waiting all this time on the green across the street, not eager to go into the house and explain to Alatheus why Amala wasn't with him. As Amala kneeled down to stroke Shindy and let him lick her face, Sippio said, "You're going to see him again, aren't you?"

Amala stood. She was in no mood for questioning. She and Sippio had made love once while Alatheus was away. She knew he loved her, though he hadn't dared tell her. Because he loved her, he felt that that allowed him to have a say in her life. If Trass or Plevna had asked her the same question, she would have turned and walked away, and never mind that they were suitors. Sippio was different. No, she didn't love him, but she was absolutely sure of him, his unswerving loyalty.

"I am," she said. "In a few days."

"I'm not sorry that Shindy almost bit the man. The dog smelled something rotten."

"You're lucky you held him back. I think citizen Breks would have used the knife. You know what Alatheus would have done if we had brought back a dead Shindy."

"He would have yelled at you, taken a swipe at me, and gone out to buy you a new dog. . . . Amala, why do you bother with the likes of that ditch-licker? You don't need him, and it's only bound to cause trouble with Alatheus."

"Don't presume to know what I need," Amala said. More softly, she added, "I'd like for you to do something for me."

Sippio sighed. "You know I won't mention anything to Alatheus about the scut. I never have with any others."

"Oh, you can tell him. That's not what I want. I want you to follow Falca Breks."

"You have standing offers of marriage from two of the wealthiest men in Beckon and Heart Hill, and you want me to prowl after that quay-stomper?"

Amala squeezed his arm, which he tightened, as if to impress her with his own attributes. Amala remembered, not without some pleasure. "Do this for me," she said, trying to keep any promise out of her voice. She'd never led him on and she'd told him there would never be a second time. He had his hopes of course, but there was nothing she could do about his longings.

"You know I will. You may not like what I find out about him."

"Perhaps not. I suspect he's not a member of the hunting club Trass finds so enjoyable."

"I don't understand you, Amala," Sippio said wearily, and handed her Shindy's leash.

"And you might not like what you found if you did. Hurry now, but keep a safe distance."

"I can take care of myself, or him, if I have to," Sippio said, bristling a bit. He loped off, a stocky, bull-like figure.

When he couldn't hear her, she said, "I'm not so sure you *could* take care of him, my friend." She knew he'd do his errand well, barring any carelessness, if only to uncover something that would discourage her from the man.

She had an idea what he would find out. Falca Breks was probably a reiver and a good one. He may have even set her up, as Alatheus insisted. She didn't like being played the fool, the poppy-head, if that was the case. But part of her was impressed with his skill. She liked adroit, competent men. Clumsiness irritated her. One could be a liar but one couldn't fake skill. She was curious to learn just how much of a liar Falca Breks really was. Any information about him would be useful, because Amala needed him. For a while, anyway.

She sat down on the steps, draped an arm over her Shindy, drawing in his warmth and affection. The dog sat on his haunches, presiding over the familiar sound of the nearby fountain, alert for the occasional passerby, protective of Amala.

The light from the window almost reached them on the step. Amala glanced back at the window. She knew where Alatheus would be in the house at this time, what he would be doing. She knew his habits as well as her own. She was certain he would be thinking of her. Once that had been the most important thing in her life. Now it scared her. The danger of the 'Roll, the reivers, cut-purses, the leering sailors that so worried him, were nothing compared with her fear of him.

There was a time when she went happily to his room, from whose windows they could see the sentries pacing the parapet of the eastern wall. Innocent visits. They gave a name to the soldier who fed gulls and saltswallows from the top of Caxen's Tower, and made up stories to explain the reason why he stopped. So many times she would go to his room down the hall from her own, in their parents' grand home higher on this very hill. She would go after her mother put her to bed, thinking another day done. But for her children, her twins, it was only the beginning. They shared a love for the night, the quiet that smoothed over the world, like fresh snowfall.

Sometimes they would sneak out at night, while their parents slept, and roam the terraces of Heart Hill and Falconwrist for the occasional adventure they would share and later embellish.

Once, near a cemetery, they were frightened by the presence of someone who slowly paced its confines. Alatheus was sure he was a Murkman and wanted to flee, but Amala scoffed at the idea. After all, the man was singing in a low, gravelly voice when he wasn't quaffing from a flagon. Murkmen weren't that jolly. Curious, Amala led the way into the cemetery, and it turned out the old man was guarding the place from vandals who'd recently stolen gravestones, many of which were over seven hundred years old. He said his name was Zever Nogg, which Amala and Alatheus later amended to "Never-Nod" because of his nocturnal vigils.

Other times, Amala and Alatheus would not venture out but share by lamplight the secrets of the day, adding and subtracting the mysteries like sums on a slate. For each person they or their parents knew they created different names to account for the secrets they supposed these people kept. The game bore a language of phrases and catchwords that had meaning only to Amala and Alatheus. It was one reason why Amala loved to speak Tongue; the Timberlimb's language had never been written down, it was a secret to most humans, including the other 'tressas, who had never bothered to learn more than a few words.

Her earlier world with Alatheus was beautiful, too, for its exclusivity, for Alatheus' dedication to it, and for Amala's greater adventurousness. But that quality of hers, which gave their separate world such life and myth, also made her see its limits, made her realize that it might not last. Alatheus needed it more than she did, she came to find out over the years. The hiding of the flina was the first break in their bond, though Amala realized it only later, when they grew older and friends intruded into their lives.

She made friends much more easily than her brother, and he came to resent them, particularly the boys. Compared with Alatheus, they were shallow and frail, and Amala gave them short shrift for a while. But one came along, Tevel Laharra, who was different from the others. He tried to force himself on Amala one summer's night by Beckon Square, and she told Alatheus about it. He beat the boy senseless, though Tevel was bigger than he. Amala was glad, and maybe a little thrilled at having someone so protective of her, someone to teach the boy a lesson. Yet the more she thought about it, the more she realized she couldn't go through life having Alatheus fight her battles.

One way or another their world was doomed. Amala came to know that, was prepared for it and wanted it to end, hence her later string of lovers that began even before Alatheus went away to Skene. Alatheus didn't want it to end. Amala had begun hoping he would realize it, too, after he went away, but he was persistent, stubborn. That had disheartened and upset her, even as she proved to be equally persistent in drawing away from him. She was not afraid then of what might happen when she pulled away for good.

She was afraid now. The flinarra had made her afraid. She could accept the demise of something whose time for beauty had passed, and salvage what remained. Alatheus couldn't. It was all or nothing for him. Like the flinarra, he would have to destroy something beautiful but flawed. She was the beauty in Alatheus' world. He was weaker than she was, with a weak person's talent for rage. Both those things pushed Amala further away.

It was all a mess; she needed a clean break.

Her deepest secret—and weakness—was that she didn't want the full responsibility for severing the bond with her brother. She prized strength, had it in other areas, but with this—no. It disgusted her to realize she wanted, needed help, but there it was. She hadn't wanted Alatheus fighting her battles, and here she was enlisting someone else. She promised herself that Falca Breks would be the last.

She didn't quite know how he could help; she only sensed instinctively that he could the day she met him. If she had been too slowly unraveling the bond with Alatheus, perhaps she needed the cut of a sword. Falca Breks had the edge, of that she was sure, no matter what else Sippio might find out about the man. She hoped Alatheus' disgust, his finally admitting that she was not perfect, would overshadow his anger and destructiveness. She saw the flinarra again, in her mind, smashing his instrument, and grew more determined to break free.

Shindy growled at men passing by the fountain. Amala hushed the dog and scratched his ears. She thought of the empty, as they were called, that had fallen into that fountain. How Alatheus took the poor thing to the crematorium without complaint. Any other man would not have dirtied his hands, or would have been afraid. He paid for the cremation, when others would merely have dumped him into a canal. Alatheus was also a good man, but he still made her feel that love was all too often a choking vine.

Plevna or Trass, with whom she had been alternating her affections, were not likely to help her. Trass was the better of the two, but also the closer friend of Alatheus. What kind of husband would he be? She'd grow bored with him in months, like most of her friends who married for station and spent their idle hours comparing lovers like they would spurroses at a garden party. Either Plevna or Trass would bring her back into the fold of Heart Hill, which she was so determined to leave.

She needed a man unlike the others, who wouldn't be afraid of Alatheus. Her manipulation bothered her, but that was where Falca Breks was perfect, apart from his physical appeal. She sensed he wanted something from her, besides the bed of course. The lure of Heart Hill wealth? She could dangle that bauble easily enough. Falca

Breks's desires undoubtedly stopped short of an offer of marriage—which Amala certainly had no intention of accepting. If Trass was one extreme, reiver Breks was the other, no doubt.

She needed Falca Breks only for a while, just like he needed her. He seemed like a man used to easy partings. A tip of that broad-brimmed hat of his would seal whatever memories they chose to keep.

There would be some, Amala thought with a smile. He might be a ditch-licker, but she liked him. He had wit to match his muscle and scars and those curious leather gloves. Anyone who could imagine a dead Timberlimb to life would have something interesting to say in the morning, more than the snoring Plevna.

So she would hand Falca Breks the flina of a past world, to smash before Alatheus did. Confronted with the pieces, Alatheus could do nothing but walk away. He wouldn't strike at her, not with Falca Breks there beside her. If she had to be cruel this one time, so be it. Alatheus wouldn't understand. But if she ever had a son, she would name it after her brother, and maybe then he would understand why she had to break loose from the greatest love she'd likely ever know.

You can't leave for Gebroan yet, citizen Breks, she thought. Not just yet. It was just as well he'd forgotten to ask for his cloak.

She began to sing the song old Nogg had sung in the cemetery years ago. Her voice carried softly and well. "Fit for lullabies," Trass had told her once, in one of his more clumsy attempts to press the matter of marriage. Well, she wanted that someday but not with a sponge-belly like Trass. Just as she wanted to do more than the work at the settlement house. She'd talked to All-Eye and Gurrus about how they came to be captured, what was being done in the Rough Bounds. She wanted to go there and help them, maybe even fight the soldiers. Was that folly? She'd asked Gurrus whether it would matter if she went, whether his people would want her there to help. He said yes. At the very least she would be of use because she knew Tongue. She could listen to the soldiers below, who didn't think anyone above knew what they were saying. She could help plan ambushes better. Her very presence there would tell his people that there were some shit-catchers who thought the soldiers wrong. If one came, maybe more would follow to help.

She despised people who assumed it was a little fancy she'd grow bored with in a year. These were the same people who judged her solely on her beauty. Well, she wanted to go to a place where her beauty wouldn't matter a fig, but her quickness, strength, and intelligence would.

Of course she was proud of her beauty, but it was a burden to her as well. She wanted to make a difference in the world as she saw it, but first she had to escape. Falca Breks would likely be the last man she'd have in a long, long time. . . .

The door at the top of the steps opened, and Alatheus stood, silhouetted by the hallway candles.

He couldn't possibly have heard her singing. More likely he'd felt her thoughts. She remembered the sudden pain in her leg months ago and knew it was the pain Alatheus suffered from the stingvine.

"Amala?" he said softly into the night.

"Yes, Alatheus. I'm coming in now."

She got up, Shindy bounding ahead of her, and took one last, deep breath of the chilly but sweet night air before following her brother into her home.

Chapter Nine

Sweet-hand

Rain began to fall as the carriage approached Raven's Gate. Falca leaned over to shutter the compartment window, muting the driver's curses, sealing off the weather. His knee touched Amala's as he leaned back, wondering if her brother would be at her home or whether they would have it to themselves.

"I'm glad we left the den early," Amala said, jostling with the sway of the carriage. "The aulosts were disappointing. So much for my suggestion for the evening. We don't seem to have much luck with music together. First the flinarra and now this."

"It was a good suggestion," Falca said, staring out the small window. The rain distorted a fire men had lit under the protection of Raven's Gate. "The dens just aren't what they used to be," he continued. "The consorts are younger than ever, and so are the blood-snares."

"I know. Impatient consorts make for hurried aulosts."

"And young 'snares don't produce the sound of mature ones used to the joining."

"Of course, if you had one of those things sucking at your arm, taking your blood, you might be in a hurry to finish playing."

Falca shrugged. "They get paid very well to perform better than they did." He thought of telling her what his uncle tried to do years ago, decided against it, then thought it wouldn't conflict with anything he'd told her before. She might be amused or feel sympathy for him. That was useful every now and then.

"I almost became a consort myself," he said.

"You're joking, Falca!"

"No, not at all. My uncle tried to sell me to the Consort's Guild when I was eight. If I'd gone, I wouldn't be here with you now," he said. "Consorts don't live past twenty-five. It's all those joinings with the parasite. There's a slow-working poison in the bloodsnare's saliva."

The carriage shuddered to a stop. Amala looked briefly out the window, then back at Falca. "You ran away?"

He nodded. "You seem amused by that."

Amala hesitated, her hand on the door latch. "I'm sorry, it's just that I ran away too. Maybe not as far away as you did. And I was considerably older. My father arranged a marriage match for me to a man I loathed. 'You're long overdue,' he said, as if I were a parcel from Slacere. 'Young women your age are married with children already,' he said."

"And?"

"Alatheus persuaded the suitor to withdraw his offer."

"How much did he pay the man?"

"He didn't. He got him drunk one night and won me back by winning the final round of a game of three-star."

Falca laughed. "What did he put up to cover a loss?"

"The deed to the family property by Slowind Lake in the mountains. It's in his name."

"Were you angry at him?"

"I should have been, but I wasn't. Too young, too grateful. Besides, it had a desperate, romantic quality to it, you know, one of those stories to tell when you're old and nobody wants you. Anyway, father blamed the failure on me, since Alatheus and I couldn't tell him what really happened. And I left. I haven't spoken to him since."

They left the carriage, and Falca paid the driver generously for the slow fare. "Should I wait?" the hooded man asked. Falca shook his head. The carriage lurched away. "I can walk back," he said to Amala.

"Not until you've been warmed by my fire and a draft or two of scorchbelly. Let's get out of this rain."

* * *

A growl greeted them in the darkness of the entryway. "You brother or the dog?" Falca said, with a grin, taking off his hat an gloves.

"Hush, Shindy," Amala said, as she lighted a lamp by the door revealing the guardian. As she was locking the door, Falca asked "Will your brother return soon?"

"Sooner or later. But he won't be able to get in." She showe Falca another key. "It's his. I took it from a pocket of his cape whil he was having his say about our evening together. I'll let him in later but only after you've gone."

Tomorrow morning, I hope, Falca thought, feeling the sweet stir ring below. He clucked his tongue teasingly. "You're a heartless woman, Amala. Locking your own brother out, one who saved yo from the chains of marriage."

"And saving your neck from his sword. Oh, he'll be just fine. H has a friend, Trass Kularrus up the street. Or he'll move further up, t my parents' home."

Falca wondered where exactly that was. He'd have to find out When the time came to approach Alatheus with his offer, he wante to know where he could find him. Another game of three-star per haps? Falca was thinking of a double fist. Get the boot-money from the brother for leaving her alone, then this house. One last visit She'd have her jewelry upstairs. Together, the two fists might just b enough for Gebroan. The thought put him in an even better moo than Amala's boldness. He had reduced his earlier wariness of her t foolishness. She had an appetite for canal-side, that was all.

"You don't really care about Alatheus, do you?" Amala was ask ing. "He wasn't exactly cordial to you before."

Falca laughed it off. "As one who's been locked out before, I fee for the man."

"I've a hunch, Falca, that you're not one to let the matter of missing key stop you. . . . Shindy, be quiet!"

"He doesn't much like me either," Falca said smiling.

"Oh, he's the same with everybody, just protective."

Amala took the lamp from the stand and shooed the dog ahead Falca followed her into the larger room. She set the lamp on the table The dog slunk underneath, his eyes following Falca as he placed hi hat and gloves on a chair.

"Get that fire alive, will you?" Amala asked. "While I get ou scorchbelly."

Falca kneeled by the hearth as Amala left the room and stirred the coals with an iron poker. He added wood from a bin formed of two brass beavers crouching tail to tail. He turned around. The dog was baring his teeth.

"Alatheus left you in charge here, did he? Don't worry, I won't hurt her."

Amala came back with two crystal bottles of differing size and two glasses and put them all on the table. "You have your choice, Falca. Scorchbelly"—she pointed to the bigger bottle with the dark red liquid—"or this."

Falca held up the smaller decanter, swirling the black liquid around. "And what is this?"

"The best translation from Tongue is Sweet-hand," Amala said.

"Never heard of it."

"They don't sell it canal-side like they do scrape, Falca," she said, and held up the decanter in front of her face, as if trying on a mask.

She knows, Falca thought. . . . But how could she; he'd said nothing. She wouldn't be here offering him a drink if she did. And he hadn't done anything so terrible for her to want to poison him. He felt a little heat in his face as she swirled the black liquid. Her brother seemed crazy enough, though, and they were twins. His wariness returned.

"So what is it, then?" he asked.

"A private pleasure, not as harsh as scrape. Did you know that back in the Rough Bounds, Limbs use scrape to help domesticate livestock they breed in pens a hundred feet off the ground?" Amala laughed.

"Quite a joke for them," Falca said.

"It is."

"Where do they get this . . . Sweet-hand?"

"Sorry. The where and how is a secret, and I gave my promise to Gurrus I'd keep it a secret."

"Should I consider it an honor that you offer it to me?"

"Only if you try it."

"Pour."

Amala gave equal measures to the glasses and raised hers. "To your Gebroanan sun that you're so eager to feel," she said, glancing at the rain-streaked windows. "And to the Timberlimbs."

Falca noted the level of her glass, waited until she'd taken a sip. Amala smiled. "Why, citizen Breks, you don't trust me, do you? Tell

me, what have you done to me that would make you think I'd wan
retribution?"

"Nothing. By nature I'm suspicious of anything I'm not familiar
with. My life has not had as full a measure of trust as is in that glass."

Amala took another sip. "That sounded honest enough. Perhaps
mine has had too full a measure."

Falca raised his glass. "To the Gebroanan sun and your Timberlimbs," he said, and drank. The liquid was sweet, musky.

"You know," Amala said, "I may go to fight with them in the
Bounds. You're the first, Falca, that I've told. *That* is an honor."

Falca was glad he checked his urge to laugh. Amala Damarr in the
Rough Bounds? She'd need more than her dancer's legs to survive.

"What does your brother think of that idea?"

"I told you, you're the first to know. I won't tell Alatheus."

"He'll be in for a surprise when he sees you along some fores
path."

She shrugged. "If he goes back."

"I've seen you with the sliver-heart, but do you know how to use
other weapons, the bow and diadem? Could you kill, even for a
cause? Have you spent a night alone in the wilderness?"

"Have you?"

"It depends on what wilderness we're talking about."

"I'll learn what I have to learn."

"Well, good luck to you, if you go. And cut your hair. It wouldn'
be very practical in the Bounds."

"You don't think I'd do it, do you? You think I'm some silly
poppy-head from the Hill, who plays at charity."

"Do you care what I think?"

Amala laughed. "No."

"Then why ask?"

"Just to see what you'd say."

He looked at her in the flickering lamplight, thinking. Rain
pattered against the window. The hand that held the glass was larger
than most women's her size. She had strength in her shoulders
her carriage. He remembered her manhandling the empty from the
fountain.

He walked the few steps to her. She didn't move, not even to pu
down her glass. With one hand he gathered her long golden hair back
from her neck. Her wide, green eyes held his. She raised her strong

chin, and he saw a little scar he hadn't noticed before. He sensed defiance and maybe anger in her and something else, something beyond him talking to her like a schoolmaster.

The leechstone glistened red in the low light. It moved. How could she stand it, having a living thing at her throat, taking from her what it needed to live.

"I'm trying to see you with short hair," Falca whispered, ignoring the growl from underneath the table. "I think, Amala, you might surprise me, not that it matters. You might surprise yourself, which does."

He released the luxuriant sheaf of her hair, stepped back, and drank all the Sweet-hand in one gulp. Amala did the same. "For a private pleasure, it becomes bitter on the tongue after that first sweetness."

"That goes away. Trust me."

He was about to place the glass on the table, but Amala caught his wrist. "You destroy the receptacle to release the dream, the wish. I forgot, you're supposed to think of something."

"We did, the toasts."

"So we did. The Limbs believe that the spirit is stronger than that which gives it form, or carries it. They burn their wooden vessels; we break the glasses."

She flung hers into the depths of the hearth, with surprising force, it seemed to Falca. He threw his glass, too, causing Shindy to rise underneath the table and growl more menacingly than before.

"I think he means it this time," Falca said.

"Perhaps we should move to a safer location."

He handed her the lamp, and she went ahead. Falca paused to bank the fire. She turned, shaking her head. "Come, Falca." She held out a hand. "The fire will take care of itself."

She squeezed his hand for a moment and then led the way from the room. He followed her, around a corner to the stairs. Near the top, he placed a hand on the side of her thigh, feeling the firm, working muscles.

"Sweet-hand," she murmured, not pausing or looking around. "It does make one eager."

His hand moved up to her waist as they entered the room. Just before she closed the door, she snapped her fingers. Falca heard the clicking of Shindy's nails on the stairs. She's no fool, he thought. In case of trouble with him, all she had to do was call the dog and it would be at his throat in seconds.

Amala put the lamp on a chest at the foot of the four-post bed. The trailing light revealed much of the small room: a shadowy wardrobe closet with a long mirror that reflected Amala; a table by the door with an enamel washing basin, gooseneck ewer, and a pouch set in the basin, oddly enough. There was a bureau with yet another mirror that filled a corner of the room by the window. Brushes, small bottles, combs were scattered over the marble bureau top. A leatherbound book inclined over a brooch. Falca couldn't have read the title if he wanted to. To the side of the mirror, a pair of skates hung by a peg on the wall. Falca nodded at them.

"My first passion," Amala said, "and a lonely one, given the climate here."

The air smelled of dried sunsbreath set in a vase, and rosewater.

Amala was lighting a candle on a bedside table. "How do you feel?" she asked.

"The Sweet-hand? If scrape is like walking on cotton, this . . . I don't know. It's good. I feel like the springs to a fine carriage, like someone's filing my bones. I want to run."

"The Limbs say it puts eyes in your hands," Amala said, sitting down on her bed cross-legged.

Falca laughed. "You seem more resistant than I. That's hardly a seductive posture. Am I supposed to reveal a secret now? You look like you're ready to listen to anything."

"I want to watch you undress."

"You're the host."

"Closer to the light, Falca."

He took off his clothes and boots, feeling uneasy, despite the facade of a grin. Even now, he didn't like being watched, observed. That was his province. Amala gazed at him as a sculptor would a model.

He bent down and transferred his dagger to a fold of his tunic. The edge of the bed blocked Amala's view. He didn't want to alarm her, but neither would he break a habit. He had to know it was within easy reach. As he gathered up his clothes and the hidden dagger, Amala said, "You're a methodical man, Sweet-hand or no."

He placed the clothes on the floor in front of the bed table. "Your turn," he said. He leaned against the wall, arms folded, just beyond the pale of the candlelight. Something poked him in the back, a wall eg and garment. As he moved, he felt it—his cloak. The leather was cool. He walked a few steps toward Amala, who had slid off the bed toward the lamplight.

She was not methodical. She left her clothes where she dropped them. He saw the point of the sliver-heart in a sleeve. He felt himself rising with the sight of her, the long yellow hair that fell almost to her waist, the dancer's legs that were more muscular than slender. He thought of the bet they had yet to decide.

She ran her hands over her breasts, her dark nipples hard from the chill of the room. She had a birthmark under the swell of her left breast. She turned her back to him, gave her buttocks a playful but sharp enough slap so that Falca could see the red from her fingers against the pale skin. "Really my best feature, don't you think?" she murmured.

"I wouldn't care to choose, Amala," he whispered, almost telling her, You're a beautiful woman, a beautiful woman. He marveled at the pleasure she took in herself, the confidence that really was her best feature, the confidence he'd sensed in her walk that first day. She was truly blessed physically. And for a moment he felt daunted by her splendor. He'd gotten lazy with the sisters. Amala deserved more than a mere tumble.

"Come here, Amala," he said softly.

She did, taking his hand. Before he embraced her, she said, "I almost forgot." She reached to the wall. "Here's your cloak," she said, laughing, as she draped it in a loose roll around the spar of his manhood, which dropped to the horizontal and stayed there, absurdly wigged. Falca stepped back, laughing too, hands on his hips.

"I've been many things, but a coathook?" He took it off and pulled Amala to him. She found him with her hand as he kissed her lips, her neck, avoiding the leechstone. His fingers ventured through the cascade of her hair to trace the path of her spine, and farther. She dropped to one knee and wet as much of him as she could with her mouth. Once, twice, then left him for the bed. She lay on her stomach, her arms outstretched, her hands bunching the linen spread, as she slowly lifted her buttocks, sinking her stomach so low that wrinkles formed in her slender waist.

"Falca..." she whispered, rising from her elbows and turning around.

He traced his tongue along the backs and insides of her legs, taking the summit of her rump again and again with his hands, spreading out the soft ends of her hair over her back.

"Falca, please," she whispered, dropping to her elbows, then lower. Her head lay to one side, her eyes closed.

When he reached over to the bed table, she sensed the momentary separation and opened her eyes. He lifted the candle from the holder, bringing light closer, bathing her exquisite body in light.

"That too?" she whispered "If you want."

He shook his head as she spread her legs wider. He didn't know why he wanted the candle, only that he saw something in his mind, in the candle, a dream, a portent. He had to have the candle, use it. It seemed so important, more important than anything else.

"Higher, Amala," he said softly, not expecting she could. She did. He held the candle above her buttocks, near the small of her back. The light illuminated the smooth grain of her skin, a beauty mark on the left, a blemish on the right, her thatch of golden hair below. He held one hand below the candle, so the dripping wax would not sting her.

She groaned softly as he entered her, gently at first, so gently the candle might have remained upright of its own accord. Then he began moving into her harder, and harder still, her skin shivering with each thrust, sometimes deep, sometimes shallow. Her hands gathered more of the spread, digging for purchase. The flame flickered with his movement, with hers. The wax spit out onto the back of his hand. He felt only brief pain each time, inconsequential to her beauty in the close, melting light, to her long, drawn-out exhalations of his name.

She shuddered, relaxed and he pierced her gently again, steadying the lowering flame over his hand. "Take it away, take your hand away," she whispered, without looking back. "I want to feel the burn too."

"No, Amala," he said.

"Please. I don't mind. I know what it's like."

He shook his head and bore into her harder, fully, causing her to groan again. His hand, spotted with blisters of wax, was her shield and he meant to protect her with it, guard her from himself, from something inside of him, the quick dream he'd had of a thousand candles.

She shuddered again, almost convulsively, and Falca moved gently but deeply in her to extract the last of her trembling. He killed the flame with a pinch of his fingers and tossed the candle to the floor. He kissed her flesh where his hand had been and withdrew from her. She rolled over onto her back, gripped his wrists, and pulled him down into her again, kissing, nipping him. Their bodies found one dance, discarded it, discovered another. They rolled over as one and laughed at the strands of her hair that were woven nuisances to their kisses.

Amala raised her arms straight over her head, and Falca saw the most wonderful smile he'd ever seen. She bent slowly backward at her knees till she lay on her legs and he marveled at her suppleness. He stroked the tension in her knees, her thighs. "Sneaking under the fence," she murmured as he rose to his elbows. The leechstone glistened in the lamplight, an ever-watchful eye half-hidden on her neck by her left breast. He found her hands and pulled her up again, and she straddled him like a cat undecided whether to eat the mouse or play with it. She teased his face, his scar, with her hair, and he suddenly grabbed a mouthful and pulled, causing her to yelp and turn on her side. Then he was on her again, beginning again, her hands on his buttocks, pulling him deeper into her.

Even when they heard the pounding at the door, outside the window and below, she wouldn't let him stop. Her eyes were open, and she kept shaking her head as Alatheus drunkenly yelled her name, demanding that she let him in. Falca was aware, again, of the rain pattering against the window, as Alatheus kept pounding on the door. There was silence for a moment, and Falca thought he was gone. Then came Alatheus' hoarse voice, closer, grainier, his calling for Amala, underneath the window.

A fierce sense of possession infused Falca as he and Amala moved together by the window. He felt he was making a claim on her, that she had made a choice and that made him drive into her harder, and her into him. He kissed her open mouth, her cheeks, then his mouth slid lower, his teeth finding the leechstone. Alatheus' gift. The carapace had the coolness of glass. He felt it move on his lips. He almost gagged. But he didn't pull on the parasite; that might have torn Amala's skin. He bit it off. She cried out, rising from the bed, her strength lifting him. He spit out the leechstone toward the window, where it made a rapping sound. Or was it a stone Alatheus had thrown against the window?

He emptied himself into her in one last lunge and lay his head to one side of hers. They both lay still, listening for Alatheus. All was quiet save for the rain against the window, and Shindy's whimpering near the door to the room. Amala held him tightly. He felt her fingers pressing into his back. He kissed damp hair by her ear.

"Amala," he whispered. "Let me see it."

She released him. He rose to his elbows. "Is there much blood?" she asked.

"Not much." What blood there was had been smeared by his skin. He licked the wound clean. Three dark beads appeared, and he cleansed those, too, with his tongue. "Did it hurt?" he said.

She shook her head and stared at him, smiling faintly. "What does it taste like, my blood?"

"Sweet. Everything about you. Everything," he said, kissing her.

"You're a liar."

"Does it bother you I did it?"

She looked amused. "Do I seem angry? If I was, you'd know it. It was time. And I've seen blood in the bed before, my blood."

Falca nodded toward the window. "Where was he then?"

"You think he was the one, the first."

Falca shrugged, feeling himself shrinking in her.

"No," she said. "Not then, or after, though there were times it could have happened, very easily, and almost did. I gave myself to a man I didn't care about, one I knew I'd never see again. I wanted to keep it simple." She laughed. "There was also another man I'd been seeing at the time, who felt cheated enough to say goodbye. A boy, really."

She said she was cold, so they got underneath the spread and blankets. Falca lay on his side, stroking her belly. "You know, Falca, most men don't like to talk about other men in bed with a woman."

"I'm the one with you now." He grinned. "But what about you? Shall I talk about other women, my first time? What I lacked in patience I made up for in numbers. The poor girl never got to sleep that night."

"Tell me about the sisters," Amala said softly.

Falca stiffened, stopped caressing her.

"Don't stop that, it feels good. Really, Falca, it's all right. If it wasn't, you wouldn't be here. Alatheus was right about you setting me up, but that's over and done with. But don't be angry that I spied on you. That would annoy me, considering you got what you deserved."

"How did you find out?" he said.

"Well, it's not as if it was very hard, though Sippio did an even better job than I thought. He told me a lot, though you'll have to tell me the name of the girl who didn't get any sleep."

"Venar?" Falca whispered.

"The little man, yes. He talked so much Sippio suspected he had a grudge against you. Of course, a little money helped. Sippio said he also tried to talk to someone else who was skulking around your warehouse home by that canal. The man ran away, though he was twice the size of Sippio. I think he must have been the one who pushed me to the street, the one I got with my sliver-heart."

Falca sat up, his heart racing.

"Did you two have a falling out?"

Falca got out of the bed. He had to stand. It was impossible, he thought. Saphrax alive?

He walked past the lamp and looked out the rain-smeared window. "When did Sippio do all this?" he asked Amala. Perhaps it was before . . .

"A day or so after I saw you last. What's the matter? Just because I had you followed?"

"No. If you want more than the lies I gave you, you have a right to find out what you want." His fingers squeaked the windowpane as he wondered why indeed he was upset. The attempt on Saphrax was shoddy work, and he detested that. He'd do better next time. If Saphrax proved more than a mere annoyance, he'd make sure to get rid of him. And in a way, it was reassuring. He *hadn't* been seeing things. It *had* been the brute by the settlement house.

"Falca . . . ?"

"I thought the man was dead, that's all."

"Don't you know for sure? What happened to him, I don't understand."

"I thought I'd killed him."

Amala was silent for long moments. Falca looked over at her, but the lamp at the end of the bed didn't provide enough light for him to see her expression. Not that he needed illumination to know what she was thinking: How safe am I with him in this room? He thought she was going to ask him why he tried to kill Saphrax, but he was wrong.

"You seem plagued by people who won't stay dead, Falca," she said.

If one imagining—Saphrax—had been real, so had the feeling he dismissed earlier about Amala. "You had me followed," Falca said. "Toward what end? Is it a game you have with men? Just to find out about me? What is it you want?"

"To be your lover and you to be mine. I want you to come back to bed. And I want something else. I was going to wait until morning. But we may as well get it over with. You'll undoubtedly be annoyed."

"You've just made sure of that."

"Go look in the washbasin near the door."

Falca took the lamp, found the pouch. Immediately he knew what it was. He walked back to the bed, put the lamp on the chest, and emptied a few of the gold roaks into his palm. "Payment? That's a first. How did you know you'd enjoy yourself so much?" If there was a trace of amusement in his voice, there was none in hers.

"Falca," she said slowly, "take that and leave the Limb mongers alone to sell their scrape without you stealing their profits. Sippio found out you're one of the biggest—what's the word?—fisters canal-side. The Limbs are allowed precious few other ways to make a life for themselves in a place they never wanted to come to. So long as you see me—and I hope you want to again—you'll leave the Limbs alone. If you do, you'll see more of what's in your sweet hand."

Falca could scarcely believe what he was hearing. "Who do you think you're talking to? Maybe your Sippio wasn't as thorough as you thought. I don't like anyone, Amala, *anyone* dictating choices to me."

"I'll tell you, Falca, who *you* are talking to. Someone who is more profitable and less dangerous than your other line of work. I'm not dictating choices to you. The choice is yours."

He felt the heat of anger in his face, the lovemaking long gone. He had a mind to rob the place now. Take everything. Show her one doesn't play with with a man such as Falca Breks. But there was the dog Amala would summon in an instant. He could kill it, but it would be messy.

He hefted the coins before putting them back in the pouch and cinching the drawstrings. He wondered if pleasure before business was always the rule with Amala Damarr.

"Your friend Sippio does good work. No wonder you keep him employed."

"Take it, Falca. It's what you want from me, isn't it?"

"Yes."

"There's much more in a safe place elsewhere. Not here. I've cashed certain gifts my brother gave me."

"You don't miss a trick," he said, thinking of his decision. The choice should be obvious. Take the easy coin. A few months of Amala Damarr and he'd be in Gebroan for good. He had finally found the One Mark. But there was a price. She'd be running his life. She already had, and he hadn't even known it. Just who had set up who? As he'd marveled at the beauty of this woman, he now marveled at something else: Given other circumstances, Amala Damarr would have been running the streets of Catch-All and Slidetown and likely he'd be working for her. Of all the men who had tried to best him, kill him, work him into a corner from which he couldn't escape, he'd finally met his match in a woman who wanted to go to the Rough Bounds to help Timberlimbs. It was almost laughable. Given ambition to match her extraordinary beauty and intelligence and family connections, she could rise to the royal court or beyond. Yet here she was, fisting for Limbs.

"Well?"she said.

"I'd better go."

"You're the first man ever to leave my bed when he didn't have to."

He shook his head in amazement that she could say something like that now. "I'd say the Sweet-hand has worn off, Amala."

He let her see the dagger as he got dressed. He picked up the pouch of gold and stuffed it into his belt.

"I'm glad," she said. "Take Alatheus' key. I want to see you again, Falca."

He let himself look at her, there on the bed, for longer than he should have, knowing, in spite of everything, that he wanted the same thing. But he had to salvage his sense of control, to walk away from hers. It was a sham of course, because he was taking the money. He told himself she was a means to an end, the most beautiful means he'd ever have.

He found Alatheus' key among her clothes.

"Any more surprises?" he said.

She hesitated enough to make him wonder what it was. "No," she said. "I think we know as much about each other as we'll ever need to know."

He opened the door wide. Shindy loped in, as if he'd been waiting all along. As Falca was closing the door behind him, he said, "By the way, Amala, you'll do just fine in the Rough Bounds."

On the landing he paused, listening to the soft sound of Amala rising from her bed, seeing in his mind her body the way he'd first seen it. He saw the falling of her hair, the swelling of her breasts as she bent over to blow out the lamp. He heard the quick puff of her closing breath. For a moment he was tempted to go back in.

In the dark he felt carefully for the first step of the stairs, then took the rest quickly.

Chapter Ten

The Lifting

Saphrax had followed Falca to the woman's house, hiding behind the far edge of the fountain of the girl. He saw Falca and the woman leave by carriage. He waited. He had no place else to go and he knew Falca would be back. He had to stay close.

Saphrax saw curtains part in windows of nearby houses and faces that briefly appeared. Passersby glanced nervously at him, giving him a wide berth. He was an intrusion in the neighborhood, but no one would do anything about it. After all, he'd broken no law. He just looked like the worst of beggars, and the neighborhood people were frightened of him. That made Saphrax feel good. A dog sauntered onto the green, and though the animal wasn't threatening, Saphrax threw a rock at it anyway. The dog yelped and ran away. Saphrax grinned with pride at his aim and thought that for the next few hours anyway, this little corner of Draica was his.

Even when the rain began to fall, he didn't leave to seek shelter under the trees of the green. His filthy, ripped clothes were soon soaked, and he trembled with the chill. He welcomed the rain as a penance, as proof to Falca of what he would endure, if only Falca would take him back. He didn't know when the moment would come when he would show himself to Falca, but surely he'd recognize that moment.

He'd watched the carriage return with Falca and the yellow-haired woman. He saw them leave the carriage and hurry toward the house, away from where he had been standing or crouching for hours, a mate for the fountain girl.

Of course Falca would go in with the woman. He always got his way. With a feeling of wanting to belong again to Falca, anger also stirred within Saphrax. Anger at Falca for abandoning his presence again, dismissing him, and anger at himself for standing mute as a statue, for not declaring himself alive to Falca.

But it wasn't the time, not when Falca was with the woman. He calmed himself, flicking his earring.

Saphrax had never been jealous of Solvie and Sincta. They were Falca's merely for rutting. He was jealous of this golden woman. She was different, if only because Falca was doing things with her, like a friend, unlike the sisters, unlike himself. She was important to him. She might even be helping him fist the Limbs, or better.

He kept wiping the rain from his eyes as he stared at the light in the upstairs window, the only light he could see in the houses around, after a while. A gentle light. It came as a gift to Saphrax, for it added the value of a vigil to his watch. He knew what they were doing, and certainly he wasn't jealous of that. Rutting was more of a nuisance; he'd never understood why Falca liked it so much.

Staring at the gentle light, Saphrax felt like a sentry on watch who took added duty without being ordered to do so. Falca would be proud that he was on guard. He felt a surge of protectiveness. That fist Falca had set up had degenerated into something else, Saphrax felt. Normally Falca would have gotten what he wanted and moved on to the next. His behavior was strange, and never mind the woman was beautiful.

A man came, one with golden hair and wearing a soldier's cape. He disturbed everything, disrupting Saphrax's important vigil. He tripped on the steps to the house. Drunk. Saphrax was so angry that he started for the intruder, intent on dragging him away. But then Saphrax stopped, realizing this might be the opportunity he had been waiting for. Maybe the man would disturb Falca, make him angry and furious.

Let the drunk do his worst, Saphrax thought. Then I'll kill him and present Falca with the body in the morning, as proof of my loyalty, my determination to make up for my mistakes.

Saphrax smiled as the man banged his fist on the door, shouting a name—Amala—over and over. So that was the quiver's name. He hoped the drunk would break the door, presenting him with an even better opportunity for impressing Falca. The man left the porch and leaned over the iron fence railings so far, Saphrax could have impaled him with a clap on the back. He assailed the second-story, where the light still glowed faintly, with the same drunken demands. Soon, however, he turned, cursing, and as he passed the steps, threw something at the door. He stumbled away up the street, his limp the invitation of an easy mark.

Saphrax followed, pausing only to steal up the steps to see what the man had thrown.

Flowers, a bunch of flowers, now strewn over stone. He must know the woman, he must be a rival to Falca. He smiled. It was getting better and better. Falca would be grateful once the man was killed. Saphrax picked up a few of the flowers and stuffed them into his belt. He'd show them to Falca as proof, for Falca surely would see the rest when he came out in the morning.

He hurried after the drunk, thinking. He could use his hands, but a weapon would be better, quicker. He had always liked the weight of something in his hand. It gave him more pleasure to strike than to squeeze. Vessa's complaint. He felt along the fence railings for a picket weakened by rust and pulled at several until he found one. He tugged hard with his strength, and the iron bar snapped off with the sound of a breaking bone. He grunted with satisfaction, hefting the two-foot length, poking his meaty palm with the point. Wiping the rain from his eyes with his other hand, he went after the drunken man.

Saphrax's mark walked at an angle in the street, between the rain-needled nimbuses of the oil streetlamps. A cat whined somewhere near. Saphrax concentrated on the stealth of his tracking, remembering Falca's disgust with his clumsiness. He was not going to fail this time.

The man passed a side alley, turned his head briefly at something there. The cat? Saphrax wondered. He stopped, held his breath, blinking his eyes as the rain hit his face. The man kept walking. Saphrax hurried ahead, taking two steps for his quarry's one. The streetlamps curved around the rising way ahead.

As Saphrax, too, passed the alley, light flared from its depths, a light so blinding, he instantly lifted his hand to protect his eyes from the fire. But he felt no heat or searing wave. The light dissipated, and

Saphrax lowered his hand to see the light shrinking, condensing into something that glittered like glass. Some powerful lantern? he thought, straining to see.

At first Saphrax was sure a woman was being raped, and he was about to go on. It was none of his business. In other circumstances it might have been amusing enough to watch, but he had business to attend to.

Then he realized it was not a man in the long cape standing over a woman, but the other way around. And that curiosity made him linger.

The man on the ground was kicking and twitching spasmodically, the way Saphrax had seen the tortured do on the prison hulk. The woman was kneeling at his side, more in the posture of succor than assault. The ball of intense blue-white light centered over the man's forehead. He kept hitting his head up and down on the paving stones, as if the woman had him by the hair and was trying to crack his skull. But there was only the ball of light, which rose and fell in tandem with the victim's head.

Saphrax had all but forgotten about his mark, so fascinated was he by this other. He walked slowly into the alley, even as the kneeling woman rose. The man lay still now, his agony over.

The woman brandished the light, and Saphrax saw that its core was contained within a knobbed head of glass or crystal. It was a mace, the length of the iron bar Saphrax still held. The light was bright enough for him to see the woman take a few petals of flowers and sprinkle them on the crumpled man's face, murmuring something Saphrax could not hear for the rain.

Saphrax was frightened, but he walked ahead anyway, pulled by awe and fascination. The woman still did not see him, still immersed in the waning moments of this strange ritual. Saphrax was mesmerized. This woman had more power than Falca ever had. She had subdued—killed?—a man with naught but light. No blows or stabs. What *was* that light? He had to know! He had to have it! He hefted the iron bar almost involuntarily, but he knew somehow that that would not be the way to get it. The woman was smaller than the man. If the physically weak could overcome the strong...Saphrax was strong, he'd shown that again and again, but he felt helpless in all other respects.

He felt as if someone had just given him a weapon.

The woman saw him now, whirled to face him, tucking the glowing mace within the folds of her cape, and in that transfer of light to darkness Saphrax saw the dagger she held in her other hand. That confused Saphrax. Why would she defend herself with such a paltry thing when she had that other power?

"No farther," the woman said.

"I . . . I meant no harm," Saphrax stammered. "I was tracking another. I . . ."

"What do you want?"

"That . . . what you have."

There was a long pause before she answered. "Do you know what I am, who we are?"

Saphrax shook his head in the dark. "I know only that I want what you have."

She took the mace out, and the brightness of it hurt Saphrax's eyes. He saw the full length of her dagger. She was a young woman, young as Falca, with the same black hair but not his blue eyes. Hers were much darker. She was smiling. "Is this what you want, my friend?" She tapped the point of the dagger on the mace-head, and Saphrax heard a sound no greater than the tapping of a windowpane.

"Yes," he said.

"You wish to join us, then. That can be done. If you succeed in giving your gift so that you may take the Gifts of others, you must know you will never be the same. Are you prepared to leave your life as you knew it?"

"I am," Saphrax said, not knowing where the words came from within him. He only knew he had to have what he had seen.

"Prepared and lucky," the woman said, her tone more casual now. "But for a few minutes, you would be lying where this one is. My luck, too, began the day I met one who brought me to the One. Now come with me. You first." She stepped aside.

Saphrax paused by the victim. In the light of the mace he saw the mark on the forehead. "Is he dead?"

"He lives, though he's given his Gift. Does it sadden you?"

Saphrax kicked the man viciously, seeing Falca's face in his.

"No more," the woman said, not yelling, but with such firmness that Saphrax instantly stopped. "He has given himself to something greater. He deserves respect for his sacrifice. Not all of us follow that rule, but it is mine and you will respect that if you would follow me."

Saphrax nodded. As if to atone for his mistake, he pulled the flowers from his belt and threw them on the man, inspired by what he'd seen the woman do.

She laughed. "You did indeed come prepared, friend. But you have anger in you. As I did. It is the beast's call that has driven you into the wilderness. But you are coming home now, to a sanctuary first, then another place, and others, but always home in the end, and you will laugh at the anger you once had."

Saphrax still wanted to kick the man, but he held himself back. He wanted to make Falca pay for what he did, for what he had always done. He saw that clearly now. He, Saphrax, would not need Falca anymore, not with the power that would be his. He looked at the mace until his eyes ached and couldn't look anymore. He would use that power against Falca before he reached . . . home.

The woman covered the mace with something, shrouding the only star of a rainy night, as Saphrax threw away the iron bar he'd forgotten was in his hand. He knew, as they began walking, that she was making him go first, like Falca always did, because she had something of value that he might want to take from her. She was careful as Falca was. There was a difference this time. This time he was going to get what he wanted.

Not far away Falca stepped out into the night. He felt something at his feet, stooped to pick up a few of the flowers on the steps. He shook his head, sensing the anger Alatheus must have felt, standing here with a gift before a locked door. What would the man say when he saw his sister's neck free of the leechstone? He just hoped Amala could handle her brother. Ferrex had gotten caught in the middle, too.

He was thirsty and considered drinking from the fountain, then remembered Amala taking the empty from its waters. He walked on, looking back once at her dark window, hearing her last puff of breath in the rustling of leaves in the trees of the green.

He headed for Raven's Gate, the clinking of her golden coins his only companion.

Chapter Eleven

On Ice

Falca was determined to learn the trick of the thing. In a few hours, when he and Amala would go yet again to frozen Ringwater, he at least wanted to be able to scuff along without falling down, without Amala's mittened hands propping him up, as if he were some hunter's decoy. He wanted to master the rudimentary skill, so that he wouldn't embarrass himself in front of her. His clumsiness infuriated him but made him try all the harder.

He wobbled along the perimeter of the circular patch of canal ice he had cleared of a few inches of snow, near where he'd thought he'd seen the last of Saphrax. Well, the brute was alive, miraculously, but Falca hadn't seen him since that day of imaginings. He was probably dead by some surer hand, or maybe he'd latched on to someone else. Falca cared only that the brute was out of his life, just as Amala seemed happy that Alatheus hadn't shown up at her home for weeks now.

Falca attacked the ice with aching ankles, flailing arms. Every time he fell, he looked up past the landing stairs to make sure no one had seen him from the street above. It was just as well he had been off the streets for a while, because if anyone he knew saw him, his reputation would go sour as pickles in a barrel. But then, he told himself, he had little need for his reputation in Draica anymore. A few more weeks of Amala Damarr and he would be able not only to get to Gebroan but set himself up in style. Perhaps some acreage along the coast south of Sandsend. With fruit trees. He had to have them, just so that he could pick off a piece of something sweet whenever he damn well wanted.

Maybe he would even send for Ferrex after a while. He would have enough. He'd told Amala about him, bared the lie. She thought it was a wonderful idea, but then she would.

And when Falca wasn't taking a chariot and pairs into the hills to hunt ("You, a canal-side man?" Amala had teased him), he'd prowl the backways of exotic Sandsend, where, it was said, ships still sailed across the Farther Water to the place called Arriosta, where Roak and Cassena came from. Perhaps he'd do that, too, someday, when he tired of the squire's life. First he wanted to have it. He wanted the feeling of growing bored with what other men dreamed of having. He would be the second Breks to ever have anything worth having. His father was the first. Not the least of Falca's anticipated pleasures would be seeing the shock and surprise on his father's face, when Falca found him, as he inevitably would. Then he would put a fist, just one, in his father's face, to shatter the surprise, and walk away.

Amala Damarr, the beautiful mark, the One Mark, was making it all possible. True to her word, she kept the money coming, every week, regular as the gull-fouled noon bell of Erisa's Campanile. So what if she'd asked him to try and learn to skate? Anything to keep her amused. Never mind that by the time he could do it without making a fool of himself, the ice would be gone with the rains.

Only once before in Falca's lifetime, had the winter weather been cold enough to freeze the canals. That was his first winter alone, after he'd fled his uncle. Even now, Falca felt a little pride at his survival, at the snug shelter he'd made on the Slidetown docks, smack in the middle of a huge pile of timber whose consignment had been delayed till spring.

The canals had been frozen for two weeks now, and all Amala wanted to do was skate in the few hours of daylight that were left after she finished work at the settlement house. "The cold won't last," she had said. "The ice will melt with the rains, and it will be twelve more years before I get to skate again."

Falca had watched her the first time, amazed at her quick and graceful recovery of the skill she had learned as a girl, at that place to the north, the one shown in the painting in her home.

The next time Falca saw her, she gave him a pair of skates, with leather straps and bronze buckles. "It's a useless enough skill for

Gebroan," she said, "but perhaps one day when you're complaining about the heat there, sick of figs and yellow-eyes, and desperate for a chill, you'll remember gliding about the frozen canals of Draica with me."

Falca kept on until he twice made the circuit of his patch of ice without falling. Then he wobbled toward the snow-encrusted hulk of the boat frozen in its ruin by the landing. He braked himself with his gloved hands and walked on sore ankles to the landing, where he sat down. He felt satisfied with his improvement, then shook his head and laughed. Amala could do the damned thing backward. He remembered how she had skated backward, under the arch of the bridge, crouching just enough to miss colliding with the keystone. She made figures in the ice for the children on the bridge. They cheered her, but Falca was the one she came to, her breath white, her face flushed with joy and exhilaration.

Even after the rains came again, Falca would never quite see the canals in the same light. The thing he would remember in Gebroan was not the green water, the poling boatmen or skipping gulls, but Amala gliding around, scarring the ice with a grace that made people stop and stare. He had to admit she made him proud. That feeling was as rare for Falca as the ice, and dangerous as falling through. Saying goodbye to her was going to be more difficult than he wanted it to be.

As he finished unstrapping his skates, Falca heard movement, voices above. He stood abruptly, holding the skates by the straps.

There were two men at the top of the steps. Someone Falca couldn't see but whose voice he recognized: "There, that's him."

Falca backed away from the landing. Two men began walking down the steps, followed by four more. Sippio and Alatheus were the last. Falca drew his knife from his boot. He looked quickly behind him. With his sore ankles he probably couldn't outrace them across the ice and snow. They would get him in the open, surround him. Better to put the high canal wall at his back, draw them away from the landing stairs, and break free.

He angled sharply to his right, surprising the lead man, who slipped trying to change direction. His sword fell from his hand and skidded, pinwheeled. The next of Alatheus' ditchies saw what Falca was trying to do and met him at the wall, a club in his fingerless gloves. Overeager, the bearded man reacted to Falca's feinting dagger thrust, not realizing the potential of the skates as a weapon. Falca swung them overhand, smashing the blades against the man's club hand, cutting the wrist badly. He howled and spun away as Falca quickly grabbed the club and tucked his knife in his boot so that he could use two hands to swing. He lashed out at the legs of a third assailant, dumping him to his side.

Falca saw Alatheus, still standing on the landing steps, his Warden's sword in hand. If he could overcome the bastard, Falca thought, the rest might scatter. He jumped back as Sippio swung a short cudgel, and was set to fling the skates in the gillie's face when someone jumped down on him from the top of the canal wall.

Grunting, Falca rose from his sprawl, flipping the leaper over. He tried to reach for his dagger, but someone else smashed a club on his arm and he cursed loudly at the stinging pain.

They were all at him now, hitting him with clubs or fists, on the shoulders, legs, his ribs. Falca stumbled toward the landing but was tripped. He fell again to a rain of more blows, though he managed to land a fist in Sippio's face, knocking him off his feet.

"Hold him down," Alatheus shouted.

They spread-eagled him to the ice, four men on his arms and legs. A scowling Sippio, blood dripping from a broken nose, held a dagger to his throat, scraping the skin. Falca smelled his breath, felt the coldness seeping into his back, legs. Alatheus picked up the skates, swung them by the straps like a clock pendulum.

"So," he said, standing between the men who held Falca's legs. "Amala has the tough Falca Breks skating like some boy. You're getting soft, reiver."

"Nine on one are soft odds," Falca said.

"Shut up," Sippio hissed, and pricked Falca's throat with the dagger, drawing blood. He wiped at his own with the back of his hand.

Alatheus extended his arm and dropped the skates on Falca's chest. One of the blades lodged against his neck, inches from the dagger. "Perhaps we'll sharpen them on the strop of your clever tongue, cabbage," Sippio whispered.

Alatheus kneeled down, his shiny kneeboots stiff. His long yellow hair fell around the curl of his burgundy cape. He tapped the point of his sword on one of the skates. Falca stared at his hand, the huge gold ring on a finger, before meeting his eyes.

"It took her but a week to learn that winter," he said. "Of course, she was on the lake at sunrise and wouldn't come off until dusk. I'd watch her from the hot springs, through the steam, watch her fall again and again, only to get up and try again until she stopped falling. She doesn't tire of things as easily as I, though I thought surely she'd tire of a scut like you by now. Roak knows I've given her enough time. Well, she hasn't, and I'm through sweating the puzzle of it. I was also waiting all this time for an offer from you. But you seem to have lost your business instincts while you've been poaching her."

"I thought of approaching you," Falca said, smiling, "But she made me a better offer."

"I'm sure she did. With the money I've given her, with everything I've given her. Well, it will end. You've intruded in our lives long enough, Breks. Amala always had a weakness for licking the gutters. Your particular stain will be washed away. If she won't do it, I will. I always have for her, and in the end she has always thanked me for it."

"You go on believing that and you'll always be banging on her door at night, out in the rain. It won't be me upstairs with her, but it will be someone else. Save yourself the ache and let her go while she still—"

Alatheus slapped him. He shook off the sting: "Free advice, citizen. Leave her be or you'll lose all of it."

Alatheus slapped him again, much harder. He bent low over Falca.

"The only reason I won't kill you now is that the loss of Amala's pet might overly distress her; she would feel responsible for your worthless life. She might do something rash. I don't want that. I don't want to see her hurt, as if one can mourn a piece of shit. So, you get a warning this time. But if you keep seeing her, I'll kill you."

He got up. "Come, Sippio."

Just like a dog, Falca thought.

Sippio lifted the dagger reluctantly, and Falca could see the contempt in his eyes for Alatheus, who was walking away toward the landing. Sippio stood, then suddenly grabbed a skate blade and ripped it across Falca's jawline from ear to chin. Screaming, Falca kicked out, twisted an arm free, and lunged after Sippio. His hands clenched air as a club cracked into the back of his head. His last sensation was a confusion of seeping warmth and returning coldness.

Falca might have frozen to death had it not been for the youths who sought to rob an easy mark. Their rough, seeking hands poked and prodded and roused him from unconsciousness. When they kicked him, frustrated at finding no coin or valuables, Falca opened his eyes to twilight, saw them walking away, one holding the skates like a dead, draining fowl. Falca heard that one say, "Can we sell these?"

"I doubts it. Who's to buy something they'll never use? Better to make knives out of 'em."

"Should've killed that empty for our trouble."

"He wasn' no empty. Empties don't use those things, fool."

"I bet he was, only someone got to him before us."

At the word *empty* Falca stirred, rolled over, lifted himself to his knees, determined to pry himself from the ice, the cold, the implications of mistaken identity. Never mind they were ditchies, he'd rather be dead than be taken for an empty. And he wasn't about to die here, within a stone's throw of his home. That was gutless. He would crawl if he had to.

The chill that permeated his body had sucked away his equilibrium, and he was so dizzy he almost fell back. He staggered to his feet, stumbled to the canal wall for support. He almost blacked out, so great was the pain in his head, his face. He felt the gash along his jaw, the crystals of ice where the blood had frozen. He had to get moving and he trudged along the wall, resting a few times, his body throbbing in a dozen places. He rested yet again at the landing steps, and by the time he had crawled up their height, twilight had deepened.

He veered shakily across the street, to the warehouse, and, once inside, collapsed on Venar's pallet. The runt, as well as the sisters, had left weeks before, once they realized Falca was no longer in business canal-side and had no intention of sharing even a small portion of Amala Damarr's money.

The place was a shambles, especially the loft that Falca hadn't the strength to climb to. Solvie, Sincta, Vessa, and Venar had turned the warehouse inside out to find Falca's cache. They had the time to search, since he had often been away for days with Amala. Falca had anticipated them and hidden the money elsewhere, at Amala's house in fact, though she didn't know it. He'd hidden it one morning when she was still sleeping.

Falca turned painfully on the pallet, trying to find a position easy on his hurting body. His head felt as if it were going to burst, and his anger didn't help any. He stared through half-shut eyes at the timbers of the ceiling, thinking that it was finally time to leave Draica.

He would see Amala once more, to get his money, to end it. Then he would find Sippio and Alatheus and kill them before he sailed for Gebroan. Never before in his life had he suffered such a beating, and they would pay for the humiliation. By the time Amala found out, he would be halfway to Sandsend. She would try to prevent him killing them if she knew.

He would have preferred another month of her to set himself up well in Sandsend. He would miss her bed, and yes, the woman herself. Now that his decision was made, he could admit that. But it was time to move on. Before he lost his hands, like Ferrex.

Moreover, her crazy brother was right. He *had* been getting soft around her. By Roak's beard, what was he doing...skating...? It was ludicrous. If he hadn't been playing, making a fool of himself for Amala's amusement, Alatheus and his ditchies wouldn't have caught him like that. He'd lost himself seeing the woman, so pleasurable and profitable as she'd been. He had even allowed her to teach him some Tongue, and never mind she had primed him for the lessons with Sweet-hand before and the bed afterward.

Enough is enough, Falca decided.

He thought to cleanse his wound, but when he reached for a basin of water near the pallet, he felt insects, killed by the cold, floating in the water. His sliced jaw was better off unwashed until he had the strength to light a fire and boil the water. Instead he pulled ragged, dirty blankets off Vessa's and Saphrax's pallets and bundled himself up in them. He placed the leg of a broken stool by his side just in case. And despite the pounding in his head and all his aches, he soon fell asleep.

He woke with a start to someone knocking on the door. He grabbed the stool leg, reeling with his sudden movement. Then he realized that Saphrax or Alatheus or any other intruder wouldn't be politely knocking for permission to enter. Still, he rose to an elbow, clutching the crude weapon.

Another knock. Then: "Falca? Are you in there?"

He sank back down to the sound of Amala's voice. He didn't answer. He wasn't sure he wanted her here now, to see him like this.

"Falca?" Another knock. She is persistent, Falca thought, and let the stool leg drop with a clatter.

"I'm here," he answered weakly.

She came in, closed the door. "Falca? Are you all right? No, of course you're not. Where's a damn candle?"

"On your right. There's a ledge."

It took her a few minutes to locate and light the thick candle. As she approached, Falca saw she was wearing his cloak, as she had ever since their first night together. She kneeled down beside the pallet and sucked in her breath at his face. "He did that?" she whispered angrily.

"Sippio. I didn't expect to see you."

"Alatheus came to the settlement house, said he'd given you a warning. I came directly from there after he left. No one followed me." She let out a string of soft curses.

"Falca, I'm so sorry. Do you want me to leave?"

"I don't know. Hurts to talk."

"Well, I'll decide for you. This is one time you aren't going to lick your wounds alone. Is anything broken?"

"I don't . . . my ribs. I feel like Roak came alive and stepped on me."

She stood. "I'm going to boil water. That cut is bad."

In time she found everything she needed. Soon a fire was crackling underneath an iron kettle suspended from the brazier pit tripod. She soaked rags in the boiling water and let them cool briefly before she began cleansing his wound. When she was done, she said, "I'll have to stitch it up. Do you have needle and thread?"

"S'all right. I'm not one of your Limbs—"

"Be quiet. Where are they?"

He sighed. "Upstairs, somewhere. Don't remember. Look, you'll never find any of that. S'a sty up there."

"I will," she said, and left with the candle.

And she came back with needle, thread, and three more candles, which she secured to the floor with wax. Kneeling, she threaded the needle, then reached into a pouch at her belt and withdrew a vial. "I knew he'd hurt you," she said. "Gurrus gave me something the Limbs use for pain. It will put you to sleep, which is good, since I haven't done this before. Gurrus says it helps him dream too. Before I give it to you, we have to talk. *I* have to talk."

"I know what you're going to say. We move up the time. Nothing more to say."

"He *will* do it, Falca."

"I don't doubt that."

"I misjudged him. He *is* mad and I don't want you to be hurt again, or worse, because of a problem that is mine alone."

"So we leave it clean."

"We go our ways. I plan to go to the Rough Bounds soon, within the week, and you, Falca, are for Gebroan."

"Already decided."

"Will you please be quiet and listen to me? I thought it hurt you to talk. When you're a little better in a few days, I want you to come by my house for the rest of the money I have. I can't bear to think of you fisting the Limbs here while I'm gone, before you go to Gebroan. You might change your mind about that. I certainly don't have need of money once I get to the Rough Bounds. I also don't want to see you try to kill Alatheus for what he's done to you. I know I don't have the right to—"

"You don't."

"But I'm going to ask you anyway. Don't kill him."

"He's the one you should be asking."

"No, he's the crazy one. You're not."

"Sometimes I'm not so sure with you, Amala. The rest of the money is a bribe, then?" He wondered how she could understand him. To his own ear his words sounded unintelligible. He could hardly move his lips.

"Call it that if you want. Surely you aren't objecting to taking more money from me."

"What's to prevent me from taking the rest of the money, killing both of them?"

"Nothing, but I don't think you'd do that. I think I know you well enough by now. Listen, Falca, you've gotten what you wanted because of me."

"Would have gotten that sooner or later."

"You might have gotten killed first."

"Almost was: Sippio."

"You know what I mean. You told me so yourself. How you were always so careful but how it could end for you anytime, on any street, any alley. Please, Falca, grant me a favor, allow me a mistake. I want to escape from Alatheus, but I don't want him dead, or Sippio."

"All right, I'll take the money. You have my promise I won't seek either man out. But if they come for me . . ."

"I don't want to see you dead either, Falca."

For a few moments they listened to Shindy barking outside.

"I'll stay with you tonight," Amala said. "And bring you food and drink tomorrow. You should be feeling well enough in a few days after that to stop by for the money. I'll take out your stitches then. I'< bring the money, but there's a greater chance of someone robbing m< than you. I'll leave the cloak. It's time I gave it back to you anyway."

He watched her draw the thread through the hot wax pooling a the top of the nearest candle. Then she handed him the vial. "Drin> all of it."

He did, and even as he gave the empty vial back to her, he won dered why he trusted her. The potion could have been some Liml poison. Dead men make the best promises. What had she to lose? N< one would miss him. He had no one except her, and Ferrex. She knev that. Alatheus would be safe, and the money could go directly to th< settlement house. Why waste it on a ditch-licker? Their few month: together were a business arrangement, sweetened to be sure by th< bed and moments of foolishness and honesty—a first for Falca Maybe it was true what she said, but he still had half a mind to forge< his promise and go after the bastards. His jaw hurt to the High Sor rows.

Amala tossed the vial into the fire pit, where it broke on th< circling stones. She smiled, and he too remembered. "That was a fin< night, wasn't it? Though it ended with business. We always seem t< end that way. But I'll never forget you trying to skate. You'll neve learn now." She shook her head and laughed.

He felt a pressing warmth. Drowsiness. Through half-shut eyes h< saw her passing the needle through a candle flame. He closed hi: eyes, but even after a few minutes he didn't fall into unconsciousness He fought it, instinctively. Because he wanted to be alive to feel hei hands moving about his face, her skin brushing his, just once more But he was slipping away, he couldn't stave it off much longer.

"Falca?" she whispered. "Falca?"

He felt the prick of the needle, the tugging of his flesh, the sliding of the needle and thread, and the pain was nothing, nothing at all. H< fell further, and when she spoke, he wasn't sure if he was actually hearing her words or whether it was a dream in which he was imagin ing what he wanted to hear from her, yet another in the plague o imaginings he would always associate with her.

"Alatheus thought I loved you," she was saying. "He said it was < waste he couldn't bear. Well, there has been a waste: you and I. He was right. I do love you, Falca, but it's no good for us. I wanted to tell you, but I didn't have the stomach for even that, just as I didn'< have the stomach to handle my brother the way I should have. Anyway you would have laughed, and I would have felt like such a fool, twice a fool.

"Because it has been a waste. You and I are more alike than any two people I know. You couldn't trust the thing even if you knew what it was. And neither can I, because of Alatheus, who showed me that love is a drowning pool, a fountain where the tiny pieces float away like that flina. Still, I'll tell you now. The beauty of this is that you'll not be able to ask me why."

He tried to rise up, but he was tied down in a hundred places. He wanted desperately to answer her, though he had no idea what the words would be or where they would come from. In a panic, he thought that this must be what it's like being an empty, with no voice, no answers.

He felt her around him, but he was heavy and lifeless as a piling in the tide-change. He let go, finally, with the consolation that dreams require no answers.

Chapter Twelve

The Earring

Four days later Amala sat cross-legged by the hearth in he[r] home. Shindy's muzzle rested on her foot, but the dog wasn't restin[g] easily. He twitched and trembled in his sleep, whimpering, whistlin[g] his breathing. Amala had to wake him to break the nightmare. Hi[s] eyes rolled open, red, and Amala soothed him. "Don't worry," sh[e] whispered. "Whatever else we do in the Bounds, I won't let th[e] Limbs infest you with pot-ticks, I promise." They were a delicacy, s[o] All-Eye told her once, and grew to the size of a large thumb on th[e] bigger dogs the Limbs kept especially for that purpose. There wer[e] some Limb customs she would never get used to, no matter how lon[g] she stayed in the Bounds.

Amala poked at the fire and glanced up at the still-frosted win[-] dows. Sunlight glittered through the ice rimming the panes. She gath[-] ered the woolen shawl closer around her shoulders, waiting for Falc[o] to arrive, and wondering just how awkward the parting would be an[d] whether she should tell him what she'd said after he had take[n] Gurrus's pain potion. On the one hand she wanted to, to end the thin[g] with an act of courage, and not the cowardice of four nights ago. H[e] should know, damn it, because it was what she felt. Still she coul[d] hear his laughter now. Or worse, the admission could muck up th[e] clean parting she wanted.

He had, also, been in a strange and wonderful mood, maybe be[-] cause his physical condition was improving quickly. She'd never see[n] anyone heal so fast, and she almost took out the stitches but decided to wait until he came to her home for the money and the final good-bye. She had never seen him so talkative, and when she laughed at a story he told about how he actually got his scar, he began laughing, too, and shaking his head because it hurt to laugh.

He asked her if she wanted to make love, and before she could say anything he shook his head and said that if you have to ask, it's no good.

"I'd say a man with a jawline of black thread should always ask first," Amala said, and they laughed together at that.

"I'll be by at noon," he said as she was leaving. "In two days. I want to ask you something else."

It was almost noon, and she was eager to leave the city before something happened, before Alatheus stopped by, saw her leavetaking, and prevented her. She told herself to be patient. It was cold, the streets icy, and Falca would be walking slowly.

She wondered what he was going to ask her. He had seemed so serious. She hoped he wouldn't confound matters and try to change her mind about the Rough Bounds or ask her to go to Gebroan with him.

For Amala was ready to go, and not to Gebroan. Everything she planned to take was on the divan. On the table was the little burlbright chest filled with gold roaks she'd promised him, the last of the money she had saved and pawned from what Alatheus had given her. Next to the chest was the pair of scissors, to snip out Falca's stitches. She'd also used them to cut her hair. On a whim, she had tied a lock of her hair with black thread and put it in the chest of coins, the color blending with the gold. On second thought, an hour ago, she took it out, and tossed it into the fire where, like the rest of the cut hair, it crackled and burned in moments. The smell had caused Shindy to back away from the fire. Amala felt a fascination with this destruction of a little part of herself, and satisfaction with her decision. It was the ending of her old self and the beginning of the new. Besides, the lock of hair was a girlish and inappropriate gesture for someone like Falca. Better he find the tiny Gebroanan flag she'd sewn herself.

Shindy suddenly lifted his head and growled. Moments later, Amala heard a knock on the door. She patted the dog's head. "That's Falca. If it was Alatheus, you'd be wagging your tails. Be good now."

As she approached the door, Falca knocked again, more loudly.

"I'm coming, Falca," she muttered, annoyed at his impatience. Then she stopped. He never rapped twice. Shindy was growling even more. But it couldn't be Alatheus. Shindy wouldn't be growling.

Amala slowly slid open the narrow grate set at eye level in the thick, iron-strapped oak door.

The visitor was a young woman, bundled up for the cold. Brown hair edged her pretty but hard face. "Yes?" Amala asked her.

"Are you Amala?" came back a question, cottoning the air.

"I am. Amala Damarr. And who are you?"

"A friend of Falca's, citizen. I . . . I have some bad news to tell you. Falca said to . . . well, may I come in?" She wiped at her eye. "It may take a moment to explain, and it's cold out here."

"If it's about Falca . . . of course," Amala said, closing the grate, a gnawing emptiness in the pit of her stomach. It had to have been Alatheus.

She worked the stout lock on the door. Still, something was odd. Something in the contrived swipe at tears that weren't there. She opened the door, but the woman didn't step forward. She was smiling. Amala instantly knew something was wrong and slammed the heavy door with both hands.

She didn't quite close it. A boot wedged between the door edge and sill, and it wasn't the woman's. She pushed wildly, with all her strength, but her weight was no match for the person on the outside who shoved the door so hard, Amala went tumbling backward.

He slipped in, slowly closed the door, grinning, and locked it.

It was the hulking man who had knocked her down on the 'Roll, the one Falca thought he'd killed but hadn't. Falca said his name was Saphrax. . . .

Behind Amala, Shindy was snarling furiously, his paws scrabbling on the rug, tearing it. Amala got up, put a hand on Shindy's stiff back fur, and let him tear into the man as she ran from the entryway, to the divan, her fingers fumbling on the buckle of the slingsack. She heard Shindy's attack, the tearing of clothing, the ripping snarls, the grunt of the man. Amala hurried over to the hearth, realizing the iron poker was a better weapon than the dagger she held, since she could strike from a distance. Dagger in her shaking left hand, poker in her right, she faced the entryway. She knew she probably should run out the back way. But this intrusion so infuriated her, she wasn't going to run away. She wasn't going to flee her own home. She was going to fight this battle herself. She knew what the brute wanted, and he was going to get hurt badly, Roak take his balls. . . .

Shindy was backing up, his bared jaws foamy and red.

The man, this . . . Saphrax . . . entered the room, slowly, wary of the dog. He was bigger than Amala remembered, and strangely passive, without the anger she expected. His blue and white cape was torn, the leather of his kneeboots ripped. He was shielding something —a weapon?—in his crooked left arm.

He was still grinning, even as he kept kicking out at Shindy, his earring bobbing back and forth. "I had to come in the day, you see," he said, loudly over Shindy's snarling. "He's with you so much at night. A simple ruse. I've been watching this place since I got back. The woman—"

"GET OUT OF HERE!" Amala screamed at him.

"In time. The woman was Sincta, one of the two quivers he kept once. She was only too eager to earn a reive for a minute's worth of work."

He kicked at Shindy, missed, and the dog leaped for his throat. He swung his huge fist, ramming Shindy's head into the wall, hard enough to shake the painting to the floor.

"GET OUT OF HERE!" Amala screamed again, and swung the poker, missing his head but hitting his shoulder, making him grunt. He grabbed the poker and almost Amala's hand, too, but she backed away as he flung the poker aside. He grinned at Shindy, who was alive but dazed, then at Amala. "You did better with the sliver-heart, I remember. But I hold no grudge. I am not going to kill you, or rut with you, like Falca loves to do. I am not even carrying a weapon. I don't need one to accept your Gift, Amala—"

"DON'T YOU DARE SAY MY NAME!" Amala shouted, lunging for the poker as Shindy attacked Saphrax again. He was weakened, though, and Saphrax kicked him aside. With a shriek, Amala swung the poker again, connected, felt the point bite into Saphrax's leg. She jerked it out, swung again as Saphrax started toward her. The poker hit his free hand, stopped him. He put the hand to his mouth, sucking flesh. "I told you I have no weapon, Amala. But if you continue to attack me, I must defend myself and the mace," he said, his voice sterner. "You may as well submit now. I am too powerful, having seen the One. That is where your Gift is destined to go. I could have taken Sincta, but your Gift is much the better, since Falca prizes it so much. When I came back, I thought he would have tired of you, completed his fist, and moved on like he always has. He has taken quite a liking to you."

Amala moved to her left, her chest heaving, heart pounding. She swung the poker again, aiming at his face, but her hand was so sweaty, the poker slipped and flew to the wall, gouging it.

He lumbered closer, and Amala let him come, then struck with the dagger, plunging it into his arm. He backed away, smiling with a wince, and plucked the knife out as he might a splinter. "You're a fierce one," he said. "No wonder Falca liked you so much."

Amala was without weapons now. She had to get out. The table was to her right. She moved behind it, putting it between her and Saphrax. She suddenly lifted the edge, spilling the chest of coins, the scissors, and bolted for the back door.

Saphrax was quicker than she thought. He lunged, his hand hitting her ankle, just enough to cause her to stumble. She recovered, but he reached out again with a long arm and caught her foot in a grip she couldn't shake. She screamed, kicked out with her other leg. He was too strong and began dragging her back while still on his knees.

He had forgotten about Shindy. The dog attacked him from behind, leaping onto his back, snapping at his neck, ripping the cloth of his cape with his claws. Amala still couldn't escape because Saphrax had rolled onto her legs, pinning her with his weight. Still, she struggled wildly, screaming as he thrashed on her, and finally he punched the dog. Amala saw the scissors nearby, reached . . . reached for them, got them, stabbed Saphrax in the shoulder. She tore them out even as he screamed. She tried for his face, but his hand caught her wrist, ripped loose the scissors, and plunged them three times into Shindy's neck and throat.

Soaked by the spray of the dog's blood and his own, Saphrax rose, heedless of his wounds, and sloughed off the dead animal. Amala was crying now in rage, futilely beating him with her fist, screaming her fury at him. He caught her fists, then wrists, and twisted her around, dragged her through Shindy's pooling blood, over the leg of the overturned table. He kneeled on her, his weight crushing her breasts, her ribs, so that she could scarcely breathe. Then he slowly unwrapped his padded, shrouded weapon.

"A wonder it is not broken," he said, his breathing heavy and foul in Amala's face. "And lucky for you, for I would be tempted to kill you if the mace could not receive your Gift."

He grinned as he ripped the dangling earring from his earlobe, oblivious of the pain, and hooked it into Amala's tunic. "So he will know I was here. So Falca will know I have risen from the ruin of what I once was. It is your plaything now. I do not need it anymore."

Saphrax shook his head, and Amala's screams became an echo to her as Saphrax pressed the bright, crystal head of the mace to her forehead.

She felt cold, a burning cold, and even though she thrashed her legs, her arms, she couldn't shake it off. He wasn't on top of her anymore, but still she couldn't escape. She had a sense of being impaled through the head, but there wasn't any pain, only a distant sound of rushing water. She began to wonder where she was. . . .

A vision shone in her mind, of the time when she was a girl and she fell down on the frozen lake in the mountains. She hit her head and blacked out, and when she awoke, Alatheus was kissing her lips —so it wouldn't hurt, he said—and he rubbed salve on her lips where the skin had come off. Then he rubbed some on his lips because he said they hurt too. Isn't that the most wonderful thing? he said. And Amala said of course it is: *You* didn't fall. And stop kissing me so much. . . .

That memory was extinguished by a growing white light now. She tried desperately to replace that memory with others, to summon the forces of her being to replace those falling, swirling, swept away by the torrent pouring from her. The visions of her family, Alatheus, Falca, the Limbs at the settlement house, her friends, lovers, Shindy —all faded, were melted by the light even as they fed its devouring brightness.

Still, Amala wouldn't give up. She summoned more visions to staunch the flow, delay it, but they, too, became unrecognizable, twisted and spun out like the thread of spinning wool into that river of light.

She slumped finally, immersed in a coldness the pervasive light should have warmed, appeased, but didn't. She felt brittle.

When the brightness finally receded and went away like everything else, she was aware of only two things. She was still cold. And she was hungry, hungry to replenish what she had lost.

Chapter Thirteen

The Fountain

Falca rapped the door-dog phallus and waited for Amala to open the door. He stamped his feet, blew out white breaths, and turned once to see if her crazy brother was hiding behind the frozen fountain or one of the trees on the green.

He frowned, rapped again. Could she have gone already? he wondered. He *was* late—a bridge had buckled over the Tears Canal and he had to take a detour. No, she wouldn't have gone and just left the money she'd promised him. There were a few words to be said before they closed it out. She *couldn't* have left. He had to ask her—straight out—whether what he had heard had been a dream or whether she'd said it. He almost hoped it had been one of his imaginings, because he didn't know what he would do if she really had spoken those words. Maybe nothing. After all, their courses were set. And there was Alatheus.

He finally used his key to open the door.

When he saw the blood, the mess in the entryway, his first thought was that he'd killed her. The crazy bastard had done it. "AMALA!" he shouted, and got no reply. He drew out his dagger from his boot-top. He cursed, sucking in his breath at the shambles.

"Amala," he called out again, nudging a little chest with his toe. Gold coins spilled out into smears of blood on the floor, the bunched up rug. He saw a dagger and . . . Amala?

For a moment Falca thought it was Alatheus, kneeling, his back to the carnage and the entryway, hunched over in the narrow corridor past the stairs, almost in the scullery. But it was Amala, he knew her shoulders. She'd cut her hair for the Rough Bounds.

"Amala? Are you all right?" he whispered, and again, more loudly when she didn't turn around. She kept dipping her head, moving her arms in a busy, working fashion.

"Amala? What are you doing?" Falca draped the cloak on the table edge. A parting gift to her.

He walked ahead, stepping in a trail of blood that led to her, in his mind forming the words, seeing the embraces he would have to give her, to help her get over the shock of having killed her brother. He was certain she had, so numb now she was aware of nothing else. "Amala," he whispered, his voice gentle and heavy. "It's all over now, it's all over." He was about to touch her shoulder, when he saw what she was doing. . . .

He backed away with a cry, so startled he dropped his dagger. She finally turned at the clotted repetition of his whispers: "No, no, Amala . . . not you. Oh please, not you. . . . "

Her face was smeared with Shindy's blood. A few wisps of steam rose from the gouged innards of the dog, who lay on his side, his eyes open and bulging. She'd severed the dog's tongue. It wobbled in her hand; she held it like a child would a candy.

It wasn't Saphrax's crude earring hooked in her tunic or the reddened scissors she held in her butcher's hand that immersed Falca in a terror he'd never felt before. It was the blankness in her eyes, darker than he remembered, that held no recognition of who he was or what she was doing. Nothing. Empty. The walking death he feared above all else. "Not you," he kept mumbling, unable to swallow. "Sweet Roak, not you." He stared at the mark on her forehead, a squared off diamond, precise as a tattoo, as he backed away. He hit the end of the table leg, whirled around so hard he slipped on the blood, the coins that she had meant for him, just as she'd meant the scissors for his stitches. On his knees he glimpsed, among all the gold roaks, a square patch of cloth with the three yellow suns of Gebroan.

The scissors snapped. She had gone back to her feeding. He wanted to rip the scissors from her fingers, shake her from this trance, but there was nothing he could do, and even if there was, he was too scared to touch her. She was diseased. She had lifted that empty from the fountain, wrapped him with the cloak, and it had happened to her. The room itself might be tainted.

And he had held that cloak too.

Outside, someone shouted, his breath ragged, a running man. "Amala?"

The door burst open. Alatheus filled the entryway, his breath cloudy, his yellow hair wild.

"YOU!" he screamed, and drew his sword.

He couldn't even see Amala, but he knew what had happened. That thought froze Falca for a moment. He hesitated, caught between the horror of Amala and one who would kill him before he could utter a single word of useless explanation.

Falca bolted, tried to leap over Amala, but hit her head with a trailing leg. She righted herself with the animation of a harbor buoy and continued gouging at the dog with the scissors and chewing on the tongue. He stumbled, crashed off-balance through the scullery, his arm sliding dishes from the counter. He yanked open the door to the alley and raced down the steps, oblivious of the pain in his leg, upsetting bowls of food Amala left for strays. He ran down the alley without looking back, without knowing or caring where he was going.

Alatheus didn't follow. The sight of his sister was a barrier he couldn't cross, even to pursue her violator. His first duty, as always, was to her. He thought at first Breks had raped her, tortured her, causing the state of numbness, shock. But, as he pulled her gently away from Shindy, he saw it was worse than that. He fought down sickness that flooded his throat.

He knew of the empties, though not how the cult, the Spirit-lifters, reived their souls.

She was one of them now, gone forever. The robber, the reiver he had warned her about to no avail, had done it. Not content with money, the pleasure of her beauty, he'd thieved the rest of her. And with it, Alatheus' world.

He thought of using the sword he still held in his hand. It would be a mercy. He dropped it, fell to his knees, and embraced his sister so fiercely that something was punctured in him, and he wept. She trembled only because he was shaking. He took her by the shoulders, tears streaming down his face, as if to see if he had imparted a miracle to her. He cupped her face, avoiding looking at her forehead. She stared past him, her eyes perfect bruises, at the light from the open doorway. He kissed her lips, tasting the blood as she had, sharing this last thing. He confronted the mark on her forehead, rubbed it with is thumb, gently at first, then harder, though knowing he couldn't rase it.

"Why didn't you listen to me?" he whispered. The feeling of vindication, of having been right about Breks, rose quickly and wasted way. "I knew something was wrong, Amala. I felt it. It hurt so, 'rass thought I was having a seizure right there in the tavern. I ran all he way from Falconwrist. I'm sorry, Amala. I should have killed him vhen I had the chance, but I didn't because it would have hurt you. 'm sorry, I'm so sorry. Did he do this because I had him beaten, ecause . . . you told him goodbye? But it was too late. . . . "

Alatheus kept rocking her as he talked.

Finally he got to his feet and pulled her up by her reddened, sticky ingers. She was shivering. He put the cloak she had worn so often round her shoulders, then ripped it off, remembering whose it was. Ie gave her his own cape and picked up his sword, wiping at his yes, and led her out the door, past a few whispering people.

She paused, and Alatheus realized she wanted to go to the founain. He took her by the hand, broke the ice with the hilt of the sword, nd cleansed her face, her forehead, her hands, and let her drink as he tared at the ice that arced out from the lifeless statue. Alatheus wung viciously at the ice, severing the form.

He thought of gently pushing her head underneath the water, :eeping it there, till she was gone. The urge passed. She flinched at he cold water, which caused him to begin weeping again. For coldess, heat, hunger, and sleep were the bounds of her existence now, ntil the day she died, or until he took her life because he couldn't tand what she was now.

It might be a week or years until he couldn't bear it anymore. Jntil then, he would care for her and love her, which was all he had ver wanted to do. Why couldn't she understand, accept the gift that vas purer and deeper than anything else she could have hoped to aave? Why had she sought to escape from something she had once reasured?

She had escaped. He would take her home, yes, and he alone vould bear the anger and grief of their parents. But before darkness ell, he would make arrangements for her care and then go after Falca 3reks. No matter where the man went, he would find and kill the one vho had destroyed his world.

Chapter Fourteen

The Swallow's Hands

Falca stopped running only when he reached the quays o[f]
Catch-All, where the masts, spars, and rigging of a dozen ship[s]
seemed like an impenetrable forest barrier. Beyond, Manger Bay lay
smooth, a carpet for the Colossus of Roak, which rose, ice-rimed, i[n]
the distance.

He leaned against a tall stack of lumber, its tarpaulin stiff an[d]
frozen, and watched the street he had just left. He knew Alatheu[s]
wasn't following him, not yet, but he watched anyway, over a row o[f]
pitch kegs, while his breathing eased. He put a hand to his ribs. The[y]
still hurt. His legs hurt. Everything hurt.

The air was heavy with salt, bilge, and smoke from braziers o[n]
the ships and more quay-side, where gangers huddled, cursing th[e]
day's work in the cold. Falca smelled cooking fish, which only reminded him of how hungry he was. But he knew that if someon[e]
came along and offered him the finest meal of his life, he'd dredge hi[s]
guts at the sight of it.

He slid his gloved hands to his armpits, more to quell their shak[-]
ing than for warmth. He could feel his sweat cold on his back. Eve[n]
more than hungry, he was thirsty. He couldn't remember ever bein[g]
so thirsty. He needed a drink, many of them, and he needed a plac[e]
where he could get warm.

There were any number of taverns facing the quay; the Glass An[-]
chor was the closest, but they knew him there, and he wanted to b[e]

alone. As he walked across the icy stone of the waterfront, he rebuked himself for his overreaction to Amala's Lifting. It wasn't as if they were husband and wife, had any blood between them, shared property, convictions, or beliefs. She had known the risks of associating with someone like him. She wasn't the poor innocent. She had used him, fisted him, as he had her. Her luck had just run out, that was all. It happened every hour in the city. His time would come too.

Of course it was a shame what happened to her, but there was nothing he could do about it now. She had known about Saphrax. Hadn't he told her? If he had known the brute joined the damned Spirit-Lifters, of course he would have warned her. Anyway, she had her brother to look after her now. In the end, after a week in the tangle and infestation and killing of the Rough Bounds she would surely have come back to him. Well, she wouldn't end up drowned in some fountain, like that other empty. Her family would put aside differences with her and afford the best of care for her. . . .

He dropped his hands from his armpits as he came to a place called the Red Gull. He hit the doorpost hard with his palms, punishing his hands for their trembling.

The tavern was little more than a scattering of benches and sawhorse tables set around an ill-vented hearth in a corner. Gray light filtered through a single dirty window. Only four or five men were drinking at this hour.

The proprietor leaned his elbows on the plank bar, talking with a burly black-bearded man sitting on a high stool. Behind the bar, a Myrcian helmet, pennon, and a severed, tarred hand were spiked to the wall. A short club hung by a rope on a peg.

Falca slapped a coin down on the worn plank and ordered his pint of ale. The tavernmaster eyed Falca's shaking hands suspiciously while he drew the pint. He slid the mug to him and plucked the coin. "If yer in trouble, bullo, you'd best drink quick and get out. This here's an honest place for workingmen."

He took a swig of the drink. It was cut-ale, all right. Not unusual for Catch-All, but Falca was more annoyed than he might otherwise have been on a better day. He looked the proprietor straight in the eye. "Honest as your asshole," he said loudly and clearly.

Someone in the corner whooped, another giggled, as Falca walked away toward the warmth of the hearth.

"Easy, ditchie," the tavernmaster called out. Falca turned to see that it was the black-bearded man who had spoken instead. He wore a hawksbill cap and was grinning at Falca, leaning forward on his stool. "The ale-puller's a friend and he likes his customers peaceful. Unless yer stupider than you look, you'd best let that slice-line heal before you get cut again. Someone been trying to sew you a better face?"

Black-beard took a baling hook from his belt and tipped up the brim of his hat. The proprietor laughed at his friend's joke as he leaned on his elbows, tapping the club on the plank.

Falca felt the familiar heat rising, expanding in him. He had walked away from worse taunts and better odds. Not today, not this day. He had fled one place; he wasn't going to flee another.

They thought him a mark. Someone in back of him laughed and said, "Careful, bullo, or you'll spill your drink. Your hands are twitching like a donkey's ears."

More laughter.

His shaking hands only made him angrier. He turned, as if to reply to the heckler, backed up a few steps to get closer to Black-beard, then whirled, throwing the ale and mug in his face. Falca kicked out viciously at his groin the moment he stood from his stool. The man grunted, doubled over in a shriek of pain, his cap and baling hook falling. Falca grabbed his greasy hair and rammed his head on the plank, breaking jaw and teeth. He slumped to the floor.

Falca ducked, sensing the tavernmaster's blow. The club missed by a hand. He tilted the plank-bar over with a crashing of sliding tankards. The proprietor stumbled back, and Falca grabbed the club from his hand, hit him on the side of the head, quickly turned, and swung, catching another man flush on the cheek. The man howled, spun away, and Falca planted a boot at his back and kicked him toward the door. The remaining patrons had already fled.

He dragged the proprietor and his friend out the door, ignoring the stares of the few passersby and gangers. He barred the door, rolled an ale keg over near the hearth, then lifted it up and set it on a table. He retrieved the baling hook and claimed the table closest to the fire by sinking the point into the oak. He sat down on a bench, dumped the ale out of a tankard, and rinsed the thing with a draw from the keg. The sorry bastards would be back, but he didn't care about when or how, or if they froze outside. They had been spoiling for a fight as much as he.

Falca's hands were calm now, and he felt that was a victory. For a few minutes he savored his tavern rousting, that old neglected terriory. It was just as well he had recovered himself, because Alatheus Damarr would be coming after him. He would be harder to deal with than a few Catch-All malletheads. Falca realized he may have missed his best chance to rid himself of the problem when he left the house with Amala gnawing at her dog. And never mind the man's rage. The next time would be of Alatheus' choosing. . . .

No, he thought, not left. Don't honey the vinegar. Fled, panicked. . . .

He ripped the baling hook from the tabletop and swung it down hard.

Never before had he run from another man. Never.

If he wanted to, he could blame Amala for that. The sight of her had so upset him, he'd lost his senses.

Falca drank. Would Alatheus follow him to Gebroan? Yes. So better to kill him while in Draica, so he wouldn't have to be looking over his shoulder day and night.

A log fell in the hearth. Falca remembered he had promised Amala he wouldn't kill her crazy twin brother, or at least not go after him. Defend himself, yes, but not seek him out.

But keep a promise to an . . . empty? What would she care about that now? She'd never know, just as he'd never know whether her words to him were real or one of his imaginings. He stared at the fire, seeing the yellow flame of her hair. He couldn't bring himself to make the decision to get Alatheus before he came for him—the first and best rule of the streets. The indecision made Falca irritable and angry at himself and at Amala for causing his confusion. She was gone, but she still pursued him with her presence, her words: "You seem plagued by people who won't stay dead." That was about Saphrax and Sorelip. Now Amala herself, dead in all that mattered.

He hated the messiness of it all. One or the other, dead or alive. But she was somewhere now in the city, breathing, seeing, maybe remembering how he'd struck her head as he ran. He hoped, beyond anything else, that she felt no sense of being abandoned, that she did not remember those quick minutes in her house that cut him like a knife.

What was he supposed to have done? Hold her while Alatheus spitted him with the sword?

Falca threw the empty tankard into the fire, to melt the flames of her hair, hair so long he could circle her breasts with a strand.

"So it happened to you because of me, because I botched the brute and didn't kill him before," he whispered. "It shouldn't have happened to you."

He lifted the hook again and brought it down again. There was no piercing force this time, no bite. The baling book clattered off the table.

Amala rose in the flames of the fire again; he saw her plainly and didn't fight this conjuring. So much for the One Mark, he thought, the only good thing to happen in my life. Where has it gotten me?

His life was a sorry mess now. Unless he was prepared to kill Alatheus, he couldn't stay in Draica and go back into, business. The Limbs were tainted with Amala. Thanks to her, he might not be able to be as tough with them as he had been before. The time he'd spent with her, away from all that, had probably cost him his streets canalside. Oh, he had enough money to get to Gebroan and live a while, but only if he could get the cache at Amala's house. A big assumption. Alatheus and Sippio would be all over that place. But when that money ran out—even if he could get it—he'd have to use the streets of Sandsend to live, unfamiliar streets, other people's territories, his father's.

He had always prided himself on his talent for survival, his ability to step back and see where he was going, where the dangers lay. It's what set him apart from all the others.

He hadn't seen the danger in Amala Damarr.

The One Mark. She had been more than he bargained for, much more, but he'd found her. He had known she was special the moment he saw her on the 'Roll.

He remembered the leechstone that first night with her, before the cold spell came. By Roak's high hand, she was beautiful. It wasn't a soft beauty, none of that flimsy fabric. She could have dealt with the streets if she had to. No, she did, with him. Again, he heard her saying how it was a waste, how she and he were so alike, saying that she loved him. It all came flooding back, but the memories would be forever marred by the sight of her gouging at the dog with the scissors that were meant to snip his stitches, by his abandonment of her, his running away like a street boy.

He had been so looking forward to one last time with her. Oh, not the bed. Just her breathing, the smell of her hair, the good hands close to him, carefully taking out the stitches, revealing the new scar. . . .

He flung the earthenware tankard at the hearth. The fire sizzled, and the thing broke, and he remembered what she had said about the Sweet-hand custom: the spirit being stronger than that which carried it.

Not in his case. He'd cleared this miserable tavern all right. But inside he was a runner. Amala was different, better. She was far from the perfect creature her brother insisted on imagining. But her spirit, the thing that Saphrax somehow sucked away like egg from a shell, was stronger than Falca's or Alatheus' put together.

Maybe that was why she was chosen to be Lifted and not him.

Empty, he thought. I'm an empty too, but in a different way. . . .

He lurched up from the bench, fled the tavern, took to the streets in a lowering afternoon sun. The only deliberate turn he made was to avoid Furrow Street and Ferrex. "Take a place beside me, Brother. I have an extra bowl for you," Ferrex might say.

He walked aimlessly in the cold, trying to escape self-pity, the memories of Amala, her caring for him when he was hurt, the silly lessons on the ice, her beauty and toughness, her turning the tables so neatly on him, the master of the fist. He knew he would have walked away without telling her what he wouldn't even admit to himself until now, that he loved her too. He wouldn't have had the guts.

Falca stopped midway on High Kear Bridge and wondered what it would have been like, without the brother, without Saphrax. A waste? She could have had any man in Draica. Would she have even given him a second day?

He stared across Manger Bay, toward Swayman's Neck and the ruins of the castle there, the old Myrcian encampment. A galliot was outward bound, coaxing a fickle wind, heading toward the arch of the Colossus' legs and the open sea. Closer, on the Valor Canal, a few skaters moved pitifully compared with Amala's grace.

With all the bay before him, Falca closed his eyes and saw himself in front of that closed door, upstairs in her home. He heard, amidst the crunching tread of people behind him, the puff of her breath as she extinguished the candle, a quick breath that for all its life, could fill the sails of the galliot. He had gone down the stairs that time; he hadn't gone back to her.

He wasn't born for greatness, born in the caul or not, falcata or not. But couldn't he manage to find the courage to tell her just once that he loved her? Then she could laugh in his face and tell him he was imagining something that wasn't there, that might exist for him but not for her.

Maybe he could show her that there was one man who wasn't a fool or weakling for loving her.

Then they could end it. First he had to bring her back. She could go on to the Rough Bounds, to fight her foolish fight for the Timberlimbs. He could move on to wherever he wanted to go.

Could he get her back? Why not, he asked himself. What was taken could be restored, no? He would find the way, if there was one, in Gebroan. The Spirit-Lifters took them all there, that much he'd heard.

And after? He couldn't think about that. If he failed, well, he'd be where he always wanted to be. If he couldn't bring Amala back, then he would fist the bastards in their lair, after he killed Saphrax. It took money to do what they did—Gebroanan authorities who tolerated a growing cult were not *that* permissive. Bribes were paid. So, if Falca could relieve the Lifters of some of their wealth, it might mean a few less empties on the streets of Draica.

He cautioned himself. Saphrax wouldn't be the brute he once knew, plucked from the prison hulks. The man had left his past pinned to the tunic of Amala Damarr, had abandoned it as Falca tried to abandon him. The change in Saphrax—his acting on his own —was extraordinary. The cult, whatever its form and territory, was a powerful lure, its poison a formidable mix to reverse a man so. Falca cautioned himself not to underestimate Saphrax and not think of him in terms of what he'd known him to be.

Alatheus? Falca could only hope he was successful in bringing Amala back, otherwise there would be a reckoning.

He couldn't risk going to Amala's home to get his cache. But Falca had an idea where he might obtain passage money for Gebroan. It was risky, but what had he to lose? First, however, he needed food and a warm place to sleep for the night.

For a few coins and as many chores, the 'tressa Beara let him have both at the settlement house. She wouldn't turn out a Limb from a pallet just to give it to Falca, which annoyed him a little. He shook his head at how far he'd sunk. Only a few months ago he'd been fisting the Limbs; now this place was his first and only choice for a meal and warmth.

He accepted a place on the floor by the hearth. At least he had some distance from the stink of the Limbs crowded in the center of the hall.

Just as he was about to go to sleep, All-Eye or Gurrus—he had trouble telling them apart—came over and squatted down beside him, wrapped in a red blanket for the cold, though it was warm enough by the fire. The Limb's gaze never left him. He kept kneading a ball of wax in his splintery fingers. He kept murmuring Amala's name over and over, the name the Limbs had given her. Falca remembered her telling him the name meant "sun thicket," or something like that. The old Limb—Gurrus, Falca decided—was concerned, obviously. How he knew something was wrong baffled Falca. Exasperated at Gurrus's unwavering stare, Falca finally spoke: "Look, I'm going after her. I'm going to bring her back if I can. Now will you let me get some sleep?"

Gurrus couldn't have known what he said, but the Limb seemed satisfied because he smiled. He took apart the wax and, glancing around once to see if Beara was about, handed Falca a chunk of something. Unmelted Sweet-hand? It smelled like it.

Gurrus left, nodding, saying something. Thank you? Falca responded, before he knew it, in Tongue. What he said was either "May your heart straighten your path"—the Limb phrase for goodbye—or "Many breaths." He couldn't remember which. He was surprised he had remembered anything at all that Amala had taught him.

Falca left the settlement house before dawn and walked back to Catch-All. The spurs—the men who ran the brothels along the quay —collected the earnings of their swallows in the mornings, he knew. He chose a house on the corner of Tidesback and Galore streets, one he hadn't been to in a while. He waited patiently on the steps leading down to the water, his head just above the level of the quay. Farther down, a tresreme creaked at its hawsers. He heard the yawn of a sailor emerging from quarters, the cry of gulls vying for slop another threw over the rails.

He spotted the spur coming down Tidesback Street, a large man, possibly Skarrian by his shaven skull and square features. He was dressed finely. His trade was lucrative.

Falca gave him enough time, then crossed the quay. He wasn't worried about the brawny eunuchs that guarded the houses. At this hour, after a night of work, they were either asleep or drunk. If not, there was always a bribe; Falca had done that more than once for extra time and favors. If worse came to worse, he'd take the spur outside, but he preferred to do this inside.

The eunuch was indeed drunk in the corridor, a flagon of wine at his side. Falca had to step over his belly to approach the spur who had just left a room. The Skarrian looked disgusted.

"I want someone . . ." Falca began, making a punching motion with his fist.

The spur kicked the eunuch, failed to rouse the man. "Dead drunk," the Skarrian muttered, his words heavy and guttural in the accent of that eastern kingdom. He cursed, then acknowledged Falca. "You're an early bull," he said suspiciously.

Falca shrugged. "I had the watch last night. The tresreme down the quay. I sneaked off, needed it quick, but your swallows were all taken. I was told they're the best. I'm back."

"It'll cost you more for what you want. Next keelcat don't want another man's bruises on his swallow."

"How much?"

"Six."

Falca raised his eyebrows. "That's a lot for one slide."

"Take it or leave it."

"All right. Which room?" Falca asked, reaching for his belt and money.

When the spur turned slightly to indicate the room he'd just left, Falca whipped the edge of his hand at the Skarrian's throat, followed with a fist to the stomach, then a quick upward thrust of his knee as the spur bent over with a loud groan. A tooth flew out of his mouth. He crumpled to the floor.

"I wasn't talking about your swallows, bullo," Falca whispered to the gurgling spur. Falca tied his hands with the man's belt, cut and ripped a long strip of the spur's cloak, doubled it and tied his ankles. He stuffed another piece in his mouth. Falca wasn't worried about the eunuch, who hadn't stirred.

He took the spur's coin-laden safe-keep, quickly checked it. More than enough.

He slid the spur's dagger and short sword in his belt and was about to go when the swallow from the nearest room poked her head out, then quickly closed the door. Falca hesitated. There was time to get what he needed.

The door wasn't locked.

She lay, half-sitting, on the pallet, staring at the dagger Falca held, her arms crossed over her breasts. Tattoos covered her body, perhaps to mask the bruises or in a pathetic attempt to imitate the speckled courtesans along the Cross Keys Canal, who served a more royal clientele.

"Do it quick and get out," she said. "No need for that," she nodded at the dagger. She stirred her legs wide underneath the blankets.

"I need a mirror," Falca said.

"What?" The swallow laughed. "Sure, ditchie. I'll just have my maid run and get one for you. Need to primp, do you, before you stir the kettle?"

"All right. You can do it, then. I need these out." Falca brushed a hand over the stitches. "Use his dagger." He tossed a coin from the safe-keep onto the bed. "You get another when you're done."

"What are you, helpless? Taila has a glass, next room. Ask her."

"You'll do fine. It's better if someone does it for me."

"Get someone else to do it."

Falca frowned. "What's your burr? I'm offering you quick money."

"I do one thing only."

"The woman who was going to do this was Lifted. She's an empty. You know what they are?"

"I seen'm. Walk like drunks, only it's not something that wears off in the morning. Tough luck, ditchie."

"I'm going to get her back. And I want these out. A whim. Yes or no?"

The whore stared at him, shaking her head. "You come in here, after knocking my man...you're crazy or stupid. Must be the weather. Yesterday I had a keelcat who had to bite off a pigeon's head before he could straighten it out."

"Yes or no."

"Give it here," she said, sighing, waggling her fingers. "And hold still while I do it."

Falca gave her the dagger and sat down on the pallet next to her.

"Ain't this sweet," she said. "Just like home. You want me to fix your breakfast after?"

"Get on with it."

"I could slit your throat, set myself up good with Scully."

"You won't. Another blade's inches from your belly. Feel it?"

"Maybe I got less to lose than you," she said, then laughed. "Don't worry. Why wreck a tender thing, eh?"

She began. Halfway through she muttered, "Don't look at me.

You make me nervous. It's tough to see the thread for your beard."

He looked away, at her washbasin, a towel, some clothes hanging up on pegs. He smelled the men on her, but still, there was more of her than them. And her hands were good. Not Amala's, but all right. She paused to brush back her long brown hair, which was getting in the way. He glanced at her crudely done tattoos: whorls of flowers, a stretching fienx, a trail of long-beaked birds drinking at a fountain— that on her belly, above a thatch of dark crinkly hair. Her forehead was high and clear, unblemished.

She pricked his skin. He flinched. "Sorry," she said. "It's this cold. And I never done this before. You'd think Scully's blade would be sharper."

She finished, picking out the last thread. "There you go, ditchie."

Falca stood, put away both daggers. "Here," he said, and handed her three more coins.

She hefted them. "That's a lot for a short time," she said, laughing.

He shrugged and smiled. "You were better at it than you thought. It's a skill, like skating on the canals."

"What?"

"Never mind." He tossed Gurrus's gift on the bed.

"What's this?" she said. "I ain't hungry."

"A . . . friend gave it to me. I won't need it. It's called Sweet-hand."

"I only use scrape. Now you better get out of here before Scully rouses."

"He won't be up till someone helps him."

She understood what he meant. "You are a strange one. No, I ain't got no one to find. But I'll keep the coin just in case."

He nodded and left, closing the door as she got off the bed to hide the coins. He checked the spur's bonds to make sure they were tight enough so that any of his swallows would have a hard time undoing them. He only needed a little time. The eunuch was still dead drunk.

Out on the quay Falca walked past the berths, limping some, hailing a few bosuns with his business. The fourth ship, a windwhipper, was bound for Sandsend at noon, and the master had room for one more passenger.

Alatheus stood on the old ramparts of the southern tower that once guarded the entrance to the Valor Canal. He watched a ship, a windwhipper, pass under the Colossus. It flew the three suns of Gebroan.

He ran a hand through his hair, which he'd just cut, on a whim, as a kind of memorial to Amala. If the man, Breks, wasn't on that ship, he thought, he'd be on another. That was where the scut was running to: Gebroan.

Alatheus was certain about the destination. He had found a hand-stitched little Gebroanan flag among the coins in the burlbright chest Amala had obviously meant to give the scut. Probably a payoff so that Breks wouldn't come after him for what he and Sippio had done to him. Well, Breks hadn't had time to take it. Maybe the little flag was a memento. She'd loved the bastard, but she didn't know what he was really like. She found out, though, and Alatheus could almost feel her panic, her despair the moment he turned on her and reived her soul.

It was Gebroan all right. Sippio had said Breks wanted to go there, relating a certain conversation Amala had had with him months ago, when it had all begun.

Sippio was bringing the baggage down to the quays. All there was to do now was find a ship for Gebroan. With any luck, they'd be on one by dawn.

BOOK TWO

THE EBONY ISLES

Chapter Fifteen

The Boy on the *Bay* of *Tyryns*

In Falca's recurring dream, he was hanging, neck broken, winging at the end of a rope. He was not alone on the gibbet. aphrax swung as lazily as he and kept whispering to Falca, his neck rooked at a grotesque angle: "Which of us will die first? One of us nust, so the other may."

Falca wouldn't die. He felt the grating of the bones in his neck, so nuch like the creaking of the gibbet beams. He knew he should be ead. What was wrong? Those below were getting impatient for his nd. They screamed curses at him, threw litter and stones, some of vhich hit him, hurt him. His neck was broken, yet he felt the sting of tones.

They were all down there. Sorelip laughed at his plight, throwing coin at him every so often. Venar looked pleased and clicked his oot heels together, mocking the clicking of the blades of ice skates alca still wore. "You don't need them, Falca," he giggled and ummed. "The ice is long gone now."

Solvie and Sincta were there below, looking expectant. As Falca urned and twisted in the air, he could see his mother, among others, n the nearby bridge, hear her screaming as they restrained her, 'Don't kill him! He was born in the caul, you can't kill him, he is estined for greatness!" Then the people holding her would let go uddenly, and she'd fall from the high arch into the canal, and no one ried to save her. And everyone down below would laugh and point

145

their fingers at Falca's useless twisting to help her, at his tears of rage.

His father always left then, after leaving the falcata on the ground near his brothers. Phalen would pick it up and hand it to Alatheus.

Ferrex sat cross-legged, the nearest to Falca, and held out his begging bowl on callused wrists, as if to catch the excrement that was slowly sliding down Falca's legs. Farther away, Timberlimbs swayed as one, chanting a corruption of the Tongue words Amala had taught him: "Too many breaths, too many breaths."

Alatheus stood with Amala, a golden pair, his arm around her waist. Her head moved with the swinging of Falca's rope, like a cat mesmerized by a dangling ball of twine. A leechstone glistened, protruding from her forehead.

Disgusted at the persistence of the two condemned men, the crowd began to disperse, abandoning Falca to his fate. Soon only Alatheus and Amala remained. Alatheus shook his head. "We can't wait any longer." He climbed the steps of the gallows and, using the falcata, cut both ropes in a single swing. He gestured for Amala to come up, and she did. "He's the one," Alatheus said, pointing at Falca. "Kill him, my love, for what he did to you."

Amala shook her head.

"Yes he is," Alatheus replied, stroking her hair. "You don't know. You can't know. You're an empty."

Still, Amala hesitated. Falca tried to call out to her, to tell her he wasn't the one, but he had no voice. He was alive but couldn't speak.

"You're an empty, Amala," Alatheus murmured, brushing his hand over her ear. "As empty as he is. You have your choice of weapons to kill him: the falcata or the scissors."

Finally Amala nodded and took the scissors. Saphrax's rope snapped. He fell, got up. As Amala approached Falca, snapping the scissors, Saphrax passed her on the steps, grinning, flicking the earring stuck on her breast, his neck still cocked at the angle of death in life. . . .

Falca awoke as Amala's blank face lowered to his, the leechstone falling off to reveal the black mark.

The ship's motion rocked his hammock. He rubbed his hand over his forehead, wiping off the sweat, and felt for the bruise near his hairline. He kept hitting himself there, the price of being tall in low, cramped quarters. His head hurt, though it might as well be the rot of the dream that had plagued him for five nights now. His curse came

...ut more of a sigh. He was getting used to the nightmare.

He closed his eyes again, swaying with the creaking of the timbers. The dream had been the only bad thing about the voyage so far. He didn't really count the bump on his head, the food given the passengers, the boy who kept appearing by his side on deck, displacing the unseen form of Amala.

He thought of her often, wondering what comments she might make about the shore, the mantle of snow on the far peaks of the Crumples, the sailors' talk, the strange boy. In his mind her hair was long again, a marker for the steady northwest wind, her beauty and laughter a source of leering distraction to the sailors. The thought made Falca protective, watchful over his phantom companion.

He was sure she would have liked the sea, she who carved the ice of the canal as the prow of the *Bay of Tyryns* carved the sea. Falca discovered he liked the ocean, the challenge of working the wind for speed and direction, the stars and compass-eye for position, though his windwhipper never strayed beyond sight of land. It was the constant effort to squeeze the most out of what was given you that appealed most to Falca. He observed Gattus, the ship's master, now and again, and suspected that he was a mediocre captain at best. If that one could become a master....

He wondered, too, what it would have been like to ship out on some windwhipper or galliot. For all the time he'd spent by the quays of Slidetown and Catch-All, with the routine purging of sailors from ships, the soup of the dock water, the taverns, he'd never thought of leaving as a sailor. A hard life, to be sure, but in time he might have saved enough to settle in Gebroan. He hadn't been queasy for long on the voyage. His seasickness had passed while other passengers—the father of the boy especially—were still hanging over the rails.

There weren't any alleys at sea. A tight run of kennels below, maybe, but on top a man could stretch and breathe. Of course, he hadn't been through a storm yet.

The shriek of a bosun's whistle roused Falca from his half-sleep. He heard the bellowing coming from amidships: "UP, UP, ALL OF YE!" It was meant for the sailors, not the passengers, but Falca tumbled out of his hammock anyway. If there was trouble, he hoped it wouldn't delay landfall in Sandsend and put more time between him and Saphrax.

He ducked a swaying lantern near his head. The hold smelled of sweat, wet wool, pitch, oakum, and charcoal. Beyond the cargo came the thumping, thudding, and curses of the *Tyryns*' sailors leaving quarters just forward of the jack hatch.

The other passengers, including the family of three nearest to Falca, had left their hammocks, too, looking sleepy and bewildered. The father had his back to Falca, blocking the narrow way. He leaned to one side. Sliding cargo had injured a leg.

"Father," his son said, glancing at Falca, though not apologetically. He eased his father gently out of Falca's path. The man turned.

"Oh, yes. I'm sorry. The leg." He smiled, giving his eyes even more of a squint, making the needless apology even more excessive.

Falca nodded. He had surprised the man drinking a bottle of scorchbelly the second day out. The son and mother had been on deck. The father had quickly put his nourishment away, looking guiltily at Falca, as if he cared.

The boy had told Falca his father was an itinerant edificiate, a public writer when he could get the business, who had gotten a posting as a teacher in Sandsend. "My father's eyesight is weak," the boy said, after Falca pointed out an uncommon sight: The Erseiyr's eastward flight far off in the distance. "It's all the books. He can't see a scratch on a pot at three paces." Whether it was his father's injury or a desire to avoid more of the lessons he gave in the mornings, the boy approached Falca more and more for conversation until Falca finally had to put him off brusquely.

As Falca passed, he heard the mother ask the father: "What do you suppose the trouble is, Kylis?"

"My guess is kreenkills, a long swarm of them, migrating in front of us. It's the season."

"Pirates," the boy said.

"Pirates, eh?" the father said, his voice indulgent, amused.

"I heard the sailors last night worrying about someone named Mangles."

"Oh, Kerros," the mother said. "They just knew you were spying on them and were trying to frighten you."

"No, they were the ones who were scared."

Falca glanced back, only because the boy said it so matter-of-factly. He went on, leaning with the motion of the ship, making his way past two more hammocks of passengers, then the bales of wool, barrel staves, the casks of pitch, charcoal, and tallow that filled the stern and amidships. Ahead, the catsteps leading up to the deck were framed by the jack hatch. As Falca rose into the morning light, he felt

e gush of salt air in his face. He hadn't taken three steps on deck
hen a sailor, shouting to another, backed into him, spinning him
round. "Get outta the way," the sailor snarled and ran for the aft
astle, where Gattus stood, screaming orders to the dozens of men
igh in the rigging and yards. The wind slapped every foot of sail,
napping, cracking the canvas. The masts creaked with the burden.

Falca skirted past two more sailors, who had jumped down from
e larboard ratlines. One of them spit on the faded red of the deck.

"Mangles or Grippa," he said. "Either way, we're meat. They're
oth squeezed from the same arsehole."

"Could still be a coastie. We've kissed the coast to stay clear of
e bastards."

The first man lowered his voice, glancing at Falca. "If it ain't, I
in't gonna stick here to greet either one. I'll take my chances over
e side. You ain't seen Mangles's cutlass worms, but I have, on the
erica, not a year ago. One bite and you're stiff as a spar for hours,
an't even waggle your tongue. By the time it's over, either the
vorms have made a meal of ye, or yer off to the Isles in Mangles's
hains. He took the *Serica* with only a dozen heaves to board, and
'm here to tell the tale only because he got a ship twice the size of his
wn and didn't want to bother with two sailors in a scatboat."

"Yer crocked, Stokie. Mangles won't be this far east."

The first sailor grabbed the other's shirt. "I ain't crocked, and
'll tell you this. Gattus may have dumped our scat in Draica for
nore swell below, but I'll oar myself to shore before I let Mangles
ave me."

A mate broke the two apart and pushed them to another task.
Maybe the boy was right after all, Falca thought. He felt a little worry
reep into his gut and hands as he leaned on the larboard rail, staring
ft. He saw the red sail, coming off the headland with some design on
e sail he couldn't quite make out. Then he noticed something else,
ike the stitching of a wound, a scar against the sky. Moments later
ame the shout from the maintop: "Stormbirds! We got stormbirds
omin'!"

This wasn't going to be a matter of simply outrunning a pirate
galley, which the swift windwhipper could do, Falca thought. He
adn't heard of Mangles or cutlass worms, but he had heard a few
tories about the stormbirds in quay-side taverns. How they had
icked children off the deck of a packet. Some said men too. Falca
ad never believed the stormbirds were big enough to do that. Nor

had he believed the claims that the stormbirds were spawned from the droppings of the Erseiyr.

He believed the stories now, though, and swore a string of oaths. The stormbirds were approaching fast, six of them, each carrying something square and dark underneath. A knot tightened in Falca's stomach. This wasn't his territory. There were no alleys to duck into and he felt suddenly trapped, exposed.

Behind him, Falca heard the clatter of swords and pikes being passed out to the crew, the panicky shouting.

". . . Plump and ready as a plattered roast."

"You know what they're carrying, don't you?"

Two sailors rushed toward the rails just aft of where Falca stood. They pushed aside the family that had come on deck, knocking the father down. The boy, Kerros, attacked the one who had done the shoving. The mother was terrified because the Gebroanan sailor wielded a sword—a falcata? She pulled her son back, even as he was pummeling the sailor's waist with his small fists.

The other sailor—the ship's cook—was about to toss an empty flour barrel overboard, but a mate rushed past Falca with a snarl and stabbed the cook in the back. The barrel fell to the deck, rolling crazily. The first sailor dropped the falcata and leaped over the rail. The mate cursed him once and ran aft, shouting orders to men still aloft.

Falca watched the sailor struggle toward the shore, his head bobbing in the whitecaps. Then he disappeared as two more sailors jumped ship.

The stormbirds were now close enough for Falca to see the curved beaks, the huge talons that gripped what looked like wicker baskets. The stormbirds had no call.

He thought of jumping too. What could he do against stormbirds and cutlass worms? He glanced across to the shore. It wasn't that far. But he couldn't swim, and even if he somehow made it, there were the Myrcians on the shore, gangers building the Long Road. He could see their tiny, swarming numbers around a half-finished mile-castle. Likely he'd be captured and put on the gang. Still, it was a chance.

He glanced down the rail, looking for the barrel, which could keep him afloat in the choppy water. The boy had picked up the falcata, the hilt and slightly curved blade ridiculously huge in his hands. He needed both to hold it.

Falca instantly changed his mind, shamed by the pathetic figure of youth ready to defend his mother and father with a sword he could scarcely hold. A falcata. Not just any sword. A falcata. He couldn't see from that, abandon that boy's courage.

Gattus was screaming for more pikes to be passed up to the men in the rigging. Falca ran to the family, who were moving toward the back hatch.

The stormbirds were circling overhead.

"Here," Falca said to the boy, holding out his hand.

The boy shook his head.

"Kerros," the father said, "give it to the man, quickly. We must get below."

"You take it," Kerros said to his father.

"I don't know how to use that thing."

"Maybe he doesn't either, Father."

"I do," Falca said impatiently, waggling his fingers. "Maybe not so well as you, but I'll manage." Somewhere, he found the briefest of smiles.

The boy gave it to him.

They didn't make it below. A screaming sailor cartwheeled down from the maintop, hit the edge of the jack hatch, and flipped back into the deck as two of the stormbirds' baskets burst nearby. Bits of wicker struck Falca like whipping branches. Kerros and his parents were hit, too, with spraying debris and stunned, as was Falca, by the squirming contents of the demolished baskets, one of which had crashed between Falca and Kerros.

The boy leaped quickly out of the way of the crawling things, followed by his mother, who was pushed to safety by her husband. He tried to follow, but slipped on one of the writhing cutlass worms. Another whipped its upturned snout. Falca shouted a warning, aghast at its seeking mouth, the ring of teeth, but was too late. It struck the father's back as he tried to scramble clear. He fell to his side with a scream, hands jerking, flailing wildly to tear it off, but he couldn't reach it. In his terror he rolled once, twice, away from Falca and the others. The boy darted toward his father, but Falca grabbed him, pushed him behind with a sweep of his arm. He began hacking at the slithering worms to clear a path to the father, kicking out with his boots.

Another worm fell from above, draping its three-foot length

around the boy's shoulders. Before it could strike either Falca or Kerros, the mother grabbed it and flung it back toward the rails and into the sea.

They reached the father. The worm was as thick as Falca's wrist and he cut the thing in two with a single stroke of the falcata. Yellow blood spurted, sprayed, stung Falca's hand. Still, the cutlass worm wouldn't let go of the father's back. The man's eyes were wide, and he screamed as he thrashed about so much that Falca had to use his weight to pin him while he gripped the worm behind the bulbous head, heedless of the puslike blood seeping from the severed end. His hand recoiled once at the raspy texture of the sand-colored scales. The worm's short, cordlike appendages brushed Falca's hand, his arm, in a hideous caress, seeking purchase. Finally Falca struck at the head twice, and it let go.

The father began convulsing, and as his son and wife dragged him back toward the larboard rail, they lost his hands several times, and Falca had to help them, even as he struck at worms slithering toward them.

The woman knelt by the rails, cradling her husband's rocking head in her lap, her arm wrapped tightly around her crying son. The father's feet kept hitting the deck, making a wild drumming. Falca kept more worms from coming close.

Soon the convulsions eased, and the father began to stiffen. His arms, his legs, his fingers straightened out. His wife kept talking to him, but he couldn't reply.

"I heard the sailors," Falca said. "He won't die, but it will be while before the poison wears off."

"We have to leave the ship," the woman said, her voice so calm that Falca was amazed at her composure. "There must be a boat."

He shook his head. "We'll find a way. But we'll have to do it ourselves."

There wasn't much time. Most of the crew had retreated to the aft castle, leaving behind a score of sailors who had been bitten by the cutlass worms. Some were still in the throes of convulsion. Others had stiffened. They couldn't even move their heads, only their eyes, like the woman's husband. They were alive but completely helpless. Falca shivered, helpless to relieve their wild eyes, the panic, the entrapment within one's own body. Some of the worms began to crawl over the dead-but-alive victims, slithering up to the eyes to begin to feed, seeking out that wildness, the only betrayal of life within. He

ould have been better if Falca could hear the screams, some release
or the agony, but they were denied even that.

Cutlass worms still dropped from the yards and lines, where the
askets had hit, spilling their contents. Falca saw one man aloft, con-
ulse, then stiffen in the crow's nest. He fell over, and his arms and
egs, straight as spars, caught in the rigging, like a fly in a web,
iving him time to think of the fall to come.

Here and there sailors still fought the cutlass worms. One sailor,
itten on the arm, whipped the worm again and again at a mast,
ogging it until he collapsed in a thrashing. Two men, a sailor and a
assenger, one stricken, one not, leaped over the starboard rail.

Many of the worms were dead, their yellow blood smearing the
eck. Those that were still alive were either feeding or seeking out
ore victims. Only a few sailors dared to venture near to kill those
utlass worms.

Above, the stormbirds, silent except for the working of their
uge gray wings, were shredding the topsails to laundry with their
dons. Because of their size, the birds couldn't reach the lower
ails, but the damage was enough. They snapped off the top
races, ripped loose the stays, and sheared off the fore and main
oyals, which fell almost to the deck, snagging the lower lines.
ne of the larger stormbirds tried to carry off a sailor from the
oreboom. For a few moments he wriggled, bait on a hook, before
alling into the sea. The stormbird wheeled lazily and came back
ow over the water, toward the stern, collapsing the group of
ailors—Gattus among them—on the aft castle.

The *Tyryns* was lost, Falca knew, unworkable, slowing. He
lanced at the gaining pirate ship, narrowing his eyes at something
amiliar emblazoned on the broad white band of its square, red
ail. . . .

He heard the boy say, "There, Mother! We can use that to get
way." Falca saw the boy pointing at the flour keg that rolled toward
hem with the ship's movement, bumped into a sailor and the cutlass
worm feeding on his eyes. The barrel rolled away again, veering
round the corner of the jack hatch. Kerros ran after it, even as his
nother shouted, "No, Kerros, let me get it. Come back." She quickly
eft her husband and ran after her son.

Falca might have gone instead, but he was caught in the dilemma
f his own fate, by what he had just seen across the water. He felt
omeone looking at him, and realized it was the boy's father. The

man couldn't speak. He had only his eyes, those weak eyes that hi son said couldn't see a scratch on a pot at three paces. Yet those eye bore into Falca's with an unmistakable, fierce demand. They flicke to Falca's sword hand, back to his eyes, back to the sword hand. Th eyes said, "By the time the poison wears off, they'll be here, an they'll take my wife and son. You know what they will do to them My wife and boy won't leave without me. I can't swim, but they can And you."

Falca shook his head, and the man's eyes grew fiercer, then soft ened to a pleading. "No, that's not what I meant," Falca said, "but I' do the other if it's what you want."

He stood over the man, straddling his waist, the falcata in both hands. He hesitated, seeing the sudden despair in the father's eyes and for a moment wondered if this, too, was an imagining, whethe he was seeing the eyes all wrong, killing someone else with the fal cata. Then the eyes hardened again, grew impatient, desperate, say ing, "Do it now. Don't let my son or wife stop you."

Falca turned his head to see them both, the barrel in front of them They were so shocked, the mother let the barrel go, and it rolled t her husband and stopped. "What are you doing?" she said.

"He wants me to kill him so that you two can escape while there' time."

"No, you don't know that. He can't speak to tell you."

"His eyes told me."

"No. Get away from him! We're all going."

"He would drown. There isn't time for—".

"NO!"

"Will you see for yourself? Come see." Falca stretched out hand.

The mother hesitated, and her son came forward instead. Falc moved the barrel for him. Kerros kneeled down by his father, his fac almost touching. For a moment he looked, then embraced his father stood and walked back to his mother, whose hands were shaking ove her mouth. She dropped to her knees, and her son put an arm over he shoulder, turning into her face, muffling her sobbing, tears streamin down his cheeks.

Falca took a deep breath, and another, then moved the barrel i front of the father so that his son could not see. He dropped the poin of the falcata over the heart and looked once more into the man' yes, seeing the confirmation, the acceptance, the wet brightness that shone like a candle flame through glass.

With both hands Falca plunged the falcata down, then withdrew it and wiped the blade on his pant let.

"Both of you," he called out. "Come here, quickly. You must go now."

He allowed the woman a moment with her dead husband, then gently lifted her up. "I'll put him to the sea after you've gone. Now, listen." He pointed over the rail. "See that jutting rock offshore? Lodge yourselves there until dark, then go ashore and go quickly south. You must move away from the Myrcians ashore. Keep off the roads, but if you take one, wrap a rag around your eyes, act the part of the blind. Or spot your faces with juice from plants for a disease. Anything to make you less desirable a mark. Do you have coin?"

The woman nodded.

"Take more," Falca said, and handed her the last of the spur's money. "Hide it well."

"Aren't you coming?" the woman said.

"No."

"Why . . . ?"

"There's no time to tell you. Put away the coins. Here . . ." Falca wrenched off the lid of the empty barrel and threw in the falcata. He had to stab the bottom deeply to make it fit. He pounded the lid back on and then ripped a strip of his tunic and wrapped his dagger blade. "Put this in your mouth. Clench tightly. You may lose a tooth, but better you have a weapon to use if any sailor would take the barrel from you. Now go. You first," he said to the mother, helping her to the rail. He gave her a push. When he saw where she surfaced, he lifted the barrel and aimed it as best he could and heaved it toward her. He lifted the boy to the rail.

"The falcata—the sword—is yours."

The boy twisted in his hands. "Why aren't you coming? You could hold on to the barrel too."

"I have someone to find. Take care of yourselves. You will have to be as brave as your father. I think you are."

Even as the boy was looking back at his father, Falca tossed him from the ship. He saw the splash, saw both mother and son struggle toward each other. The mother reached the barrel first, then her son. She still had the dagger between her teeth.

They might make it, he thought, though the odds were against them reaching some town safely. Still, the woman was tougher than she looked, and the boy . . . he was a good one.

He turned away and watched the pirate ship coming closer still. He wondered about his decision, if by staying he would be getting closer to Saphrax—and Amala—than he would by going ashore and running the risk of capture by the Myrcians as he made his way to Gebroan.

Had he seen what he thought he'd seen on that sail? Or was it another trick of the eye?

He would be taken by the pirates, of course, this Mangles. They wouldn't kill him, unless he put up a fight, which he wouldn't. They wouldn't have gone to all the trouble of the cutlass worms if they only meant to board and begin killing. They were after a prize ship and slaves to sell.

It crossed his grain to deliberately put himself in danger, to limit his options. The odds weren't good. But if he had weighed odds, he wouldn't have gone after Amala Damarr in the first place.

He wasn't fleeing this time. His sense of purpose had a taste of Sweet-hand, or so he imagined. He stared at the sail as it came closer, feeling closer to Amala, despite everything. His eyes hadn't tricked him.

For on the ship's sail, smooth now with the wind as Amala's skin was to his touch, was the same mark he'd seen on her forehead, the mark of a mace-head.

Chapter Sixteen

Grippa's Island

On the morning of the fifth day since Mangles took the *yryns* in tow, Falca saw a peculiar cloud low in the sky, just off the dge of the galley's sail. The stoneskins brought aboard to guard e cargo had seen it also. From their lively conversation, Falca uessed that the cloud was no cloud at all. He remembered hearing omewhere of a volcano in the Ebony Isles, Cloudscrag or something ke that. The blossoming, vertical whiteness in the blue sky could be s steamy exhalation.

Wrapped in a blanket to ward off the cold, Falca spent the next ours at the starboard rail, watching the mountain form on the hori- on, followed by a string of dark green humps, the Ebony Isles. own toward the bow the sailors were watching too. If they were inking of jumping ship that night, Falca heard no talk of it in their wn listless conversation. They were resigned. There was no hope in scaping *into* the lair of Mangles and this Grippa. And the Spirit- ifters? Falca counted himself the only captive to feel a sense of xpectation in approaching the foreboding Ebony Isles.

He wondered about the coupling between the pirates and the ifters. It was all the more strange since everything he'd heard about he cult placed them in Gebroan. Was it solely a matter of a slave ade? The pirates bringing the Lifters captives, who were returned as mpties, docile oarsmen for the pirate galleys, who would feel pain ut no resentment at the oarmaster's whip? Whatever, it was a fair guess the Ebony Isles were some gruesome depot for the Lifters Falca was uneasy about it all, but not discouraged. There was a way in; there would be a way out, a way to get to Gebroan if he couldn' fist the Lifters in the Isles. If nothing else, all the years on the street had taught him about finding the escape routes.

At sunset that day the ships passed the first of forested islands Above it, Cloudscrag's distant western face was bathed in golds reds, and pinks, the white plume of steam now twilight pastels. A tower rose darkly from a clearing, silhouetted by the faraway peak A beacon came to life on the tower, a brilliant flickering eye in th waning day.

On the shore a village clustered about three ramshackle piers Falca saw no lights, no sign of life among the dozen cottages and hovels, the handful of moored boats. The place was empty. Falc wondered how many village sons now pulled on Mangles's oars There was little wind, the evening seemed to be holding its breath and Falca could hear the whispering rhythm of stroking oars marked by the drumbeat. Was it better or worse that the oarsmen, the empties were not capable of recognizing their village? He decided it wasn' better.

That night, before he fell asleep, Falca saw another light in th black: a spearpoint compared with the swaying lanterns on the gal ley's stern. Another signal tower. The Isles were probably laced wit them, so that this Grippa—Mangles's overlord, according to th sailors—would have plenty of warning in case of attack.

The next morning they passed yet another signal tower, its beaco made smoky by daylight visibility. Two more villages, nestled i rocky coves, appeared to be deserted. High above the hilly ridge o the headland, two stormbirds rose in ever-widening gyres, joined by third.

The galley swung to the west, around the point, and the *Tyryn* followed in a wider arc, its towline teased by gulls. The entrance t the long inlet was narrow, pinched on one side by shoals that rose to rocky outcropping frosted by gull droppings. At the very end stoo the last of the signal towers. It was more formidable than the others Falca saw as they passed. There were actually two towers. Th higher, more slender one contained the cresset beacon. The lowe broader tower was closer to the open water, an effective platform fo archers to ignite the sails of intruders with fire arrows. A mace-hea flag, red on white, fluttered from a pole on the lower tower. Sentrie waved at the galley. A few sailors on the *Tyryns* answered with ruder gestures.

Smaller boats dotted the inlet, fishing the calm, green waters. The men who cast and hauled in the nets were empties, four or five to a boat. Their listlessness, even in work, was unmistakable, in contrast to the single overseer in each boat who shouted instructions or prodded them with a broad stick. It was no consolation that empties could be taught simple tasks, such as rowing or netting fish. What would Amala do if he was not successful in bringing her back somehow? Weave baskets for the rest of her life?

Horsemen rode along a road on the near side of the inlet. The riders scattered a pair of animals Falca had never seen before. They were graceful beasts with long legs, outsized ears, and they fled into their forest haven that rose up steeply to the crest of the ridge. Falca watched as the horsemen paused to shoot arrows at the fleet animals. They missed and continued on their way. It was an odd thing to give Falca hope, but it did. He savored it only a short while because the sight of Mangles's stronghold stunned him like a blow to the head.

The castle rose from a rocky base, diminished only by the lofty escarpment behind and the monstrous gouge of a quarry from which the gray-white stone had been taken. Stormbirds circled lazily high above the four towers. Smoke rose from a dozen chimneys, and Falca's keen eyes saw the sentires on the ramparts. It was a new fortress that would have made any noble of Lucidor proud and testified to this Grippa's growing wealth and power.

Two smaller towers at the end of a downward slope of crenelated wall guarded the quays. Two of the docks speared out below the castle, with four more along the shore. At least fifteen ships nestled along their lengths—tresremes, galliots, windwhippers, sturdy bawleys.

Closest to the quays sprawled the pirate town, where perhaps an old fishing village had been, like those Falca had seen deserted in the coves. The buildings were of timber, though some of the larger ones were of the same gray-white stone as the castle. Just beyond the town was a fenced enclosure, a place for prisoners. Falca saw a sizable group of them, guarded by patrolling sentries. The catch of Roak-knew-how-many ships.

Between that pen and the quarry was a larger, more permanent-looking palisade. Falca couldn't see the entrance, but along the road to this second pen there were groups of herded men and women, and

he guessed this enclosure was the empties home. If the size was any
indication, there were hundreds of them. These were the ones Falca
saw on the quays, hauling and lifting, sweating, the brute work that
could be learned through repetition and the club. The females among
them would be used by Grippa's galley-heaves until they were thrown
away like so much spoiled meat.

And perhaps the wagon Falca observed moving up a track toward
the heights was filled with those empties who had finally been worked
to death. Stormbird fodder. Falca saw the caves, several hundred
yards away from the town, cut into the hillside. The forest had been
cleared of its firs and hangbark, the trees stacked to form giant terraces. Falca watched the moving forms of the birds within the nests.
One stormbird came out, flaring its wings, frightening the team of
horses below. After a few minutes the animals were calmed enough
by the drivers to unhitch the wagon and leave it at the end of the road
below the terraces. As the men hurried away with the team, the
stormbirds engulfed the wagon.

He turned away in disgust as the *Tyryns'* towline was cut. The
windshipper drifted in alongside the galley, snagged to a final
thumping berth by hooked lines pulled by dockmen.

The stoneskins herded Falca and the sailors off the ship, allowing
them a few moments to get their land-legs before marching them
down the quay, toward the road leading to the town. The road was
crowded with carts, prisoners, gangs of empties, and the ever-present
overseers, dockmen, stoneskins, and galley-heaves in red-stained
leather. As Falca trudged along with the other captives, he saw what
could only be the Spirit-Lifters.

Some were coming off a galliot, others walking along the road in
groups. Most were dressed in blue trousers, tunics, and long gray
capes for the cold. He saw a curious design on their tunics—a
golden, slightly concave line with the mace-head in its curve. Some
of the Lifters wore a white cape, and Falca guessed these were some
higher order of the cult. But what caught his attention most, and
convinced him that these men and women were indeed Lifters, were
the long-handled maces secured at the belts. Several times as they
talked and gestured, their swirling capes revealed the mace-heads to
the bright sun. The jewellike flashes hurt Falca's eyes. He wondered
if it was for that reason alone that the nearby toiling empties seemed
to cringe and shy away from those Lifters carrying the maces.

No, he decided, flinching with a sudden understanding. His eyes closed almost against his will, and he saw in his mind the terrible brightness in Amala's house. When he opened his eyes, he saw, over the slumped shoulders of the sailor in front of him, the brute who had caused it. Falca stopped, only to be pushed ahead roughly by the stoneskin behind him.

Saphrax approached along the road, with three other gray-capes. He was talking, though Falca was too far away yet to hear his words. Saphrax was making some conversational point in such an assured, confident way, Falca thought for a moment it couldn't be Saphrax. But it was. He had put on weight, and his face was rounder, but there was no mistaking the misshapen nose, the tiny eyes, the ruined ear-lobe.

Saphrax waved an arm from the ships, back toward the castle looming over all. Falca saw the mace, its flashing crystal head big as his fist. Falca knew, felt to the core of his heart, that Amala was here, her spirit, her essence trapped within the mace-head.

His anger and fear began with the sweat of his clenched fists. Amala, Sun-thicket, the best part of his life, was slung at the brute's hip like a pouchful of coins.

Chapter Seventeen

Saia's Dowry

It was all Falca could do to restrain himself from lunging a Saphrax. This might be the only chance he had for the brute, but there had to be a better one. He forced the image of Amala eating her dog the earring pinned to her tunic, from his mind. Still, if he knew fo certain there was no way to rejoin her spirit to the husk of her body he would have bolted from his captors, and smashed Saphrax from the quayside walk and killed him in the water before they got him.

Saphrax and his companions had already passed when Falca called out sharply to him. A stoneskin jabbed him to punish him for the outburst, but Falca shouted again, more harshly: "Saphrax!"

The brute saw him then, began walking back with the others, even as Falca was pushed roughly ahead by the stoneskin. He kept looking back, wanting more than anything to smear that smiling face.

When Saphrax caught up, he ordered the stoneskin to loose Falc from the rest of the prisoners. "I'll see that he gets to the crib, Saphrax said.

The stoneskin was reluctant. Saphrax raised his voice, annoyed "He won't escape. He wants what I have. You could give him a ship oarsmen, and free passage and he wouldn't escape without this, yo fool." Saphrax patted the mace. "Isn't that right, Falca?"

As if to underscore the point, Saphrax turned without waiting fo Falca to reply and walked off the road, closer to the water. The stone skin, who probably hadn't understood a word Saphrax had said stared at Falca, waiting for him to bolt. He could have. But to where? The brute was right. He followed Saphrax, leaving the stoneskin shaking his head before resuming the herding of the prisoners.

Saphrax was smiling, too excited, it seemed to Falca, to lean against the hawser bollards like his three companions were doing. "I knew you would follow," Saphrax said. "But I thought we'd meet again in Gebroan. Bad luck to be captured by Mangles."

Falca glanced down at Saphrax's belt. The core of light hurt his eyes.

"What did you do, Saphrax?" he said. "Why her and not me?"

"Don't talk to me like I'd just botched one of your fists. Who do you think you are? *I'm* the one now in the position to rescue you from the prison hulk of your life. You need a lesson. Giver Blave, show my old friend what the mace can do."

Blave took a few steps toward Falca, unsheathing the mace. Falca backed up a few steps, puzzled because he could easily keep out of range of the mace. Blave dropped the mace-head to the vertical, then lifted it quickly to the level of Falca's chest.

The blow cracked like the butting of rams, smothering his scream, lifting him to darkness. The next thing he knew, he landed on his back, his head thumping the stone of the quay. He opened his eyes to a wheeling stormbird in the darkening blue of the afternoon. As he waited for the weight on his chest to lessen, he heard the laughter, and that forced him to get to his knees.

Blave stood no closer than a couple of yards, sheathing the mace.

"It all depends on the speed you use it, Falca, and the direction. Soft, overhand for that woman of yours. Quick and up for an enemy."

Falca wanted to rush him, snatch the mace, and never mind his ditchies or whatever they were. But he couldn't, even if he didn't feel like a giant boot was pressing down on his chest. He could still hardly breathe. No, he needed to find out what happened. The best way was to let this strange incarnation of the brute play the turnkey, let him savor his revenge for Falca's attempt on his life.

He rubbed his chest as Saphrax smiled. "The mace changed my life. I changed my life, that's what I did, after you botched my death. Giver Agona took me here with others she found in Draica, for the initiation into the Curve of our god. Maradus himself was present when my mace was given to me and charged by the Prism, but he's left now for Gebroan."

Falca coughed. "The Prism?"

"Surely you've heard of Roak's Prism of Empathy, surely you saw the mark on Mangles's sail. The Prism is the fountain of all you will see here, both Grippa's and ours," Saphrax said, still tugging at his ear, the vestige of the earlier habit. The mangled flesh was still red where he'd ripped off his earring.

"So I was given my mace and went back to Draica for the sweetest fist of my life. Of course my mace is filled and cannot be used for a weapon, though Blave's and the others' can. Theirs are empty, but have been charged by the Prism. They won't be empty for long. Maybe you would like to offer your Gift to one of them and join your woman in union with the One, at the Crucible of Souls."

Falca stood finally, as Saphrax went on. "Personally I think that would be a waste. You would be much better suited as a disciple of Maradus, our Father of the One, as a Giver—voals, we call ourselves. Which is perhaps why I chose her and not you," he said, laughing, "to answer your question."

"I want her back," Falca whispered. It was stupid, he knew, but he didn't know what else to say to the brute's babbling.

"Of course you do. But everything has its price. I knew that even before you took me from the river hulks. Tell me, have you heard of our Maradus?"

Falca shook his head.

"You will. In time all the Six Kingdoms will have heard of him and his inspiration. Would you care to hear?"

What Falca cared to do was kill the brute. The edge of the quay, the water, was a mere body's length behind Saphrax. Finish him off in the water for good this time. But lose Amala forever.

"You've come a long way from the hulks," he said instead.

"Maradus did too, perhaps farther. He began as a castrated servant to a young princess years ago, a Gebroanan princess named Saia, who was to be wed to Rekèlever in the Great Hall at Cross Keys Island. The matching of the western kingdoms, a merging that would have caused Myrcia fits. Her dowry was none other than the Prism of Empathy, which, next to Cassena's Nimbus, was the softest of Roak's Six Gifts. You know about the Prism, Falca?"

"It was long ago, Saphrax."

"They've taught me much. You should attend to your education too, sometime, Falca. It is said that Roak had the Prism made in order to keep himself humble. In the far land of Arriosta, our motherland, Roak would summon peasants and tradesmen and craftsmen, people f all kinds, and the power of the Prism let him see and feel how they ived, let him experience their days of fears and wants. Good rulers nake as many enemies as bad, and Roak was no fool, for the Prism ould also ferret out treachery.

"The Prism was a tool for purity and truth. Those qualities, like he Prism itself, have long been undervalued and perhaps that was vhy the Prism was chosen as Saia's dowry, a fitting adornment to her nnocence."

Falca had to stifle a laugh. "They've given you a tongue, aphrax," he said. If he could keep him talking, sooner or later he'd ind out how the process of Lifting could be reversed, if it could.

"I had it all along, waiting to be discovered. You have treasures vithin as well; we all do. Those who think themselves complete are he greatest fools. That is your greatest fault, Falca."

My greatest fault was in botching your death, Falca thought. "You vere talking about this Saia," he said.

Saphrax smiled, almost mournfully, as if lamenting a weakness e'd seen. Falca wanted to slap him.

"She was scarcely more than a child," Saphrax said. "And one of er favorite things was a crystal mace, given to her by her father, who ired all boys but her, brothers who preferred iron, not fragile crystal n their hands.

"Her ship and escorts never made it to Draica. A storm drove hem off course, to the Ebony Isles, and they foundered. Most of the urvivors were killed later by a petty chieftain, a shore-licker who trangled his own fowl for dinner. . . ."

Blave and the others snickered. The contempt in Saphrax's voice urprised Falca, for he knew who the pirate was. "And his name was Grippa."

"It unfortunately still is," Saphrax said. "He captured Maradus nd Saia and took the Prism. He soon discovered, by clumsy acci-lent, how the Prism can charge weapons, swords, so that one need tot have to cut or thrust for the weapon to be effective. All that is teeded is the close presence of a wild spirit, a ruptured soul. That was nd is Grippa.

"Grippa was thinking of ransoming Saia, but the power of the 'rism changed his mind. It exceeded his wildest, most ambitious topes. So he decided to have his way with Saia.

"Our Blessed Maradus had long been in love with Saia, and that light he heard her being ravished, heard the screams that turned his

tears to acid, channels of sorrow that one may still see to this day. O
Blessed Maradus hated Grippa even more and wanted to save Sai
from him, prevent him from hurting her again. Better to kill the or
he loved than have her endure a life of degradation and rape. His onl
weapon—for he couldn't bear to use his hands on her throat—wa
her crystal mace. He charged the mace and contrived to be alone wit
Saia later.

"As our Father of Souls was about to bring down the mace t
cause her death, his heart welled at the sight of her sleeping form, an
he relented and let the mace fall gently to her forehead as he wep
Quickly he was astounded by what happened. He realized he wa
hurting her, but it wasn't any worse than what had been done to he
He wasn't even touching her. And he felt, so he has said, such
strength, a potency, he had never felt before. He knew in his hea
that she was sacrificing herself for something greater, and he accepte
that, as a lover accepts what another gives. He was awed by th
power, the blinding light that seemed to purify his taking. As lover
are spent after union, so was Saia, totally as was the Father of th
One in his own way. For he had been in union with her, let there b
no doubt, and she gave birth to a vision that brought our Blesse
Maradus to tears again."

Blave nodded gravely. He had been mouthing the exact sam
words as Saphrax. He was giving a recitation beaten into every init
ate, Falca thought. It was so much honey-covered dung. Tears, m
ass . . . Maradus's vision was now slung at Saphrax's belt. Falca
contempt hardened to an anger and rage that he could scarcely con
trol. He kept seeing the room, then glimpses of Amala gliding on th
ice. He felt her hands at his face, tasted the salt of her skin after thei
union, heard her laughter. . . .

Saphrax stood before him, so close Falca could almost reach ou
and touch Amala's mace. The brute slapped him so hard he lost hi
balance, fell to his knees. As Saphrax stepped back, his companion
closed, ready with their charged maces.

"Are you listening to me, Falca?" Saphrax whispered. "There ar
no other stories but this one. Perhaps Blave's mace will force mor
respect from you."

Falca tongued the blood of his cut lip.

"The vision was of a god," Saphrax said softly, "an infinite mo
saic of Gifts, whose creation would be the only tribute possible t
Saia and our Blessed Maradus's love for her. Through that love an

he attendant seneschals of sacrifice, discipline, and purity, all other
vorshipers would be humbled, so Maradus foretells: the Myrcians
vith their greedy, arrogant Erseiyr, the Attallissians with their thiev-
ng Kraken, the Skarrians with their crude deification of dead war-
ords, the Gebroanans with their vulgar sensuality, the mountain kings
f Helveylyn with their obsessive search for immortality.

"Blessed Maradus knew he was alone in a den of wolves, who
vould kill and scavenge his dream before it began. He knew that for
t to ripen, he had to submit to an alliance with the one he hated so.
hat was a great but necessary sacrifice, for Grippa controlled the
'rism.

"Grippa was outraged when he saw the lifeless yet living Saia,
s Maradus knew he would be. Before the pirate could kill the
'ather of the One, Maradus said, 'I am of more use to you if you
end me to Gebroan. You have seen what happened to the princess.
maginе an army of men like her, men to oar your ships, build you
 fortress the envy of kings. I know how to give you that. But I
teed to go to Gebroan to fashion more of what I need, to mate
vith the Prism. I ask only to have access to that Prism and to keep
vhat I shall take from those who will follow in the sacrifice of
'aia. You have no use for what I want. You are a man of the earth,
he senses. Keep those I empty—to arm, to work, to fornicate
vith. I am a man of the spirit.'

"Grippa agreed and sent Maradus to Gebroan, thinking that at the
ery least, he was getting rid of a foolish man-child who kept a
hild's toy clutched to his breast.

"And so it began," Saphrax ended, his words echoed by Blave and
he others.

Still kneeling, his face yet tingling from Saphrax's blow, Falca
tared at Amala's mace, whose light had become even more luminous
s the daylight waned. He was supposed to be impressed by this
 anal-muck, impressed with Saphrax for his acceptance into this guild
f abominators. The brute was trying to sway him—why else take the
ime? The choice was coming: join the Lifters or become an empty.
Ie thought of the animals he'd seen from the ship, who had escaped
he hunters' arrows. If he could bolt, run as he'd never run before,
nake it to the forest to hide. . . . He'd have to come down from the
orest for food—he wouldn't last a week otherwise. He'd lived in the
ity all his life. Then how would he get to Gebroan? That was where
aphrax was taking Amala. This place was only a way station. How

would he get there? He couldn't very well steal a forty-oar ship.

Saphrax came closer to Falca, close enough for him to see th‸
planes and bevels of the mace crystal, the myriad tiny suns. The ligh‸
hurt his eyes it was so close. He reached out a hand, expectin‸
Saphrax to slap it away, but he only moved Falca's hand away with n‸
more force than a parent would redirect a crawling infant fro‸
danger.

"I have broken the rules for you in telling you this sacred recit‸
tion, which took me so many hours to learn, I am not ashamed to sa‸
A voal such as I may normally give the recitation only when on‸
decides to join the Curve of our god. But I think you might so decid‸
You were always practical, as thieves are. I offer you the chance f‸
your life and a chance to experience countless others, as I will ‸
Gebroan. Join me there. Your rutting with the woman would be ‸
nothing compared with what Maradus promises his new voals. B‸
come one of us. Otherwise you'll surely die here or wind up on one ‸
Grippa's galleys, your only distraction the keening of gulls, with n‸
more life in your heart than the beating of the oar drum."

Falca looked away, as if considering the offer, but he was searc‸
ing for the start of the inlet road, measuring the thickness of the fore‸
beyond.

"I am different, Falca. You must be able to see and hear that. ‸
have been taught much in a short time, as have we all, for one ‸
Maradus's goals is enlightenment through the One. I have yet to giv‸
my Gift to the One, though that will happen soon enough in Gebroa‸
I have changed. You haven't. You're searching. Why else did yo‸
follow me? It wasn't just because of the woman. Without my hel‸
your search will end in folly, in the time it takes to walk from thi‸
quay to the stockade. You saved me once from the hulks, I offer yo‸
the chance to let me save you."

Only that? Falca thought. Surely after the attempt on his life he'‸
want revenge. Getting Falca to join the cult would be revenge ‸
sorts.

He looked into Saphrax's eyes, curious at the tone in his voice tha‸
was close to a plea. He didn't have to be that way. He could kill Falc‸
here for that revenge. The brute wanted something else, somethin‸
even more than for Falca to follow him into Maradus's sty. What wa‸
it? Acceptance? Falca could hardly believe that after all that had hap‸
pened, he and Saphrax were still on the streets of Draica. Even Blav‸

nd the other voals were looking troubled, embarrassed. Saphrax was
till conferring some power on him, as a younger brother might to an
lder. Falca kneeled like a beggar before him, but there it was.

He shifted, searching the end of the quay for the beginning of the
oad. A stormbird took to the air in the distance. He was wondering
whether Saphrax's coming rage would end it all here, on the stone of
he quay. He felt something at the side of his face, touching the place
where Amala had sewn his flesh. Saphrax turned Falca's face toward
him with the helve end of Amala's mace. His one huge hand almost
ompletely covered the mace-head, the light edging his skin in red.

Falca recoiled in revulsion at this pressing, at what seemed like a
aress. Then his anger rose with the vision of that huge hand pushing
down on Amala's face, smothering her. He tried to stand up, but one
f the voals pushed him down again to his knees.

Falca spit the words out. "You know what I followed you for."

"The woman? Is that what you want?" Saphrax said, the soft,
leading voice gone. "You trouble yourself so much over the woman
who gave her Gift to me. Here, is it that brief sweetness you want?"

Saphrax whirled away, grabbed a passing empty, a woman, and
mashed a bundle from her hands. He dragged her over to Falca by an
rm, ripped off her ragged clothes. She was so dirty the black mark
n her forehead seemed more like a smudge. She stared blankly at a
pot over Falca's head, her blue eyes never blinking. Saphrax poked
t her patch of hair with the same end of Amala's mace he'd used to
ouch Falca's face.

"Saphrax, stop it!" Falca shouted, only to have Blave cuff him
ard on the side of the head. The woman slowly lay down and spread
er legs, turning her head slowly to look at the sun emptying itself
nto the water of the inlet. Her arm grazed the nipple of her left breast
s her hand plucked a bright stone.

Saphrax kicked her away. Falca's curses were drowned out by
Saphrax's shouting: "And if not women, what then? Power? Is that
what you want?"

Saphrax grabbed Blave's mace and strode over to a gang of emp-
ies stacking casks along the quay. He brought the mace up sharply
nd blew one of the empties into the water, eliciting an angry shout
rom the overseer. Saphrax ignored the man and walked back to
Falca. "Isn't that what you yearned for, really, as you fisted those
nimals, the Timberlands, on the streets of Draica? As you eyed the

carriage that time by the canal? I saw you. I knew. I wasn't the do
you thought I was. I can give you power or, at the very least, a poi
to your meaningless life."

Falca shook his head.

"You want nothing besides... this?" He fondled the head c
Amala's mace, eclipsing the brilliant light.

"Just that, Saphrax."

"Then you're a fool," Saphrax said, and handed Blave his mace
He put his own back into his belt. His anger had subsided as quickl
as it came. So much had changed about him, Falca thought, and s
little. "I just might give it to you," Saphrax said, "if you would joi
me in serving the One. What do you say to that? How much do yo
love her, Falca?"

The word sounded strange to Falca coming from someone else
and stranger still from Saphrax. Was there a measure of love? H
didn't know. Either you did or didn't.

"How much, my old friend?" Saphrax said, grinning, tauntin
now. "There is a simple way to rejoin body and soul. That could b
arranged, provided you follow me into the Curve of our god. Ther
are others whose Gifts I could take to the One in Gebroan. There are
hundred, at least, in the stockade."

Falca swallowed hard. Was this his chance? Could he play alon
until Amala was... safe? But he didn't know how far he'd have t
go, how deeply their hooks would sink in him. In the end he wa
fearful of that, the alley from which he might not be able to escape.

He loved Amala. But that didn't require him to sacrifice himsel
Wasn't that what her brother had required of her? No, he had to se
this through on his own terms, in his own way.

He shook his head once again, staring at the light of the mace
telling her without words that he loved her, that he was sorry.

"She would be disappointed," Saphrax said. "I must take her Gi
with me to Gebroan, then. And you to the stockade. Perhaps Blave c
Kemris here will have the pleasure of your Gift. Many will be take
tonight. Get up."

Falca did so. "You've not changed at all, Saphrax. You've onl
replaced me with another."

"If so, it is an infinitely greater replacement."

Chapter Eighteen

Caged

Falca stood near the gate of the stockade watching a few Lifter voals lighting cressets marking the corners of the paved square. In the middle, two white-caped priests talked to each other by a waist-high dais that could only be the place where prisoners would be Lifted later.

He spat between the timbers of the palisade, thinking hard, working his tongue at the spot where the scrape sore had been. It had healed weeks after he met Amala Damarr, but he tongued it anyway.

There wasn't much time. He hadn't seen Saphrax again, or Blave and the other voals who had thrown him into this pen, where over a hundred other prisoners waited and wondered if they would be among those culled for Lifting. He would not go quietly if he was taken. Mace or no mace, he promised himself to take a few of the bastards before they got him.

He glanced over the huddled prisoners, to the larger stockade on a rise of hill close by the quarry: the empties' home. In the fading light Falca could see their arms draped through the slits of their palisade.

No, he thought. Not quietly. Saphrax would be somewhere in the square, watching, when the time came, and Falca would break for him, kill him with his hands before they could use the charged maces to subdue him. Saphrax would have only Amala's mace, and that would be no protection.

Still, he couldn't resign himself to an end here. The timbers of the

171

stockade only angered him. He hadn't escaped the river hulks i
Draica year in, year out, only to wind up in this crib, next to
stoneskin who was—Falca shook his head in disgust—scraping hi
arms with a sharp-edged rock. There had to be a way out. His onl
ally so far was the coming darkness. He could use it to escape to th
forest along the inlet, then work his way to one of the deserted vil
lages he saw on the way in. He could steal all the provisions he coul
carry, find a boat or gig, point the thing south, and hope for the best.

But first things first: Get out of the pen.

The last light of day bathed the tops of Grippa's castle towers. A
Falca watched activity by the castle gate, he felt something at his leg
turned, saw a Timberlimb not two feet away, sniffing at him like
dog, chattering something Falca didn't understand. The surprise a
seeing a Timberland here gave way to his somber mood, and h
waved the Limb away.

She was a female, that was obvious. Her soiled red bandy scarcel
covered her pointy breasts. Her black hair was longer than most Lim
females he'd seen in Draica. She wore only one little boot.

The Limb came closer, craning her neck to catch more of hi
scent. Falca was in no mood for this and pushed her away. She wasn'
discouraged and advanced again, though not close enough to ge
pushed. Falca turned his back to her excited singsong, unnerved b
the Limb's ability to smell her own kind on him through the mask c
his own stink. It was a reminder of what he'd promised Gurrus at th
settlement house the night before he took ship.

He glanced at the stoneskin, who was still gazing through th
timbers. He had his top leathers off, despite the cold, and stroked hi
huge arms with the rock, again and again.

Falca tried to calm his irritation. It was stupid to be irked by suc
things, when in a short while he'd be trying to salvage his life. An
Amala's. No one else around seemed to mind the incessant scraping
but it was driving Falca crazy. Here he was trying to think of a wa
out of this pen, and this . . . shale-head was calmly grooming himsel
if that's what it was. He'd never before seen a 'skin do that. An
anyway, what in the name of the High Sorrows was a stoneskin doin
in the pen?

Falca moved away, but the scraping sound dominated the lo
whimperings, whisperings, the stamping of cold feet of the other pri
oners.

The Limb followed Falca to his new spot, keeping her distance

The 'skin went on scraping, and Falca couldn't take it anymore. The shalie might pound his skull with those sledge-hands but he didn't care. He walked back and yanked the rock from his hands and flung it away, hitting someone, who yelped a curse.

The stoneskin turned slowly, matching Falca's movement to the right. Falca tightened his fists, taking a step back, eyeing the iron band around his neck, knowing there was no place on the man where he wouldn't rip his knuckles. Before Falca and the stoneskin could settle the matter, the Limb darted in between the two, chattering vociferously, almost angrily, and pushed first at the shale-head and then at Falca, as if to separate them. Neither man moved, though the tiny hand Falca felt on his thigh was surprisingly strong. The Timberlimb kept at it, talking furious gibberish to Falca, pushing, unafraid of the cuff from either man that could send her sprawling.

The stoneskin grunted. "She don't want us to fight. What about you, roaking?" He shoved the Limb aside with the back of his hand.

Before Falca could answer, the Limb darted back between them and tried to push Falca away. "She's made up your mind for you. You stink of something she likes," the stoneskin said, and turned from them both.

The intercession of the Limb had taken the edge from Falca, and he walked away, feeling foolish for starting something he didn't finish. It was just as well. The shale-head stood a head taller than he and had arms like wharf pilings. Soon Falca heard the scrape-scrape again and resigned himself to the annoyance.

He gave his attention to the square. Scores of Lifter voals and priests gathered on one side, and Grippa's heaves were on the other, separated by an avenue the width of the dais. Perhaps, he thought, the two factions didn't like each other. Everyone in the square seemed to be waiting for the wagon that was creaking slowly down the castle road toward the gathering. A profusion of torches surrounded it, the light more wild and diffuse than the hard, brilliant jewels that marked the maces. More voals were coming from the town that sprawled toward the quays. Falca tried to find Saphrax among them all, but darkness had fallen, and a pair of patrolling heaves blocked his searching.

Was the uneasy alliance between Grippa and the Lifters the key to his freedom? Impatiently he wondered how he could use that. He glanced over to the stoneskin, who, as always, was looking toward the square. He'd stopped his scraping, and his hands gripped timbers.

He looked like he was strong enough to snap the thick poles. Falc
heard him spit through the slits. Perhaps the shale-head could giv
him answers. Make a little peace with the giant and get him to talk.

"They bring you off a ship?" Falca called out.

The stoneskin glanced in his direction, the resumed staring at th
square.

"Why aren't you out there like all the other stoneskins?" Falc
persisted.

He didn't reply, and Falca looked around at the other prisoners fo
a better prospect. The Limb was sitting almost close enough for Falc
to touch her. When he tried to shoo her away, the stoneskin finall
spoke.

"Leave her alone, roaking. She done you a favor before."

"She pick your stones out for you?" Falca said.

"What's your burr? You haven't got much time before they suc
you dry."

"I suppose Grippa keeps you in here to keep the peace."

"The Roach keeps me in here because I killed two of his 'stone
and three of his heaves."

He walked closer to the stoneskin. "You mind telling me why?"

"You'll see the answer soon enough."

Falca cleared his throat. "What's going to happen tonight?"

The stoneskin swung an arm behind him. "Grippa and Vaxxa—"

"Vaxxa?"

"The Lifter priest who runs the voals here. Both of them wil
divide us up. Usually it's half and half. Grippa does the choosing
since he's got the Prism. They'll haggle a while for the show of it, bu
it's the Roach who has the last word. Vaxxa doesn't like it much
He'd chop his lumber off to get the Prism."

"They don't like each other, do they?"

"Hate's more like it. They're two dogs at either end of a bone
One of these days it'll come to a head, but so far . . . I been here thre
years and it hasn't yet."

"So you were one of Grippa's . . ."

"One of the best the bastard ever had."

"What's your name?"

"Ballast. I had another in Helveylyn, in the High Vales, where w
come from. They got to calling me Ballast after I hired out to
sealord in Slacere."

"Roakings?"

"What you are, what anyone is, who doesn't wear the band." He clunked his iron collar. "We fought you when you came to the Vales, and now we carry a sword for those who can pay us. But you haven't got time for that story. What's your name?"

"Falca. Falca Breks. Which half will you be tonight, Ballast?"

"I know which half I won't be. And praise the Caves for that. Grippa holds grudges tighter than bark to a tree, but he won't allow me to be Lifted tonight. I'll fetch him too sweet a price with the Myrcian slavers. Who knows? After crushing a few miles of rock for the bed of the Long Road they're building, I just might wind up in the Sanctor's bodyguard. He has two thousand 'skins in his household guard alone. Two of my four brothers are with them."

"For someone who isn't worried about the Lifters, you seem to be staring mighty hard at what's coming."

"Never mind what I'm waiting for, roaking. Look to your own. You might get lucky, though. You're a good size, and you'd put a fair pile in the Roach's hand. You might even wind up on the same road gang as me."

Falca shook his head. "There's a voal out there. Someone who used to work for me in Draica before he joined the Lifters. He Lifted a woman I knew. I followed him here. He knows I'm here."

"So?"

"So I tried to kill him once. Now he wants to make me a Lifter, in return for the woman."

Ballast was silent for a moment. "A woman and a poor chance, is that it?"

"A poor chance to get her back," Falca said, "But I will."

"Sure you will," Ballast said. "You've maybe an hour to do it."

"A lot can happen in that time. It's why I'm talking to you. You know about them."

Ballast shook his head. "You're a fool, roaking. But tell me the woman's name anyway."

"Amala."

"Mine's was Mag, Marf Mag," Ballast said softly. "You want an idea from me? Tell your man you changed your mind."

"No."

Ballast jabbed a thumb to his forehead. "Then it's the quarry for you, or maybe an oar for Mangles. Here"—Ballast picked up a rock and tossed to Falca, who caught it—"save yourself the trouble and wash your head in now," he said, laughing.

The rock was cool. He kept it, the closest thing to a weapo
he had.

"I'll tell you this . . . Falca. If you're ass-ways of a Lifter and yo
haven't the heft of a 'skin like me, you're gone, you're dry. No on
can help you, not even that Limb who saved you from my hands
You've as much of a chance as she does. She's too small to work th
Road and she'll probably wind up as feed for the stormbirds. She'd b
up there now, except she's been creased by a few pus-hearts who wai
some more of it. There's some that like the fit of Limbs; I know a fev
of 'em by name. I just wish I had my hands on them now. They're a
roakings like you, which makes it a puzzle why she's taken to you so
It's like she knows you're going to do something and she's waiting fc
it to happen."

Falca shook his head. "She smells her own kind on me, that's all
The woman—Amala—worked with them, taking care of them. Sh
wanted to go to the Rough Bounds to help them fight against th
Wardens."

"Then it's even more of a shame what happened to her," Balla
said. "Those people and mine were here long before your Roa
dropped his anchor. What we have now is no more than the last of th
butter in the frying pan. My kind hires out to fight and die in roakin
wars now, but her kind doesn't even have that to save them, nothin
worth anything to the roakings."

Falca moved away from the stoneskin's tirade. He hadn't bee
much of a help. His bitterness wouldn't help spring him. He looke
out at the processional nearing the square, feeling the spread of poo
ing desperation.

Torchbearers surrounded a tight cordon of stoneskins, who in tu
shielded the wagon that bore the Prism of Empathy. The rumbling c
the wheels grew louder.

Ballast called out to him. "You want me to do it for you?"

"What?"

"Do you want me to kill you? It's better than letting the Lifter
empty you. I'll do your neck. Hers too," he said, pointing to the Lim
female, who stood close to Falca. "It'd be better for her than th
stormbirds. It won't hurt either of you but quick."

"You're serious, aren't you?" Falca said.

Ballast nodded toward the square. "Ever seen what happens whe
they Lift someone?"

Falca gripped the rock tightly. It was warm from his hand.

"No," he said. "If I go, I want the pleasure of taking a few of them with me."

"You won't have the luck, roaking. If you change your mind, the offer still stands."

Falca shook his head in the darkness. They might have been discussing a minor matter of debt or lodging.

"Don't wait too long to decide," Ballast added. "There's my Mag now in the cage with the Prism. You see her, Falca? If you see what she is, you'll know why I'm in here."

Falca watched the Prism wagon finally enter the far edge of the square. He heard, to his right, the scrape-scrape of Ballast rubbing his skin again with a rock from the stockade ground. He was rubbing faster than before, and the stroking, it seemed to Falca, had all the rhythm and purpose of combing one's hair before hurrying away for a tryst with a lover.

Chapter Nineteen

Marf Mag

A gang of twenty empties pulled the Prism wagon along the far perimeter of the square, prodded by the short staffs of overseers. The huge wagon creaked along on its six wheels, each as high as the accompanying torchbearers. It finally stopped in a corner. The empties dropped their ropes and were herded past the cresset fire, beyond the assembled Lifters, there to remain until they were needed again to pull the wagon back to the castle.

The cordon of stoneskins and torchbearers parted, peeled back to reveal the full length of the wagon. The only break in the bars of the cage atop the wagon was a set of doors. The largest was scarcely big enough for a man to crawl through. The smaller and lower was a mere horizontal grate. The bars of both were more closely set together than those of the wagon itself.

Smoke from all the torches stung Falca's keen eyes, making them water, and he wiped at them to clear a better view of the young stoneskin female who stood in the cage. Her hands gripped the bars of the door, her curving fingernails half again as long as her fingers. She was naked, her only modesty the knee-length black hair that fanned wildly over her body.

That hair suddenly swirled to life as she began pulling and pushing futilely on the bars, emitting a wail—a ferocious yet plaintive cry—that cut across the murmuring of the Lifters and heaves.

Falca glanced at Ballast, saw him angrily throw away his stone and grip the timbers of the cage. Falca wanted to ask him about this woman, his connection to her, but he didn't dare, not now. Ballast's anger boiled off him.

Falca saw two flenx in the cage also. One lay curled around the base of the Prism, which was set in the middle of the prison on wheels. The Prism's light trapped and augmented the flickering illumination of the torches, making its brilliance the beacon of the square and focusing the entrapment of this young stoneskin female.

The other flenx, aroused by her keening, brushed the woman, dislodging her momentarily from her hold on the bars. She turned angrily, spoke harshly to the predator, which could have killed her instantly with a flick of its headhorn, a swipe of claws. The animal slunk back toward the other. The woman pressed even more tightly against the bars, and Falca narrowed his eyes at the bar that rose from the thatch of her loin hair, to spear the cleavage of her breasts. She had a strange and sad mastery of the cage, whose bars matched the color of her skin. Maybe it was the light, or the wildness she exuded, or his own imprisonment, but Falca saw a beauty matched by only one other he'd seen: Amala. Seeing this young woman made him even more desperate to get out, to get Amala back. When he put his hands on the timbers in front of him, he could feel the tugging of Ballast's hands, a link to himself that finally gave Falca an overriding urge to ask about Marf Mag.

"Tell me about her."

"What's the use, roaking? The story, like all those of your life, will be sucked from you soon, just as your woman's were."

"Maybe that's why I want to know."

"You're a strange one. Your last hour would be better spent thinking of your own life."

Falca said nothing, felt Ballast's hands leave the timbers. But when they gripped again, the stoneskin began to speak, so softly that Falca had to move closer to him.

"I brought her here myself, along with three others I bought with Grippa's money from a Helyn factor in Castlecliff. The Roach sent me for the buy because I was one of his best 'stones, and most trusted. I was the one who told him more females were needed for us. The men were grumbling, and so were the few females already in service here. It isn't just the stoneskin males who hire out as mercenaries to kings and nobles and scut like Grippa. Without the greylas—the females—and our mating with them, the males would eventually lose their skin, their roughy, and with it, their value as soldiers.

"I'd contracted for three greylas, and Marf Mag was the fourth, a throw-in from the factor, who'd said she'd caused him too much trouble.

"She caused trouble here, too, so much so that Grippa had a mind to dump her too. She wouldn't let no one touch her, and her ferocity shrunk even the hungriest of the 'stones. I told Grippa I'd square her, since I brung her. It took some doing, but I was patient, and over a few weeks talked to her more and more.

"Homesick, that's all she was, for a place that, turns out, wasn't far from my own home. The more she talked, the more she made *me* homesick, and I never thought that would be possible to do. I been away ten years now. Never wanted to go back. It's the way with 'skins.

"You see, roaking, she had spirit and a gentleness no one saw but me. Whether it was that, or that talk of home . . . what I'm trying to say is, it became the two of us, and we kept on about going back to the High Vales together. My contract—it's called a hand—with Grippa was up soon."

Ballast fell quiet, as if suddenly aware of how much he was gutting himself for a stranger. Falca hadn't expected such an outpouring, something he'd never heard from another, except Amala. That he wanted Ballast to go on talking even now, with Grippa coming down from his castle, was in part his old habit of reiving. He was getting something he wanted, needed, from the stoneskin, something from a foreign territory: his heart. The difference was he had this odd desire to give something back to the 'skin in return.

Marf Mag had quieted as a litter borne by heaves approached the square, to a chorus of shouts from those soldiers on the square. Falca took a deep breath, squeezed the rock in his hand. "So what happened, Ballast?"

The stoneskin didn't immediately begin again, as if he was deciding whether he wanted to rub the wound again. Falca waited, watching the square.

"Problems, that's what. The hands for two other females were up, and they left; another died of skullsies. Many of the 'skins were jealous of me—and of my roughy. The difference was a big one, my leather to their paper.

"Before Mag and I could leave, twenty-five of them broke into

ur quarters, took her away. I went crazy, tried to fight them all off,
but there were too many. I wound up in chains until Grippa sent me
away on a long raiding voyage. When I got back, she was as you see
her now. She'd been used so much, something broke inside her. I
tried to free her anyway but failed, and I had to settle for vengeance.
Any other would have been put to death for the killings, but I was
worth too much to Grippa. They would have put Mag to death, too,
for castrating the last one who tried her, but Vaxxa had the idea to use
her in the cage.

"They twisted her out of shape. Someone like her is always
needed near the Prism, to take the maces in hand and caress the
corruption with them, someone to prop the dead against the Prism.

"When Mag's anger and rage and insanity are all used up, they'll
stick another in there, and when that one cracks his bell . . ." Ballast
hit his fists together.

"All she wanted to do was go home. 'We'll roll the stones down
on the roakings,' she laughed, 'from the poor fields they've left us,
there to crash against the walls of the mountain slides they call castles
and wake them from their sleep. And when your roughy, Ballast, is
the marvel of the Last Vales, I'll leave you with your pride, as many
flagons of ale as the number of sons and daughters I've given you—
for you'll need one to work the other—and raid the roaking pens as
we used to raid our vale-foes and show you how the Fallow Queens
used to hurry home the stolen shag-horns and dare the waiting men to
do as well. All the better that these shags will be roaking shags, for
there are more of them than us now anyway, and they can afford the
loss of a few to keep our winter fire spitting with dripping grease.'

"I told you all this, Falca, to keep your mind off what's going to
happen to you and to let you know that the thing you see now in the
cage was someone who told me her dreams in the morning. I'll hear
no finer dreams for as long as I live."

"I'm sorry," Falca said.

"No, none of that. I'm the one who has the life ahead, not her, or
you."

"I was thinking of another Fallow Queen as well as Marf Mag,"
Falca said.

"I wish you had more time. There," Ballast pointed between the
timbers. "There's all the time you have. Do you see Vaxxa—he's the
tall one—going to meet Grippa in the litter, to haggle. If I had a god,

I'd put in a word for you, because you seem a decent sort for a roaking and because that Limb female behind you has taken a liking to you. She's had it rougher than either of us."

Falca watched a group of priests, the white capes bleached as bones in the torchlight, walk across the square toward the litter. They paused before a row of stoneskins. Vaxxa stepped forward, hushing the murmur of Lifters and heaves crowding the square. It was so quiet now that Falca could hear the priest talking, but couldn't make out the words. The only other sounds came from the stockade and cage, where Marf Mag sat, her hair pooled in the basin of her lap, singing a song of words Falca didn't know, but guessed must be the language of the High Vales. Ballast turned away and sat down with his back against the timbers, his boots almost touching the Timberlimb. Falca knew the song was one the stoneskin must have heard before. Soon Falca heard the scraping of Ballast's stone.

"You're losing it. The roughy you had with her?"

"It'll come again, with some greyla in Myrcia. But never as fine. I'd strut around pale as you, soft-skinned as a fig, to get her back. It itches now. Scraping helps. There are stories told of the old days, of famine in the Vales, when the Queens decreed the greylas deny their men so that their roughies would shed. The greylas would collect the leavings each day to feed the young and animals first."

Ballast threw the rock. "What're they doing now?"

Falca brought his mind back, from a time when Amala took needle and thread to the cut of his face. Even now he could feel the working of her hands, the tugging of his flesh. "Grippa hasn't come out of that covered litter."

"He won't." ·

"Why not?"

"Doesn't trust anybody to get too close, least of all Vaxxa and his voals. The Roach has to hide, has to have the feel of cracks and creases and walls around. He won't even let them in his castle for the Prism ceremony, so it's done here, with all his men around. The more he's gotten, the more he's become scared of someone taking it away. He's rotting. The Lifters boast that one day they'll put him in the Prism cage."

"Vaxxa's finished now," Falca said. "He's walking back toward that stone, the platform in the middle of the square. It's hard to see in the light, but I don't think he was smiling."

"A good sign for you," Ballast said. "That means Grippa didn't give him all he asked for. The Roach is in a sour mood. His gout's probably bothering him again."

"The Lifters don't like it much either," Falca said, as Vaxxa raised an arm and turned his hand to offer a sign. A rumbling of disapproval welled in the square. Soon two voals led a man from the multitude of Lifters. Ballast got up to watch when the shouting began. He shook his head at the strident cries, the bleating of indignation. "A greedy lot. I never did like them, not from the first. I've seen them bring out three or four men for the cage, enough to charge a hundred maces."

"What happens to them?"

"You'll see."

The shouts from the Lifters became more sporadic, but the tension in the arena was still palpable, heavy as a tool . . . a weapon. Falca watched more stoneskins tighten the cordon around Grippa's litter. The soldiers and galley-heaves hurled back insults, taunts about Maradus's sexual deficiency.

Falca's mind raced. The dogs were chained in the same kennel. How to loose them at each other?

The voals paused with their man by Vaxxa and his priests. The captive was bound, hooded, and loosely hobbled, so that he could take only small steps. Vaxxa touched him on the top of his head, and he was led toward the cage, his sad, mincing shuffle depriving him of the dignity of a proper stride to his fate.

Vaxxa signaled again, and two more voals emerged from the crowd of Lifters carrying a long, deep box. It looked to Falca like a small coffin.

"The maces," Ballast said, as the voals followed the others toward the cage. One of them opened the larger door, then helped the other raise and shove the hooded man inside. They quickly shut the door.

Marf Mag approached the man and gently, like one undressing a lover, undid his hood, his bonds, his hobbles. Falca glanced at Ballast, wondering how he'd stomach this. His hands were on the timbers, high over his head, as if they'd been tied for a flogging.

The flenx rose from around the base of the Prism pedestal, their back fur stiffening. They didn't approach; Marf Mag was too near the intruder. He knew his only hope, however brief, was in keeping close to her. One of the flenx pawed at his headhorn.

It was a dance. Marf Mag moved, he moved with her. She seemed to enjoy the play of it, the man's desperation, the prolonging of this mating. His left hand kept seeking her flesh, to secure the proximity that would keep him alive for seconds more. Since his eyes were always on the flenx, he was as good as blind as his hand reached out to Marf Mag, to her hair, her waist, the flare of her hips, her buttocks.

Falca's loins tightened, hardened, and he was instantly repelled by his reaction. He felt something had intruded, entered him, something akin to the thing that moved the Lifters to their abomination. It was more than just the naked, sensuous young greyla, the hidden expectation that she might rut with the man before he died. That feeling was bad enough, for that was the last thing on the victim's mind. And there was the rub of betrayal of Ballast, who had told him so much about his love for Marf Mag before they'd put her in this cage, twisted her inner wire to this teasing pose, this parody of a Fallow Queen.

It was more than all that to Falca. What gripped him against his will was the expectation of someone's coming death, the certainty of that death and the fascination with one who had the power over the timing of another's end. He had never taken pleasure in killing. Saphrax had, and Falca felt himself suddenly closer to the brute than he thought possible. Had Saphrax felt like this when he Lifted all but the heartbeat from Amala? The thought frightened him with the same intensity he'd felt in Amala's house that day.

He watched Marf Mag's game with the man, the promised toy. She sidestepped only just enough to keep him near, keep his hand at her.

"It's not her you're seeing," Ballast whispered fiercely.

But what did Falca know of that? Maybe the Fallow Queen was a conjuring of the stoneskin's. It could be, for all Falca knew. His doubting disgusted him, for it measured how swiftly he had fallen, could fall away from another's pain at the loss of a great love. It held the possibility of his own abandonment of Amala Damarr.

Marf Mag's laughter came in short bursts, as keenly edged as the scissors Amala had held over her dog. The laughter stung Falca like a slap, and he turned violently away from the timbers, to get away from his doubts, his fascination with the cage. He saw the Timberlimb female, an arm's length away, staring at him. The torchlight glittered in her eyes. Ballast was still gazing at the cage, as were most of the prisoners. Only Falca and the Limb were not looking now. So he did not see Marf Mag suddenly tire of the game and dart quickly away giving the flenx striking room even as the man tried to close the distance to the dancing Marf Mag.

His screams drew Falca back, screams that ended when one of the flenx impaled the man on his headhorn, lifting him and flinging him against the bars of the cage with a vicious, shedding motion. The man crumpled to the floor of the cage as the Lifters shouted and clapped their approval.

Falca felt sick, not only for the death, but for his part in it. The anger that filled him was a loathing, for himself and the ones out there, beyond his own timbered cage, who had stained this night, who had turned a Fallow Queen into something that danced at death.

Something touched his leg. He whirled. That hand that held the rock hit something: the Timberlimb. "I'm sorry," Falca said, kneeling down to her. She didn't back away, but only shook her head, saying something he didn't understand. She touched his leg again, and he let her hand stay there, needing it, needing this small and tenuous connection with Amala, who would have understood what she'd said.

Marf Mag clapped her hands twice, and the two flenx slunk reluctantly away from their feeding. Her long hair was a shroud for the dead man as she dragged him toward the base of the Prism. She turned him over on his stomach with little difficulty and lifted him up so that his face was pressed against a plane of the Prism. It was as high as Marf Mag was tall and caught the torchlights, weaving and twisting them into a single great beacon.

Ballast whispered again, "It's not her you're seeing, it isn't."

The corpse slipped a little, and Marf Mag propped him up again against the Prism. Grotesque though the dead man's position was, it reminded Falca of someone peering closely into a storefront to inspect the merchandise. He remembered the awe he felt as a boy when he saw the glass fronts to shops in Heart Hill and Beckon. He could not afford what lay behind, displayed so wonderfully, but he turned the glass to his advantage. While the well-to-do passerby paused, preoccupied by the offerings, Falca would stroll past and lift whatever his nimble fingers found.

He had a sudden longing for that time, the sureness of his skills, his speed and quickness of foot, if the man in front of the glass window suddenly turned.

How often he had twisted things to his advantage before. If only he could do it again now. He hadn't lost his gift. Now that he really had something at stake, the gift couldn't have deserted him. What he had felt before, when the Prism man still had life, wasn't really what he was . . .

The voals had opened the smaller door to the wagon cage and were passing the maces to Marf Mag, who carried them two at a time to the Prism and propped them against the side facing the dead man. The Prism reddened. The flenx moved to a far corner of the cage and began howling, pawing at their jaws. The mace-heads began filling with a paler red, which turned slowly to orange, then yellow-white, as Falca watched.

"You want to know the odds, Falca? I've been counting. There's thirty of the maces. Over a hundred of us in here. With a little luck. . . . It's too bad that Lifter knows you're here. Maybe he's forgotten."

"He hasn't," Falca said, as Marf Mag began bringing the maces back to the voals at the cage door.

Vaxxa called out names. Falca heard one: Blave. The chosen voals strode eagerly toward the cage to accept a charged mace. Then they lined up by the dais, cradling the maces like newborns. The succession of glowing mace-heads had a symmetry that Falca wanted to smash, like he would ice formed over a puddle.

Vaxxa signaled again with a raised arm, and five voals walked from the mass of Lifters, accompanied by two torchbearers. One of the five was Saphrax, his height and bulk unmistakable.

"They're coming for us now," Ballast whispered to Falca. "It isn't too late. It won't take but a few seconds. The Limb too."

Falca's hand tightened around the stone as Saphrax left the group and walked over to talk with Vaxxa. The high priest nodded and sent a man over to Grippa's litter. After a moment the voal came back to Vaxxa. Falca felt a sudden chill at the priest's nod. That was me, he thought. Saphrax has his mark, his One Mark. . . .

Thirty of Grippa's heaves, armed with swords and axes, accompanied by more torchbearers, joined Saphrax's group, and they all proceeded toward the stockade.

The prisoners nearest the gates scuttled past Falca, to the depths of the crib. "You'd better bury yourself with the others," Ballast said.

Falca shook his head. His hope had all but fled him. His mind was a blank. He couldn't think of a way out. There was no alley to dart into.

He had no choice but to face the brute. It had come to this—his mother's insistence on great deeds for him, his father's naming him after the falcata.

Saphrax would ferret him out in the mass of prisoners if he hid there. Falca had no desire to merge himself into their panicked, bawling numbers. He had always known his time would come, was sure it would be in some crease of the city. This would have to do. He wished only that Amala could somehow know that he'd tried, that in the end he hadn't abandoned her, that he loved her more than anything else in his life. And he hoped that she might forgive him for what he was going to do. But she wouldn't know. She had no idea of forgiveness now. He could no more save her now than Ballast could his Mag. Like the stoneskin, he would have to be content with vengeance.

The rock was heavy in his hand, heavy enough to smash Saphrax's mace, releasing Amala into the night before he used it a second time to smash the brute's skull. He felt the heat rising in him, the familiar heat of that quayside tavern and a hundred other times in his life.

Ballast and the Timberlimb stayed with him. He gestured for her to get behind him as the stockade gate opened. Ballast took it one step further and swept her behind him with his arm.

For a moment Falca thought the voals and heaves might be stupid or overconfident enough to leave the gate open and unguarded while they chose the victims. Falca slipped along the stockade timbers, with Ballast and the Limb following, but stopped when someone ordered three heaves to close the gate and wait there.

Three torchbearers led the way. The flames were given tongues by the brisk wind that rose with nightfall. But, the densest, brightest light was that of Amala's mace at Saphrax's side. Falca never took his eyes off it. Voals walked in front and behind the brute, with the armed heaves ranging ahead. Falca knew he could get close enough to Saphrax, but he had to strike before Grippa's soldiers ringed him with sword points and closed for the kill.

Falca blew on his cold hands to warm them for a better grip. He could have stayed in the darkness until Saphrax found him, but he stepped forward into the pale of light from the nearest torch.

"This one seems eager enough to give us his Gift," said a voal, laughing. "Shall we take him first, Giver Saphrax?"

Saphrax paused, smiling. He moved his hand to the mace-head at his belt, to let Falca see. The edges of his fingers, his palm, glowed red.

"He's too sturdy, too big," said another voal. "The Roach wouldn't pass him."

"Oh, he will," Saphrax said. "Vaxxa has gotten that favor from Grippa for me. What say you, Falca, my old friend? Would you like to go now?"

"I'm ready. Come get me, Saphrax," Falca whispered.

Saphrax laughed. "Beware that dog. He schemes at a last chance."

"Giver Saphrax, we mustn't delay," the first voal said impatiently. "We have thirty to do, and if we aren't quick about it, the Roach won't even let us have that. You know what he did to us the last time."

"Patience, Giver Horel," Saphrax said. "We have time." He caressed Amala's mace. "So you're that eager to join your woman in the Crucible? I thought you might have come to your senses and decided to join me in accepting the Curve of the One."

Falca had to have him closer, without the heaves. "I have something to say to you about that. Alone."

"It is I who summon you, Falca," Saphrax said. Then he laughed. "Maybe you need more time to change your mind. I think you'll decide to save your life and join me when you see what happens to the first ten who give their Gifts. We'll save you for the next group."

Falca started to rush him, but a hand clamped on his shoulder from behind, gripping his tunic. Falca strained, and the tunic ripped, but Ballast anchored him with his other hand.

Saphrax and the others moved on, the torches illuminating the huddled prisoners. Falca watched them advance, and his rage gradually eased. The brute was toying with him, as surely as Marf Mag toyed with the Prism man, and he still wanted to feel the shattering of Saphrax's skull with the rock he had. But Ballast was right. Falca told him to let go, and Ballast did.

A few prisoners scurried along the stockade walls, trying to escape the heaves. But Grippa's men spread out, using their swords to force the prisoners back. It did not take them long to cull ten of them. Four went willingly enough, resigned to their fate. The others kicked and screamed and had to be dragged and manhandled. Saphrax walked at the head of the group, furthest from the prisoners, lest one kick or strike at the precious mace at his belt.

The prisoners were led past Grippa's litter. Evidently he approved, for all ten were then brought to a point opposite the waist-high dais and the line of voals cradling their charged maces. One prisoner tried to escape, but he didn't get far and was chosen to be the first lifted. As soon as he was pinned down on the dais, voals at his hands and feet, Vaxxa gave a signal, and the nearest mace-holder stepped forward from the line.

"You better not look," Ballast said.

Falca shook his head, but in truth he didn't want to, didn't want to run the risk of weakening. He had shored himself up before, resigned himself with an eagerness to kill the brute, but he hadn't counted on the game Saphrax was playing with him. Maybe Saphrax knew him better than he thought, knew that Falca Breks was, if nothing else, a man who would do anything to survive. The man Saphrax had once known would have taken any way out.

But Falca wasn't quite the man Saphrax would have known, just as the brute, too, had changed. So Falca watched, in the end, to see just how Amala Damarr had been taken from him. Gradually a defiance filled him, surprising him with its weight. He felt the Timber-limb next to him and put a hand on her tiny shoulder; the other held the stone.

The voals at the corners of the dais had to lean heavily to keep the victim under control. He thrashed and kicked, shaking his head from side to side in a futile attempt to avoid the closing mace-head. When the light was inches from his eyes, his head suddenly stopped moving, hooked, bonded with the light. The voal who held the mace lowered it until it touched the man's forehead. He still screamed and jerked his arms and legs, but his head was locked in place, tight with the harness of light. It seemed to Falca that a spike had been driven into his forehead, impaling him to the stone below. The voals at the corners let go as the mace-head began filling with a light so blinding that Falca had to shield his eyes. Beside him the Limb female cried out as if in pain. Ballast was shaking his head.

Falca closed his eyes, forcing himself to see what had happened to Amala in her house, to goad, drive him toward the way out for her, for him. He said her name over and over and whispered his love for her. When he opened his eyes again, the macelight had subsided as the man's body quieted with the stillness of lost dreams.

The voal stepped away with the mace, holding it aloft to a chorus of cheers from his fellow Lifters. He walked back to the line of thirty.

The light from his Gifted mace shone greater than that of the others.
Soon they would be all the same, Falca knew.

The empty was led away into the darkness by a single heave, to
join all the others in their "town" beyond the stockade. Another victim was dragged to the dais.

Falca looked away to the voals in line and counted. The eleventh
mace—held by a woman—would be his, assuming Saphrax would
pick him first in the next group. His throat was raspy and dry, and he
swallowed hard, remembering the empty drinking from the fountain
outside Amala's home. He realized that his hand on the Limb was
trembling, and to compensate for it, he gripped the rock in his other
more tightly. Again he whispered Amala's name over and over as an
incantation to shatter the hardening fear within him, the acknowledgment of the beauty in that line of glowing maces, the symmetry of
brightness denied even the stars overhead.

The second victim began thrashing, screaming on the dais. Falca
was cold. As he shivered, he remembered a time when he had accompanied Amala to Ringwater, where she wanted to skate. The path
through the snowy street was brown and dirty, no wider than a cart. A
row of icicles hung from a low eave of a nearby house. It was a sunny
afternoon, and the spears of ice were melting. Falca walked over to
them, took off a glove, and touched the tips of several, feeling
pleasure in their fragile sharpness. He brushed a finger over them,
caught a few drops of water, and brought the moisture to his lips.

Amala had laughed. "Hardly enough for a thirsty man," she said.

He swept an arm through the icicles, scything them in half. Amala
huffed in surprise and disgust as the pieces fell without a sound into
the snow below.

She shook her head. "You admire beauty, then destroy it. I'm
afraid that's an all-too-common trait of men."

Falca had smirked then at her opinion, her scolding tone, that she
could feel moved to words over something so trifling. Perhaps, he
decided, she had been thinking about the flinarra.

Now, as the light from the dais flared with another's Gift, he
didn't shield his eyes this time. The blazing, brief flight seemed white
as snow as he stared at the line of maces. They were straight as the
eave of a house, so delicate in the arms of their bearers, delicate as
flina, ready to be filled with the music and discord of thirty lives.

An alley formed in his mind, a way out. It wasn't the escape
Saphrax offered, but Falca clearly saw him standing at the end of it.

Chapter Twenty

Ballast

The roaking's idea was crazy, and doomed to fail, but Ballast began scouring the ground for rocks anyway, with great sweeps of his arm. Most were no bigger than a thumbnail, but here and there Ballast netted a fist-sized stone. It felt good to scrape his arms on the ground. They itched to the point of burning.

Not far away the roaking hunted for rocks, too, his pale arms and back twisting, turning. He'd taken off his tunic, to use as a basket. Ballast glanced at him, wondering if it could work, not daring to hope that a shower of rocks from the stockade could free Mag. The Timberlimb couldn't have known what was going on, but she must have sensed Falca's desperation and was imitating his example.

Ballast would have ignored any other roaking who'd offered such a foolish idea for escape. But this one was different. He'd begun with, "We'll roll the stones down on the roakings, from the poor fields they've left us, to crash against the walls of the mountain slides they call castles and wake them from their sleep."

Ballast had been startled by Falca's recitation. Any other roaking would have forgotten those words of Mag's, dismissed them as inconsequential in the face of a coming death. Falca had used them to give life to a hope—crude and futile—but hope nonetheless. He told Ballast more of the plan, speaking so quickly that Ballast almost couldn't understand him. He made the promise to free Marf Mag if all went well. "I need your help to do this, Ballast," he'd said.

Crazy though the scheme was, Ballast wished he'd thought of ▮ There lay the difference between roakings and stoneskins. Without ▮ roughy, a roaking had to employ other means to lessen his vulnerab▮ ity: wits, cleverness, deceit. The first roakings to challenge the Val ▮ were slaughtered, but the survivors and successors learned from tho▮ early, crushing defeats and adapted. The tactics of scorched earth a▮ starvation were not the least of the means they used to overcome t▮ roughy and the Fallow Queens. In victory or defeat, the roakin▮ wasted little time with boasting or laments but planned and scheme▮ and that was why they ruled the best of the Vales now.

And that was why Ballast now hunted the dark ground for ston▮ to shatter maces.

He saw Falca twist the ends of his tunic and lift the basket. "Le▮ go to the others," he said.

Falca quickly told them about his plan. When several prisone▮ laughed derisively, Falca spoke more loudly, harshly.

"If anyone else thinks this foolhardy, that you run the risk ▮ getting killed, think about what's going to happen to us. Either t▮ Lifters will rinse our minds from our bodies like those poor scuts o▮ there or Grippa will sell us to the Myrcians, who will work us ▮ death."

No one else laughed. "Take the rocks we're going to give you a▮ go to the gate. Those who don't have a stone, find one, find ten, pi▮ them by the gates. When I give the signal, throw them and ke▮ throwing hard. We must enrage the bastards enough to come and op▮ the gates to stop us. When they do, stand your ground and ke▮ throwing at them. We must seize control of the gate."

Ballast handed out his rocks to the prisoners and pushed the▮ toward the gate. He gathered more as Falca gave out his. Some pri▮ oners dropped the stones, but Ballast and Falca didn't waste time w▮ them. Soon, scores of captives were streaming toward the gate▮ When their hands were empty, Ballast, Falca, and the Limb hurri▮ back, urging the rest of the prisoners to follow. Most did.

At the gates they collected more stones. Ballast looked up once ▮ see the next victim begin led away. One more to go. The man w▮ hysterical and kept trying to twist free of his captors, but to no ava▮ The Gifted maces were brilliant. Mag was sitting in her cage, wra▮ ping, then releasing, coils of her hair around her arms. Her work ▮ done, Ballast thought. And he feared suddenly that she wouldn't re▮ ognize him when they came to take her from the cage. He was p▮

pared for the months and maybe even years necessary to bring her back, but there had to be something, *something* to build on, some tiny but glowing cinder he could gently breathe life into. Though his roughy was now thinner and more vulnerable than it had ever been since he was banded, he had no fear of wound or death. His only fear was that his Mag had already died. Was the unexpected hope of recovering her clouding his senses, making him see a flicker of the Mag that no longer existed?

Falca walked along the perimeter of the gathered, silent prisoners, telling them to aim for the line of thirty voals.

"Where's your man, that Lifter?" Ballast asked Falca, as he passed.

"He's standing by Vaxxa and the others."

"Tell the prisoners to aim away from Vaxxa. The mace of your woman mustn't be lost."

"It's a danger," Falca said softly. "But there's nothing we can do about that risk. I'm afraid it's all we can do to throw the stone, between the gate timbers or over. Are you worried about Marf Mag? Don't be. She's away from where most of the stones will fall."

"They'll hurry the Prism wagon away when the trouble hits. We have to be quick to get her."

"We will."

"They're bringing the tenth to the slab now."

"Wait," Falca said. "We'll wait until he's there."

It seemed to take forever, for the man kicked and thrashed even more than the others. When he was finally pinned to the dais, Falca spoke loudly to the prisoners. "Aim your first throws as best you can. They'll be protecting their maces soon enough."

The tenth voal approached the dais, holding his mace high, to acknowledge the cheers of all the gathered Lifters.

"NOW!" Falca shouted, and flung his rock. Ballast hurled his. Together they hurried along the perimeter of the prisoners, urging them to keep throwing.

And they did. Some poorly, some well. They hurled shouts and curses. A few rocks hit the stockade timbers, ricocheting back, but most went through the vertical spaces or over the top.

Ballast threw a second, a third rock, then paused to see the formations of the two camps—Grippa's heaves and the Lifters—shift in surprise and confusion. The line of voal's broke in disarray, the Lifters grunting, shouting as the rocks hit them. Then Ballast heard the shattering of a mace, saw the spear of light shoot into the night. The voal grasped wildly for what she had been holding.

Falca's whoop of triumph was drowned out by the cheers of the prisoners around him. Ballast clapped him so hard on the back that he stumbled. Ballast lifted him up by an arm, worried for a moment that he'd hurt the roaking, but he saw only the broadest smile on Falca's face. "More," Falca shouted. "We need more of them, Ballast!"

The Timberlimb, knowing she couldn't throw with sufficient force, had gathered up more stones and dropped them at Ballast's and Falca's feet. Falca clasped her tiny shoulder and said, "When we leave this damned island, she's coming with us."

"I'll carry her myself!" Ballast shouted.

Another mace disintegrated, giving the night another arrow of light so distinct, it seemed to Ballast to have an edge. "KEEP THROWING!" he roared to the prisoners, but the encouragement was not needed. They were in a frenzy now.

The man on the dais tumbled from the slab, fled his confused captors, and ran right through the milling voals and priests. "That's it, you lucky scut," Ballast shouted. "Run, run!"

He saw Vaxxa pointing in the direction of the stockade, ducking falling stones, shouting at his voals. One of them tripped over another who was clutching his head on his knees. His mace broke on the paved square.

The light from the first two shattered maces still hung in the night, glittering but slowly fading as the wind carried the gossamer over the Prism cage. Marf Mag jumped up and down in her cage, clapping her hands at this unexpected excitement. "Soon, my Mag," Ballast whispered. "We're coming to get you, soon as we're out of our cage."

A mob of voals and heaves streamed toward the stockade gates now, and the prisoners began throwing directly at them. "That's it!" Falca yelled. "Hit them hard!" Ballast hurled rocks with all his strength. A few voals spun away with a cry as stones smashed them in the face. Torches bobbed, one fell, and was picked up by another bearer. The swords and axes of the heaves glinted in the torchlight, the glare of the voals' charged maces. Several broke, their flaring light revealing the fury of the Lifters.

They closed on the gate, but didn't open it, not wanting to loose the prisoners. But they stabbed through the gate with swords and poked the torches through to push back the taunting prisoners.

"We need one of the torches," Falca said. Ballast hurled a rock the

THE MACE OF SOULS   195

size of his fist, point-blank in the face of a torchbearer. It hit him in the left eye, and he screamed, dropping the torch. Ballast thrust his long arm between two timbers of the gate, grasped the burning end of the torch, and whipped it back. A galley-heave stabbed his sword through, but the point scraped, slid off Ballast's wrist. Ballast scarcely felt the burn on his fingers and palm. His roughy was still thick there.

The prisoners shouted, screamed triumphantly at Ballast's prize, but above all that, Ballast heard Falca's voice: "Take it to the back. Set fire to the timbers there!" Falca threw another stone. Ballast took off running, feeling the streaming heat of the torch in his face.

No one was at the far end of the stockade. Even the most apathetic of the prisoners had joined the throng up front.

Ballast rubbed his arm against the timbers, to roughen the wood, then put the torch against the abraded area. He ripped off his jerkin and fed half to the flames. When he had his fire, he started a second the same way in a different part of the stockade. By the time the bastards saw his work, he thought, it would be too late to put it out. He propped the torch against yet a third timber and ran back toward the gates.

He only got halfway. The prisoners were streaming back from the gates, brushing him, stumbling by him. One sailor threw out his arms and fell in a heap, an arrow sticking out of his back. Another prisoner screamed, whirled, and grabbed at a shaft that had pierced his thigh.

Arrows whined through the air. One nicked Ballast's leg, etching a furrow through his trousers. He dropped to his stomach, not wanting to chance the fate of an arrow finding the softening parts of his roughy. As he crawled toward the timbers, looking for Falca, another prisoner took an arrow through his neck and fell so close to Ballast that blood spurted over the stoneskin's hand. Ballast moved on past the man's glazing eyes and twitching body.

Lying low by the timbers, Ballast saw Falca moving in a crouch, shadowed by the Timberlimb, dragging a body in front of him for protection against the archers. Ballast called out to him, twice, and Falca shifted direction to join him, dumping the corpse in front of them all. The Timberlimb kneeled between the men. It didn't look good to Ballast.

Forty or more prisoners lay in clumps, some draped over each other, some still alive, moaning, screaming in pain. The galley-heaves were still shooting arrows through the gate, but the easiest targets had fled. In the rear of the stockade the remaining prisoners whooped and still threw rocks defiantly at the heaves and voals who were bringing water buckets to douse the fire. The flames were beyond control, Ballast judged with pride. But the heaves could ring the stockade with archers and kill everyone within before the fire collapsed the timbers. And Mag's cage would be long gone by then. Ballast even heard someone—Vaxxa?—argue that he wanted to kill all the prisoners for the desecration of the ceremony. Someone else wanted only to subdue the rebellious prisoners. There were still plenty. Once cowed and chained, they would be valuable to Myrcian slavers.

The shouting at the gate grew more strident, and then, to Ballast's disbelief, the heaves and voals began to attack each other. He felt Falca's hand clap his back excitedly. "I knew the dogs would turn on each other."

Swords glinted in the torchlight. A voal wielding a charged mace blew a galley-heave against the gate. The fire behind them grew in intensity, the flames licking over the top of the timbers.

The flare-up didn't last long. Vaxxa called off his voals, who were outnumbered by the better-armed galley-heaves.

"Here we go," Falca whispered as the soldiers unbarred the gates. "Wait till they're all through. Sink into the earth like you're dead, Ballast, until they're past us. They're after the others in the rear."

Ballast nodded and gently squashed the Limb down to her stomach. Without moving his head, he watched a hundred of them storm past, the stockade firelight oiling their faces. The gate was empty of all but a handful of heaves and voals.

"Ready?" Falca whispered.

"Yes," Ballast said. "You and the little one keep behind me."

"All right. You're the ram. When we're out, we take a voal first. You'll see what I have in mind. We have to get the dogs at each other's throats again."

"Let's go," Ballast said and surged up from the ground.

It was only a short run to the gates, and Ballast charged into the nearest heaves, driving them back through the gate opening. He took two sword slashes on his neck and arm, but neither did any damage. He sidearmed one heave, knocking him unconscious with a blow to his head, and ripped a sword loose from another, taking it by the blade. The soldier fled. Two others lunged at Ballast, spearing with their swords, but Ballast parried one with an arm, the other with his sword, and kept after them, until both turned and ran.

They were through the gates now but didn't get far. Two archers saw them, took aim, and fired. Ballast lunged ahead, to shield Falca and the Limb. Shafts popped out of his left leg, not deep, but enough to cause Ballast to twist and fall, and drop the sword. He cursed, not from the pain but in anger that his roughy hadn't protected him. Before, it would have blunted the iron tips. Even as Ballast struggled to his feet, jerking out the arrows, Falca was rushing the nearest archer before he could shoot again. He rammed the first bowman into the second, tumbling them both to the paving stones. The Timberlimb darted around, pulled the bows from the thrashing heaves, then came back to throw herself on one of the men, who had Falca by the neck. Ballast roared his encouragement at the courageous Timberlimb. Her distraction was enough to allow Falca to struggle free. He rammed the head of the archer to the stone. The other heave escaped, but Falca let him go and hurried over to Ballast.

"Can you walk?" he said, his breathing heavy and ragged.

"Yes," Ballast said, disgusted.

They made their way to a corner of the stockade. It was darker now in the square, the torches dispersed, though the fire in the crib raged higher, the crackling roar leavened by the fighting, the screams within the stockade. The Prism wagon and Mag seemed impossibly far away to Ballast. It was still guarded by 'skins, though others had left to hurry Grippa and his litter back to the castle. Ballast heard overseers screaming, shouting, enraged at the empties who had drifted off into the night, in the confusion. There weren't enough to pull the wagon.

The Timberlimb raised a shout of warning just before a group of heaves and a voal attacked them. Falca was closest to the Lifter, and before he could react the voal swept his mace up and blew Falca back against the timbers, where he slumped with a groan. Ballast punched one of the heaves, knocking him to the ground, and looked wildly around for the sword the soldier had dropped. Behind him the Limb shrieked something, and Ballast turned to see her offering a sword, a different one she'd gotten from somewhere in the dark. Ballast grabbed it, pushed the Limb back toward Falca, who was rising from his daze, shaking his head. Ballast moved quickly to protect both of them, parrying the cuts and thrusts of the heaves. He recognized one from before—a man who'd used the Timberlimb. That and the image of Marf Mag in the cage whetted his frenzy and Ballast went on the

attack, taking sword slashes on his arms to get better strikes of his
own. His roughy was thickest on his upper body, and he used it as a
second weapon, giving the battle cry his father taught him at his
banding. He killed the Limb's violator with two cuts and wounded
another heave in the knee, disabling him from the fight.

Falca had retrieved a fallen torch and was waving it crazily, his
only weapon. Ballast remembered that he'd wanted a voal and was
determined to give him one. "Do you want one dead or alive?" Ballast roared.

"Either way! It's the mace I need," Falca shouted back.

Ballast kept on, smashing a backhand to the face of a heave whose
sword stab missed him by a hand's breadth. He killed another heave
to get to the voal. Ballast swung what he thought was a killing strike,
but his weakened leg buckled with his overeagerness. He couldn't
recover quickly enough to prevent the Lifter from using his mace.

A giant fist hit his face, a blow so powerful that it whipped his
neck and body back. His head hit the stone, and a brilliant flash of
light collapsed into dark.

He woke again to a reemergence of light. As his eyes focused, he
saw the core of light inches from his forehead. Over the white, blazing rim of the mace, Falca's face appeared, the scar a white worm
nestled in his beard.

Ballast shook his head at the pulling, trying to shake off the sudden betrayal. "NO!" he shouted, and aimed a fist at the mace. He
missed as Falca quickly moved it away, the only light in the immedi-
ate vicinity.

"Easy!" Falca said sharply, his face bathed in the brilliance of a
lost soul. The Timberlimb stood just inside the pale of the macelight,
her eyes flicking between Falca and Ballast.

"Get that thing away from me, roaking," Ballast growled, fighting off waves of dizziness as he got unsteadily to his feet. He leaned
on his good leg. "By the Caves, I thought you were going to use it
on me."

"Are you crazy? I was only trying to rouse you, you dolt. Dragging you way from the stockade fire didn't do it. You're a damn
heavy load."

Ballast felt the back of his head and winced. "What're you dressed
like a voal for? You're bloody convincing as a Lifter."

"What do you think? I have to get close enough to Saphrax to get

Amala's mace." Falca flipped the hood of the gray cape over his head. "The fit is tight, but it'll have to do."

He tossed the bloodstained sword to Ballast, who caught it. "I finished what you started with the Lifter," Falca said. "You ready to go? They're taking the Prism wagon away and herding the prisoners to the other pen. First we have to get your Mag, then Amala. To do both, we have to bring the dogs back together again."

Ballast looked around. The stockade was a skeletal inferno. The other concentrations of lights, torches, marked the leave-taking of Lifters back to the quay-side compound, the heaves with the prisoners. And the wagon, Mag's cage-wagon, back to the castle. Ballast heard the creaking of wheels, saw the glinting of the Prism catching torchlight, saw half the small silhouette of his Mag.

"Ballast, we have to hurry," Falca said.

"My leg, I have to walk my leg for a moment," Ballast said, and limped out of the macelight into the darkness still punctuated by shouts and screams.

It wasn't his leg. He didn't trust Falca. The mace had been too close. Maybe, he thought, it was the old distrust of the pale roaking kind, whose soft skin covered a pit with stakes.

Yet this Falca still wanted to get his Mag, keep his promise. He was out now and could hunt down the Lifter Saphrax, forgetting the promise. Ballast felt a sudden anger at the roaking. Where did he get such a belief that he could bring all the lights together, to clash and merge toward his own purpose?

Ballast almost wished he would forget, felt like walking on. If Falca had discarded his promise, it would confirm Ballast's idea about roakings, that they either paid you or betrayed you. But he knew there was another reason for his lassitude, his hesitancy about going on with the roaking. Was it the old trait of stoneskins that preferred laments to victories? He feared that Mag wouldn't leave once they opened her cage, feared that she was indeed completely gone, more lenx than greyla. Deep down, he didn't want the absolute certainty of knowing she was lost to him forever.

Falca was forcing him to find out, one way or the other, leading him to either victory or defeat when what he wanted was neither. He'd killed to get out of the pen, yet here he was, quailing at the thought of going on, to confront his Mag.

In a way he was a mercenary to *this* roaking now, to his inexplicable determination, that sheathed him like roughy. There was no con-

tract, no money to weight his hand, only the hope, however futile, o
recovering the Fallow Queens.

"Ballast, it's time to do it," Falca called out. And in the darknes
he felt something brush his hand, grabbing a thumb. Fingers. Th
Timberlimb.

He didn't know why, but he let himself be led back to Falca an
the nimbus of macelight by this smallest of creatures.

"Here's what we'll do, Ballast," Falca said, as he led the wa
toward the Prism wagon and Marf Mag.

Chapter Twenty-one

The Prism of Empathy

Falca walked quickly after the Lifters leaving the square. They were taking it slowly, in small groups, the light of their maces tenser than the wild flames of the heaves' torches.

Maybe it was the mace Falca held in his hand—he didn't know—but he could feel the anger of the departing voals and priests, anger at the meager allotment of victims Grippa had allowed, the disruption of the ceremony, the destruction of the maces. Soon, he thought, I'll harness that anger, let them array their maces against the swords and axes of the heaves . . . and maces too. Some of the heaves and stone-kins guarding Marf Mag's wagon held maces.

He looked in the direction of Grippa's castle. The litter was half-way to the gates, the torches illuminating the winding, rising road.

The gang that pulled the Prism wagon was composed mostly of prisoners, since the empties had wandered off during the rock fall. Prodded by overseers, they turned the wagon around in a wide arc and approached the beginning of the castle road. The wheels of the wagon creaked, rousing Marf Mag from a sitting position. Her hair trailed over the dead man inside the cage. He had slumped away from the Prism, and the flenx were feeding on him. Marf Mag had her back to their meal. She sang a plaintive song. Snatches of it carried over the square, over the grunting of the straining prisoners, the curses of the overseers.

Falca looked back to make sure Ballast was following. The stone-

skin was silhouetted by the stockade fire, making the best of a limp
eager now for Marf Mag. A strange one, he thought, but brave. The
Timberlimb walked beside him.

Falca angled past the dais, walking quickly still, threading his way
through the grumbling, muttering voals. He pulled the cape hood low
and kept an eye out for Saphrax, the only one of them who could
recognize him in the fitful light of the square. The bulk of the Lifters
had already left, but all Falca needed was a dozen or so at first, tinder
for the fire. What were the words Saphrax had used? It unsettled him
at how quickly he remembered.

As he passed three voals, he said, "Givers, we must get the Prism
now. Follow me to the wagon if you wish to Give the greatest Gift to
our Blessed Maradus."

He walked on, more slowly: "We must have the Prism tonight.
Walk with me. I have the word of Vaxxa for the command."

He brushed by more voals: "The Roach must be punished for our
disgrace. It is time we took the Prism for our own, as a Gift for our
Father of Souls."

Some voals paused, some ignored him. A few whispered after him
if Vaxxa had indeed given his command. Two voals argued briefly
with a third. One kept on walking, but the others hurried after Falca.
Then another.

Falca turned briefly, smiling, and kept on. "We get the Prism
tonight. For the One, for Blessed Maradus," he said, passing a priest
and four Lifters. "Follow us to enrich our god."

He walked toward the wagon, which had entered the road. At
least twenty stoneskins surrounded the wagon and half as many
heaves. Their backs were to the square now. The last thing they expected was trouble from the Lifters. Most of the guards, Falca saw,
had maces as well as swords. Only Marf Mag was facing the square,
a hand on one of the bars, to steady herself as the wagon rumbled on.
She seemed reluctant to leave, Falca thought. Or had she finally seen
Ballast?

He glanced behind him. Five voals and a priest followed. Three
had charged maces. One of those who didn't stopped, evidently losing heart. Beyond, a dozen others stood, undecided, waiting.

Falca said softly as he walked, "Surprise will be ours, Givers.
Strike at the rear guards quickly, capture their maces. Never mind the
swords. Strike quickly again once you have their maces."

He stole a glance to his left. Ballast and the Limb approached, according to the plan. Beyond them were the last of the heaves taking the prisoners to the empties' pen.

The square, so close to being emptied, would soon be a battleground. Falca felt like he was gliding, gliding on ice. He had never felt so good in his life. The shroud of the hood concealed a broad smile. He would live, he had to live, if only to boast of these . . . fists, the greatest he'd ever done. He was bestowing Gifts tonight: freedom to the prisoners, Marf Mag to Ballast, life again for Amala and for himself. The mace seemed the fount of it all, both cold and hot in his grip, its weight the hammer of his fullness, his surging confidence.

The rearmost stoneskin, trudging alongside a creaking wagon wheel, saw Marf Mag's sudden arousal from lassitude. He turned just as Falca lifted his mace. An invisible ram punched him in the stomach, lifted him off his feet, driving him into the guard next in line. The two fell in a heap. Even as those farther ahead broke from their single file, shouting, drawing swords and maces, Falca used his on two more stoneskins, sending them crashing against the wagon. A mace broke, its light piercing the night.

Two unarmed voals, screaming the name of Maradus, darted past Falca, rooting for the intact maces among the unconscious stoneskins. They found one, and a voal swung it up at a pair of charging 'skins, leaving them apart like melon halves.

The Prism wagon stopped moving. Marf Mag was jumping up and down, clapping her hands at the renewal of conflict. Behind her, the lenx growled, stabbing the air with their headhorns.

As Falca ran back deeper into the square, he saw the prisoners who had been pulling the huge wagon. They fled in all directions, dodging stoneskins, their overseers, galley-heaves. Falca waved his mace in the air, screaming over and over, "GIVERS TO THE ONE! THE WAGON! THE PRISM! THE PRISM WILL BE OURS!"

The cry was not false; his exultation rose from his very core. Falca's purpose and that of the Lifters were one and the same, for the moment. He felt as if he could conquer anything now. They were all doing his bidding. He alone, of anyone in the square, was in control. Not Maradus, or Vaxxa, or Grippa. He, Falca Breks, directed fate, with no weapon in his hand but the crystal mace and the light of an unknown soul.

They were running now toward him, all those who had lingered, waiting for success or failure. They drew back the greater numbers o Lifters, Vaxxa among them, who had left the square. By tens, the twenties, they rushed past Falca to the fighting by the wagon. H waved them on, exhorting them, horses to the finish of the race. H thought he saw Saphrax in the distance, the lumbering gait illum nated by a passing voal carrying a torch. Whether it was the brute o not, it made Falca remember his purpose. "You're mine," he sai aloud.

He turned, looking for Ballast.

The galley-heaves guarding the prisoners were only now chargin back into the square, leaving but a few men to keep the prisone from escaping. Those few, Falca saw, were quickly overwhelme however, and the prisoners broke free, scattering across the squar past the burning stockade, yipping and shouting with sudden freedom

He joined the stream of Lifters hurrying to the fray. He saw Ba last looking wildly around, sword in his huge hand, pushing awa those who fought or stumbled too close, trying to protect the Timbe limb. Falca shouted to Ballast, but in the din he couldn't hear. Falc sprinted to him, twisting left then right, through the melee. When was only a few feet away, Falca yelled, "Quickly, the other side!"

The doors to the cage were on the side of the wagon opposite th square and most of the fighting. As the three came around the wago —Ballast at the rear because of his leg—they confronted a doze stoneskins, heaves, and voals fighting in the glare of torchligh splinted and enhanced by the nearby Prism.

The ferocity of Ballast's charge stunned even Falca. He scattere many of the heaves with a dozen quick swings and thrusts of h sword. Falca used the mace against two stoneskins, blowing the away from the side of the wagon. A third raised his own mace but to slowly, having made the mistake of a moment's surprise at seein Ballast, a past comrade. Falca used his mace and blew away th 'skin. He dropped to the ground an instant before another guard use a mace. Falca heard, felt something crash over his head. A voal be hind him spun off into the darkness, having caught the mace blo Ballast came at the stoneskin guard from the side, calling out th 'skin's name—Vlax—before smashing the sword down on his wris The blade snapped off, a glinting silver sliver that escaped a mome before the mace fell, shattering in a blaze of light. As Ballast stepp away from the discharge, his broken sword blade passed through th

fiery spear of light which cut in half what remained of the blade—
and the guard's left arm.

More voals appeared. Most did not have maces, but they charged
into the remaining stoneskins, flailing with their fists, their numbers
making them more than a nuisance to the armed guards, who could
use their maces only once before the swarm.

Ballast threw away the useless stub of his sword, gripped the cage
door, and tugged and pounded with his fists. Marf Mag was only an
arm's length away from him through the bars. Over the growling and
keening of the flenx, the screams of the wounded and dying, the
hoarse cries, Falca heard Marf Mag say Ballast's name, his other one?
She'd stopped jumping up and down, now held the bunched end of
her black hair to her mouth, shaking her head in disbelief.

Ballast wasn't getting anywhere trying to rip the door off its
hinges, though his strength buckled the metal. Half-carrying, half-
pushing the Timberlimb ahead of him, to get her out of the way of the
fighting behind him, Falca shouted at Ballast, "Get away! It's no use.
Let me use the mace!"

The voals in back of Falca were screaming so loudly for Falca to
get the Prism that Ballast couldn't have heard him. He kept tugging at
the door in a fury, his great strength trembling the wagon, calling out
Marf Mag's name again and again.

Falca shouldered Ballast out of the way, yelled at Marf Mag to
move to one side. She didn't. Ballast shouted at her, in Vale-tongue,
and she moved, but too far. She was frightened.

Falca lifted the mace. The door ripped loose from its hinges, flew
across the cage, crashed into the far side where the flenx attacked it,
spearing through the bars.

Ballast rushed to the door, shouting at Mag to come out. But she
only stepped back. "No, Mag! Don't be afraid. You're coming with
me. Please don't be afraid. I've come for you!"

The voals were still screaming for the Prism, while others were
trying to pull it away. Falca had to push two voals back from the
cage. "Ballast! Go in and get her. Hurry! There are men coming down
from the castle." As soon as he said it, before Ballast began trying,
Falca knew he was too big to fit through. He backed away with such a
look of helplessness and fear and despair that Falca took only a moment to decide. "Hold the mace," Falca said, "and use it on the flenx
when the time comes."

As Falca climbed up and began wriggling through the doorway, Marf Mag ran to the far side, turning around finally with terror marring her face.

"No," Falca shouted. "It's all right. I'm not going to hurt you. You're coming to a safe place."

Mag's hands pulled on her hair, kneading it, as she shook her head, even when Ballast called out words she could understand.

"She's gone, Falca, she's gone," Ballast said. "Why won't she come out?"

"We'll get her," Falca said, but he knew Ballast couldn't hear him. Without the mace he felt defenseless, vulnerable.

A flenx growled behind her, and she reached out to its stiff back fur, as if seeking an ally. The other flenx crouched to Falca's right, ready to spring. Marf Mag and the animals were tiny, distorted in the depths of the Prism that rose in the center of the cage, the scattering of bones of the Lifters' victim stiff worms in that Prism.

Falca called out to her again. If he moved farther into the cage, the second flenx would charge.

He extended a hand to her, calling as softly as he could, but loud enough for her to hear him over the shouting behind him. Even that gesture was enough to cause the flenx to attack, though he carried no weapon. Someone—Ballast or a Lifter—used a mace. The flenx stopped in its tracks, headhorn a foot from Falca. The force of the mace charge curled the flesh away from the predator's fangs, shut its eyes, roughed its fur like a brush against the grain. The flenx collapsed to its side, shaking its head violently as if something was caught in its throat.

Falca lunged past the flenx to Marf Mag and almost caught her. There was no more time for coaxing. She was too quick, too frightened. She escaped to where there was no place to flee. She screamed when she impaled herself on the horn of the flenx behind, her cry merging with Falca's and Ballast's.

The beast shook its head, slid her off with a paw, and raised its head. It keened, confused.

Falca heard more shouts then, the voals eager to get the Prism. He stood, fully, and walked over to Marf Mag's body. He didn't fear the flenx now. It had nothing to protect anymore. The beast even backed away from him, snarling halfheartedly, its image receding in the nearby Prism.

"GET IT, GET THE PRISM," came the voals' shouts.

"PUSH IT CLOSER, BRING IT TO US."

"SHUT THEM UP, BALLAST," Falca shouted back, furious. He dragged Marf Mag back to the cage door. "Take her, Ballast, bring her through."

The stoneskin shook his head. "She wanted to stay." He touched her hand once, then her face. He lashed out once at the voals pressing him close against the wagon. Then he took a sword and cut a length of her hair. Falca avoided the blank stare of Mag's eyes, and in doing so, an image of Amala entered his mind. He looked to the Prism and saw himself: tiny, contorted, squeezed, as if he had just been born. With a shroud, a caul.

Outside the cage, fighting raged in the square, myriad individual battles illuminated by the stockade pyre. And suddenly, as if the Prism had allowed his eyes greater focus, he saw Saphrax, sword in hand, his back to the dais.

He had to get out. As much to get Saphrax and the mace as flee the cage. He feared the door would be blocked, sealing him inside, trapping him as the next servant to the Prism, eroding him so completely he would not want to leave either, preferring the world as he would come to know it, to what had been.

Ballast pulled him through, as if delivering him from the womb.

The Timberlimb, next to Ballast, held the mace, and the sword.

The voals pressed, pushed all around, shouting at Falca. Some were angry that he'd shown so little concern for the Prism; others were bewildered. Falca didn't care. All he needed was to get to Saphrax.

The voals shoved and screamed, and one bowled over the Timberlimb as he tried to get to the cage. Falca hit him with a backhand fist, sickened by him, by them all. The Limb wasn't hurt; she bounded to her feet. She understood that she stood in danger of getting trampled and allowed Falca to sling her over his shoulder. He let Ballast do most of the work clearing a path through the swarming voals and priests. Whether from the stoneskin's raining blows, the great sweeping motions of his scything arms, or their eagerness to gain possession of the Prism, the Lifters soon gave the three room to escape.

They stopped near the cresset that marked a corner of the square, away from the fighting. Panting, out of breath, Falca nevertheless kept his eye on Saphrax. His eyes had always been good at night. Ballast, too, was fatigued, though the Timberlimb seemed fresh as ever. She still carried both sword and mace in the crook of her tiny arms.

Ballast stared in a different direction, at the wagon, now filled with voals pushing, dragging the Prism toward its release. They'd already killed the flenx and heaped Marf Mag into a corner of the cage.

"We could have gotten her out," Ballast," Falca said. "Given her a burial."

Ballast had tied the sheaf of her hair around his belt. He shook his head. "We've neither the time, the tools, or ground soft enough to do her the respect. From a ship is no good. It's not our way. Stoneskins expect no burial when they die away from the home ground, least of all a Fallow Queen."

"You tried to get her, Ballast. She didn't want to come."

The stoneskin spoke softly, his eyes still on the cage. "I didn't want to find out. You forced an end to it. It's finished now and it wouldn't have been otherwise. It's better this way—for her and for me. I'll never forget you went in there to bring her back to me. Never will I forget, roaking. She is gone now. It's time for you to get Amala's mace. Do you want my help, or is it something you must do alone?"

"Go on to the quay. Find a ship. There will be other prisoners there, enough for a crew. Wait for me there, take the Limb. Wait until you can't wait any longer."

Ballast nodded, looked away. "Someone's loosed the empties."

Falca looked. The fighting went on. More stoneskins and heaves had come from the castle. There seemed to be more of them than the Lifters. But Falca judged the Lifters' fanaticism would get them the Prism. If they did, their pestilence would spread. And he was the one who opened the foul vial and spilled the contents.

"Go on to the quay now," he said to Ballast.

"We'll wait until you come, with Amala's mace. We'll not leave without you."

Falca gestured to the Timberlimb for the mace and sword. She handed him the weapon readily, but held back the mace and even stepped back.

"I'll need it to get the other, to get close to Saphrax," Falca said.

"Will you? How close do you have to get?" Ballast asked.

The stoneskin couldn't know what was in Falca's mind: that the mace he had held over Ballast's forehead *had* been too close. That for the time of a few heartbeats Falca had borne the temptation to let the mace-head drop, to feel what it was like to Lift another's soul. But Ballast did know, or suspected. That made him uneasy. No one, save Amala, had ever held knowledge of such weakness, that secret place in him.

Still, Ballast asked the Limb for the mace, and she gave it to him, perhaps thinking he wouldn't give it to Falca. He did and walked away with her. She looked back once, her eyes glittering in the light of the mace. Falca raised the sword in a salute to the first friends of his life. He wished for all the world that Amala might someday ferret out the mystery of that Timberlimb, who had kept both he and Ballast on a road whose bounds she seemed to know better than they.

He ran through the confusion in the square, scanning the fighting for Saphrax. The influx of empties, like moths to the flame, made the search harder. He avoided the countless melees and was surprised when a heave attacked him, then remembered he was clothed as a Lifter. Instinctively he used the mace to dispatch the soldier. Consciously he reminded himself that the mace was only a means to an end. Still, it was pleasurable to be holding the thing, having that much easy power in his hands.

He didn't see Saphrax among all the hundreds in the square and feared the brute had been killed, or that he'd left. He began to wonder if he had seen him at all, whether the Prism had tricked him into another conjuring.

He ducked, dodged the grappling heaves, Lifters, and stoneskins and their rasping, thudding swords and axes. Here and there a mace broke, geysering light into the smoky night air.

Then he saw him, just after the near wall of the stockade toppled, breaking apart in a showering of flame, sparks, and cinders. Saphrax rose from the ground not twenty yards away near the dais, withdrawing a sword from a thrashing heave. An empty blundered close to Falca, blocking his view. Falca ran to his left, sidestepped another empty, who sat cross-legged by a dead heave, hitting him with the wrong end of an ax.

Surrounded by three voals, Saphrax, his back to Falca, was swinging a sword at the nearest of four galley-heaves.

Falca hefted the mace and sword. One or the other would do, but he favored the mace. Once he got Amala, he would use it on Saphrax.

Once it was filled with his miserable life, he would fling it into the pyre of the stockade. The thought came as a promise to the Timberlimb.

Only one of the voals around Saphrax had a mace. Falca used his on that Lifter first, then another. Both voals arched back, sprawling into the attacking heaves, toppling two. Once again, Falca felt the joy of using so effective and powerful a weapon. The voal's mace exploded in a flare of light. Distracted, the third voal was killed by a heave as Saphrax turned into the point of Falca's sword.

He was confused for a moment, not immediately recognizing Falca in the Lifter cape, hood, and tunic. Falca took the opportunity to topple two more of Grippa's soldiers, attacking from his left.

Falca raised the sword to Saphrax's neck, the point rising and falling with his breathing. "Drop the sword, run out beyond the fire," he said, "and don't stop until I tell you to."

When Saphrax smirked, Falca felt like killing him, but he couldn't. Not yet. He needed to find out about Amala first, the process of rejoining soul to body. He drew blood with a flick of the sword point, and the brute finally did as he was told. Loping behind, he had to prod Saphrax with the sword to keep him moving fast enough.

He fended off more heaves with the mace, pushed aside empties blundering into his path.

He directed Saphrax wide of the intense heat of the stockade fire. He could feel it on his face. The acrid air, the stench of roasting bodies made Falca cough.

The rocky ground rose. "This will do," Falca said, circling wide around Saphrax so that he could see the road below, the square. He didn't know if any Lifters had followed and he didn't want to be surprised. The sound of the fighting was distant now, but clear. Torches linked castle to the scattered light of the square. The wagon had moved in the direction of the quays, taking with it the greatest concentration of fighting. Falca didn't care who won now. He had his man.

"Is it you we have to thank?" Saphrax murmured.

"Drop to your knees," Falca said, pricking Saphrax's neck again.

The only light around was from Falca's mace in his left hand, more than enough illumination to see a smile that infuriated him. Everything else about the brute was the same—the misshapen nose, the ripped ear where the earring had been—except for the smile.

Saphrax kneeled, still smiling.

"Now, take Amala's mace from your belt. Leave the leather hood on. Put it very gently on the ground before you and crawl backward away from it."

Saphrax nodded, placed his hand on the covered mace-head—and stopped.

"I think that I've indulged you enough, Falca. You picked me from the gutter once because of my strength. You know my grip. I could crush the mace-head in a moment, in the time it takes you to run the sword through my neck. My guess is that you would rather I didn't crush your Amala. You have done a great deal tonight, but you won't get all you want.

"So I'm getting up now, Falca. Kill me if you want, but all you'll get from me are pieces of crystal and a charred scrap of leather and bits of my hand."

Falca's thoughts raced, but the sword never wavered from Saphrax's neck. The point rose as the Lifter did. Falca knew, even as he desperately tried to salvage his position, that it was lost, a victim of the very vulnerability of a thing that had such power.

He dropped the sword point, stepped back, and felt the salt wind blowing over this rise of ground.

Saphrax took the leather off Amala's mace. Light flared, hurt Falca's eyes, bathing him and Saphrax in the same brilliance. Saphrax covered the crystal with his huge hand, fondling it gently as a woman's breast.

"So fragile a thing. If I fell on it, my weight would break it. And so simple a thing. All it would take to bring her back—retrieved, we call it—is to place the mace on her forehead again. Simple as filling a ewer with water. It is done all the time in quarters at the Crucible in Gebroan. Amusing to put a woman's soul and memories back in the body of a male empty, or vice versa. It is done to empties when Givers are copulating with them though Maradus frowns on that. It heightens a crude pleasure."

Falca raged within herself. He'd botched this fist, the most important of his life. He should have tripped the brute to his back somehow, gotten the mace to him, snatched away Amala. The knowledge of retrieval could have been squeezed from any voal. He cursed himself. Why was he so stupid? Saphrax's assurance, patience, his control infuriated him. It was as if there was another man inside the body of the brute he'd known. There was nothing he could do now. He might as well have been wrapped in chains.

"Why tell me now about how to bring her back?" Falca said finally.

"Oh, you deserve at least that reward for helping us get the Prism. Which we shall. We have greater purpose than Grippa's mercenaries and are prepared to die in greater numbers for it." He swung an arm back. "They're doing so now. We were like Grippa's mercenaries back in the alleys of Draica. You are still. Maradus tells us a man or woman is not whole until he is prepared to die for something. You still count the odds, Falca."

Falca ignored the taunting. "You have them now. Perhaps not in Gerbroan."

"Your following me there would be a gift. You might get her back; there is always a chance. But you needn't go to all that trouble. Join me in our purpose and you can have her mace. I'll go back with you to Draica and retrieve her myself if you like."

"My answer to that hasn't changed, Saphrax."

The Lifter grinned. "Nor has my determination in trying to change it. You taught me the rudiments of persistence in my earlier life." He patted the mace and laughed. "I think you're halfway to me anyway. You wear the cape and sign of the One, you hold a charged mace as if you enjoy the possession of it. You feel its power and pleasure and probably have wondered what it would be like to fill it with someone's Gift. No, in your effort to get Amala back, you have come closer to us than you think, my friend."

Falca flicked the sword up, catching Saphrax's chin. The brute's hand was tight around Amala's mace, his fingers red, glowing, tense.

"So delicate," Saphrax whispered, his voice throaty from the pressure of the sword point. A little blood trickled down. "So delicate. But a god such as ours is made from many such delicate things. Yet the resulting strength and power is a wonder to behold, the most beautiful thing you will ever, *ever* see. What you feel from that single mace in your other hand is pitiful, puny compared with the Gathering of the One in the Crucible."

Falca wanted to kill him, purge his life of this stalking brute, once little more than a beast, but a beast now who had been given greater life by this . . . One . . . the abomination of the maces . . . all the wandering empties. He wanted so badly to drain the life from Saphrax,

ut the mace to his forehead. But his vengeance would make him one
f them, would seal Amala's fate. So much as a tremble of his sword
and . . . and Saphrax would instantly close his around the light and
fe of Amala Damarr.

He lowered the sword.

"You'd best be on your way, Falca," Saphrax said. "To the ships, I
ope. Save us the sturdiest galliot for the Prism, will you?" He
aughed. "And when you get to Sandsend, follow the aqueduct road
o the lake and the lesser road through the mountains to the desert.
'ake the mace you have in your hand. You'll only have to hold an-
ther to get this one back. Take it as a Gift."

"You may be right, Saphrax. Until then, I won't need it." Falca
Iropped it and was surprised it didn't break.

"Such fortitude and will," Saphrax sneered. "Such virtue. Really,
'alca, what's come over you? Don't you feel now a sense of loss at
uch an instrument of strength and power? Only steel for Falca Breks,
s that it?"

Falca wiped his hand on his trousers. He would have thrown off
he Lifter cloak, too, but it was cold and would be colder at sea. He
egan walking away, toward the quays. Saphrax wouldn't use the
harged mace on him. The brute wanted him to come to Gebroan. He
vould have his wish. Saphrax was right. Part of him did want to go
ack and pick up the mace, to feel its weight in his hand. But it
vasn't the better part of him, the one that went into the Prism cage for
Marf Mag. Anyway, he smiled to himself, chances weren't good the
nace would have survived the voyage to Gebroan. Something told
im the Timberlimb would have tossed the mace over the side before
andfall. He had to find out her name. Surely, in time, he and she
ould work out each other's names.

Saphrax called out after him, and Falca turned to see the Lifter
ick up the mace. "There will be many more like these," he said. "So
nany Gifts for the One." He shattered the mace on the ground. Light
hot up, almost liquid in intensity and straight as a spear. Saphrax
ripped the helve and passed the length repeatedly through the light.
Sections of the helve dropped one after the other, like the paring of a
ausage.

"How weak the crystal," he went on. "So like ourselves, Falca.
Who is to say which is the weaker?"

Falca stared at the light, the slow dissipation, wondering who the
erson had been. The empty at the fountain? Or some villager from

one of the hamlets he'd seen coming into the Ebony Isles? He saw hi
Amala, the stranger still, a mark to him, before the flina player, th
candle in her room that first night, before the ice. He saw her bendin
over to lift the empty from the fountain with her deceptive strength
that tough fiber of her beauty.

He carried another weapon with him now, and he spoke its nam
to the brilliant core of Amala's light that he would carry back to he
husk, or die trying: the words that he had wanted to tell her but neve
got the chance. He hoped that weapon would be enough in Gebroar
Until then, it was enough to breathe deeply in celebration of anothe
retrieval, with only a sword in his hand.

BOOK THREE

GEBROAN

Chapter Twenty-two

The Racing Station

Freaca preferred the place high atop the dead tree, an enclosure not much bigger than the tub her mother used to bathe her brothers. She could almost hear them—and herself—squealing from the coldness of the rainwater. This place reminded her of home, as high as the racing stations the males used to loft their prize birds in the summer contests. She had sneaked up to one of the stations once, and her later punishment was well worth the sight of the green cloth of the forest stretching all the way to the distant mountains, so much like this endless water below her. The trail of this boat reminded her of the Road, which disappeared and reappeared in the rolling of the green. Even the creaking of this dead tree she stood atop reminded her of the swaying timbers of the Road, whose lashings and supports were her father's constant worry. He cared for a longer stretch of the Road than any other male in the village, and she had always been so proud of that.

It made her feel good that Falca had allowed her to climb this high, to a place where only men—shit-catchers—normally went. She knew his reasons were not just a matter of allowing her roaming freedom. This racing station was also the safest place for her on the boat, far above the quarrelsome shit-catchers. Sometimes a few would climb close, to tend ropes and the things Falca called sails, which snapped and grew taut as a drumskin with the wind.

Freaca spent all of her time now in this racing station because she

didn'   it them to hurt her again. If they did, she would die. And
she didn't want Falca to have to come to her aid again, as he had the
second day out. A shit-catcher had tried to rape her below, at night
Falca had caught him and was so angry he threw the man into the
water. Freaca easily sensed the other 'catchers' anger and unease a
what he had done. Even the rock-man, the friend Falca called Ballast
had words with him, but he wasn't angry like the rest. When a few
men tried to hurt Falca later, Ballast had taken two of them and
rammed their heads into this very tree, as easily as one might crack
nuts. No, the 'catchers' didn't like her, and she didn't want to cause
Falca any more trouble. That would only delay her getting home
delay Falca's getting home.

His helping her had surprised her perhaps as much as it had surprised the other men. Falca couldn't know she was torn inside. The
blood flow had stopped, but with every movement she could feel the
wound. It was much better now, but she knew she would never bear
any children. That saddened her, so she tried not to think about it.
Eight times it had happened, since she and Leila and Eoka and the
other females had left the village: once on a boat like this one, twice
within sight of the home forest, and five times at the place where
Falca and Ballast had also been captive. Different shit-catchers from
different clans, but the end was all the same. They emptied their stink
inside her, over her bruised legs and breasts. Their skin was like that
of snakes that crawled along the ground, like that of the bark of trees
overtaken by swamp. Her people had named them shit-catchers for
their loathsome habit of putting their hands—sometimes filled with
leaves—between their legs when they relieved themselves.

Freaca tried not to dwell on how much she hated them, for that
only brought up the memories and made her hurt inside more. They
were not all bad; there had been a few who approached kindness.
Then there was Falca. She didn't call him shit-catcher, though he was
one. His name, when she had eked it out the first day on the water,
had made her laugh because it sounded like the noise her kinsmen
made when they slapped lazy onax on the rump to get them moving
with a load along the Road. She hoped she hadn't offended him with
her laugh because he had seemed so eager to know her name. He
called her Frikko, which was close enough. They had worked out two
other names. One was Ballast, who stroked himself so often with a
knife, and tossed the gray shavings of his skin overboard. His illness
—what else could it be?—was a strange and awful one, though oth-

erwise he seemed healthy. Ballast was scraping himself now below, with Falca next to him. They were talking as they did constantly, and that made Freaca feel good, too, seeing their friendship grow, as it had from that first time when she prevented them from coming to blows. She had thought it might end—just before Falca went into the cage of beasts, to get the woman, Ballast's woman, who had the hair like a river. Their friendship was close now, one of the few constants in Freaca's life. She valued it greatly.

The other name Freaca learned was Amala, who Freaca thought of as the Absent One, who slept with Falca. She might as well have been present for the look in Falca's eyes when he spoke of her. She was his mate, or something close to it. Freaca had confirmed this by pointing to her sex and then Falca's. He reddened in embarrassment, as if feeling his reaction more like an unbroken youth's. Then he nodded and smiled.

Freaca had thought for a while to name another herself: Styada. She hadn't. He had been, true enough, the only male in her life, but now, more than ever, she knew they wouldn't be mated for life. She could have named him to Falca out of loneliness, but it wouldn't have been the truth. Falca wouldn't have known any better, or cared perhaps, but Freaca did.

They shared names and a desire to get home. They had enemies and had shared captivity. Did that all mean that Falca's home, his clan, were being attacked, too, being killed and captured by a people as powerful to them as the shit-catchers were to her own? Probably not, she decided. She had seen, in all the time she'd been away, no indication of a people who were slowly gnawing toward the heart of Falca's kind, with the possible exception of the ones who hunted with the sun-boughs that broke so easily. There was danger there for Falca, but it couldn't be like the soldiers, the shit-catchers who were killing and enslaving her kin, who stank like the swamps.

Falca carried a strong odor. And he was a soldier, good enough to make others follow his orders. It was not just his skill and readiness to kill. She had sensed no enjoyment when Falca killed the man who tried to rape her. Still, she would not want to be his enemy. Freaca was not afraid of him, but she did not trust him when he had held the sun-bough. There was poison in it.

Falca was different, yes. Freaca had known it immediately in the place of wailing shit-catchers, the pen of close trees. She had smelled Patient One on him, the faint but unmistakable scent of Sweet-hand

that she had grown so used to with old Gurrus. It shocked her that
such a scent would be on a shit-catcher, but she was thrilled, too, for
here was a link, a road—the only one in a year of captivity and
degradation—to home.

Freaca knew she would probably never find out how he came to
carry the scent of Sweet-hand, which the Patient Ones guarded so
closely. Gurrus's hoven had reeked of it, but he would have never
even considered sharing any with her, given her age, no matter what
his hopes for her.

Had Falca, if he used to be a shit-catcher soldier in the home
forest, taken some Sweet-hand before burning a village, before herding kinfolk away to the Stone Forest? Had he found some there perhaps? Patient Ones lived now in the shit-catcher's Stone Forest,
among all the others, perhaps even Gurrus. No, she decided. Wherever he got it, it wasn't through hurting her people. He had thrown
one of his own kind to the sea because of her. She would tell that
story in her village when she got back, and they would laugh in her
face in disbelief.

It was enough that he carried the scent, enough for her to be
curious without knowing. There were those who were like roads, to
be followed, though one might not know the destination, only that the
path was necessary, the clearest way through the trees.

Some females in the lodge had said that about her, almost in defense of her youth, against those who thought her idea of traveling
beyond the forests for help was foolish. Freaca had persisted and led
Leila and Eoka and the other three Outside. She was the only one left.
She had been foolish, but she did not regret her desire to help her
people. Her treasure, she knew, lay in the attempt. Those who came
with her knew the danger.

She did not want to lead again, though. She wanted to hurry
Home. For she felt now she carried within herself the help for her
people she had sought from others. The surest route was Falca, who
carried the scent of a Patient One. She had been most frightened not
when he was fighting the shit-catchers and rock-men, but when he
held that sun-bough. It was like a fire under the Road, or the rot that
weakened its lashings. She could sense his confusion and struggle
when he held it. He was other than himself, enjoying something like
anger, only greater and sweeter, sweet as the poisonous resin that
had been her chore as a child to leave out each night to tempt climb-
ing horn-tails.

She wanted to keep it from him because she wanted to get home,
as she knew he did. She didn't think either of them would, with a
un-bough in his grasp.

Ballast knew it too. It was not hard to sense that. She felt sorry for
the rock-man, though that was odd enough: like pitying the strength
of a lodge tree or distant mountains. He had lost something at the
age of beasts. The woman who had the hair like a river. He followed
alca, too, like a road. Was that because he had no home, not even a
ome that, like hers, was slowly dying?

It had been dying from the soldiers even when Freaca had been
orn. She knew of the rot when she came of age, though her village
ad still been untouched by the war. The day after the runner came
ith news that the Farolas' village had been burned, the people killed
r taken away, she was already in a kind of mourning. That was the
ay she knew that Styada would not be her mate. Though older than
he, he was still a young male who mistook—how could he know
therwise?—her willingness to nestle with a wildness of spirit.
Wasn't she the youngest in the village to lie with a male, and one
om so important a family? Freaca knew differently. She was curious
nd, yes, adventurous, but she knew even at that age that she didn't
ave the wildness the males prized. Oh, Styada had proudly showed
er bites on his neck and shoulders to his friends. He didn't know
ow deliberately, how consciously, she had done it—purposefully as
weaving cloth—to please him, to let the man she loved brag. He had
anted to seal their bond with the ceremony—the threat of the shit-
atchers made it seem urgent—but she told him to be patient. He had
een angry, as if he was unsatisfactory to her. How could she tell him
was not him she was disappointed in but herself? She feared the day
hen he would find her out, grow bored with her, and finally leave
er, to find greater pleasure in eloe dung or in the gaming boards of
he males' lodge. She was unhappy for days, and not the least of her
easons was that her father was eager for the match, despite her
outh, and irritated at her reluctance.

So she went to old Gurrus—the Patient One of the village—for
olace and counsel, telling him all between coughing fits, for the reek
f Sweet-hand was thick as mist in his tiny hoven off the Road. He
eard her out without interruption, then smiled and lifted from her
houlders that which was not there, telling her:

"The greatest burden one can bear—when one has the hunger as
ou do, Freaca—is to know oneself better than the other knows him-

self. Truth can be a burden but harmful only if one seeks to brir
oneself down to the other's awareness, to dull the senses in the nam
of love or loyalty. One will stoop in time, chafe under a lighter load.

"You and Styada are young yet, Freaca, and as such are apt to fe
any differences between you. It is the way. But hold yourself proudl
have faith in your heart, trust it for no other reason than because it
yours and therefore a truth.

"Keep part of your heart for yourself and revel in that part yc
give him or another. And who knows, you and Styada may yet sett
on the same branch, Freaca, if that thought warms you. Though yo
weights are unequal, together on the branch yours and his will caus
the leaves to move as one."

Freaca went to talk with Gurrus often after that, not out of need s
much as pleasure. Often it was she who did most of the talking and h
the listening. At one point he chided her: "Your tongue, Freaca, is t
the wind as loam is to the rain." Then he smiled. "As one said to m
once."

There came a day when he thrilled her by saying she had the see
of a Patient One in her. He spoke in a whisper, as if realizing th
precedent. A female Patient One? Once, long ago in Boughbreak
but never in this backward village near the mountains, where th
Road ended at the lake.

Gurrus said, "Your path may indeed be different than the res
Perhaps you are one of the lucky who value wisdom above all els
For wisdom, Freaca, is that which cannot be burned or consumed.
is strong as the vines, as resilient, and its many strands can be wove
simply, or intricately, according to the need, for strength or delicac
Its nourishment lies in the seed of the pod, not the bright husk. For a
these reasons it can be greater than love, can conquer hate, though i
plumage very often suffers in comparison."

Freaca paused in her thoughts, saddened about Gurrus. Belov
Ballast was taking a turn at the smooth, straight branches Falca calle
oars that helped move the boat. All the shit-catchers took turns pul
ing the oars; Falca made sure of that. His turn usually came afte
Ballast's. He waved up at Freaca, and she waved back, pleased at hi
attention but still in the grip of her mood.

For Gurrus never came back from a visit to Boughbreaks, th
large village along the northern road, where he had an ailing brothe
The males in the racing stations had seen smoke drifting over the tree

the distance. Freaca went with Styada and a score of others to see at had happened.

At least he wasn't among the dead in the burned village. Freaca ght have searched along the Road beyond the ruins, but the fire had stroyed a portion of the Road. There was no place to look but wn, and so she went, shaming Styada who, like the others, had her no stomach or no interest in searching for the dead. Females ln't usually go below, but rules were changing in the home forest. e shit-catchers with their metal weapons and torches were changing m.

Freaca could have searched for a year and never found him in the gle of forest and undergrowth to either side of the hunting path low the Road. The burned village far above, the dead bodies, were t the only scents Freaca smelled of a closing world. She smelled the t-catchers and their captives, the survivors of the battle and burning Boughbreaks. She caught the scent of a Patient One—Sweet-hand but it could have been One of the village, not Gurrus. From the dergrowth came sounds of predators devouring the dead who had len from the village or Road: a poor fate, for the Cloud Hands ver reached souls that far below, or so it was thought. Freaca mpsed down the path a small flenx pulling at an arm.

She climbed back up and walked, alone, back to her village. ada shunned her. She didn't care. She didn't want to see him that ht.

She hated the shit-catchers for what they had done, though she nembered well enough Gurrus's words: "Hate only what you may d in the touch, Freaca. And if you are able to touch something, you ly find there is no desire to hate after all."

What good did that advice do you, Gurrus? she wondered aloud to wind that snapped the sails. The idea was born of a time before coming of the soldiers, an idea that only made it possible for so ny of her people to be taken away to the Stone Forest, to be hunted the limits of the Road.

Styada came to her later and they talked. For once he agreed with r on something. "It is not enough to hate only what you can touch," said. "To survive, our eyes, all our senses must be as weapons."

Those were among his last words before he went away to ambush shit-catchers who were coming up the river, the scouts said, in ats so much smaller than the one of Freaca's later captivity and now

her freedom. Styada and fifty other males dropped from the Road t
was slung across the river, their goal only to capsize the boats a
swim for shore and let the 'catchers drown or get devoured by krila

Whatever had happened, only ten males—Styada among them
came back. They claimed victory, boasting that all but two of
boats had turned over, drowning many 'catchers.

Freaca turned away from their pitiful boasts, saddened, angry.
this was victory, there was no hope. Styada told her nothing mc
The news came from others. He was not visibly wounded, but son
thing had happened to him. All he did when she visited him v
stare, eat little, and remain silent, and though Freaca wanted to
him of her idea, she knew it was no use. It was like talking to a tr
She asked other males of the expedition what had happened and o
one would tell her anything, and even he was reluctant. Freaca v
persistent and found out that Styada had not dropped from the bri
with the others. He had frozen and joined the survivors later.

She did not feel the shame she was supposed to feel at this c
grace. She felt sorry for him, for the low place he would occupy n
in the males' lodge, if they would even let him in. Some said her i
was borne of the shame Styada brought her, that she wanted to lea
because of it. But her idea had come to her before she found out ab
Styada's cowardice.

She gathered the females of the village in their lodge on a spur
the Road and told them their only hope lay Outside the forests. S
reasoned that the shit-catchers must have other enemies, who mi
deliver her people if only to kill their enemy. Her voice was as full
loam after a rain.

She counted it as a success that even five of the females agreed
go with her. When she told Styada what she planned to do, he or
shook his head and stared past her, and his hands remained at his si
when she stroked him.

Her mother and father tried to prevent her departure and even h
her eldest brother stand guard. "Where would you go, who wo
know you seek help, and if they did, who would want to help withe
the favors you could not possibly give them?" her father said. "Y
are foolish, Freaca. We will move to the end of the Road. The sl
catchers' season for war will end, as all seasons do."

She answered, "What is more foolish, Father, than one in ev
five males returning from waging war against the soldiers and clai

ng victory? The shit-catchers don't count seasons as we do. Theirs will not end until all of us are either dead or captured."

Freaca believed with all her heart that beyond home there was help. At the very least she might find another home where there were no shit-catchers. And so she escaped with the five, leaving her own home as one might flee the enemy.

She knew now there was no other home, no place free of the enemy. The shit-catchers were more plentiful than grubs in a tree. Her mother and father were right, but at least she had tried the one way, found it held no hope, and now could try another. Gurrus had a lesson for that too: "The true test of the ripeness of fruit, in the end, is in the tasting."

She would hold her head high when she returned. She had learned much about the shit-catchers, more than any of her people, and she would put that to good use in the struggle ahead. She would counsel them that they had to abandon their villages high along the Road, even if it was at the end, for such places were nothing more now than the traps her people themselves set for animals. Below, they might hide, use the density of the forest to ambush, to discourage the shit-catchers. Dangerous and unprecedented a move, but necessary. She would encounter much resistence. She already had an answer: "Does not the dripping-bird lose its color to mask itself from predators?"

Freaca sensed the nearness of land before she saw it low on the horizon—a washed-out green, so unlike the rich color of home. She felt the heat of that land under a sun that seemed so much brighter and hotter than the one she knew before. She smelled the dryness of the distant land in the wind.

She called out to Falca below, pointing. He and the others were excited, rushing to the edge of the boat, clapping each other on the back, pausing at the oars. Freaca wondered if this place of sun was Falca's home. The thought confused her feelings. She was happy for him, that he was coming home, that his road had ended, that he would no longer have to be content with the Absent One sleeping within him.

But who would lead her closer to her own home?

It was such a long way.

She would have to do it herself, she thought. A Patient One, as Gurrus would have told her, is she who truly marks the path to follow.

A seabird flew by closely, keening. It reminded her of all the changes that awaited her arrival home. Freaca sighed. If only she could change her color, mask her smallness in such a large world when she left Falca and Ballast. She would make her own Road. But that would not make it any less dangerous.

Chapter Twenty-three

Sandsend

"Maybe that's him," Sippio said, pointing over the iron balcony railing at the ship. The sleek, black-hulled galley was rounding the promontory that shielded the outer harbor of Sandsend.

Alatheus shook his head, momentarily more annoyed with his gillie's denseness than the heat. "I told you before. I checked with the harbormasters in Draica. The last four ships to leave there before ours were either Gebroanan windshippers or galliots. That isn't one of those."

"He could have left after us," Sippio said.

"Not likely, not for one so eager to make his escape." Still, Alatheus followed the ship as it approached the curled finger of rock that formed the city's inner harbor and upon which rose the whitewashed fortress of the Gebroanan King, Dehèglia.

He had a clear view of the bustling quays and all the ships crowded closely as the forests of the Rough Bounds. It had taken Alatheus awhile to find not only a proper vantage point to look for the bastard but also one that wouldn't offend his sensibilities. He picked a third-story room, in a fairly clean inn owned by a talkative master Alatheus found entirely too jovial. There had been a better room available, but it was closer to the vulgarity of the street below.

In the middle of the wide central quay, a four-faced water clock graced a slender tower. The clock wasn't working. For a day now, Alatheus had stared at the same time. The clock probably hadn't worked for months. It was just like the Gebroanans to tolerate the disrepair. It wasn't for lack of water or a rusted mechanism. Alatheus could see, if he craned his neck, the twin pools at the terminus of the great aqueduct in the city's central square. A narrow trough ran down the middle of the tree-lined thoroughfare. The water was a glistening, taut rope at this distance. At the end of the promenade rose one of the three seaward gates to the core of Sandsend, where Alatheus had men watching for Breks.

He shook his head at the bronze hands of the clock, annoyed at their immobility. The tower had no more function than shade now for beggars and infants publicly abandoned by these Sandsenders: a beautiful, useless thing.

The oppressive heat also fouled his mood. The hour couldn't be noon yet, and already Alatheus was sweltering under the balcony's sun-bleached awning. The harbor breeze helped only a little.

He stepped back from the railing and finished off the water from a flagon on a table. At least the water was good—better than Draica's, he had to admit. Sippio eyed him, knowing his mood, but his obvious concern about the tardy arrival of Breks still nettled Alatheus. He could see it in the gillie's small eyes, a worry that this mission was failing somehow, as if Alatheus wasn't doing all he could. The judgment was close to impertinence. Sippio's boldness, Alatheus felt, was due to Amala's influence. The man had changed while Alatheus was in the Rough Bounds, killing Timberlimbs, burning their wretched villages high in the trees.

Sippio had been with the family too long.

"We should have seen Breks by now," the servant said. "Suppose he's slipped by us?"

"He hasn't," Alatheus said, and turned his back to Sippio. Carts rumbled in the street below, vendors hawked an amazing variety of wares. The smell of cooking meat drifted up. They butchered animals in the street, mixed blood with wine and sold it. He'd even seen mothers selling their milk. Still, he was hungry, and the exotic smells gave an edge to his appetite. He'd have to send Sippio down for food. And water. His throat was already parched again.

"But suppose he *has* slipped by us?" Sippio persisted.

The questioning infuriated Alatheus, and he wanted to slap the gillie, to remind him to show more respect. Alatheus barely controlled his urge. Hitting Sippio would only send him into a sulk of orse. He needed the gillie for a while longer yet. Perhaps it was the loseness of the voyage, but Alatheus was sick of the man. He had lways been more of Amala's servant than his and now that she had . . changed, there was little need of Sippio. Alatheus consciously oftened his anger to a sigh.

"Sippio, if he has slipped by us, we will pursue him. But he asn't. I have increased the number of men watching the quays. here's twenty now. They have the scut's description."

Sippio ws impressed. "Twenty? That's good. But maybe Breks as disguised himself?"

"Look, he isn't expecting us to follow him here. He won't be on is guard. He must feel he's made good his escape. Even if he is still autious, even if he's cut his hair, dyed it, put a patch over an eye, he till can't mask that scar you put on his face. Also, the men have an dded incentive to look sharply for him. I have increased the reward the one who leads me to Falca Breks. Does five hundred gold clats meet with your approval, Sippio?"

The gillie's eyes grew wide. Alatheus knew what he was thinking. ippio could live for ten years on that sum.

"And I'd pay five times the amount for the absolute certainty of etting Falca Breks," Alatheus added.

"So would I," Sippio whispered. "If I had the money. What he did Amala—"

Alatheus cut him off. "You'll do your part in getting him. But I an't let you down to the quays, though you know I'd like to give the eward to you. Breks knows what you look like. We can't risk that, an we, Sippio?"

"No, I understand. I never said I wanted the reward."

"It's all right. I know you were thinking that you would be best uited to look for Breks, since you've seen him before with Amala."

"No, Alatheus. I could indeed watch for him without being seen. I id it for Amala once. But you're wrong about the reward. It is a reat sum, but all I want to do is run my knife"—he patted the hilt at is belt—"across his neck, for our Amala."

Alatheus felt sudden heat at the back of his neck and stared at his illie, who'd turned away as if wronged. "Our Amala," Alatheus epeated within. She and Sippio had spent much time together. He new that, just as he knew the servant, loyal as a dog, had worshiped er. He wondered just how much. And though he tried to close the memory shut, he heard these sounds again, from the night he stood in the rain, pounding hard at the door to the house so that he wouldn't hear Amala's moanings and urgings upstairs.

Sippio too?

The gillie would indeed play his part in getting Breks, and more than he knew.

"A word, Sippio," Alatheus said, the harshness of his voice drawing the gillie around. "I'm as eager as you to get Breks. But we must be careful not to tip our hand. This cesspit of a city has many cracks for an insect like Falca Breks to scuttle into if he senses our tread. We will follow him and wait for the right place to get him, a place where he can't escape from. We will work together to get him, you and I."

The gillie nodded.

A web drifted down, the sun marking the spider as bright as a jewel. Even as it floated in the breeze, the spider scuttled from end to end, searching for escape but sensing nothing. For the first time in a day, Alatheus smiled, amused at the spider's predicament. As the web landed on the railing, curling down over it as if melting, Alatheus drew his Warden's sword, plucked the web before the spider could move to freedom, and dropped it over the edge.

"Falca Breks, too, will come to the place," Alatheus said, "and we will deal with him similarly, eh, Sippio?"

The gillie smiled, the tension between him and Alatheus gone for the moment. "The innkeeper says the webs come from islands off the coast, which are inhabited only by celibate monks. They cut loose the webs and cultivate the spiders with as much enthusiasm as they do the crops and mulder bushes the webs foul."

"Is that so, Sippio?"

"Yes, the man claims the monks are a spiteful lot who know the wind will take the spiders to Sandsend and punish the city for its wickedness."

Sippio laughed. "One of the things drifted through the keeper's window at night just last year, and the spider bit him on his backside while he was enjoying his mistress. Said he was sick for a week from the bite. When I asked him why the King or city magistrates don't just clear the islands of the nuisance, the innkeeper shrugged and said, 'The Myrcians pay tribute to their Erseiyr. We suffer the web each year in the way of tribute to our consciences. It's a small enough price to pay.'"

"Well, perhaps Breks will get bitten and make things easier for ."

Sippio nodded. "This is a strange place. I'll be glad to leave. Give e the fog and rain of Draica, thank you. The sun curdles the senses re. Staking Falca Breks out in the sun would be a pleasure, though I ppose the knife will have to do."

"Any way will do," Alatheus said softly. "Just so long as I get m." He lowered the wide brim of his hat, masking his eyes and oughts of the hour when Sippio would find out that he'd be staying der the Gebroanan sun for the rest of his life. Alatheus felt only a tle regret at having sold Sippio to the slave monger while the gillie as on an errand for food and drink.

It was necessary. Alatheus would need the extra money to pay for e additional men and reward. His father had given him a consider- le sum for the killing of Breks, but it hadn't been quite enough, ven the bastard's late arrival.

Alatheus had gotten only a hundred fifty for the gillie—half then, lf on delivery. The price was an insult, given the man's muscle, perience, and docility, and certainly much less than Alatheus had pected. Of course, he didn't have the time to haggle, and Sippio dn't been present to be properly assessed.

The slave monger had hesitated about the transaction. "This isn't y usual way of doing business. But I understand you have a last use r the man before you sell him to me. And you look like a gentleman ho keeps his word, a man of substance." He nodded at Alatheus' othing, then shrugged, as if sorely burdened. "I would like to give u more, understand, as I am a merchant of some fairness and repu- tion myself. But business is poor. The Spirit-Lifters are running me t. They turn these empties loose on the streets, and the King's men ke them to the labor camps. The damn Lifters don't care about aking a profit on them. They could use me and a few others as iddlemen, and we'd both profit. But no, they just turn the sorry stards loose. No wonder the King won't do nothing about the fters. Well, you get what you pay for. It'll take the city a lot longer finish building the spur of the aqueduct with the empties doing the uling, than with slaves—like your man—who can take an order d keep it in their heads."

Alatheus took his money from the monger, not caring in the least r the merchant's problems, which were probably a lie anyway. That

there might be empties like Amala in Sandsend didn't surprise him
though. Falca Breks, who probably got a bounty from some Lifter fo
Amala, would undoubtedly be trying his luck again here. He wouldn'
get far.

Sippio was shielding his eyes with a hand, gazing at the harbor
searching, the hard muscles of his hands bunched and tight. Alatheu
wondered again if Amala had reveled in the embrace of those powe
ful arms. If she had, that memory, along with every other one she ha
ever had, was gone, wiped away, her memories of Falca Breks too. I
a way it had been like a cleansing. If only Alatheus could wipe awa
his memory of that night in the rain, when she locked him out.

His most secret thought, that he had acknowledged but immedi
ately buried, surfaced again: He was glad there would be no mor
nights such as that one. For it brought her again to him, opened th
door, let him come to Gebroan on this mission of single-minded de
votion.

This is all for you, my love, he thought. He might even tell Sippi
that when the monger's men hauled him away. The gillie might eve
come to accept it. There could be no greater purpose to his shallo
life than to help his master get Breks. Surely Sippio felt that now, i
his eagerness to kill the bastard.

For all of his cautionary words about being too impatient
Alatheus was just that: eager to get back to Amala and care for her, t
take her away from the family estate in Heart Hill. He'd be doing hi
parents a favor. Perhaps he'd take Amala to that lakeside village i
the mountains where they went as children. No, that would only re
mind him of her foolishness with Breks and the skating. Perhap
Slacere, down the coast, or the Isles of Sleat.

There was no one else to look after her, other than the elderl
couple he had hired to care for her in his absence and keep away th
Timberlimbs who loitered outside the fencing, reminding everyone c
Amala's waywardness. The couple was the best he could find on suc
short notice. The woman in particular seemed kind and protective an
not overly intimidated by his father.

The old general had sold the four other servants, just so that the
wouldn't talk to others in the neighborhood. Alatheus' mother ha
gone into seclusion, wrecked by what her beautiful, spirited—an
rebellious—daughter had become. It had been bad enough whe
Amala spurned her social station to work in that Timberlimb settle
ment house. But this . . . their poor mother would never recover from

he embarrassment Amala's condition would cause her in the salons of
Heart Hill.

And his father? He had said little more than, "Bring me the hand
of the one who did this, or don't come back to this house." And he
gave Alatheus the pouches of money. It was almost as if he blamed
his son for what had happened.

What had truly happened, Alatheus realized after grieving, was
the rebirth of a union his parents had never understood, had tried to
inhibit because of their typically vulgar fear of something incestuous.
Well, Alatheus thought, they needn't worry now. It would be like
making love to a rag doll, though others might take advantage of
Amala's condition, finding pleasure in her total passivity. One of
Alatheus' friends had taken a drunken dare and copulated with a
woman only two hours dead from drowning in the Valor Canal. Only
Alatheus stood between Amala and such desecration. Perhaps in time
he might elicit simple responses from Amala, recognition of him,
maybe even memories of him alone with her, memories to come. She
was his life now, even more than before.

She had been sucking on her hand like a newborn the day he left
for Gebroan, staring out the window at the gray sky, never even turning or acknowledging the strokes of the brush as he combed her short
hair. It would grow again. He could keep it as long as he wanted,
keep her plump or slender as before. She was always hungry, he'd
discovered, and especially thirsty. She could never drink enough, and
she relieved herself in the room as often as a drunken sailor. When he
left her with the elderly couple and said goodbye, she didn't say a
word. She snared a buzzing bluebite with reflexes quick as before. He
closed the door to her room as she slapped the insect into her mouth.

The only thing he worried about now was that someone else
would kill Falca Breks first. He had spent many hours during the
voyage to Sandsend sharpening his sword. His father wanted Breks's
hand. Well, he'd give him the head. He'd roll it out from a sack, like
a bowl and pins, all the way down the expensive Helyn carpet that
Amala had once been scolded for soiling. Falca Breks's head would
knock against the door to his father's study; he'd open the door and
look down to see the eyes staring up at him.

He reached for the flagon of water, then realized it was empty. By
the High Sorrows but he was thirsty under this sun . . . and hungry.
Sippio left the railing reluctantly when Alatheus ordered him to go
below for food and drink. Alatheus thought, with a smile, that Sip-

pio's errand would probably be his last. Alatheus would have to fend for himself soon with Sippio gone.

He wiped his forehead of sweat, lowered the brim of his hat, and stared into the blue of the harbor. Another ship had passed the pharos. The oars worked spasmodically, out of rhythm, as if the men were inexperienced or weary from something that had delayed their land-fall.

He fingered the hilt of the sword. The ship was a windwhipper. It could be. This could be him. He would know soon enough. Tratraig had orders to send a man to the inn as soon as Breks was seen. Alatheus wondered if he should let Tratraig use his sliver-heart on Breks when the time came. Perhaps an eye. No more. The final cut will be mine, he thought.

"Amala," he whispered as he followed the ship's progress toward the quays. "I think our spider has just drifted into harbor."

Chapter Twenty-four

The Falcata

Falca had seen the sign of the weapons shop as he hunted along the quay for a buyer for the ship. Within an hour he was in the shop, his share of the prize money in hand, ready to keep a long-held promise. Ballast and Frikko waited for him by the water-clock tower down the way.

He had a desperate thirst and hunger—the last few days at sea were nothing more than hard biscuits and stale water. But the sweet Gebroanan wine, roast fowl, and fresh bread he could smell could wait. He had to make sure he had enough of these six-sided Geroanan splendents to buy the falcata.

"Let's see your shine," the merchant said, yawning, expecting little. After the voyage from the Ebony Isles, Falca looked more like a begger than a buyer. He spread his offer on the nicked counter, surprising the merchant, who grunted and turned to decide which of the swords Falca could have for the price. He scratched the stump of his left arm, surveying all the swords that hung from pegs by their hilts.

Falca had his eye on a beauty, a falcata with a gold snake-head hilt and silver inlay, but he wasn't too disappointed when the merchant brought another down for him to look at.

To afford the snake-head, Falca would have had to accept the actor's offer to buy not only the ship but the crew as well. They had all remained on board, to ensure possession of the prize. If Falca hesitated, it was only because any one of the crew would have accepted the buyer's offer, had one been in Falca's place. They would have loved to see him sold as a slave. He might have saved them from Grippa, but he had killed a man because of a mere Timberlimb and also insisted on five shares of the coming prize money to their one each. He also insisted on a share for Frikko, a demand for which he had almost come to blows with the friend of the sailor who tried to rape her.

Thinking Falca reluctant to sell men he assumed were friends, the factor amended, "Just the stoneskin, then, and that other thing, whatever it is, up in the rigging."

Falca shook his head and took his money for the ship.

The falcata he bought had no inlay or hilt design. It was just a standard issue that some Gebroanan soldier had sold for a week's worth of ale or whores after the Myrcian war. But it hadn't a streak of rust on it. And it was a thing to marvel at. No straight sword of Lucidorean or Myrcian design could match it. Falca's father had always said that the falcata had made the difference in the war.

The long, slightly curved sword was single-edged for half its length; the remainder of the blade was double-edged and tapered to a sharp point. The single-edged section had a thick, heavy back, useful for cut and thrust. The hilt was forged as one piece with the blade and it curved around and back toward the blade to protect the hand. The scabbard was leather, with darker brown splotches from dried blood, and could be suspended by rings from a waist belt. Falca had to pay extra for that, along with a whetstone. He smiled. Ballast could use that to scrape himself until he found a greyla to renew his roughy. Somewhere in this city there would be one.

He stood outside the shop, underneath the point of the dangling swordsign, the sun hot in his face. He buckled the belt and drew out the falcata. The hilt was cool, comfortable, though his hand was blistered and sore from all the hours at the oar bench. He marveled at the falcata's balance. He had held no finer thing in his hand. No wonder his father had been obsessed with these Gebroanan swords.

Falca could have bought or stolen a falcata in Draica from any number of drunken Gebroanan sailors over the years. It wouldn't have been the same, though. The one he'd used on the *Tyryns* had been for the boy. Falca had promised himself only one when he got to Gebroan.

Maybe it was the weight of the sword, but he felt he could sense his father's presence now, somewhere in this sun-baked city of stone, whose heart was at once speared and nurtured by the aqueduct coming down from the mountains to the east. His father would be old. He would have had many years now to forget all about the sons he'd abandoned for the dream of Gebroan, the dream Falca adopted as his own. But he was alive, Falca was sure of that. He remembered his father's physical strength, strong hands, the quick mind that could shift so easily from humor to anger. As a man who could laugh so easily, he chided his boy for dourness. "What do you expect?" Falca had always wanted to tell him. For just when he was ready to laugh with his father, the anger would come quickly over a trifle, quick as a mist on a mirror. Falca learned to trust only the unpredictability of his father's mood.

Unencumbered by his sons, his wife, Barla Breks would have prospered here. Falca wouldn't have been surprised to find out he owned one of the villas he saw from the ship coming in. Perhaps that beauty nearest the pharos on the ridge that shielded the harbor from the sea. Whichever, it would face the harbor and this crammed city, its back to the ocean and far Draica. There would be girls to keep him young.

Given enough time, Falca was sure he could find the old man. But Falca didn't have the time, not now. Perhaps, after this was all over, he would come back for that confrontation with Barla Breks. Now he couldn't risk more than a day in Sandsend, where once he wanted to finish out his life in the sweet stupor of wine and women he, too, had promised himself. There was the aqueduct road to take out of the city, into the Crumples Mountains, where the road ended at the lake that gave this city its life.

Beyond stretched the desert, where Saphrax said the Spirit-Lifters' Crucible lay, whatever it was. The manifestation of their god? Where Amala would be. Falca didn't know what route Saphrax and the Lifters took to reach the heart of their corruption. He was certain, however, that it wasn't through this city. The Lifters only stole from the crowded pens of the western kingdoms, but the predators didn't linger to be seen or caged themselves. Falca expected to see empties, evidence of their hunting here, but not Saphrax and Amala's mace, or the Prism of Empathy. They could hardly haul Roak's stolen gift through the streets of Sandsend.

Falca gripped the hilt of the falcata tightly as he threaded his way along the busy harborside toward Ballast and Frikko. The scabbard tapped at his left leg. It felt good, this weight, the residue of all the years of dreaming. He couldn't hear the jangle of the scabbard rings as he walked—the bustle of the quay was too great—but he knew the music was there. He felt more confident about his coming intrusion into the Lifters' desert lair carrying the sweet edge of his falcata.

As Falca, Ballast, and Frikko headed for the central gateway to the city, the Timberlimb stopped so suddenly that Falca stumbled into her. She wouldn't move. She was staring at a man leaning against a sun-bleached fresco of the archway. He was staring back, working his teeth with a metal toothpick. His fingernails were sharp as dagger points.

He turned to disappear into the crowd flowing through the way, just as Frikko flung a chunk of paving stone surprisingly hard at him. It missed, hit a woman in the back instead, who whirled angrily. To Falca's astonishment, Frikko took off after the man, and Falca had to hurry to stop her. He could feel the tenseness, the anger in her shoulder.

"The bastard was watching her, waiting for the moment to snatch her," Falca said. "That's two now who've wanted her—the factor and this scut—and we haven't hit noon yet. Enough is enough, Ballast. We have to keep a closer eye on her."

The stoneskin nodded. "No fault of hers, but the little mottle draws trouble like a sponge to water. Was it this sun poaching my eyes, or did that roaking have a toothpick long as my hand-spread?"

"It wasn't a toothpick," Falca said, as they continued through the archway. "In Draica they're called sliver-hearts. The footpads like them because they're cheap and effective, and the women because they can be easily hidden in a sleeve catch until they're needed. Amala had one."

"She ever use it?"

"Once, that I know of," Falca said, thinking back to the first day he saw her. "A good strike, but not good enough."

Chapter Twenty-five

Barla Breks

The sweet wine they bought put Falca in a better mood. It was called leg-up, and every vendor they'd passed served it in rounded earthenware chalices the size of a large pear. Falca finally asked one of them why this was so. The vendor shrugged. It was the custom going back to his grandfather's time, he said, to Queen Hyrie, King Naavan's second wife. The first died tragically young, and the king made a cast of her breasts and then two gold chalices from the cast, so that he could drink his wine and remember. Queen Hyrie was jealous of the first, so when the king died, she ordered that every drinking vessel in the kingdom be made from those casts. In her words: "So that all the citizens of Gebroan may suck at her breasts, like the harlot she was."

It was, Falca thought, typically Gebroanan.

They stopped in front of a baker's shop, after Falca announced he was still hungry.

"You're what?" Ballast said, shifting his load of clothes and new boots to his other arm. "By the sweet Caves, Falca, you ate more of those sausages and bread than me and Frikko together. You eat more and you're going to have to go back to that clothes-man for bigger boots and tunic."

"So I've got a sweet tooth."

"You got a worm in you, is what."

"Here," Falca said, grinning, and dumped his purchases on top of

Ballast's. Of course he wasn't hungry at all. Mix all the food they'd eaten at half a dozen places along this tree-lined avenue with the heat and leg-up and he could have slept for a week. He felt like satisfying a different sort of appetite. Through the open window of the shop he had seen the design of a phallus, scorched on its lower portions over the oven door inside. Falca could almost hear Amala laughing: "Draican bakers could use that inspiration, Falca, to make their breads rise as well."

He came back with four honey cakes. He offered one to Frikko, who smelled it with disinterest and pushed it away to resume her perusal of the passersby along the thoroughfare.

"She's still looking for Sliver-heart," Falca said. "You want hers?"

"Well, since you bought them," Ballast said, and put down his load. He didn't ask who the fourth was for, and Falca tossed it to the boldest of the harbor gulls nearby, thinking of Amala.

"So where're we going to put these on?" Ballast said, picking up the bundle of clothes and his boots. "You'd have thought the clothesman would've had a place for his customers."

"I'm listening to a man who's spent years in barracks, pissed on campfires and off Grippa's wall-walk? There's your privacy—shade's all you get, and precious little of that, under those trees by the watercourse, across the way."

"You pointing where that jack is selling more of those winged pricks?" Ballast scratched a coin-sized flake of skin off his arm. "I never seen the like of those things and I've been sober in three of the Six Kingdoms."

No sooner had Frikko changed into the child's smock Falca had bought her than she jumped into the water channel that extended all the way up to the aqueduct square in the distance. She splashed Falca and Ballast, who were sitting on the trough edge, lacing their new half-boots.

"Now, why didn't she do that before she put the new clothes on?" Ballast said.

"Maybe she wants the wet to last longer on her," Falca said, softening the stiff felt of his new hat. "Where she comes from, she's got more shade and rain than sun." He noticed that the red color of the smock was bleeding, staining the water. "Frikko, get out of there," he said, gesturing.

"You're getting superstitious, Falca," Ballast said.

It was even worse when Frikko got out to stand on the trough edge, for once taller than the sitting Falca. The dye dripped down her legs and began pooling at her feet. Falca couldn't stand it and began wiping the red off with his old clothes.

Ballast suddenly slapped his shoulder with his hat and pointed at a man approaching. He wore nothing but a loincloth, sandals, and a bell that jingled on his right ankle. Behind him, a canopied litter of yellow and maroon diverted the steady flow of pedestrians. The woman lounging in the litter turned slightly for Falca's benefit. She wore the typical cutaway gown that cupped and shaped her breasts. She gazed at Falca as she played with her dark, tightly woven braids, issuing an invitation to him even before her man did so.

Falca smiled, not at her, though she was comely enough, but at the yawn of her second man, who squatted behind the rear thrusting rails of the litter, bored with his mistress's frequent habit.

The jingling of the slave's bell stopped. Before the man could open his mouth, Ballast waved him away.

"Not you," the slave said.

"I *know* she's not interested in me. You think I don't have eyes? He"—Ballast jerked a thumb at Falca—"isn't interested."

The slave looked at Falca, who shook his head.

"I see," the slave sneered, and left.

"No, and it isn't *that* either," Ballast shouted after him, half-rising from his perch.

"I can do my own talking, Ballast," Falca said. He watched the lady shrug away her rejection and order the litter onward.

"You got yours," Ballast grumbled, scratching himself. "Well, half of her anyway. I'm only looking after you."

"I'll let you know when I need your help, like I did on the island."

"Look, it's just that you told me on the ship how you always wanted to come here to rut away in the sun till you couldn't lift your lumber anymore. I'm not going to let you dribble it away until you get the other thing done. Leastways so long as I'm with you."

"And how long's that going to be?"

"Until the square, where I strike off and find what *I* have to find. You're stuck with me till the square. Someone could try to snatch Frikko again, or you could turn another head."

Frikko, who had watched it all with a tiny hand on Falca's shoulder, hopped off the low wall, as if signaling them to get going.

"And when I'm not around to keep you straight, she will be,"

Ballast said, nodding at the impatient Timberlimb.

"Enough," Falca said. "You've made your point." He slid off the water wall. Who was it, he tried to remember, who once told him that only a friend has the right not to trust you? His father? No, of course not. Amala. It had to have been Amala. Well, he had no intention of going with the woman. Why had Ballast thought he might? It was like that time on the island, when he had the mace. Ballast and Frikko had acted so strangely. . . .

They saw the litter by the vendor who was hawking the winged phalluses, holding them up like strings of sausages. He fanned out the iridescent wings—easily three feet across—for display, then stroked the long, slender body. Falca saw the thing's hooded eyes blink lazily, the eyes of river eels.

The woman's slave bought one of the large ones, and the vendor put it in a wicker cage. As Falca passed the litter, the lady glanced at him ruefully, as if he'd disappointed her. He was close enough to see the moisture between her breasts, smell the sweet but sharp fragrance of perfume: elixith and something else. She had the tiniest of tattoos in the same place Amala once had the leechstone: a stretching cat.

Falca suddenly had the urge to walk the few steps to her and give her what she wanted, in front of all these people. He was startled by the power of his desire. Maybe it was the heat. He wanted to brush the useless if beautiful wings of that living phallus over her thighs, toss it away, and ride into her, the carriage to her gate. He wouldn't take long; he had to move on, after all. She might even pay him. Amala paid him, hadn't she? No, that had been to keep him from fisting her Limbs. He would have done it with this woman if not for Ballast and Frikko.

He walked on, resentful of them, and even of his self-imposed purpose of going into the desert to recover something as formless as light in a lantern. Long before Amala, he'd had his dream of coming to Gebroan for the reward of so many years of watching over his shoulder, putting up with ditch-lickers like Saphrax and Venar, of work that could have killed him any minute. Now he was walking away from the first of that reward he'd promised himself, from something not formless but of flesh and blood and a desire he ached to match. And what was he walking away toward? Probably his death. At the very least failure. All Saphrax had to do was drop Amala's mace and it would shatter as easily as glass.

It all seemed so foolish. For a man who had stayed alive in one of
ie roughest parts of any kingdom by not taking risks, the desert
:emed foolish beyond measure.

Besides that, he told himself, wasn't there an appeal to letting
.mala lie safely in memory, remembering her as she was, that time of
:e outside and the warmth of the hearth and her body inside—with-
ut running the risk, the futility of storming the Lifters' stronghold?
Vherever it was. It could be anywhere in the desert. And really, what
vould happen? He might die there in the attempt. Or if he succeeded
nd brought Amala whole again, who could say he'd be happier?

He loved her; he couldn't hide that from himself. But did he have
> run the risk of her devouring that offering as she had devoured the
og that meant so much to her? She might hate him, hold him respon-
ible for what had happened to her. She had every right to do so.
aphrax had been his man, as surely as Sippio had been hers. Likely
he would sink back to her brother, the safe, constant thing.

Why risk anything else? And maybe she would be crippled in
ome way, not quite whole, even though he might be successful in
ringing back her mace. So that to love her, he would have to nurse
er constantly, the good memories eroding week by week, month by
1onth, till he came to hate her.

As suddenly as these thoughts, came a self-loathing. No, the best
eason for not going into the desert was that he simply wasn't worthy
f her. How easily his purpose had been deflected by an idle if beauti-
ul woman who would just as soon substitute a winged phallus for a
1an. He was a street beast as much as that thing. How did she know
hat? Did it ooze from his skin?

He spit with disgust at himself, unworthy of the superb falcata
lapping his leg as he walked, unworthy of his companions' loyalty.
Ie felt like walking away. They were right to have their doubts about
im. It didn't matter if Frikko didn't have the words to tell him. She
aid more with her eyes and gestures than most people with their
lapping mouths. And it was a relief to know that Ballast would soon
·e leaving: one less witness to failure. He had gotten them off the
sles, to be sure, but he felt now he had come to the end of his limits.
Amala would never know the difference if he walked away into Ge-
·roan, letting the sun gradually darken his skin to a disguise.

Falca heard laughter that stopped him as surely as if he'd run into
ι wall. It was a laugh he could never forget, having heard it last when

he was a boy. The laughter came again, off to the right of Balla
ahead, deep and powerful. Falca searched more closely, trying t
pinpoint it among all the people around.

His eyesight, upon which he had relied so much for his surviva
didn't fail him this time either. He saw two men. One was his fathe
Beyond, Sliver-heart, who looked startled, since there was no reaso
why Falca would have suddenly looked sharply to his right. Th
watcher hurried away. And Falca stared at his father, who laughed b
a stand of vegetables and fruits with a woman half his age.

A driver cursed Falca, swerving his team and wagon around hi
and blocking Ballast and Frikko from view. They had kept on, think
ing Falca right behind.

His hands began to shake, and within the time of a dozen hear
beats, he knew two things: Amala's brother was in Sandsend. Slive
heart could only be a watcher, and there was only one explanation fo
that. Frikko was nowhere near. He wasn't after her. Sliver-heart wa
watching him, as he had been by the city gate. Frikko had known i
sensed the malevolence. Alatheus was waiting for him somewhere
and Sippio too, no doubt.

And there was his father, no more than a canal-boat length away,
falcata at his side.

Falca took a step closer, staring at his father's profile, hearing th
laugh again as Barla Breks picked up a melon and compared it to th
young woman's breasts. Her smile couldn't quite cover her embar
rassment. It was something his father would do, Falca thought, jus
like bringing home a woman a week after his wife died.

He drifted in time, pushed, shouldered, and cursed at by thes
strange, bronzed Gebroanans, whose way he blocked. Someon
called him a drunk, another an empty. . . .

After his mother had died, there had been a string of them
some hardly older than his oldest brother Varro, who had his fa
ther's blue eyes. Falca remembered the look his father gave Varr
then, a mixture of defiance and wariness, as if his eldest son was
potential rival for the girl. Falca listened to his father all thos
nights, with only a woolen sheet between him, his girls, and hi
sons, and always Falca wished in the morning that he'd falle
asleep like his brothers.

Phalen Breks would taunt and castigate his brother about hi
needs, but the only time he and Phalen came to blows was whe
Phalen rudely pushed Falca for some trifle—a word or a look. An

Barla Breks rose to such a fury that Varro had to pull him off Phalen, lest he kill him.

Barla Breks now moved down the display of fruits, pausing the way the women had paused to choose among the babies abandoned underneath the water-clock. Barla's hands were smaller than Falca remembered, but he thought it was the perspective of years. Barla's gray hair was long, in defiance of the Gebroanan style, nor did he wear a hat.

Falca walked closer to his father, who had left the long stand without buying anything. Falca's fist sweated as he clenched and un-clenched, getting ready. He tried to calm his heart so that whatever words he could manage would be said forcefully, clearly, without all the years clogging his throat, thickening his tongue.

He couldn't help rushing the last steps. Barla must have heard or sensed his approach, for he turned just as Falca was about to lay a hand on the square shoulder.

His eyes were not blue, but black, and the first thing Falca thought of as the man knocked away his hand was how the Gebroanan sun could have ruined, darkened, his father's eyes.

Falca backed away from his anger, trying to ask the question. The other's hand hesitated on the silver hilt of the falcata. "Get away from us, you ditch-licker. Go on with you!"

Falca couldn't move, couldn't leave.

"What is he waiting for?" the young woman asked.

"Roak only knows."

Falca didn't know. He was waiting for the eyes to change, for a sign of recognition, of softening. Anything. He blinked his eyes, striving for a focus he knew would never come.

"Why, Rhodri, I do believe he's crying," the woman said, as if she'd just seen a dog do a trick. She giggled. "Oh, give him a splen-dent, Rhodri. That's all he wants. That's what he's waiting for."

Rhodri shook his head. "Not from the look of his clothes and stiff boots and that falcata, unless beggars are different here than in Myr-ia. Whatever he wants, it's not money. Come, Jezza."

They left. The man, Rhodri, looked back once, his eyes still dark, judging Falca not as a street threat anymore but as a fool.

Falca still stood at the end of the produce stalls. People glanced at him quizzically. He scarcely heard the vendor grumble, "You! You here! Move on with your weeping if you're not going to buy."

He moved, thinking of Sorelip and Saphrax and Amala's words:

"You seem plagued by people who won't stay dead."

He knew now his father was dead. He had died twice. Once long ago and just now. He knew he could spend the next twenty years searching the long length and narrow breadth of Gebroan and never find him. Barla Breks had never made it to Gebroan, he'd never abandoned his sons except through a careless death that his brother, Phalen, had sought to profit from.

What sort of choice had there been for a boy? To accept either that your father was alive, though free of his sons in a place to which he'd always talked about going, or that he was dead in some tavern, his throat cut from behind in a dispute that had gotten out of hand. Even now Falca wanted to believe that his father was alive, but he knew better. It was time to know better.

He walked listlessly down the sweet-smelling stand of fruits, the vendors' strident hawking filling his ears.

His eyes were so keen, how could they have deceived him yet again? He wondered if he had imagined the threat of Sliver-heart. No. That was real, confirmed earlier by Ballast and Frikko. Alatheus *was* here. And Falca's father had saved him. If he hadn't heard, sought out, the laughter he remembered so well, he wouldn't have seen the scut.

He had been saved by a plaything of Barla Breks'. Gebroan had been his ale-dream, to be forgotten in the morning with a girl and the following days until his restlessness fermented yet again. Falca never forgot. Barla's Gebroan had been the boss to the son's shield, the iron center to cracked leather and splintered wood. In a way Barla had brought Amala to Falca.

His father hadn't known what he was doing, but then father didn't, couldn't know what their sons chose to remember. He thought about the boy and his father on the *Tyryns*. How could the father have known that his weaknesses would forge a boy of such remarkable strength and courage? No, Falca's father had no design other than getting drunk and spilling his seed into the loins of other men's daughters.

Still, sons fashion their fathers' lives after the fact, as much as the fathers do their own. Even if the boy on the *Tyryns* hadn't witnessed his father's last heroism, he might have changed that day. A son was allowed to tamper with the little deaths that comprised memory, wasn't he? Falca had earned that right, hadn't he? Maybe Barla had earned, so long after his death, the right for his son's forgiveness.

The smell of the fruit drew Falca closer. He'd never seen such an
ay, not in Draica. Another vendor looked hopefully at him, sug-
sted the red-bellies. Falca took one in his hand, pressed a thumb for
ripe softness, and, within, heard his father say,

"I named you after the best-crafted sword in the Six Kingdoms,
lca. The streets didn't get you because I gave you Gebroan, and
n sorry it took till now for you to find out that was the only way I
uld tell you that I loved you. That's a short-pole, as our Draican
nalers would say, but . . . Look, I know I'm not one to give advice.
t a man can't do everything for his son. A man should leave the
ighest part for his boy after giving him a nudge. Otherwise, he'll
n out to be no more than the dock bollard for other men's hawsers.

"Keep after the woman, Falca. She's no short-pole, no, by Roak
e isn't. The bastards have riven her from what she truly is. Most
nes we don't need people to do that to us. We're cursed with the
ent, most of us, for doing it to ourselves. I did it myself, but that's
ne, and you'll have to live with it. See, we're all at *least* two kinds
people, and the trick, as I see it, is to walk as the one you would
e the best, not necessarily the one you *know* the best. You won't do
at by staying here in Gebroan, which is only the means, by Roak,
t the end.

"I know you love her, Falca. I loved your mother, though it's true,
r memory wasn't enough for me after she died. I suspect your
nala loves you too. But make no mistake. She isn't the one waiting
r you at the end of this. You are."

Falca took a bite out of the melon, tasting its coolness and tart
etness.

Someone shouted to him, behind. "You can't walk away without
ying for that!"

He turned, realized what he'd done, and smiled at the vendor's
ger. He walked back and paid the man, then placed the red-belly on
p of the display. "I can't sell that now," the vendor complained, and
ssed it away.

Falca shrugged. "I paid for it. One bite was all I wanted."

He saw Ballast up ahead, looking for him. Likely he had Frikko
v the hand, keeping her close. Falca couldn't see for all the people.
therwise, her sense of smell would have led Ballast to him by now.

Falca turned and walked back the way they had come, keeping to
e thickest clots of pedestrians, using carts and wagons, the litters of

the well-to-do, as shields. It felt odd avoiding his friends, as if the
and not the others, were his enemies. But he had to confront Alathe
by himself. It wasn't Ballast's problem or Frikko's. Likely, in t
coming rip-up, they would be hurt or killed. If Ballast was hurt, ho
would he get his roughy back from some Sandsend greyla far fro
the High Vales?

Falca knew that if he told them of what was going to happe
Ballast would insist on helping. Frikko, too, without words. She
known all along. Her prescience was remarkable and unsettling. Pe
ple regarded her as little more than a pet, an oddity. Falca knew sl
was leading as much as being led. She had her own purpose, a
maybe someday he'd find out what it was.

If he survived Alatheus, he'd find Ballast and Frikko of cours
and bid a proper goodbye. If not, the stoneskin would take care of t
Timberlimb. Or was it the other way around? Falca smiled.

He crossed over to the other side of the watercourse and heade
up toward the square. Over the heads of the passersby he could s
the white tongues of the aqueduct road spilling into the great circl
He'd keep walking until they came for him. He would let the
choose the place. The odds weren't as bad as they could be, he d
cided. Sliver-heart probably knew that Falca suspected somethin
Human nature being what it was, however, he wouldn't tell Alathe
and admit he'd botched his job. Falca would be ready for them. Ho
many? At least three, possibly more. It would be hard not to tak
Alatheus first, go for the head of the beast. But he'd take a few of t
others, Sippio certainly, and hope for a moment to shout sense in
the brother, so at least he could truthfully tell Amala he tried to e
plain what really happened. Futile and very dangerous. The ma
hadn't come all this way to be reasoned with. Still, he vowed he'd t
before Alatheus closed on him and thus sealed his miserable fate.

Falca felt confident, though he would be outnumbered, though b
sword hand was still red and tender from the oars. Maybe if he hadn
worn gloves all those years in Draica, his hands would have bee
tougher. Sore or not, they would have to do.

The falcata slapped his leg as he walked, his eyes working th
crowds as if for a mark. This time, he was it.

Chapter Twenty-six

The Aqueduct Road

A dozen stone turtles supported the roof of the fountain pool at the terminus of the aqueduct. Since each turtle was much larger than life-size, the gap between pool rim and roof allowed Sandsenders to draw water with buckets. Falca paused in his walk around the pool. He dipped a hand over the rim and looked up, past the splashes and play of the children and thirsty elders, at the men following him. They still had not closed on the pool, but they had seen Falca go around it, presumably heading for the road.

As Falca sucked two mouthfuls of cold water from his cupped hand, he saw how badly he was outnumbered. There were seven others beside Alatheus, Sippio, and Sliver-heart. They walked boldly as a group, not bothering to split up to go around the fountain pool so that Falca couldn't elude them. Sliver-heart hadn't told Alatheus a thing, Falca guessed. They were confident he didn't know he was being followed.

Even as Falca hurried away from the pool, he thought of confronting them in the square, perhaps with his back against the statue up ahead that parted the road traffic. There were hundreds of people around; that could work to his advantage. He decided to let them have the aqueduct road, probably Alatheus' chosen place: the straight line from which there was but one way to escape. With nine men, Alatheus could run down his prey if need be. That dimension might be useful to Alatheus, but another was crucial for Falca. Throw a man down on the square and he gets up and attacks again. Shoulder a man off the aqueduct road and he falls to his death. Or her death. There was a woman, as burly as any of them, among the nine.

Falca walked quickly past the statue of some kneeling Gebroanan monarch, eager to attain the height of the aqueduct road, which served as the lid to the aqueduct channels themselves. From the fountain square, the road rose gradually to the city walls and leveled off just after crossing the battlements. Its width shrunk from three wagons' worth to two where the twin branches of the aqueduct veered off at an angle, to empty their flow into the reservoir towers within the city below.

The foot traffic was light on the road, interspersed with the occasional carter, dray wagon, and litter. The wall to either side was waist high, a useful height, Falca thought. It was covered here and there with scribblings and crude drawings. He could read none of it, but a drawing done in charcoal caught his eye: the Prism? over a much larger, cresset-shaped object. The Lifters' Crucible?

He went on. He didn't want to risk looking directly back, but he had to know how far away they were. He seized the diversion of a family, obviously moving to the city, their creaking wagon piled high, pulled by a scrawny horse.

"What is the weather like today, my friend?" Falca asked the father.

"What? Are you blind? See for yourself," the man replied, his eyes narrowing under the wide brim of his hat. Falca did just that, out of the corner of his eye. Alatheus was coming all right, fourth in line, next to the woman, not a stone's throw down the road. Sliver-heart looked an eager first.

Falca thanked the man. "My pleasure," the father said, and as Falca walked away, he heard him mutter to his wife, "Will they all be as crazy as that one?"

Falca's senses were so edged, he could feel the sluicing water in the aqueduct channel below the road. He slowed, as if savoring the view from the height. The narrow Gebroanan plain rose to the foothills of the Crumples.

His pursuers were so close. He guessed that some of Alatheus' men would rush past him, to cut off his expected flight, to surround him on the narrow road. He moved closer to the left-hand wall, so that they would have but one lane to run past.

He felt their approach in the worn stone beneath his feet, then eard the quick tread of boots. He waited, time now a matter of breaths. When he heard theirs, he whirled sharply to his right, though n control, keeping low, his weight forward. He rammed Sliver-heart ust below the waist, lifting him over the wall, braking himself with is knees.

The second man was so startled or daunted by Sliver-heart's sudlen departure that he swung his sword weakly. Falca sidestepped, larted inside, grabbed the man's loose tunic, and hurled him back gainst the other wall, catching Alatheus' shoulder and spinning him way. Falca lunged, gripped the ankles of the man who foolishly icked out in desperation and hastened his topple over the road wall.

Falca turned with the scream, in time to face Alatheus closing on im. He swung his sword viciously, but Falca ducked under the whisling strike and scuttled away on all fours, his boot slipping once on he dropped sliver-heart. He drew his falcata as he rose, and that topped the charge of a third Gebroanan.

"Call them off, Alatheus!" Falca roared. "Or you'll never get Amala back. I'm not the one you want, but I'll tell you who is!"

"Get him!" Alatheus screamed back. When no one dared move irst, he pushed the nearest man at Falca. Committed against his will, e swing his sword clumsily, and Falca countered it easily with his alcata, coming up underneath, into the man's stomach. Even before ²alca could withdraw, Sippio bulled through Alatheus' reluctant hirelings to cut off Falca from retreat, which, in any case, was blocked by handful of frightened travelers.

Falca backed away to the wall. They came at him then, stepping ver their dying companion. Falca swung at the nearest, then parried thrust from Sippio, then back again at the first, slicing deeply into he upper arm. But as he brought the falcata back again at Sippio, the voman swung a cudgel down on the falcata, connecting near the hilt. The sword skewed away toward Alatheus' boots. As Falca lunged for t, oblivious of Alatheus' sword, Sippio tripped him up with a swipe t the ankles, and he careened into the wall past Alatheus and a sword trike that sparked metal to stone. The force of the collision thrust his rms over the top, and in that instant before Alatheus yanked him ack by the hair to a nest of swords, Falca saw his falcata shine in the un as it cut the air, falling.

"Why'd you do that?" shouted the woman at Sippio. "I deserved t. I got him."

"Get it later," the gillie yelled back. "After he's dead."

"Shut up both of you," Alatheus said. "You'll each get a chance to do whatever you want to the bastard. I don't care what, so long as you don't kill him before I get to him. Anyone does gets thrown over the wall. Sippio, you're first."

The gillie stepped forward, hefting his sword for a better grip, his grin showing gaps in his teeth. "Wait," Alatheus said, his hand moving to Sippio's thick forearm. "Wait till they pass."

The Gebroanans hurried by, taking fearful glances at Falca. A dog sniffed the boot heels of the ditch-licker Falca stabbed in the stomach. He was groaning.

"Toss him over the wall," Alatheus ordered. "Get him out of the way."

"He ain't dead yet," the woman protested.

"He's your friend, Brissa. It's a quicker mercy."

As they were doing it, Falca's mind raced. He knew he had only moments. He had to talk, say anything. Drive a wedge. Hadn't Amala said that Sippio and Alatheus disliked each other? Could he use that? Drive the wedge between them as he had with the Lifter and Grippa. With what? Where was the weapon?

Sippio put a boot heel on Falca's forehead, driving his skull into the road. Through eyes squinting with pain, he saw nothing but the pleasure of hate in those small eyes. "How does it feel?" Sippio whispered. "You put something to her forehead, too, didn't you, scut?"

The boot heel was a vise, and Falca couldn't even move his head to indicate no. He managed to croak out the words, "You loved her very much, didn't you?"

The gillie looked like he'd been stunned with Brissa's thick cudgel. Falca felt the crushing weight of his boot lessen. He'd found a weapon. . . . It was probably the only time Sippio's love for Amala had been acknowledged.

Falca spoke quickly. "I love her as you do, Sippio. There's still a chance to bring her back. Only I can do it." He could smell the boot leather, the stink of Sippio's feet.

"Sippio," Alatheus said. "Take out his tongue for spewing such nonsense."

The boot came off Falca's forehead when Sippio whirled and shouted, "No, *you* shut up for once. It's *not* nonsense."

Even as Sippio glared at the surprised Alatheus, Falca spoke rapidly.

"I had no more desire to hurt her than you, Sippio. The one who
d hurt her was named Saphrax. The size of a small horse. You saw
s mangled nose, the earring. You know who I'm talking about. You
w him when you followed me for Amala."

Falca's hands were sweating.

"Enough of this, Sippio," Alatheus said and tried to shove him
vay from Falca. Sippio was a rock and wouldn't be moved. "No,"
: said. "It's my turn. You said we could do whatever we want to
m. Maybe I want to listen to what he has to say before I cut him."

"Come on, toad," Brissa yelled. "We were hired to kill this Lucie,
t jabber with him."

"You shut up," Sippio said, and whirled with his sword, nicking a
linter out of Brissa's cudgel. She would have struck him if another
an had not stepped in front: "No fighting. It's what he wants.
latheus, get your man to hurry up. I want my money."

Alatheus, aware that Sippio's instability could quickly unravel
ings, tried a placating tone: "Listen, he's only telling lies to save
mself."

"Not lies, the truth," Falca said hurriedly. "I came to Gebroan to
t her back from the Lifters. I found out how to do it at Grippa's
land after the pirate Mangles captured the ship I was on."

Sippio grunted, sword ready in his hand. "He *was* late in getting
re, Alatheus. We waited a long time."

"He's lied enough, I tell you! Now let's be done with this and go
me." Others grumbled their assent.

Sippio shook his head and pricked Falca's neck with his sword.
Keep talking." Falca didn't need the urging.

"The Lifters—Saphrax is one of them—take the maces, the
ings they fill with the souls, into the desert somewhere. Amala's
ace will be in the desert, at a place called the Crucible. That's where
was going—"

"You knew we were coming," Alatheus said harshly. "You were
nning away. You were working for this Saphrax."

Falca forced a laugh. "Running away? Into the desert? There are
ore pleasurable and profitable places to hide than the desert. You
ink I'm with the bastards, sold Amala's soul to them? Do you see
n me any profit? You kill me now, Alatheus, and you'll never get her
ack. Nor will I," he added, defiantly.

Sippio turned to Alatheus. "What've we got to lose by letting him go? If he's telling the truth, fine. If he dies in the attempt, I won't shed a tear. If he's lying, we'll find him again and kill him."

"You can't let him go," Brissa shouted. "He's killed three of ours."

"He's not going anywhere," Alatheus said. "He's talked long enough. I'm sick of his lies."

"What?" Sippio said, wide-eyed. "Are you crazy? If there's even a small chance to get Amala back, we should try."

Falca broke in with all the contempt he could muster, lying flat on his back. "I'm not sure you want that, Alatheus. The three of us—you, Sippio, and I—have come a long way because we love Amala. Only *you* don't want her back the way she was. Because if that happened, you'd lose her again, wouldn't you? You want her to stay just as she is, an empty. If she can't speak, has no will, she can't say no."

To get at Falca, Alatheus had to go through Sippio, and the gillie was no match for the rage Falca had unleashed in the man. Alatheus shoved Sippio aside so hard that he crashed into the Gebroanan behind him, who tumbled against the road wall. But Alatheus got his free hand cut by the sword Sippio raised to protect himself. Falca had no time to roll away and get to his feet. Alatheus dropped the shaking point of his sword between Falca's eyes. The only thing delaying his death was Alatheus' anger with his gillie. The blood on Damarr's hand only infuriated him more. He struggled for control. "Take his sword," he ordered Brissa, who was only too glad to do so.

Sippio let them have his sword, and Falca closed his eyes. No, he said to himself, and opened them. Alatheus wasn't even looking at him, though the sword point was still a finger's width away from his eyes. Alatheus was shaking and screamed at the rising Sippio.

"I ought to kill you, too, for your betrayal! How dare you, HOW DARE YOU whine so covetously about my love. Who are you to do that, WHO? YOU ARE NOTHING, DO YOU HEAR, NOTHING! I paid you to walk Amala's dog! I won't kill you, fool. You're going to the slave monger's. I should have sold you to him before and this wouldn't have happened."

"That's where you got the extra money," Sippio broke in. "You sold me! We talked and planned, and all the while you'd already sold me as a slave. You . . . YOU dare to talk to *me* of betrayal? You're Amala's real enemy!"

Sippio charged him like a bull, weaponless. Alatheus had only to

ld his ground and let his gillie impale himself on his sword. But
atheus, senseless with a fury equal to Sippio's, closed on him,
ldying an overhand strike that would crumple Sippio to his knees.

The blow never came. Still on his back, Falca did the only thing
could do: whip his legs against Alatheus' ankles and trip him.
atheus stumbled.

Sippio struck his chest so hard that Alatheus lost his footing and
l to his back with such force that Falca heard the gush of breath
m Alatheus' lungs. He lost the sword, which clattered against the
ll. Sippio fought his way through his master's hands, found the
:oat.

Brissa and another kicked Falca for his intervention, and he rolled
vay from the thrashing pair, to the wall, as the Gebroanans tried to
parate them.

Falca tried to get to his feet, but his guard shoved him down. The
ners couldn't loose Sippio's hands from Alatheus' throat. They
lled, pulled. One man crooked an arm around the gillie's neck,
gging it back. Another yanked at his hair, screaming, "Get him off,
t the bastard off our money!"

Alatheus kicked wildly, his face and neck shading darker and
rker. But his ditch-lickers couldn't rip Sippio from him. Even as
ey began hacking at Sippio's hands with daggers and swords, the
llie held on to his killing grip. Blood poured everywhere from Sip-
o's wrists, coating Alatheus' arms, hands. By the time Brissa swung
r cudgel down twice on Sippio's head, it was too late. The gillie fell
vay from Amala's brother with a sigh and convulsions. Brissa
vung a third time to the side of his face. One glazing eye survived
e pulping and stared past Falca. Blood oozed from Sippio's ear.

One of the men kicked him in disgust, causing the blood to spurt
omentarily from Sippio's ear. "Now what do we do? The both of
em are dead. The one who had our money and this one." He kicked
ppio again. "Who could have at least told us where he kept it. And
atraig's dead, who knew where both of them were staying, so we
n't pilfer the load."

Falca's guard waggled his sword, scraping the side of his neck.
Ve oughta do this Lucie. He's the one what caused all this."

"Except Flear don't take dead men, you dolt," Brissa said.
Maybe it ain't too bad. With Tratraig, Dolo, and Lamear dead, we
ould be able to do almost as well selling him."

"I hear Flear ain't buying. Heard he's marking empties."

"Yah, he would. Well, if Flear won't buy this one, we'll t Pliato. He'll fetch a good price from someone. Check Damar pockets, see what he has. What a mess."

A couple of them scuffed through Alatheus' clothing. One held a small leather pouch and shook it.

"It's a start," Brissa said. "Let's get going."

Falca felt his own money in his boots as they prodded him to h feet, shoved him ahead, over the outstretched arm of Sippio. H wrists hung at grotesque angles, the tendons white as worms. Fal had no intention of letting them take him past the square. He wou make his move near the fountain pool, where he had room to run a separate the bastards. They would have to spread out to surround hi on all sides. With only five of them now, they wouldn't be able double up on him. He'd be one man away from his freedom. A they wouldn't be quick with their swords because of his worth at t monger's. Besides, they were stupid. They hadn't even checked hi over for a money pouch. They'd missed, incredibly, the ring th Alatheus wore, smeared, masked as it was with blood.

Brissa had taken Alatheus' sword. "Let's see you go down and g the other, toad," she said to Sippio, kicking him.

Falca was looking forward to depriving her, all of them, of the money. He chanced a look back before a sword point turned hi forward again. Sooner or later someone coming along the road wou dump Sippio's body over the wall to get him out of the way. Ev now, people were stepping over the men, shielding children's ey from the grisly sight.

Sippio deserved better, Falca thought as he trudged down th road. The gillie would have slit Falca's throat as easily as any of t others, but still . . . the man deserved better than to be dumped belo to be picked away at by birds and wolves.

As his captors approached the branching of the aqueduct, Fal saw none other than Ballast and Frikko hurrying up the road. Th Timberlimb was ahead, obviously impatient, and had to stop twice f the lumbering Ballast to catch up. The stoneskin's leg was still bot ering him.

Falca shouted to Ballast and got a cuff to the head as a result.

The stoneskin whipped out his sword, ordered Frikko back, a she had sense enough to obey him once she saw Falca's predicamen

allast hurried along a father and child, then effectively blocked the
ad with his great size. Falca's guards slowed as they formed to the
nt to meet Ballast, leaving one man behind Falca, sword poking
s back. Not insurmountable odds, Falca thought, though there was
mething to try before swords clashed. Ballast's casual scratching at
s leg gave him the idea.

"You don't want to get near him," Falca said loudly to Brissa,
rectly ahead of him, loudly enough for Ballast to hear.

"Shut up."

"It's for your own good. He's diseased. Look at him."

Come on, my friend, Falca urged silently. Pick this up.

After a moment of puzzlement, Ballast did. He rubbed a skein of
in off his neck with an exaggerated motion.

"But please," Falca said, as loudly as ever. "In the name of sweet
oak, don't let him have me." He added a pleading whine to his
ice. "I'm the one that got him into trouble, and he vowed to get me
hen the magistrate ordered him to leave the city."

"Just give me the scut," roared Ballast, "and all of you can pass
e free and clear. I've no quarrel with any of you, only him."

"You called out to him," Brissa said.

"I was alerting you to the bastard," Falca said quickly.

"He's *talking* again," hissed the Gebroanan behind Falca, and
ked with the sword as if to emphasize his skepticism. Falca was
tting tired of the scut doing that, but he held his mask for this
me.

Ballast rubbed a few more shreds of skin into a sizable roll and
uck it on the point of his sword, as if it was a fish ready for the fire.
e advanced a few steps, in tandem with Frikko.

"Get back, you fools!" Falca warned, his boldness with his cap-
rs making the lie all the better. "If that skin touches you, you'll be
ad within the week. There's no cure for the Stoneskin Disease. He
as run out of Helveylyn. . . ."

"I tell you, he's just talking, like he did before!"

Ballast tossed the skin shred at the front men, who recoiled back
to Falca.

"Maybe you're willing to take the chance, Blyre, but I'm not,"
id Brissa. "We have the pouch. It'll have to do. Roak's balls, look
that shale-head!"

"Don't let him have me," Falca whined, clutching at Blyre. He

dropped to his knees, hoping he wasn't overplaying it. He grabbed
Blyre again when the Gebroanan cuffed him in disgust.

"You deserve a slow death. Get away from me!" The guard spa
and turned away, abandoning him.

As soon as Blyre left, Falca bolted away from them all, as muc
to finish out the ruse as get away from the ditch-lickers before any o
them changed their minds. He slowed soon, to let Ballast and Frikk
catch up, and watched the five hurry away down the road.

Ballast and Frikko were grinning ear to ear when they greete
Falca. The Timberlimb wrapped a skinny arm around Falca's leg
then backed away, imitating the cutthroat's reaction to Ballast's dar
gling skin. The stoneskin, hands on his knees, puffed heavy breath
then shook his head at Frikko. "I've never run so much in my life
But she found you all right. Why'd you take off?"

Falca told him everything, except the incident with the man h
thought was his father. That he couldn't explain, even if he wante
to. "Thanks, both of you," he said finally, and gave Frikko a hug.

"Well," Ballast said, "I know you're a good liar, and I suspecte
you could whine, but so convincingly?"

"No, you're the convincing one—and quick."

"Maybe a theater troupe after this is all over," Ballast said, grir
ning.

"I hope you don't mind the inspiration," Falca said.

"Do I look angry?" Ballast's smile lessened but didn't quite disap
pear. "In a way I am diseased, Falca, though it's nothing I'll die o
As a stoneskin with a poor roughy, all I'm good for *is* a theate
troupe."

"Go take care of that. I'll walk with you a ways before I take m
leave, Ballast."

The stoneskin shook his head. "I've thought about it. I hate cover
ing the same territory twice. I'm going on with you, unless you wan
different. Besides, the city back there is no place for a diseased man.

"What about your roughy?"

"It'll keep for a while. So long as Frikko keeps her nose in the a
for danger and you, roaking, keep coming up with ideas to get us ou
of trouble, I can make do with what's fading." He scratched a piece o
skin off and flung it to the wind. "Anyway, you'll never get Amal
without us, me and Frikko."

Falca clasped Ballast's arm and held it long enough to make th
stoneskin embarrassed. "You may be right, my friend."

"Are the bodies up ahead?" Ballast asked. "The brother and the other one?"

"If someone hasn't tossed them over the wall by now."

With Frikko in the middle, Falca and Ballast walked back. Overhead, carrion birds circled.

Chapter Twenty-seven

Amala's Room

Ellele poured the last of the hot bath water and returned th
iron pot to the hearth. She stoked the fire so that the room would b
warmer for Amala when she took her bath. She lingered by the fi
for the sake of her old bones, too. More and more she was feeling th
damp of Draica these days.

Amala sat in a chair, facing the oak tub, close enough to wave
hand back and forth in the steam that rose from the tub. Ellel
watched her bring a finger to her lips, as if to taste the wisps. Whe
Amala got up to step in the tub, Ellele hurried over and gently put h
back in the chair. "No, child, you know how we do it. You have
take off your clothes first. It will feel better that way." Still, Ama
wanted to bathe now, and Ellele had to use more strength to discou
age her. "Your water is still too hot. See?" Ellele dipped a finge
drew it back quickly, and made a face. "We always wait a bit after
pour the water."

Amala slumped back in the chair. Ellele went to the double wi
dows. It was raining hard and the smear and run of the drops again
the panes provided all the privacy one needed. But when a woma
takes a bath, you close the curtains. Before Ellele did so, she rubb
away a circle of mist to see if they were still outside.

They were, four, their small shapes melted by the rain, distort
by imperfections in the glass, though distinct enough to see, squa
ting, facing the bars of the gate from the outside.

Ellele sighed. She and Hallys had given up trying to keep the mberlimbs away from the gate. The disgusting little things were ven away easily enough. Hallys might be old, but he still had ough sinew left from his soldiering days to wield a rod of burl-ght. Yet no sooner would he scatter the mottles and return to the use than they'd come back—usually an older one and three young.

Ellele should have expected they'd be out there in this weather. A lting rain might shrink the size of a king's funeral, but fickleness as one attribute the Timberlimbs evidently didn't have.

She walked back to test the bath water. "Not quite, child." Really, lele told herself, she had to stop calling Amala that. It was dotty ough to talk to her all the time and get no reply of course. She'd erheard the Master and Mistress discussing that eccentricity in dis-proving tones. Amala was no child, though her condition prompted comparison. She was a woman whose beauty had stopped Hallys his creaky tracks the moment he saw her.

On the fourth day, though, Hallys had been shocked when he me in to see Amala masturbating as she stared idly out the window. e didn't know what she was doing really, only that it felt good, as lele told her husband.

They had an argument over it that night. Hallys thought Ellele relict in her duty not to stop Amala from doing that. Ellele told him was none of his business, or hers, for that matter. If it gave Amala a ker of pleasure, so be it. After that, Hallys rarely came into nala's room, contenting himself with the outside work.

No, Amala was no child, but Ellele couldn't keep from calling her at, any more than she could solve the puzzle of the Timberlimbs' rsistence outside the gate.

Hallys said it was their sense of smell. The why was more of a ad scratcher. Ellele hadn't known Amala before, though she had und out soon enough that she once worked at a settlement house t cared for the Limbs. So Amala had been good to them, they were ateful, hence the vigil. But you keep a vigil, you persist, only if ere is hope. How could the Timberlimbs know there was any hope r the child? There was no one to tell them no. They couldn't see r. Once, Ellele was tempted to bring Amala out, let them see her as e was now, even though the Master forbade Ellele from doing so ach as taking Amala for a walk in the garden in good weather. It d seemed to Ellele, however, the only solution to the Timberlimbs' tering.

She had once thought it an embarrassment to this fine neighborhood, easily the best she and Hallys had worked in. Ellele would see
them—all the fine carriages—when she was out in the garden picking winter greens to grace Amala's room. She'd see the pointing
fingers, the faces in the carriage windows, the heads that nodded in
satisfaction. It came to anger Ellele so much that once she threw a
clod of garden soil at a passing phaeton. Hallys saw her and scolded
her, but Ellele wasn't chastened. The child was nothing to be laughed
at. A terrible thing had happened to her. From then on, she felt more
of a kinship with the Timberlimbs, though she still thought they had
some disgusting habits. She never did bring Amala out to discourage
them. Maybe they knew something she didn't know, saw something
she couldn't see.

The water was ready. "Come on, then, child," Ellele said briskly.
"Off with your clothes." Ellele helped her out of the soiled garment
and into the tub. It always bothered her joints when she had to move
Amala or bathe her, for the young woman was bigger than most. She
couldn't trust Amala not to do something like drink the bath water, or
gnaw on the soap, or slip underneath the water. She was so much like
a baby.

It would have been easy to neglect Amala. The brother who'd
hired her and Hallys was away. The parents—Master and Mistress—
rarely came in to see their daughter, though the room was only down
the hall. They wouldn't know if Ellele bathed their daughter once a
week or never. Ellele would. It mattered to her that Amala was clean,
and that required daily bathing. It was a point of pride that she tried to
instill in her own children: Do what is best, not just what is easiest. In
a way, it was like the wonder of Cassena's Chalice, reputedly Roak's
wedding gift to his queen. Ellele had seen it once as a girl when it
was on display, carefully guarded by a dozen stoneskins in Cross
Keys Square on the King's birthday. In order to view it, the guard
tied one's hands.

Ellele had annoyed one guard by asking him to turn it upside
down. She wanted to see every inch. Ellele never forgot the beauty,
the workmanship on the underside of the Chalice—the part of it no
one could see, which meant as much or more to Ellele than the curving sides, open to glory.

Ellele smiled as she soaped Amala down. Hallys was different
from her in that respect, and they'd had their spits and snorts over the

ars about it. He was the one, for all his outward deference to their
ployers, who would sweep the dirt under the rug or put the bread
ck on the trencher after it had fallen to a dirty floor. His barracks
bits, Ellele called them. At least he had learned not to do such
ngs in her presence anymore and risk her wrath.

So Ellele bathed Amala once a day. The child seemed to like it,
ich would have been reason enough. But there was, for Ellele,
other reason, a more private one. She loved to see and feel the
oothness and tautness of Amala's skin. It reminded her of what she
d once had, and that gave her joy in thinking back. It also made her
ittle sad when her hand or arm would rub next to Amala's, and she
uld see the difference, see her own loose, wrinkled skin, the spots.

She knew Amala's body almost as well as her own. The only flaw
e had found—the black mark on the forehead didn't count—was
e scar at the throat, possibly where a leechstone had once been.
sides that, a mark here and there.

Amala was a beauty denied the world, a voice and spirit too, one
at could still command such a strange vigil by the Timberlimbs,
d the parents into seclusion and a devoted brother on a mission of
venge. She fervently hoped he would find the hireling of the Lifters
o did this to Amala and hang him by his heels.

Ellele scrubbed Amala's back, arms, her breasts gently. Amala
red past at the twin portraits of herself and her brother, done when
y were children. As Ellele washed her legs, she had the sudden
tion that Amala's skin would always stay as it was now, that she
uld never grow old. Because what was there to make her old, her
in crinkly and spotted as Ellele's own? She'd see nothing more of
e rigors of the world than this room and a succession of caretakers.
r brother would have his own life to lead. Ellele imagined Amala
uld stay smooth as a silver brush kept as an heirloom in a bottom
awer, never to be scratched, nicked, dropped on the floor, or slid
ross a bureau by a young woman eager for the world, the evening,
a lover.

The waste of it all welled up in Ellele and she stroked Amala's
ad, her golden hair darker now with damp, held it to her bony
oulder till the wetness damped her clothes.

Amala stiffened in Ellele's embrace; her head jerked away from
e old woman's shoulder as if she'd heard something. She gripped
e tub rim, her knuckles whitening.

"What is it, child?" Ellele said, staring in disbelief at this arouse Amala had never done anything like this before. "Do you hear som thing?"

Ellele heard nothing, only the rain, but then, her hearing wasn what it had been.

Amala rose from the rub so quickly, she knocked Ellele off th footstool. She climbed out, dripping water, as if pursued, her ey wide, seeking a distant focus. Ellele was too shocked even to get t immediately, could only stare at this flicker of life.

"What's the matter?" she whispered as Amala took two steps th way, three that, drops of water spraying off her breasts.

The fear in Amala's eyes roused Ellele painfully to her feet, an she hurried to the window. Were the Timberlimbs doing somethin unleashing some long pent-up anger Amala sensed? Ellele quick parted the curtains. No, they were still huddled beyond the gate.

Amala was so agitated, her hands and elbows so active, that Elle was fearful of going near to calm her, lest Amala knock her dow But when Amala began soundlessly mouthing a word, struggling give it life, Ellele went to her, first snatching a robe from a chair.

"Amala, Amala," Ellele soothed. Amala's hand hit Ellele's hea then the fingers went to her mouth, as if she was trying to draw wor from within. Ellele managed to drape the robe around her shoulder though Amala was much the taller, and this finally seemed to qui her. She slumped to the floor, taking Ellele with her, and as Elle rocked her, the tears began streaming down Amala's cheek.

Stricken with wonder, Ellele wiped them away with the edge the robe, to make sure they weren't mere water dripping from th curls of her short hair, her generous eyebrows. The tears poured for as Ellele held her tightly and as Amala tried to speak. "Say it, chil bring it out," she whispered.

The tears were a beautiful and painful thing for Ellele to see. Th had to be shared, she decided. The Master or Mistress had to see wh was happening, to give them hope, to bring them back to their daug ter again. She thought of calling Hallys, so that he could bring the to the room, but she remembered he was on an errand.

Amala's eyes held the fear of abandonment, which Ellele tried assuage. "I won't be long. I'll be back quickly . . . but your father an mother should see you. I won't be long, child, I promise."

She disengaged herself, thinking to do it gently, but Ama gripped her tightly, and Ellele had to be more forceful than sh anted. She got up, leaving Amala on the floor, her arms crossed, nds kneading fistfuls of the robe. Again she told Amala she'd be ght back and walked to the door, opened it, looked back once at mala's tear-streaked face, and hurried down the hall to the Mas- r's study. Her side hurt from the low fall, but that was of no nsequence now.

He wasn't in the study, and for the first time in years, Ellele rsed. She moved on quickly to the kitchen, shouting for him, and st before she got there, he emerged, looking annoyed. There were umbs in his beard.

Rapidly she told him what was happening. He bolted past her, wn the hallway, almost slipping on the rug. Ellele followed, and by e time she got back to Amala's room, the Master was already com- g out. There was a sound behind Ellele, and she turned to see the istress in her bedclothes coming from her bedchamber. The Master oved to place himself between his wife and Ellele, and from the ger and disappointment in his face, Ellele knew something had ppened. Her heart began thumping even more. I never should have ft her, she thought. She fell in the tub and drowned. . . .

"You'll say nothing of this to the Mistress," he said.

"I don't understand," Ellele began. "What happened? Is she all ght?"

"There's nothing, nothing at all. I saw nothing. Amala is un- anged."

"But I saw. . ."

"What you *saw*, Ellele, was my daughter's face wet from the bath. don't know what you *think* you saw—you haven't been drinking or d smell it on your breath. I'll thank you not to have any more of ur . . . visions. It's cruel to us."

"I know what I saw," Ellele said firmly. "I'm sorry, but I know. 's true she was in the bath . . ."

"Havaarl, what's the matter?" his wife called out.

"Nothing, Serisa. I'll be right there." To Ellele: "See what you ant to see; sometimes it happens when one is overly sympathetic— careless with the bath water."

He left. Ellele looked from the doorway to see Amala, sitting by e tub, her face dry, as if she'd brushed away the tears, no longer anting them. Her mouth was closed, calm, as she stared at the low re in the hearth, too far away for the heat to have dried the tears ready.

Ellele walked into the room. She heard the Master's fading trea
in the hallway, his explanation to Serisa. "It was just a few spark
from the hearth that frightened Ellele. She's an old woman."

Ellele closed the door and uttered a few oaths that would hav
reddened Hallys's ears.

She wasn't saddened at all. "I know, child, I know," she said to
Amala. "It will have to do, this. I just wish you could tell me wh
they were for. Yourself or someone else, or both."

To Ellele the fact that Amala may have wiped away the tears wa
as remarkable as the tears themselves.

When she told Hallys tonight, likely he wouldn't believe her ei
ther and make some comment about her failing sight or some sucl
nonsense. Her eyes were as good as ever, about the only part of he
that was. The only ones who might believe her, she thought as sh
stared at the curtains, were the Timberlimbs. But she could no mor
talk to them than Amala could talk to her.

She took Amala over near the hearth, got the brush from the man
tel, and sat down with her to slowly brush her hair. There was nothin
else to do. When Amala reached out toward the flames, Ellele caugh
her hand and whispered, "No, child, you'd burn yourself, just lik
your father would believe."

She held Amala's hand and shared the heat of the fire, the dancin
figures in the flames. "Maybe next time, Amala, you'll laugh o
smile. We'll wait together for that, you and I. And your Timberlimb
outside."

Chapter Twenty-eight

The Castellan
of Kingstear

Falca, Ballast, and Frikko were among the last to be let through the tower at the end of the aqueduct road before the gates were closed for the night. As they led the pony and cart—laden with the bodies of Alatheus and Sippio—onto the causeway over the lake, Falca saw overseers below, directing gangs of empties up from two pumping stations close to the lake edge. The empties were herded into barracks grafted onto the inner face of the wall encircling Kingstear Lake. Then two more gangs of empties, replacements, were led from more barracks o the other side and down the long stairs, toward the great spokes of the pump wheels and circular track underneath. Soon the empties would be walking around and around, pushing the spokes to drive the pumps, forcing water to the sea.

"They're not shackled," Ballast said.

"They don't need to be," Falca replied.

The last of the travelers passed the cart, hurrying to make the second closure of gates at the end of the causeway, where the city rose from a promontory reaching halfway into the lake.

"No wonder the Gebroanan king doesn't do nothing about the lifters," Ballast said. "They need to work the pumps night and day. It's the sweat of those poor bastards that brings Sandsend to life."

"It's beast work is what it is," Falca said, and spit his digust. After I get Amala, we'll end that."

They walked on, slowly, with Frikko still leading the pony. Falca

267

looked back in the dusk, but he couldn't see the empties. He though
of that time he watched Amala from afar in the rain, bending over th
fountain by her house to retrieve the empty whose thirst had been s
great he'd drowned.

"We'll bury them here," he said to Ballast. "In the lake."

"You going to take that?" Ballast asked, nodding at the ring o
Alatheus' blood-smeared finger.

"No," Falca said. Amala had given it to her brother. The rin
wasn't Falca's to take.

"The finger's swollen, but you could hack it off for the ring."

Falca hefted Alatheus' body off the cart in answer.

Ballast shook his head, then reached for Sippio's body. "This su
has poached your senses, roaking. First you pay that old carter for hi
blind pony and wagon, when we could've just taken them, and hi
falcata too. Now you'll give the lake that piece of gold."

"Neither the ring nor the falcata will help us in the desert, Bal
last," Falca said.

Frikko did not want to sleep in the wagon, preferring a spot be
tween Falca and Ballast against the low rim of the causeway. Th
pony brayed and stomped until Frikko began feeding it the stales
bread and handfuls of grain. After this was done, Frikko fell asleep i
minutes. Ballast, too, was soon snoring.

Falca couldn't quite make it. For the others, the quiet hastene
sleep, but the night on the lake was anything but restful for Falca. H
could plainly hear, from across the lake, the creaking of the wheel
and pump, the trudging of the boots of the empties who kept the wate
flowing to a city Falca was glad to have left. He would never forge
it; too much had happened. But it was only a means to an end—h
smiled—just like his father said, and not the end itself. Wherever tha
was, it was going to include Amala. For all her own sensuality, sh
wouldn't like Gebroan, where they abandoned babies. Too much of i
would anger her, and a land of so much sun was no place for one wit
as fair a complexion as hers. Gebroan was, too, the place that ha
allowed the Spirit-Lifters to spawn, that even now used them, thei
discarded men and women, to give it life. Falca would come back bu
once, on his return from the desert, to get a ship for Draica. He woul
keep her mace so close to him, buy the softest muslin in the market
then wrap that in leather to protect her on the voyage back.

"Only a little while longer, Amala," he whispered aloud.

Frikko stirred, and Falca spoke even more softly. He had to talk to her, sound her name over the tramping boots and grinding wheels that kept him awake.

"He's gone now, Amala. Sippio too. I did what I could for both, took them to water. I'm all you have left. I hope it will be enough."

Gradually the rhythm of the empties' work across the water began to lull him, pull him to drowsiness, and he fell asleep, dreaming first of open eyes and mouths that kept drifting down in dark water and a dead, smothering quiet. Something forced that from his dreaming, and he dreamed next of Amala's first words when she'd rouse from her own walking sleep. He couldn't make them out, only knew that she was saying something. He knew what he would say to her.

At dawn the gates opened with yawning keepers, and they went into the city of Kingstear. Much smaller, it had little of Sandsend's bustle, given even a busier hour. The city had more the feel of a military outpost, and indeed, its reason for being was to protect the source of water for Sandsend and the narrow plain. The street from the gate widened into a market whose businesses were just beginning to open for the day.

Falca sold the cart and pony to a sleepy merchant, who either didn't notice or didn't care that the pony was blind. Even so, they didn't get much. Falca used the money to pay for used wool cloaks—a child's for Frikko—and other supplies for the mountains, which loomed over the eastern wall and towers.

Falca took advantage of a merchant arguing with his wife to steal a leather slingsack to carry the supplies and food. Ballast shielded the theft, and Frikko created a diversion by jumping up on the display table and pulling off several hanging woolen belts. By the time the vendor poked her off with a stick, Falca was walking away, with Ballast still shielding him and the prize.

That Falca had any qualms at all about reiving was remarkable. Two months ago he would have taken what he needed without a second thought. As Frikko bounded up to them, Falca shook his head woefully, smiling. "I'm afraid I've come to prefer paying for what I need, Ballast. I'm sinking low, I tell you. I have this urge to reimburse the man on the way back."

"Now both of us are diseased," Ballast said. "You expect to take money, treasure, back from this Lifter sanctuary in the desert?"

"We'll have to take back something to pay for passage to Draica. I can't steal a ship."

"You did before."

Falca laughed. "That I did. Strange, isn't it, Ballast, how when diseases such as ours strike, we can least afford the affliction."

Within the hour they reached the mountain gate of the city. Nearby a half-dozen empties stood or sat against the wall, guarded by a few soldiers waiting to take them to Sandsend and the labor camps. Falca glanced at them only long enough to see the black marks on their foreheads: the abominations of entry point and exit, dark as the gate ahead.

A bow-legged castellan strode from the sentry door of the near gate tower, pocketing a pair of dice. Two other sentries poked their heads out, then went back in. As the castellan approached Falca and Ballast, he said, "You want out this way?"

Falca nodded.

"You know what's out there?"

"We do," Ballast replied.

"Have to ask, y'understand. You don't have the local look." He glanced at Frikko with some curiosity. She smiled at him and he returned it. "Heard of their kind, but never have seen one. Friendly, isn't she?"

"She's adopted us, after a fashion," Falca said.

"She's a long way from home."

"We all are."

"Business out there?"

"You might say that."

"So it is," the castellan said, hooking his thumbs in his belt, from which hung a falcata. "So is this. A poor job it is. I'm more like an executioner, I am. You'd be surprised how often I open this gate. Mind if I look in your slingsack?"

Falca shrugged. "You won't find any maces, if that's what you want."

The castellan glanced at him sharply. "I don't *want* the damned things. I have to look for them. I'm the only one who does anymore." He shook his head. "Check for Lifters, is the word, but don't hunt too hard."

"The water has to keep flowing, eh?" Falca said. He liked this talkative soldier.

"Yah, and stone has to be hauled," the castellan said, and finished searching. "Why *are* you going out there, friend?" He waved an arm at a man above in the gate tower. Soon the thick drawbar began sliding back into the wall.

"To get back something I lost," Falca said.

The castellan grunted. "Well, it ain't none of my business anyhow. Just watch yourselves. Even the mountain brigands that used to keep us on our toes have been snatched by the Lifters. Everyone knows the danger, and it don't seem to matter. Maybe it's the light that attracts them. Sometimes at night, if the air is keen, you can see the glow from the wall walk."

"The glow?" Ballast said.

"That's what we see: a whore's blush, if ever there was one. Don't ask me what it *is*. You could ask them"—he nodded at the empties—"but you wouldn't get no more of an answer, the sorry bastards."

"Which direction is this . . . glow?" Falca asked.

The castellan smiled thinly. "The way you're going I'd say. But steer a little to the north." He spit. "It's a damn shame. They go out, and none come back the same way. They wander back, rooting for water and food. Sometimes we go out to get them. Easy as plucking berries from a vine. Sometimes I think they want it to happen to them. Out there, I mean."

"No, they don't," Falca said sharply.

The castellan was surprised at Falca's vehemence, but still he muttered, "Well, why else go out there? Unless, of course, you're looking for something you lost. Which may be the same thing. Some of them ask me how far it is. I just tell'm to follow the road till it ends. Beyond that, well, it's probably just as far and near as those empties over there."

Two soldiers had pulled back the gates, and the passage loomed open, dark as the thickness of the wall. Falca could suddenly smell the scent of the forest beyond. "Let's go, Ballast," Falca said, then nodded at the castellan. "You do a poor job well."

"I hope you find what you lost, friend. Now you better get on, or your little companion's gonna get there ahead of you." He pointed to the gate, and Frikko, who was already in the shadows of the passage.

"Never even saw her sneak ahead," Ballast grumbled. He and Falca hurried after her. When Falca looked back, he saw the castellan, hands on his belt, staring after them, shaking his head. He plucked the dice from his pocket, tossed them in the air, caught them with a swipe, and turned away.

Chapter Twenty-nine

Thefts

It took Falca, Ballast, and Frikko five days to follow the road out of the mountains. Always there were markers for the trail: wandering empties who sought with listless arms and vacant eyes the food and water Falca couldn't spare to give; remains of bodies, the bones gnawed clean, bleached by the sun; shreds of cloth clinging to brush—a boot here, a cap there.

As the weather grew hotter, they bundled the wool cloaks that had served them well in the mountains and put them to the side of the track, for use on their return.

The land soon became hilly, though to the south and east it stretched flat to the horizon. The track led over scrub hills and disappeared in gravel washes but always resumed again on the hillsides. Toward sunset of the seventh day they passed the charred circle of a campfire and the bones of an empty.

Falca didn't want to camp in the vale, near that skeleton, so they walked up the last, steep hill for the day.

At the top Falca halted, sucked in his breath, dropped to his knees, and waved vigorously at Ballast and Frikko behind him to do the same.

Falca counted six Lifters, two of whom were hacking with swords at some of the larger scrub bushes in the vale ahead. Another was going through bundles on the ground, readying food and utensils for the evening meal. Two others stood over the six maces laid side by side on the ground, not far from the road that curved in the glen and disappeared around a rise. One of the Lifters pointed in that direction, as if telling the other how far they had to go.

"Is your man among them?" Ballast whispered.

Falca shook his head.

"Too bad. Would've saved us a lot of trouble."

"I know. But where there's six, there'll be more at the end of the road. It probably starts at the coast north of Sandsend, a shorter route and safer, and all their own."

"We follow them now?"

"I don't know. Let me think."

"What else can we do, Falca? It'd be one thing if your Saphrax was down there. We could wait till they're asleep, kill the guard if they post one, go in and out quick with the mace. But your man isn't down there. Why take the chance with a scuff before we have to? You get hurt or worse and it's over before we start."

Falca thought it over as he watched the Lifters finish preparing their camp. They were so careful around the shrouded maces lying on the ground in a neat row, like corpses ready for burial. He frowned. Just following them *was* probably all they could or should do now. Yet it wasn't enough somehow to merely trail after them, the way the empties had followed them, begging for water and food. So they followed the Lifters to their Crucible and then what? They would still be on the outside, looking in. They had to *get* in somehow.

The idea that came to Falca was not new. He'd done it before and didn't want to use it again. But there was no other choice he could see.

"Ballast," Falca said, "go back down to that campfire and bring back a handful of charcoal."

"What for?"

"I'll tell you more when you get back."

The stoneskin left, grumpy at the walk down and back. Falca glanced over at Frikko. She undoubtedly knew that the men down there were the enemy and that he was going to do something about them, though she couldn't know what. For some reason he felt, again, like she was worrying. She had it in her eyes. She moved closer to him, saying something he couldn't understand, frustrating him that way, as always. He put a hand on her tiny shoulder. "Sometimes the most dangerous way, Frikko, is the only way. I have to

ecome like them to kill them, do you understand. To get Amala
ack."

She put a hand over his, looked away to where Ballast had gone,
hen smiled at Falca in the deepening dusk. "Ballast and I will go
down after it's dark," Falca whispered to her. "I'd like you to stay up
ere; this isn't your fight, Frikko. If it goes badly, well, someone has
o get home."

Ballast and Falca left the crest of the hill, stepping carefully
oward the eye of the beast below. Beyond, the light of the sanctuary
eemed like dawn, but it wasn't diffuse enough. Still, there came the
alling of birds, fooled by the false dawn.

"She didn't want to stay," Ballast said.

"But she did," Falca whispered back. "She knows the danger. Do
ou know what to do?"

"Circle around the campsite, and after you draw the Lifters away,
ill anyone who remains by the fire."

Falca nodded in the darkness. "Some will remain. They all won't
ome after me. Also, the ones who stay will have their backs to you.
The important thing is to split them up. Get at least two of the six
naces, and two of their capes and tunics."

"All right, but I still wish you had that sword."

"I don't need one, not in the dark. So long as I don't move, they
on't be able to find me. We don't have to kill all of them. Chances
re, any who get away won't recognize me later; light's too bad. They
on't recognize you because they won't have seen you. No more talk
ow; we're getting too close. I can hear one snoring."

They approached softly, quietly, and Falca was thankful they had
o animals, whose keen senses might arouse the bastards. They
arted as planned, gripping arms in a brief, silent farewell.

As Falca waited for Ballast to circle around, he unclenched his left
and. The ground-up charcoal that Ballast had earlier taken from the
ampfire was damp from sweat. He spit into his palm, mixed the
lack dust with a finger, and daubed more of the paste on his fore-
ead, directly over the bridge of his nose. Ballast had done this earlier
n the last light of day and deemed him, with a tense grin, to be as
lose to an empty as he should ever hope to get.

Falca kneeled, wiped his palm on the ground. Close would have
o do. The crude ruse had only to last briefly. The Lifters' campfire

burned low, he saw, as he stood, providing just enough light to see where the maces were, but not enough for keener observation.

He walked ahead, trying to picture in his mind the movements, the unfocused but searching eyes of all the empties he'd seen.

The Lifters had posted a guard all right. He sat closest to the fire, a sword across his knees, head on arms. He was asleep. Next to him lay the row of maces, the heads shrouded by cinched leather hoods. The other voals slept close to the fire, in pairs.

For a moment Falca was tempted to rush the campsite while the guard slept, grab two maces, and flee. If he was quiet about it, he could probably escape easily. But he and Ballast also needed the Lifter garb and to get them, to allow Ballast to do his work, the Lifters had to be aroused and divided by a chase. There was one more thing. If any of the scuts later was left alive, he wanted to give them the memory of the "empty" who stole maces from them. The idea was useless, quirky, but it pleased him to think of the bewilderment it would cause the Lifters. Anyway, he had the damn mark on his forehead; he might as well use it.

Quietly he circled around so that he'd have a straight run ahead when he grabbed the maces. Ballast was behind him somewhere, waiting.

Falca breathed deeply and walked into the pale of the campfire. He scuffed his boots, sending a few stones into the embers. He made a rasping sound in his throat.

The guard bolted upright, whirled, his sword cutting an arc. "You!" was all the voal could manage. Falca made sure he could see his forehead, then turned to rummage among the pile of packs and water skins. The voal took a few steps toward him, as other Lifters awoke, their heads rising, turning.

"What's the matter, Gossark?" said a Lifter.

"An empty. Brazen bastard he is."

His head down, Falca eyed the maces. They were maybe ten steps away. He'd have to go over one of the Lifters. The point of the voal's sword was five steps away, to his right. He pretended to search for food even as the guard stared at him, uncertain what to do.

Three of the five were staring at him, sleepily.

"Well, don't be a dolt, Gossark," said a Lifter. A priest? "Either give it some water and send it on its way or take it from here and kill it. Whatever you do, be quiet about it. We need sleep; we must be fresh for the Crucible."

The Lifter closest to Falca yawned. "Better kill it. It'll just come ack for more, and we can't spare the water or food. It is still two ays to Blessed Maradus."

"Very well, Giver," Gossark said.

Falca stood. Out of the corner of his eye he watched the voal pproach, holding his sword low, in his right hand, ready to prod alca out into the darkness to his death. When Falca felt the sword oint in his right side, he knew he had the proper distance. He spun, a alf turn, and connected a backhanded fist to Gossark's face. Even as ie voal fell back from the blow, Falca grabbed the sword he dropped nd lunged toward the maces. The nearest Lifter shouted, but got no arther than a sitting position. Falca swung the sword at his neck, felt bite halfway through, and left it to free his hands.

One less for Ballast, he thought, as he scooped up two of the iaces and sprinted away from the Lifters' cries. He looked back. iossark was still flattened, with a Lifter standing by him, pointing, creaming in Falca's direction. Another tended to the dying Lifter.

Three came after him.

He ran hard, veering to his right, feeling the rise of the hill that ulled at his roaring heart. He stopped, though he wanted to race on, :lt he could run for miles. His breathing couldn't get too labored, or iey'd hear him. He began walking, slowly, consciously trying to alm himself. He glanced up at the moons, to reassure himself that ieir light wasn't enough to give him away. Then he checked the iaces, to make sure that their masking shrouds were tight.

All was darkness, except for the glow of the sanctuary that seeped ver the far hill.

Falca listened to the shouts of his pursuers off to his right and felt) good at the panic in their voices that he wanted to laugh. He hefted ie maces, feeling the wonderful weight again, his doubts about hold- ig, possessing them vanished. He'd forgotten how good it felt since e'd held that first one on Grippa's island. They filled his hands better ian the falcata. He briefly wondered who the souls had belonged to. didn't matter. Having the maces was the most remarkable thing he ould imagine, holding the years of two lives as weight.

The thrill of possession stirred him higher. He said silently to his lind hunters, You'll never get them back. They're mine now, keys to ie lock. He laughed just as silently at their clumsiness and felt the nveloping night as a friend, sealing him off from harm as tightly as ie soft but thick leather bound the mace-heads. Without their maces,

the Lifters were lost in that dark trying to retrieve what he'd stolen
Comparing all the fists of his life, this surely was the most pleasur
able.

Cradling the maces, he watched Ballast enter the campsite and
quickly kill a standing Lifter as the voal turned to face him. Ballast
hesitated over the unconscious Gossark.

Go ahead, kill him too, Falca urged, and frowned. He was going
to kill me.

Evidently Ballast couldn't bring himself to dispatch the helpless
voal, but he did strip him of his cape. As the stoneskin was doing the
same with the other, Falca pointed, shook the maces at him, suddenly
angry at what he felt was Ballast's weakness. Gossark suddenly
stirred as if roused by Falca's shaking maces and anger and attacked
Ballast. But he had no weapon, and the stoneskin killed him then.

Falca nodded, satisfied. It would be better, of course, to Lift the
'lickers, like they did Amala, instead of killing them. But the maces
were full, Gifted. There was no place for their corroded spirits to go.

Ballast stole away back into the darkness with the rest of the
maces. Good, Falca thought. More.

He could hear his clumsy pursuers, who hadn't even seen what
was going on below, so eager were they searching. But one of them
noticed now, and Falca taunted them silently as they ran back down
the hill to discover the newly dead.

His smile vanished in a rush of fear as he felt something on his
shoulder. In an instant he cursed himself for miscounting the number
of Lifters, waited only a few heartbeats for the burning steel to pierce
him. How had they found him? The point of the sword moved, in
almost a caress, and he knew what was beyond him just as the whisper came, "Falca . . . ?"

He twisted around, stood abruptly, feeling foolish, embarrassed at
his imagining of the Lifter he forgot to count. How could he have
mistaken the touch of Frikko's hand? He cast it off, his chagrin sour-
ing to anger. She didn't back away; he could smell her nearness. Her
lack of fear annoyed him further.

"Frikko, I told you to stay on the ridge." He could have shaken
her. She said something. Whatever it was, he didn't care and turned
away from her in disgust, his victory marred by her having found
him, finding the weakness in his power of disguise. He'd hidden from
the Lifters, but he couldn't hide from this mottle's sense of smell, her
acute hearing. Why hadn't she stayed where she was supposed to?

e'd understood the danger. He didn't need her. Everything had
ne according to plan. He had the maces. The first step to Amala.

He watched the three remaining Lifters hurriedly leaving camp,
king to the road. Their shadows passed the campfire. He decided to
alk back to the top of the hill to wait for Ballast. Frikko followed
m closely. As they neared the ridge, Falca heard a crack, and a
ear of light shot up into the night. As the hard edges of the flare
adually diffused, Falca saw the silhouette of Ballast.

He was angry at the stoneskin, too, now. The Lifters could have
en that from afar. Ballast could have called softly to him. Such a
aste, to use something so wondrous as a Gifted mace merely to find
friend in the darkness. Was that any way to spend someone's soul?
at mace could have been Amala's, for all he knew. Maybe Saphrax
d gotten killed, his mace given to one of the six Lifters.

When he strode up to Ballast, the stoneskin said, "I didn't know if
u still had the two maces, so just in case I took the others."

"Don't ever use a mace for so trivial a reason again, Ballast, do
u hear?"

"What?"

"You heard me. It was a waste."

"What are you so angry about? You got more of these things than
u need."

"Where are the other three maces?"

"They're on the ground, between us. Take them before I smash
em. By the sweet Caves, I don't know what's got into you. No, I
. But it's a thing to be settled in the morning, when there's light to
e a man face to face."

Falca kneeled, found the maces, and gathered them into his arms
d walked away. When he couldn't hear Ballast's grumbling, he
pped and lay down, keeping the five maces close to him, facing
em, like he would a sleeping lover. Amala. The feeling of posses-
n and protectiveness was as comforting as a firm pillow for his
st, but he didn't allow himself to go to sleep immediately, though he
as bone tired. Ballast was wrong. The Lifters might steal back,
ving seen the flare of a mace. There was no telling what Ballast
ight do in the night. Leave?

Falca didn't care now if he did. He had the maces, and Ballast
rely wouldn't take the Lifter clothing. Falca had all he needed to
t Amala back.

* * *

Falca woke with the dawn, cold and damp and stiff from tʰ night. It was a moment before he realized that three of the maces weʳ gone. The theft woke him fully, instantly, and he quickly grabbed tʰ two remaining and raced down the ridge, his anger pushing him harᵈ

They were up, seemingly waiting for him. At their feet lay tʰ three maces, the crystal heads crushed, the leather hoods nearby. Bᵃ last was scraping himself, tossing bits of his roughy onto the maᶜ hoods.

"You or her?" Falca demanded, breathing hard.

Ballast jabbed a thumb in his chest.

"You're lying. You're too clumsy; you would've woken mᵉ You're protecting her."

Frikko stepped forward, sadness in her large, dark eyes. Ballᵃ blocked her way with an arm. His other hand stayed hard on hⁱ sword.

"I won't let you hurt her, Falca. She did what I should have doⁿ —took them, like you took the others, and a better theft it was. ⁱ crushed them myself—see the black streaks in the saw grass wheⁿ the power and the light went. You don't need them all. I wish yᵉ didn't need any, but you probably do, to get into the bastards' laⁱ You're right about that at least. If you want to do something aboᵘ what we did, you and I will do it, but it will end here. You have ᵗ know that. Amala will end. Otherwise, put the maces down and we'ˡ go on."

"I have to take them."

"I know that. But you shouldn't be the one to carry them, not unᵗ it's time."

"Who will?"

"Frikko. I don't know why she cares so much about you, but sʰ does. You'd have thought the stink of the Draican Limbs would'ᵛ worn off you by now."

Ballast rolled another piece of his roughy and threw it after all tʰ others.

Suddenly Falca knew why Frikko came off the ridge to find hⁱ the night before: to help him. How? He didn't know. Just to be wⁱ him, to break the effect of the maces on him by her mere presenᶜ The weight of the maces seemed a burden now, not a part of him, aⁿ he placed them on the ground.

"All right," he said softly.

Frikko came forward, without hesitation, and picked them up. Each was over half her height in length.

"If she gets tired carrying them," Ballast said, "I'll do it. They don't seem to affect me as they do a roaking. Don't ask me why. Maybe it's the roughy." He peeled one more piece off his arm and tossed it away, trying to smile, but wearily. "Shall we go now, Falca?" He gathered up the slingsack and gave it to Falca to carry. "I'll manage these," he said, folding up the blue and white Lifter capes and tunics. "No sense in putting them on until we need to or see someone along that road."

Frikko was already walking down the hill, the maces tilted over her right shoulder. "She's more determined than I," Falca whispered. "She wants to go home."

The stoneskin nodded.

"I'm scared, Ballast."

"You'll get her back."

"I have to use the maces to do it. I can't see any other way."

"Don't underestimate yourself. You gave them up just now, when you could have walked away from us. You'll do what you have to do. You always have."

They walked after Frikko. "One more thing," Ballast said. "You won't be alone in there. I'll be with you."

"You could have walked away too."

"One of us has to push the rocks down on the damned roakings, with or without a roughy."

"You don't need me to get home."

"Maybe, maybe not. But a stoneskin always feels better letting someone else lead, whether it's a Fallow Queen, a roaking, or"—he smiled—"that little one down there."

"I think she knows the way better than either of us."

They gained the road below. Falca glanced over at the Lifters' campsite. Flies had already settled on the corpses. Before day's end, the carrion birds and predators would have their feast.

Chapter Thirty

The Crucible

The land was now a wasteland whose only feature was the twin black columns at the end of the road. Heat distorted the horizon, and the wind carried sand and grit that kept Falca's eyes watering so that he couldn't discern any more detail of the columns. But it was enough to know that they marked the Lifters' sanctuary. The glow was invisible in the glaring wash of the day. The night before, however, the light had filled a third of the sky, masking the moons, making dusk of midnight.

Frikko fared the worst in the desert heat. Ballast tried to shield her with his bulk, but it was of little use. Falca and the stoneskin sweated buckets in the Lifter camps and tunics, and they wanted to take them off. They couldn't, not with so many Lifters on the road. All were hurrying, impatient, and so not overly curious about a Timberlimb carrying two maces, or a stoneskin whose garb was far too tight a fit. Falca could sense their excitement and expectation even when they weren't talking with one another. He knew why.

Earlier in the day he had overheard a conversation as four Lifters passed by. The Prism had arrived four days before, and tonight or possibly the next, Maradus would dedicate it.

Falca had mixed feelings about the news. On the one hand, it probably meant that Saphrax was already at the sanctuary, since he would undoubtedly have accompanied the Prism from Grippa's island. It also meant that Falca would not encounter him on the road.

'alca would have to retrieve Amala's mace in the den of wolves.)espite the knot of fear in his belly, he was as impatient as any Lifter n the road to get to the sanctuary. Whatever chance he had to get Amala back would happen tonight. He set a pace faster than Frikko ould manage, and periodically Ballast picked her up, maces and all, ɔ catch up.

The sun had finally settled below the horizon when they stopped t road's end. Ahead rose the twin obelisks, rising within a dip in a ɔw ridge, a stone's throw away. Each was finely hewn, thrice the ,eight of a man, silhouetted against the light of the sanctuary. The ,low seemed to come up from the earth; Falca could see no edifice, ɔ point of origin. No longer was the glow diffused by distance but vas a curtain of light, whose edges had the definition of a sword's. ſe looked up into the darkening sky, and only there did the illuminaion feather out to the stars.

They walked ahead slowly. The fear in Falca's gut twisted, urned. It seemed as if they were approaching an abyss. The Lifters n front dropped, in ranks, to one knee between the obelisks, bowed heir heads, got up, and then moved to the right or left and . . . lisappeared, making room for those waiting behind.

Where were the walls, the towers, the guards of the stronghold? ʻalca wondered. The approach was as easy and terrifying as walking ›ff a cliff. When he finally glimpsed the nature of the Lifters' sanctury, his awe pulled him ahead so that he bumped into the voal in ront. He stepped back, his mouth open, and heard Ballast's low vhistle of amazement.

The sanctuary was a vast round depression, a hollowed-out fruit in his wasteland. The shimmering cylinder of light—the heart of the ›east—lay at the bottom, dominating the center. It was like a volume ›f water that had retained its form without the vessel, pouring upward nto the heavens. The tiny figures of men below marked the depth and ˙astness of the sanctuary. A long ramp extended down from the lip of he crater and the obelisks, all the way down to the opening in a wall hat encircled this home of the Lifters. Falca saw towers, buildings, ˙urving rows of trees and . . . water? Stairways, broad as the ramp but teeper and shorter, flanked that smooth tongue, and on these, Lifters lescended, leaving pack animals and supplies at the top.

Somewhere down there, Falca said silently to himself, was ›aphrax and Amala. . . .

He felt a nudge, heard the whisper of his name. Ballast nodded his head down. Yes, of course, Falca thought. They were dressed as voals; they had to begin acting like them. As he knelt, his hand brushed a side of the obelisk. He'd never felt stone cut so smoothly, perfectly, smooth as glass. How had they done it? Then he remembered how the light from the mace Saphrax broke had cut through the helve like butter. They used souls like masons' saws to work stone. How many lives were spent to make these markers for Lifter pilgrims? The abomination of it outweighed the marvel for him, and he felt tainted within the Lifter cape and tunic.

Frikko had remained standing as Falca and Ballast knelt. No one behind had said anything, but even so, the two moved away quickly to their left before a voal or priest could question them.

It was the longest, slowest descent Falca had ever made. He said not a word to Ballast; he wouldn't have known what to say. There was nothing like this sanctuary in the Six Kingdoms. He tried to ward off the wonder, feeling it a betrayal to his purpose, a worm ready to feed, but he couldn't help the assessment. After all the days in the desert, the wasteland, this place seemed almost a reward. Whatever else the Lifters were, there was a beauty and symmetry and order in what they had built. Even as Falca stepped down, shaking his head in awe at this inverted city, he kept telling himself how many hundreds or thousands of lives were taken to make it possible.

There was water. Where had the Lifters gotten it? Wells, dug by empties? A broad band of water circled the Crucible, whose light made the water dance a color as gold as Alatheus' ring. Short causeways spanned the circular fountain at top and bottom, linking the Crucible with raised platforms, daises, each in perfect alignment with the other, though the far dais was bigger than its opposite. The sheer of the Crucible's light distorted Falca's view, but he could see something resting on that far dais, and he guessed it could only be the Prism of Empathy.

Beyond, clustered in a concise arrangement, were seven towers, six of which were of identical shape and size. The seventh was much larger, and two-thirds of the way up there was an opening, a balcony. The top third of the tower was thicker than the lower portion, and it seemed to Falca nothing more nor less than a phallus, whose height was exceeded only by the scintillation of Crucible light. Falca wondered whether the tower was the residence of Maradus himself, the much who had conjured this all from a dream.

Scores of Lifters had already gathered in front of the near dais, but many more were walking from the two long buildings set back to ther side of the circular watercourse. A row of trees bordered the ar of the buildings and curved around behind the seven towers. The aves glinted gold in the light.

Beyond the trees were tethers for stormbirds. Falca saw six and uessed that that was how the Lifters supplied the sanctuary, though ere appeared to be gardens bordering the inner sweep of the low all.

They neared the end of the steps, when Ballast said, "We should ave Frikko someplace. We have to go on alone; she'll give us way."

Falca nodded. "Somewhere near the steps." As he looked to his ft, he saw the empties, the countless shapes that moved among rude dwellings, tomblike, scarcely distinguishable from the talus and ebris of the crater's sloping sides. The rough terraces seemed almost nimate with the listless meanderings of the empties.

"I never even saw them," Falca whispered.

"Nor I," Ballast said. "They're forgotten in all this."

"Frikko will be safe there, behind that rock, until we leave."

"Safer than us, my friend."

They let three Lifters pass them on the steps before jumping down rom the edge and walking, with some difficulty, over the sloping round to the large rock. Its inner face was bathed in the Crucible ght, the opposite dark. Just beyond, a group of empties squatted ver a pile of something—food?

Falca shook his head in pity, his wonder and awe at the beauty and ymmetry of the sanctuary lessening. Here was the labor that hauled nd lifted the blocks of stone, who ate their cold scraps of food in the ight of their own souls. Falca was convinced that the Crucible had omething to do with the maces.

The three of them stood in the dark behind the rock, and Falca nally spoke. "No goodbyes. We're all going back up those stairs."

"And at a run, I'd wager," Ballast said.

Falca thought Frikko would not want to give him a mace. She did, anding it to him, speaking something he wished he understood. When this was all over, he would learn their Tongue. He heard both is name and Amala's, and he knew then that the wonder of this place, which had seemed like a fertile oasis, was secondary to th marvel of Frikko's understanding of him and what he was tryin to do.

Falca handed the mace to Ballast, as much to delay its effect o him as to embrace the Timberlimb. He held her, her face in his stom ach, for long moments before letting go. "That's not a goodbye. It' for getting us here, Frikko. When you see us running for our lives u the stairs, you join us quickly."

She nodded, as if she understood the words, and then pushed a him, and then Ballast.

As they picked their way back to the steps, Falca whispered, "Yo give me a mace only when you have to. We'll know the time. Witl any luck, I may not have to use it. You know what Saphrax look like?"

Ballast nodded. "He's hard to miss."

Falca began looking for the Lifter even as they walked down th last of the steps and joined a dozen voals heading for the gateway Falca glanced back up the steps, searching, knowing that Saphrax wa inside, waiting for him, knowing that he had what Falca wanted Falca realized he was hesitating, cringing inwardly at the prospect o going ever closer to that light with nothing in his hands, no falcata not even a mace. But he kept moving, he had to keep moving. He was too close now.

The rim of the crater loomed high all around, supplanting half th night stars with the stark shadow and brightness cast by the Crucible As Falca and Ballast angled toward the opening in the wall—whicl was only slightly higher than a man—Falca heard the sound tha seemed to merge with the tension within him: a humming, approach ing discordance, that reminded him of a flina's high note. The soun grew louder, and as Falca and Ballast came to the opening in the wall Falca knew where it was coming from.

The Crucible's light was so powerful that he had to shield his eye: for a moment, as did Ballast. As Falca's eyes adjusted to the brillian curtain, he saw myriad maces fitted upright into...what? He couldn't tell. The base of the Crucible didn't seem like either stone o wood or metal. The sides rose above the dais in front, the surroundin; fountain whose calm surface was like the finest beaten gold.

"There must be a thousand of them," Falca whispered.

"A graveyard," Ballast murmured.

"Only it's not quiet," Falca said. He realized that the humminį

is the music of those souls condensed within the cores of all the
ices, seeping out of each brilliant individual prison, to ricochet
inst the crystal mace-heads all around.

They were arranged in concentric circles, with only a narrow
thway down the center, linking the daises at either end. There was a
ght rise to the path, the gentlest of hills: the Curve of the One.

Falca kept waiting to feel heat from such illumination, but he
dn't. If anything, there was a coldness, or maybe it was just the air
at was so crisp, so clean, it smelled better than earth after a rain.

He touched Ballast's arm. "This way," he whispered.

Too many Lifters were convening in front of the steps to the fore-
is, all of them carrying maces. Falca wanted to see Saphrax first,
id not the other way around. There were hundreds of Lifters and an
jual number of empties, wandering around like unwatched pets,
inking from the fountains in front of the barracks or the circular
atercourse. Some carried burdens, on errands.

Falca saw one tall, lanky empty wandering among the voals gath-
ed around the near dais and steps. If he got too close, some Lifter
ould push him away. It seemed strange to Falca that the Lifters, who
id built this place with such precision and care, would tolerate the
eanderings of the ones whose souls they'd stolen. Elsewhere, the
npties were penned or kept away. Here they could obviously go
here they wanted, until needed for work or the Lifters' pleasure. It
emed like a mixture of utter contempt, disregard, and leniency,
hich said, "We took your souls, but you may go where you like,
ink where you want, wander up the stairs and into the desert, all the
ay to Sandsend if you like. We won't stop you. There's more where
ou came from."

It was the worst of fates, Falca thought, this invisibility, worse
an death. The tall empty now moved as one unseen among the
oals, who were talking enthusiastically, gesturing toward the Cruci-
le with their maces, or up at the tallest tower. Falca could feel the
xpectation in the air. Maradus would be appearing soon. Falca
lanced up at the stairs, the ramp. Only a few Lifters were hurrying
own to join the swollen ranks below.

Someone pushed the empty toward the steps, then turned back to
ontinue her conversation. Falca watched the empty stumble up the
tairs, walk unsteadily across the dais toward the narrow rising path
iat bisected the Crucible. He held out his hands, as if fending off the
ght. He faltered, his body jerking spasmodically as he entered the

outer edge of the Crucible that wasn't yet filled with maces. A vo
noticed him then, someone pointed, heads turned, but no one move
to stop the empty. Surely they considered him trespassing, his action
sacrilege, Falca thought.

The empty's hands broke the plane of the light curtain first. H
was drawn in and a moment later exploded, instantly butchered into
hundred pieces like so much ice dropped from a height. A blackene
chunk of him landed near Ballast, formless as a cinder spit from
fire.

Maybe it was rage that made him tingle, seemed to turn his fir
gertips into daggers, but Falca saw the brute just then, the drawn-bac
hood of his cape an obscene cushion for that grinning profile
Saphrax.

Falca pulled his own hood as far forward as it would go.
severely narrowed his field of vision, but that didn't matter now. He'
spotted Saphrax. He was sure the brute hadn't seen him. His eyes
like all the voals', would be staring ahead, eager for Maradus. Falc
would be right behind him, and when he grabbed the mace or lifted
from the belt loop. . . .

Falca nudged Ballast. "He's here. This is what we're going to do
We leave one mace here, take one, which you'll give to me as w
work our way through the bastards, until we're behind him. The m
ment after I grab Amala's mace from him, I give it to you. By th
time Saphrax reacts, turns around, all he'll see is me holding a mace
You turn your face and slowly work your way back through them
Once you're at the very back of them, use your judgment to eithe
keep going or wait until a better time."

Ballast frowned. "All right, but that leaves you in the nest of rat
Falca. What're you going to do after we make the switch?"

"The plan ends there. I don't know. I may pretend I've joine
them, give the mace back to him, saying that I wanted to show him
could take it. Or I might break the mace over his head. I may run."

Ballast shook his head. "You won't get far. There has to be an
other way."

"I can't think of one. We can't stay here trying. We're running o
of time. Something's going to happen soon."

"Where'll I put this?" Ballast said, holding up one of the maces.

"Behind the trees over there. Hurry."

Falca was walking toward the Lifters as Ballast caught up to him
Falca's eyes were dead on Saphrax. "You remember what I told yo

out the mace and the retrieval of an empty?" Falca asked.

"Yes."

"Get her out of here if it doesn't seem like I'll be coming back
ith you, Ballast."

"You know I will."

Falca smiled. "Imagine what a few rocks would do, tossed into
e Crucible. Or rolled down the hill, to crash into their castle and
ake them from their sleep."

He felt Ballast's hand on his shoulder. "Do you think Frikko will
e all right?"

"She will," Falca said. "We'll get out of here, all four of us."

The crowd of Lifters stretched almost to the gateway of the wall.
hey fell silent as Falca and Ballast worked their way toward
aphrax. Three men had appeared on the balcony of the high tower
st beyond the far dais. The one in the middle was dressed in white
bes, his arms braced by the other two. Maradus? Falca wondered.
e seemed like he was blind. His priests led him to the railing care-
lly, then stepped back. Maradus slowly raised his arms, his head
. A roar erupted from the hundreds of Lifters. Each raised a mace.
allast did, too, with a look at Falca, who kept going, slipping,
ueezing himself past the voals, who were too caught up in Mar-
dus's appearance to notice that he wasn't carrying a mace.

Falca's eyes bore down on Saphrax now. The Lifters had surged
rward, which aided Falca's approach, but it also carried Saphrax
vay from him. Falca moved as quickly as he could, eager now, his
patience and aggressiveness interpreted by those he passed as
erely desire to get closer to the man who gave birth to the One.

He glanced up at the tower to see Maradus nod to the men who
anked him, then he stepped back. One priest held a writhing snake,
e other a bow and arrow.

The Lifters were closely packed; Falca had tougher going the
oser he and Ballast came to Saphrax.

The brute was close now. He glanced up at the tower to see a
iest impale the tail of the snake on the arrow, even as the archer
ew the bow. The Lifters were so quiet, Falca could hear the release
ver the humming of the Crucible. He looked, as did they all, at the
gh trajectory of the shaft that entered the upper reaches of the Cruci-
e light cylinder. He saw it drop beyond the wall, a wriggling worm
om heaven.

The Lifters were silent, still, expectant. Falca moved ahead, his eyes on Saphrax. He could almost hear him breathing over the chorus of souls, or so he imagined. When Falca looked back, to gesture to Ballast to give him the mace, he stopped.

A sliding rustling sound began to grow, soon drowning out the Crucible keening, the breathing of the Lifters around Falca. He heard the cracking of masonry, saw something bright and seemingly wet pass and obstruct the gateway of the wall. The sound grew harder, the scraping of stone. Ballast caught his eye. The stoneskin shook his head in disbelief as scales, glittering in Crucible light, rose like flood waters around the circular dike of the sanctuary wall, soon doubling its height.

As the scraping ceased, and the monstrous snake reared its head above the gateway, the Lifters gave a roar of approval at the manifestation of the Crucible's power. A tongue the size of an oar flicked out the eyes black stars given life by the One.

Falca saw Ballast curse silently amidst the shouts of the Lifters, the jabbing of the maces.

Falca stared in disbelief at the snake.

He and Ballast were trapped. Even if they got Amala's mace there was nowhere to run with it. Trapped, in the middle of a horde of Lifters, with Saphrax so close that he could see the mangled ear where he'd ripped the earring to pin it on Amala. The brute speared the air with her mace.

As Maradus stepped forward, the sanctuary quieted. "Once again we have sealed our nest," he began. "I have brought us ever closer together, on this night, when we finally have what is ours, the Prism of Empathy, with which we will hasten the cleansing of all of the Six Kingdoms, giving the gift of our purity and purpose to multitudes as yet diseased with faithlessness, mired in lives lost in the wilderness of the flesh, far from the path they wish to regain but know not how. As we are close to the One, so shall all be bathed in our Light.

"Let us now begin."

Chapter Thirty-one

Falca's Walk

Two blind priests walked unaided up the steps of the fore-
is, in a way that counted ritual and habit as eyes. They turned as
e, smiling, to call forth their voals.

There was no rush or confusion. At each utterance of, "Come
ead to join with the One," two voals walked up to the priests. Falca
tched them pause, unhood their maces, and drop the coverings at
e priests' feet, like dogs dropping fowl at their masters' boots. The
als touched the glowing mace-heads to the outstretched hands of
e priests and walked ahead together down the central pathway. As
ey entered the curtain of Crucible light, the maces flared, and the
olytes' bodies were sheathed momentarily in sparks of light. The
als separated, taking meandering paths through the vast halves of
e Crucible, heading for the periphery, where they would give their
fts to the One.

Falca's eyes ached terribly from the light. Did all the Lifters wind
blind from gazing too much at the Crucible? He'd seen many older
iests, Maradus himself, who were blind. He remembered a snatch
conversation on the desert road. A Lifter had rebuked another who
iced fears of going blind. "We will take care of you. Remember
is, the Gift of two eyes to the One is a small price to pay to see with
housand."

Still, the ache was not enough for Falca to avert his own eyes
om the Crucible. To do that would mark him as an imposter. He

needed time to think of a way out. Beyond that, he *had* to look, as
Ballast was too, at the shape-shifting that was the most beautiful and
terrifying thing he had ever witnessed.

As the voals walked through the Crucible, their forms seemed to
change a hundred times. Maybe it was just the trick of the shimmering light, the veil of souls, but Falca saw the voals as different men,
as women. They shrank to the size of young boys, then rose again,
only to collapse to old men like boughs weighted with snow.

Was Ballast seeing the same things? At first Falca couldn't believe
his eyes. He wondered, too, if he had a premonition of this, with
Sorelip and the man he'd thought was his father. Had he somehow
been affected by the Crucible, betrayed a predisposition to its power
long before he came to the Sanctuary?

When the voals reached the perimeter of the Crucible, they left
their maces, shaft first, vertically in perfect alignment with the nearest
one. They didn't struggle to secure it in the . . . body? . . . of the Crucible. They left the maces as easily as one would lean a staff against a
wall. The moment the voals did this, the two priests called forth the
next pair without turning around. They felt the Gifts being given,
Falca was sure, because they smiled each time with an arrogance, a
confidence he wanted to wipe off their faces: the satisfaction of a
herder whose dogs had brought in the last sheep. They couldn't see,
and they couldn't hear the giving of the maces, for there was no
sound other than the humming of the Crucible, a keening that increased with each mace delivered.

By the time two voals had joined others on the far dais, two more
would be walking their different paths through the Crucible. The ones
who had been through stood to either side of the Prism and its
attendant priests. Above, in the high tower, Maradus stood over all
with the same satiated smile as his followers. A few voals collapsed
like soldiers in the sun too long. They were neither helped nor
abused.

Only a few more Lifters remained in front of Saphrax. Falca
looked back and caught Ballast's eyes, which spoke plainly enough.
What are we going to do?

Above the wall the snake head, its eyes big as shields, moved
sideways, as if seeking targets. Below, the tapering end of its tail
twitched, silently beating on the earth the rhythm of this convocation.

Falca knew he would have to walk; there was no other path for
him to take, no alley. The part of him that resisted had the full

knowledge that he would not be the same man once he did. If anything, the transformation would be greater than the voals', who had come prepared, eager for the union with the One. His plan seemed fragile as crystal: walk the Crucible, get Amala's mace from where Saphrax would leave it, threaten to wreck the Crucible if Maradus didn't destroy the snake and let Ballast free with Amala.

He had to walk, if only to run out that slim hope for her. As two more voals left, Falca gestured to Ballast to come closer. But the stoneskin misinterpreted his meaning and turned away to begin walking back through the Lifters waiting to walk. As Falca shouldered through the voals, he wondered how Ballast could have made the mistake. Was it the stoneskin's own desire to get away? Had he matched his fatalism with what he thought was Falca's surrender?

Falca felt a flicker of temptation to use the mistake as an excuse, to keep on going, find a place, and wait for Maradus to cast away the guardian snake. But by then it would be too late for Amala. . . .

He caught Ballast's arm, gripping him to a halt, bringing him near enough to whisper in his ear. No one around looked at them suspiciously. All eyes were on the Crucible. "I'm going in," Falca said.

"Because you want to or have to?"

"Maybe it's the same now. I'll need the mace."

"Falca, I've never seen your Amala. I've come far with you. If you go in, you'll get neither her out nor yourself. It's over. You'd just be destroying yourself."

"Ballast, grab another mace from someone when I shout your name and come forth. I'll give you Amala's. They will let you free or I'll destroy the Crucible or as much of it as I can before they kill me. Take Amala and Frikko and get out of here."

He grabbed the mace and felt, in Ballast's reluctance to give it up, all of his friend's despair, sadness, fear. But the stoneskin finally relinquished it. "Good luck, roaking."

Falca took his place again, just one man behind Saphrax. He lifted the mace, expectant now. Part of him weakened with its possession; the other grew stronger. He wanted to walk now and he sounded Amala's name over and over, soundlessly, to convince himself that he was doing this for her and not himself, to smother the part of him he didn't trust, the one that did not feel revulsion at the Crucible but a desire to walk its gentle grade. It was the temptation of beauty, of belonging, of final rest but not death, of possession of a gift he had longed to give and receive.

He still sounded Amala's name when Saphrax's turn came. Falca had never before concentrated so hard on anything as he did on the brute's path through the Crucible. He took the right half of the One, off the central pathway. Maybe it was the fierceness of Falca's gaze, like that of a hungry predator tracking prey over a winter field, but he never saw in Saphrax the shimmering changes that occurred in the others who walked. Maybe they happened but he didn't see them, or didn't allow his eyes, which had tricked him before, to see them. All he saw was Amala's mace, and the exact spot where Saphrax gave it to the One. His eyes didn't follow Saphrax to the far dais to mark his location among all the others, nor did he follow the voal, whose departure left Falca face to face with the Crucible. He only allowed the voal into his field of vision when the Lifter gave his mace.

Amala's would be the second in line along the curving outer rim of the Crucible, just one more star in the heavens, but one he had to bring earthward with a reach that spanned an abyss he was now eager to bridge.

Distantly he heard the priests' calling and stepped forward. He walked up the dais steps and unhooded his mace without looking, for his head was still turned in the direction of Amala. He felt a moment of panic when the flaring light of the close mace-head momentarily blinded him from the view of her mace. He found it again as he held the mace out for the priest's hand.

He walked on, trembling at the approach of the curtain of Crucible light, his eyes slitted but still true to Amala's location. He expected to feel the heat of the light, but he only shivered with a chill. Only when he stepped into the Crucible, penetrating the cylinder of light, did he feel a sudden heat that matched the greater incandescence of the mace in his left hand. The waves of pleasure were so intense that his legs buckled for a moment, and even after he steadied himself, it didn't end. He had entered into union with the One, but one of many thousands, and the feeling that was almost too much to bear was not his alone, he realized, but pleasure once experienced by all the shining Gifts around him. When it finally began to subside, his first thought was that he had to have this again, that he would do anything to gain a second penetration. Then he was repelled by the desire, for in that time he had almost lost Amala. There she was at the edge of all the others. He said her name and that helped him turn off the central path to the right heart-chamber of the Spirit-Lifter's god, his god now.

He felt like he was walking a warm beach, with a summer's wate

irling gently around his ankles. He couldn't see it, but he felt it
essing him, lulling him. He didn't know what he was treading
on, but there was a give and softness in its foundation. It was like
shing one's hand along the flank of a sleeping lover, inert but alive
breathing, and Falca suddenly knew that this thing, this Crucible
stolen life, was alive. Maybe it was given life by some seeping
charge, the soul-seep dripping down from the mace-heads, like the
ter on a glass on a hot day.

He remembered the candle from that first night with Amala, how
wanted him to remove his hand so that she, too, could feel the
at of the dripping wax, the evidence that gave a mortality to the
idlelight revealing her beauty with shadow and brightness. That
idle, the mace, were one and the same. He hadn't wanted her to
the sting of the wax, but he had used the candle, tempting the
ne so close to her skin. Her beauty and spirit were matched with
t of this Crucible-god. He knew he would have to choose between
m.

Falca saw her mace now as a lit candle, one of thousands that
rounded him, rising like that first one from her beauty. He sounded
name, his truest defense against himself, and suddenly feared for
loss of his Amala. Then he thought: Surely there hadn't been time
her to seep away, trickle precious drops down the mace-shaft, to
il and mingle with all the others that gave the Crucible keening
, that was even now giving him lives. No, she'd only just been
ven to the One. There wasn't time for loss, but in time . . .

He took no meandering path through the maces. That gave him
ie. He walked the shortest route, more frightened than he had ever
en. One moment of distraction and he might lose her mace among
the identical others, become disoriented. There was nothing spe-
about her mace, or the light of her soul from its crystal head. Her
queness lay within him, and far away, and would flower again
y if he kept the door to his memories open. Yet so many more
re being flung open too.

What would happen if he made a mistake, took the wrong mace,
all the way back to Draica, only to join the soul of a stranger to
aala?

Those doorways were so wide! He was at once spectator and par-
pant in births, deaths. He felt himself being constricted, pulled,
hed toward a light greater than even the Crucible, and colder. He
a roughness abrading his skin that made him want to cry out, a

cry that turned into the matching pain of the deliverer, not the delivered. He felt the fatigue he so wanted to end, the pain he thoug
would never cease, heard the urgings of those around him, t
squeezing of his hand, something cool on his forehead, and then th
last of the unbearable pain, and he collapsed with such relief and je
he would never feel beyond the confines of this field of light.

He walked on with nothing but his mace, but its weight grew in
moment, its form changed and gave voice, and Falca spoke to
softly with warmth and love and wonder and pride. The fullness
this swirled away without names, and he became the source of th
love that had never come to him before. He saw through weak ey
the blurred faces, then the smiles as two people came closer. His fea
eased, faded away for a moment with a contentment he couldn't nam
but knew was there, as someone picked him up and rocked him. Fal
wanted to linger here, but this fullness, too, slipped away of its ov
accord, and he felt different arms holding him. He walked on but w
on his back, feeling weight on his loins, eager but fearing the pen
tration that dissolved expectation to a sharp, brief pain. He closed h
eyes to this different fullness, felt the racing heartbeat matching hi
the sweat of the boy who whispered a name into his ear: "Kris
Krisa, Krisa..." His encircling arms that slid over the sweat on th
boy's back began hitting, pounding against another as he walked. I
screamed with rage and fury at an act forced on him by a man wi
stinking breath and strong arms; screamed at the violation, the man
reeking anger.

The heat in his face, the helplessness within, became a differe
terror, and he watched the death of his wife in childbirth, calling h
name over and over as she rocked and bucked, screaming at the bab
to come out, come out, screaming at him to do something because
hurt so.

He walked on, turning here on weak legs to see Draica before th
Colossus was completed and jumped up and down as a boy, holdi
his father's hand, feeling the wind of the Erseiyr's departure with
wagon load of treasure, hurrying like all the others after the go
coins that slid off past the talons gripping and the rising, risi
wagon.

As a girl he stumbled and fell in a shed, cutting his arm on
spade, and as a young consort, drew in his breath at the sucking pa
of a bloodsnare finding purchase in his arm. He heard the wild ap
plause of patrons in the den as his blood filled the drones of th

nare, beginning the slow music of the aulost that was his gift and the
oung parasite's gift to the world. The weakness from loss of blood
ecame the weakness of his legs taking first steps.

He was drunk, laughing in the hold of a swaying ship, and laugh-
ig again in conspiracy with others at the scorn the lady of the house
eaped on her husband behind closed doors. He opened another and
ished he hadn't, to see the infidelity he never suspected from his
usband. He rushed away, and his anger turned to tears, but he was
ioving faster, and the wind quickly dried the tears, and he used the
rop to urge his horse faster, pulling away from the other racers to
ictory.

Falca walked on, nearing the curving edge, feeling regret at the
uick passing of the good, relief at the bad. The lives swept by him at
ie pace of a heartbeat here, a dozen there. He felt it all, but each
me rose above it, moved beyond, a carriage stopping at all the inns
iong the way, the same carriage he'd yearned to possess that day by
ie canal. Above all, he felt, there was a sense of power,
ivulnerability, for he was at once part yet apart from it all, plunged
ito this river of souls but always lifted out before he drowned. His
ands, his mind, possessed equal measures of control and abandon-
ient. He was both a god and a supplicant in the Crucible, horse and
der, walking the seams of twilight and dawn between night and day.
le expanded to everything he wanted—and didn't want to be—and
one of it. The exhilaration that hammered at his heart was like that
f eluding pursuit.

He approached Amala's mace and stopped, as if her standing light
as the haven where he was safe from hunters. But was it? Through
ll the walk his eyes had never left her mace, though his mind and
ody had entered and passed through a hundred lives. Now that he
as this close to her, his eyes strayed to the place just beyond in her
w, the smooth, never-turned earth of this living cemetery, where he
ould place the mace he held, adding one more burst of light and life,
iother few steps to a Path.

Falca felt tired, as weary as an old man running through his mem-
ries. Always he was the one who had to watch over others, look over
is shoulder. There had been no one, ever, to look after him, to be the
rong one, to allow him the rest he deserved. He laughed in amaze-
ent at the thought that never in his life had he truly rested without
orry. That's why he'd always wanted to go to Gebroan. He grew
sentful. Didn't he deserve something now? Why not let someone

else carry the load? He could rest, and surely the Spirit-Lifters would watch his back.

Something told him not to give it up, what he'd just been through, the most wonderful moments of his life. Moments or years, he couldn't tell. Why exchange a thousand lives for one? What bargain was that? And more were being added all the time, increasing the Paths one could take for Union with the One. He himself would be adding a Gift. With so many Paths, it was no bondage or subjugation but freedom to choose within the One. How paltry the common union when one could experience the hard and soft of so many, one moment offering, the next accepting, or discard the shy lover for the sensuous in the space of a few steps. Caress or be caressed and held.

He walked past Amala's mace, closer to the rows of maces than hers, to offer his Gift. Before he did, he looked back at her mace, whose light was indistinguishable from that of the next in line, or the one Falca held. He wondered why he had come so far to recover a light the same as all the rest.

He placed the mace upright, and it stood of its own accord, on the end of the helve. With his hand still on it, he felt it slip downward, as if into the softest, most fertile earth. It stayed there. As Falca accepted a rushing of pleasure at giving a Gift to the One, he looked up at the dais, where they were all waiting for him. The other voal was now walking toward the steps, and Falca felt an urge to follow him, to join him and all the others, felt the eager anticipation of Lifting a soul for himself, for surely there was an even greater bond in giving a Gift you had taken yourself.

Something held him back, as if he'd left a house forgetting... something he'd meant to take with him but he couldn't remember what it was. He was trying to recall, when he saw Saphrax looking at him, nodding happily as if he'd received a gift. Falca was surprised because he had never seen such happiness on Saphrax's face. He was saying something to Falca, then leaned over to another and spoke.

Why is he so happy? Falca wondered. Was it his own walk through the Crucible? No, that wasn't all of it. Amala?

Amala? He said the name again, recovering for a moment its familiarity. That was what he'd forgotten, what Saphrax was so happy about, why he was gesturing him to walk on to the dais and join all the others. Saphrax, too, had felt all that was Amala. He had shared with Falca the memories of her that were still cloudy but getting

earer. He had possessed her, too, and in that lay a tempting kinship
ith the One.

What had Saphrax told him once: "You took me from the river
alks, the gutters once, saved my life, gave me a first life to bide me
l I found a second, better one. The least I can do is repay my
lvation with yours."

He was offering it to Falca even now, vigorously gesturing with
s hand: "Come forth, come here, join me and we will walk the
reets of the cities together to find Gifts for the evergrowing One, as
e stole from fools and those reeking animals, the Timberlimbs. We
ill walk many Paths through the Crucible hereafter. What is one
hen there are thousands to be part of, my friend."

Falca couldn't hear the words but knew he'd spoken, so close was
e bond, and he felt himself nodding, accepting the deliverance, the
omise. But instead of walking ahead, he went back to Amala's
ace. To say goodbye, to join with her, as her, a last time. As he
me closer, he hesitated, sensing danger within himself. She would
ill be here for all those times to come. Why do this now? He felt
ar at this new temptation, something within himself that drew him
ick to her, though he wanted to be with all the others. As he stood in
e pale of her light, a nimbus like all the rest, he realized with the
uickness of a snapping branch that Saphrax had only meant to lure
m to a place of abomination, where only moments before he wanted
go. The bait for the lure was Amala. She was the sacrifice. He was
e sacrifice. And he felt, as she had, the terror of the last moments
rashing on the floor of the room, the hearth, the dog, the windows,
e divan all at crazy desperate angles. He smelled the stink, the
vful purpose of the huge brute, saw the dangling earring, struck out
ith fists in a ferocious but futile attack, wildly determined not to
eld but knowing she was losing, losing herself, wondering where
alca was and why, oh why, he hadn't come to her earlier to say
oodbye.

Chapter Thirty-two

Freaca's Gift

Freaca was too edgy and apprehensive to stay in the plac
Falca and Ballast had left her. She didn't like Falca when he held one o
the sun-boughs, and here he was facing a forest of them, surrounded b
shit-catchers thick as grubs in a dinner bowl. And not only that. She'd lo
sight of Falca and Ballast when the nightmare snake materialized fro
the darkness to encircle the place below. She had almost gone down the
fearing the snake would begin constricting, crushing Falca and Balla
within its sliding coils. But it had stopped, merely linking its tapering ta
to its rising neck and head that remained motionless, high as a racin
station, no doubt as transfixed by the light as the shit-catchers were. Tha
was an odd thing to Freaca, for she had grown accustomed to the
impatience. Yet here were so many, as passive and tightly lashed togethe
as timbers on the Road.

She climbed up the steps she and Falca and Ballast had walke
down from the awful treeless land. She moved farther up those step
so that she could once again see Falca and Ballast below. She felt a b
better, no more. Something was going to happen. She felt it lurking
as real and as shadowy as the silent shit-catchers, those walkin
stones with the winter eyes, that prowled the darkness near her. It wa
strange how she didn't fear them.

This place was a puzzle and not a good one, and certainly it hel
mysteries she could never understand. It was definitely not Falca

ome, though a destination. Maybe a home to the extent, any-
ay, that he had come here to make Amala, the Absent One, less
stant in his heart and mind. Perhaps after here, Falca would move
to his true home, and Freaca comforted herself with that
ought.

She tried to quell her misgivings with the question of whether the
rest of sun-boughs could be all bad. Certainly Falca was not himself
hen he held one. Could they all be bad? Gurrus had once told her
at the very trees of her own home, the ones that nurtured the ani-
als and climbers, the ones that gave their boughs to the Road and
e dwellings of her people, had a special life all their own. They
uldn't talk or run or do anything a person could do, but they had
eir own spirits. For if they burned down, or were cut, would there
ot be loss? Would not the animals—indeed her people—go else-
here for sustenance?

She wondered if there was a connection between Amala and the
un-boughs down there. Why else would Falca have come here, to be
nong all those shit-catchers he despised? They were enemies. He
d Ballast had killed some.

Could it be that this place was a kind of birthing place for some of
alca's kind? The sun-boughs the seeds that would grow into
atchers? Even the monstrous snake might be only the guardian of a
est. Freaca had seen that much at home. Most shit-catchers were
uel, voracious creatures, and maybe that was because their birthing,
nlike her own kind's, was devoid of the flesh, its warmth and blood.
laybe Falca had come to take the birthing seed of Amala to his
ome, where she could grow.

No, that couldn't be right, Freaca thought. Amala was good, oth-
wise Falca wouldn't love her. She was sure that Amala, though
bsent, existed, had already been born, had loved Falca as he did
er. How could one love something not yet born?

Freaca was sure about only one thing. Falca had come for Amala
d would leave with what he came for, whatever it was. He would
ke something. He was a hunter, a good one, and such a hunter
oesn't return home with nothing.

She kept waiting for him to take one of the sun-boughs. Amala?
he one he had come for. When she saw him walk as the others had,
e whispered to him, urging him to do what he had traveled so far to
o. He didn't. He was doing exactly like everyone else before him,
l those 'catchers he despised. He was dressed in their garb, held the

sun-bough she and Ballast had kept from him until he needed it.

She had to help him. She had done it before and would do it again, even if it meant going down there among all the shit-catchers and calling to him. Or whatever else it took to make him remember.

She wasn't scared; too much had happened to her since she left home. The only thing that frightened her was not being able to get home and save her people before the 'catchers killed them all. She knew she would never be able to make it home without Falca's and Ballast's help. It was too far; there was too much of the Road to walk before the trees appeared again on the earth, before the terrible heat lessened and raindrops dripped from leaves.

There was all of that down below; she could almost smell home. Not even the stench of the god-snake and the shit-catchers could mask the smell of the water circling the forest of sun-boughs and the trees around the water. And with Falca down there, it seemed the shorter, easier route back home to save her people. The other Road, no. She shook her head and took a few steps down. Too many shit-catchers on that longer Road who would pin her to the ground. She didn't want that to happen again. She needed Falca. Ballast too, who had so often been her shade in the desert.

Falca was intertwined with her home. Was his home hers now, or was it just the time together on the Road that made her feel that way? Was it just her love for him that made it matter so much to her that Falca bring home Amala, the Absent One?

She hurried down the steps, shaking off the questions that might never be answered, knowing that she had to act quickly. For she saw Falca leave a sun-bough near the far end of the forest of light. He began to walk away without taking anything. He had forgotten why he had come here. Was it like the sun-bough he had held before that made him forget who he was?

Freaca lost sight of him before she reached the bottom of the steps, and that made her more desperate to reach him before it was too late. She gagged at the bottom-of-the-forest stench of the night mare snake looming like a wall ahead of her. She didn't pause from fear, she was too small for it to notice her. As she ran around the twitching tail—big as her hoven back home—its head dropped. She could feel the shift in the wind as she ran through the small opening underneath the rising curve of its neck and one side of the gateway.

Something wet and raspy pushed her ahead so hard, her feet left the ground and she tumbled, skinning her hands and knees. She

oked back as she quickly got to her feet, ducking the darting tip of
e monster's tongue. She ran from the red eyes, big as moons, the
wline that seemed to be smiling at her violation of this place. She
ept on running, waiting for blackness to envelop her, but the snake
dn't strike. Maybe she was too small, or maybe it was all the shit-
atchers around her, who were crying out in fear at the lowering
east's head. No 'catcher tried to stop her; they were looking past her
the snake.

She darted past the last of them and raced up the steps Falca had
ken into the forest, hope rising in her heart, for soon she would be
le to see him, call to him.

They were shouting at her now, but one voice alone made her
ause as she reached the top of the steps, where two more shit-
atchers stood, their heads and arms moving to block her way.

It was Ballast, shouting at her, lunging toward the steps she had
st taken. She saw him grab a sun-bough from an astonished shit-
atcher and wave it at her, offering it to her, obviously wanting her to
ke it. But Freaca didn't want to have anything to do with the thing,
hich contained the poison that made Falca forget. She didn't have
me to puzzle out why Ballast wanted her to have it. Maybe he, too,
ad forgotten.

Angry shit-catchers were coming after her now. She ran past
e clumsy pair, toward the wall of light that hurt her eyes. All she
uld discern was a dark shape, a familiar shape in the distance to her
ght. Falca. He was there. He hadn't left yet. Was he coming back
ward her?

She smelled anger, overpowering anger, but it wasn't Falca's. She
new that. The anger was of something chained, contained for too
ng.

Freaca called out to Falca, repeating one of the only words she
new he would understand, the word she hoped would bring him—
d her—home at last.

She felt no pain as she died in the space of a heartbeat. The last
ing she felt was joy that she had called to him in time, before he left
e forest of light without taking anything with him.

Chapter Thirty-three

Amala's Mace

Frikko's calling of his name, Amala's name, was like a reflex that snapped Falca's hand over the final distance to Amala' mace. He lifted it up and turned in the same motion, to scream a warning to Frikko. It was too late. She disintegrated within the curtain of Crucible light, scattering as a sudden gust blows embers from a fire.

He saw Ballast kneeling on the dais, head bowed, flanked by the blind priests, who were calling for calm to those below. Falca cradled Amala's mace tightly, to protect it not only from his anger at this place but from his despair at his own weakness, which had made Frikko come forth. He whispered a promise to her, for mourning, and two more: one to keep now, the other later. He told her fiercely she would not be forgotten. He held the mace as if it were her dying body. For this moment, Frikko and Amala were one and the same.

No one had ever held the mace of someone they had loved, for no one would ever do such a thing as Lift the soul of a lover, a daughter a husband, a father. Holding Amala now, finally, it all came back to Falca with the speed of skipping stones, and he felt such a strength, a union, and a triumph that his face ran hot with tears for Frikko, who had sought to make sure that would happen.

He saw Amala as a girl, severely scolded for the small mischief of soiling a favorite carpet of her parents but defiant as she walked away. He was with her in a graveyard where an old man stood guard at night over the tombstones. He felt her love for her brother as she embraced him, the night she gave him the ring. Falca knew what it said, for he was with Amala—*was* Amala—when she composed the inscription. Only now did he fully understand the love between Amala and Alatheus, its depth and tightening constrictions that drove her to the surface, and air.

His skin shivered as hers did the winter night she lost her virginity to a handsome, convenient young man; felt her eager, defiant thrill at keeping this secret from Alatheus. He felt her contempt for the men of her social station, the ones Alatheus bullied, and felt pity at their fear. She might have yearned for her freedom, but there was such comfort in knowing that a certain one would always protect you, even die for you.

She sought escape eventually, and Falca understood that she saw herself an outcast by design as much as by accident and felt a kinship with those outcast in a much harder, crueler way—the Timberlimbs. He took the same sneaking pleasure she did at circumventing the stern 'tressas' rules by shutting an eye to trysts between lovers at the settlement house. He heard Gurrus give her the secret of Sweet-hand and was with her and Sippio as she practiced with the sliver-heart and wondered how much skill she'd need to survive in the Rough Bounds.

Falca had Amala's eyes that first night together, and her body, and he saw himself making love to her. The greatest pleasure he had ever had now was in knowing, truly knowing, the pleasure she took in him. He knew by her laughs at his clumsiness on the ice, he knew she loved him, knew the words she was going to say the day she became an empty.

It took no more than a dozen heartbeats to glimpse these colors of her soul. Though he had an eagerness to know *all* her secrets, he returned the gift of this knowledge with an equal desire to return to her the privacy of her soul. He wanted now to know only what she would later choose to give him, let him know and see and hear. For there was mystery in this and chance, unpredictability and risk—all those things that were, along with a fierce devotion, the better tinctures of love than possession of the soul and all secrets. That was the mixture Alatheus had tried in his own crucible.

They were shouting at him, so many of them, from both daises, priests and voals—and Saphrax. Falca heard Saphrax above all the others: "Put it back. Join us, Falca. You transgress. It is not too late to Give yourself to us and so transcend yourself. Something better awaits you. It is not too late to save yourself, my friend. . . ."

Others screamed at him, "Abandon your god and you abandon yourself!"

"Do not betray what you are now."

"Don't abandon what you could become."

Falca knew he had the power to destroy this thing because he held Amala's mace. He had to destroy the abomination of the Crucible. It had killed Frikko. Its servants and creator wouldn't let him go free with Amala and Ballast.

Falca tucked her mace beneath his tabard, protecting it with his left hand. With his right he lifted another mace from the Crucible as easily as pulling a weed from soft earth. He paused to look at Saphrax and all the priests and voals who had rushed down from the far dais. They had no maces and stood helplessly before the Crucible's light, shouting, flailing their arms as if at a river's edge where their enemy had just safely crossed to the other side. High above in the tower, a frenzied Maradus screamed at them to stop Falca. At the other dais, voals gathered to do his bidding. Only those who had not walked the Crucible, who still had maces to give to the One, could safely enter.

Falca thought, They could only want to be released, these souls stolen by the Lifters. He smashed the head of his mace against another's and ducked, though careful not to stumble and smash Amala's mace, which he held close to his heart. He felt the spray of crystal shards, but the released souls ignored him, shot off in surging, narrow arcs that bent, swooped; hawks after prey. They crossed once in the air and leveled off, one boring through the stomach of a Lifter standing near Saphrax, the other rising to shear off the head of a voal. The head rolled down the steps of the dais, bouncing like a child's ball. The soul-light didn't stop. One ray sliced through a corner of Maradus's tower; the other cleaved a column in the Lifters' barracks.

Falca began a measured walk, lifting a mace from the Crucible, smashing another. Again and again. It was as easy as taking a stick to icicles hanging from the eave of a house. A deadly lacing of light stitched the night.

Falca glanced back at Ballast, who stood like a giant where the blind priests had been. He'd thrown away his mace and taken his sword. For all their number the voals were no match for him. He stood his ground, cleaving Lifters right and left, shouldering them off the dais, tripping others, screaming at more to come. Most of them had no weapons; their maces were Gifted, not charged, and they had to hold them to get into the Crucible, to Falca. By holding them, they were easy victims for an enraged Ballast.

Falca smashed more maces. Lifters, desperate to stop him, charged down into the wavering curtain of light but met the same fate as Frikko and the empty before her. One voal was struck by a ray of soul-light as he ran toward the Crucible. It sliced through both knees from the side, and he fell back, his stumps wriggling in the air, leaving his feet and lower legs like boots set out for polishing.

Falca saw Saphrax standing rigidly as Lifters around him were being killed by the weaving streams of light. Saphrax kept shaking his head, as if Falca had betrayed him. Only then did he turn and walk away, the soul-light arcing by him, above his head, but never touching him.

The voals facing Ballast had fled, and Falca turned at his roar of triumph to see the stoneskin grab a mace from a Lifter he'd gutted and wade into the Crucible, smashing with sword and headless mace, adding still more spears of light to the sanctuary.

Few Lifters remained around the Crucible now as Falca and Ballast kept on smashing its maces. Falca could feel a shuddering beneath his feet, but whether it was the death agony of the One or the reverberations from the sanctuary's towers and barracks, he couldn't tell. Scores of Lifters fled to the protection of buildings, running inside or hiding behind. They couldn't escape. The released souls tore through stone, cut through stone to get at each one, or curved around the corners, like bright ribbon around a box, to strike at their huddled groups. The material—flesh or stone—didn't matter. Only time wore down the rays, the dissipation a rising, golden dust, a final gift to the night.

Each soul found a mark, Falca was sure. The One Mark for each. The killing wasn't random. Was it rage, retribution? The rebound, the completion of a terrible union that each Lifter had begun with his or her victim?

Falca and Ballast continued smashing maces, watching the searing light escape to begin hunting. Within moments came a scream or a hissing of cutting stone as the light pared off huge chunks of the towers, the barracks. The fiery bolts lopped off trunks of surrounding trees, which fell back toward the wall, or forward, smashing into buildings or the towers behind that of Maradus.

At the end of it all, Falca knew that he and Ballast would have to destroy the Prism, the fount of the Spirit-Lifters' corruption, which lay at the base of Maradus's tower.

He worked his way toward Ballast, near the dais where Frikko died, when the stoneskin shouted at him. Falca turned to see Maradus's tower, weakened by all the strikes of soul-light, begin to fall. He sprinted away, over the bodies of Lifters, down the dais steps toward the gateway.

The snake Maradus had summoned withered away to the size of a cutlass worm, and Falca and Ballast leaped over it, turning only when they reached the first steps leading up to the land.

The tower fell in more of a slide than a topple, obliterating the moaning and crying of dying Lifters. Like the bursting of a dammed river, the tower broke apart, engulfing the dais and the Prism, its great stones heaving into the ring of water. Others tumbled like blocks into the Crucible, smashing hundreds of maces, which in turn scythed through hundreds more, sending out myriad ropes of light that tightened and curled and brightened the basin of the sanctuary to daylight, seeking out the Lifters.

Kneeling, his great arm and shoulder shielding Falca's head, Ballast offered himself as protection. Whining shards of crystal flew through the air. Though he huddled behind Ballast, his hand over Amala's mace, Falca felt the sting of cuts. Ballast caught the worst. Falca wondered if he had forgotten that his roughy was no longer as good as a shield, that he bled as easily now as Falca.

The storm of light ended, and they stood, staring at what was left, as they picked splinters of crystal from themselves and each other. They daubed the worst of the cuts and let the rest bleed.

"Is she all right?" Ballast asked.

"Yes," said Falca.

The rubble of the sanctuary was shrouded in a mist that clung to the ruins of amputated towers, the barracks, the trees that were little more than an unevenly cropped hedge of stumps now. The water of the fountain ring had overflowed, displaced by so much of Maradus's tower. The water pooled all the way to the corroded wall that surrounded everything.

The mist of souls gradually rose, taking with it the light that had once bathed the sanctuary. The Crucible still contained a few score maces that escaped destruction. "We may as well get the rest of them," Falca said.

Bodies sprawled everywhere. Some Lifters were still alive, beg-
ing for help or water. Falca went on. There was little he could do to
lp them, even if he wanted to.

As he and Ballast entered the Crucible, no brighter now than the
mplit street by Amala's house, he saw shapes coming from his left,
en right, converging on the Crucible in the listless manner of emp-
es.

Ballast backed toward Falca, drawing his sword, but Falca put a
and on his arm. "They're not coming for us."

There were almost a hundred at least, and they took the steps of
e dais like condemned men or women would those of a gallows.
hey spread out, passing by Falca and Ballast with scarcely a look,
d took their paths to the remaining maces, their bare feet making a
ttle sound on the litter of crystal. Some cut their feet, but seemed not
notice, and as they turned and left with their prizes, they left tracks
f blood that veined the Crucible. Given their numbers and the bodies
f Lifters they had to step over to get back, Falca expected some to
umble, fall, and break the maces. None did. Those who didn't get a
ace merely turned around and followed the others. A group of them,
long with a few who had maces, used the ruins of Maradus's tower
cross from the Crucible, over the water ring. There, by the edge,
ith great blocks of stone looming over them, they passed the maces
om one to the other, letting each satisfy his or her curiosity in turn.

He and Ballast walked over to watch them. Falca wondered what
e odds were of any of them holding up his own soul. He shook his
ead as Ballast pointed. "Care to buy a ship for the voyage home?"
e stoneskin said.

Two empties sat on halves of a chest, whose contents had spilled
ut over the ground, glinting in the light of the half-dozen maces
ther empties held. Most of the gold and coins and jewels had fallen
to the water, whose surface shimmered in the light. "Maradus had
ore on his mind than the Crucible," Falca whispered.

The chest might have contained gravel, for all the empties cared.
hey were more interested in the maces, the light that was cool to the
ouch, and in drinking from the water. Falca remembered the coins
e'd flung into the fountain at Rhysselia's Garden, after the flinarra
layed his last song for Amala. She would have that memory back,
ith all the others too. Soon.

"Shall we get the maces before the empties go too far with them?"
allast asked.

"No," Falca said. "Let them have them."

The empties left, straggling away, taking the last light with them. Already Falca could see the gleaming maces in the darkness of the sanctuary basin moving slowly, like restless, earthbound stars, the only treasure the empties would have.

"Maybe we should help them, then," Ballast said softly, speaking what was on Falca's mind.

"If only we knew, but we can't know. Do you understand what I'm saying?"

"Yes. It's too bad, though."

"Maybe it's just better to let them have what they find. They are scavengers, but this place is theirs now, and they've been lords of nothing else before. They will rule here. There's water and food in the ruins, for a while anyway. It's a better place for them than the camps outside Sandsend or the aqueduct pumps."

Ballast shook his head. "Without the Lifters to give them food, they'll starve."

"Maybe," Falca said. "But there's also the pack animals up top, supplies. We'll leave most of that for them. As long as there's water down here, animals will come. If they can kill them, they'll have food."

Still, he truly didn't know if it was right to leave them as they were. Would it be better to give an old empty, a male, the life of a girl, or a young woman all the life and memories of an old man? Or would it kill the empty if such a cross-matching was made? Also, there were ten times as many empties as maces, at least. What about all those who would be left behind? Falca didn't want to choose, play the god as the Lifters had done. If he did, what would he say to the woman in the man's body, who saw herself squatting before a fire, staring blankly at the flames?

He decided finally: It was enough to have made sure the nightmare would never happen again.

It was dark, but in the absence of Crucible light, the moons—Suaila and Cassena—seemed brighter than Falca remembered. He allowed himself the thought that maybe the moons seemed brighter because the motes of souls had risen already to that height. He saw movement among the ruins; not an empty. One of the few surviving Lifters. He remembered that there would be a few because not all the maces had been destroyed.

The Lifter continued on, and in the short time before he disapared behind the rubble of the towers, Falca saw that it was Saphrax. ne moonlight revealed his shambling gait.

"He's there, Ballast, Saphrax. It's strange. I saved his life by king Amala's mace."

"You want to finish him?" Ballast said, reaching for his sword.

Falca was tempted. Even now the memories, Amala's memories, : her Lifting were so strong that he felt a surge of anger at what aphrax had done, the absolute violation that would never happen ;ain.

Falca realized he had a part in that. It had begun the day he bought aphrax off the river hulks. Though the brute had been rabid before en, Falca had used him, supplied the length of chain that finally napped because Falca didn't want him anymore. Saphrax had been ter him, and Amala was the means. The brute deserved punishment, ıt maybe these ruins would be enough. If Falca had never known m, the decision would be clear-cut.

Falca put a hand on Ballast's and slid the sword home. "He came long way, too, for something. Let him have the ruins; it's little ıough. Without the Prism, nothing can be resurrected."

"He could follow you, seeking revenge."

"I don't think so. There's no one here to take him from the hulks ;ain."

They went down to the water to collect Maradus's gold. Ballast und a Lifter's cape and spread it out. He used two hands to scoop ie treasure onto the cape; Falca watched him, content to let him do ie work. He didn't want to risk Amala's mace.

They took the steps slowly in the dark; the only sounds were the linking of the tied-off cape of treasure against Ballast's back, the ind, and the braying of the animals above.

Along with the food and water, they'd also need a blanket or :ather to protect Amala's mace until Falca got something better in ingstear. The castellan there would be more than happy to supply im with something.

"I wonder what the castellan said, there on the parapet, when the ght disappeared far in the distance," Falca murmured.

"Well, we'll just have to ask him that, in a tavern of his choice."

Nearby in the enclosure, animals stamped and rustled. Falca and allast went over and picked the most docile of the packhorses to arry food, water, and the gleanings of Maradus's treasure.

As they took to the road under the stars, Falca could feel the heat of the land, what was left from before and what was to come.

Ballast felt it too. "I'm going to miss being her shade."

Falca remembered how she'd kept getting up, coming back when he pushed her away at Grippa's island, how she could never stay away. He felt, in a way, that he was taking her home, bringing back what she'd sought by leaving her home.

How he longed to tell Amala about Frikko and ask her if she would share the promise he had made to the Timberlimb.

First he had to get her home, safely. What was it the Limbs had called her? Sun-thicket. He smiled and held the mace tightly and imagined his heartbeats stirring her soul within.

Epilogue

Ellele saw the two men approach the gate as she stood before the window, enjoying the first sunny day in a week. Hallys was working in the garden, spade in hand, preparing the spring soil for the spurroses Ellele had gotten permission to plant. The Master and Mistress were in Falconwrist for the afternoon. It was just Ellele, Hallys, Amala—and the Timberlimbs of course. Ellele had given herself the fancy that the house and grounds were just hers and Hallys's, when the men broke her reverie.

At first she thought they were just going to taunt the four Timberlimbs, or worse. It happened periodically, and there was little she or Hallys could do about it. But the smaller of the two men merely nodded to the four by the gate, looking unsure, as if doubtful of the address. Then he gripped a bar of the gate, though he must have been able to see that it was locked.

Ellele watched, curious, as the old Limb got up and walked over to the man, to stand not a hand's width in front of him. Ellele expected the man to push the Limb away. He didn't. The old Timberlimb's head moved from side to side. Did he nod? Ellele couldn't be sure, given the glass and the partial obstruction of the gate. The Timberlimb then turned away and began walking down the street, followed by the younger Limbs.

Ellele licked her lips, puzzled, and not a little excited by this mystery.

They had ended their vigil.

Why now?

It was as if the Timberlimbs had been *waiting* for these two men. . . . Ellele shook her head, baffled. The men looked anything but savory. They were dressed in clothing scarcely better than rags and had the soiled, weary appearance of travelers who'd come a long way. The big man—fully a head taller than the other—was a hulking thing, a stoneskin perhaps, but his skin had not the usual gray tinge and was, if anything, paler than the other, though with dark splotches on his neck.

The smaller man's hair and beard were unkempt, and he seemed nervous. He held something long and bulky beneath his loose tabard, which worried Ellele. A weapon? The bigger man had a sword, which he obviously felt no need of hiding. She watched him take it out after a word with his companion and rattle it between the gate bars to get someone's attention. They could have shouted for someone, but they chose to use the sword. Aggressive men, Ellele judged, and here for a specific purpose. They must be friends of Alatheus who'd served with him in the Rough Bounds.

Ellele watched Hallys take his spade over to the gate to talk to them. After a moment he shook his head, then put the spade down and headed for the house.

"What do they want?" Ellele asked him when he came into the room.

"A strange pair. The stink of them is so bad, no wonder the Limbs left."

"What do they want?" Ellele repeated.

"Said they were friends of Amala's, wanted to know if she was here. I said she was, though I probably shouldn't have. The smaller one, with all the black hair, said he had a gift for Amala and news about her brother. When I asked him for both, he'd neither give me the gift nor tell me the news. So I told them to leave."

Ellele glanced through the window. "They're still there."

Hallys sighed. "The Limbs finally leave, and now we get these two. Well, I'm going back to work. We'll let the Master deal with them when he returns."

"Hallys," Ellele said softly. "Tell the smaller man to come in alone with the gift he has for Amala and this news about her brother."

"Ellele, I don't think it's wise. . . ."

"Think about it. Do you suppose if they meant any harm, they'd be going about it this way? The Master will want to know about

Alatheus. Besides, this man out there, whoever he is, is the first person who's even mentioned Amala's name since we came here."

"Ellele, you know the rules here. The Master will dismiss us quick if he finds out."

"He and the Mistress aren't due back till the end of the afternoon."

Her voice was so firm that Hallys knew better than to argue. As a last resort she was prepared to go out and do it herself, but Hallys sighed in resignation and left.

She wondered if she was being foolish, even courting danger. No. The Limbs had left. That was all the convincing she needed, though if someone asked her to explain her instinct, she couldn't. Whatever their rough appearance, these men had something for Amala.

Ellele watched her husband talking with them again. The smaller man shook his head, and Hallys stalked off again to the house.

"He won't come in alone without the other. Says if we're worried, they'll leave the sword outside the gate."

"Go let them in."

"Ellele, this is ridiculous! I'm not an errand boy. . . ."

"I'm sorry, Hallys. I'll do it myself."

"No, no," he muttered. "Honestly, Ellele, sometimes I wonder how we've lasted this long together."

"You take the sword just in case, and be careful," she called after him, and smiled. There was but one reason why they were still together. She and Hallys loved each other, that was all, and knew what was important to each. She didn't always get her way. But this was important to her.

She turned and walked the few steps to Amala, who was sitting on the floor, tying knots in a length of rope. She would do it for hours. She was almost done with the coil of rope Ellele bought her only last week. She'd have to get more.

She stroked Amala's golden hair. "I think you have visitors," she said softly. Amala looked up briefly, acknowledging Ellele's hand, her presence. At such moments Ellele thought that Amala was on the verge of smiling, but all she offered was simple recognition. Ellele wasn't disappointed. She couldn't be. The child was who she was, no more nor less.

Nor did the man, Falca Breks, seem disappointed that Amala gave him only the quickest of glances, as she might curtains suddenly ruffled by a breeze. He sat on the floor opposite her, holding the crystal mace as if someone, even now, was going to grab it, take it away from him. The light from the mace brightened the room better than the sunniest of days, and Ellele had occasionally to avert her eyes for rest during the time he told his story.

There was no doubting him. Sitting in the chair, Ellele kept her gaze on Falca, who in turn never took his eyes off Amala. He spoke in a low voice, which occasionally dipped to a whisper. He was not trying to convince anyone of the truth of what he said, Ellele felt. He was speaking to Amala, though he knew she wasn't listening. She kept making her knots, her long, working fingers not an arm's length from the one who had come so far to love her.

When Falca was done, Hallys cleared his throat. He was standing by the door with Ballast. The sword leaned against the wall near the hearth. "I think, Falca, that you'd better get on with it," Hallys said, gently and firmly. "Before her mother and father return." Ellele had never loved him so much as she did now, and she'd tell him so, later.

"Do you want us to stay or leave?" Ellele asked Falca, thinking of the birthings of her own two children and her preference to be with only Hallys and the midwife. For this seemed to her a rebirthing, Amala's reemergence into the world.

"It's not what I want," Falca said. "But we can't ask Amala what she wants. Stay, all of you. Will you hold this a moment?" he added to Ellele.

She took the mace, while Falca got pillows from the bed and put them on the floor, where Amala's head would lie. The mace was surprisingly heavy to Ellele. Maybe I am getting old, she thought. She passed a hand over the brightness of the crystal, as much to shield her eyes as to feel the coolness. Falca had spoken of the effect the maces had on him, and not just in the Crucible. Ellele didn't expect a cascade of visions from Amala's life. But before Falca took the mace back, one question was answered for Ellele. She knew now who Amala had wept for that day: her brother.

Falca asked her to lay Amala down, to ready her. Ellele got up from her chair to do so, talking softly to Amala. Even when her head was resting on the pillows, Amala didn't stop with the knots, looked at nothing but her working hands. Ellele brushed her wrinkled, spotted hand over Amala's forehead, as she had done the mace-head, and stood.

Falca took a deep breath to calm himself and kneeled at Amala's
ide.

He took a second breath and slowly lowered the mace-head to
.mala's forehead, covering the black mark, the indelible mark that
.llele had tried to scrub out in the bath those first days with her.

Amala's eyes grew wild, then closed, slowly. The knotted rope
ell from her hands as the light began to swirl in the room, coalescing
ato a narrowing rope of brightness that sought the source of the
aace-head and the concentration of greater light there. It coiled
round Falca so thickly that he was shielded from Ellele, though she
tood only steps away from him. It curled around his hands, the
ength of the mace, like a vine, feeding the mace-head, making it ever
righter, before the light within the crystal began fading, entering
.mala, disappearing into her.

She remained perfectly still, except for her hands, which reached
ut toward Falca. He kept his hands tightly together on the helve, not
vanting to risk—Ellele could see—any movement save the tears that
vere welling in his eyes. Her hands, her arms fell back to her sides as
he trembled now, ever so slightly.

The light Falca had brought to the room was gone, leaving only
hat which entered through the window behind Ellele. The rays caught
he empty mace-head, twisting through it, giving the crystal color
vhere once there had been trapped the sun.

Falca held the mace on Amala's forehead for long moments after
he opened her eyes, long after Ellele could tell she was back in the
vorld. Ellele wanted to tell him it was all right now, but he had to do
t himself. She knew he wanted to make sure, that in laying aside the
nace forever, he wouldn't be abandoning even a day of Amala's life.

Amala pushed it away in the end, and Falca lay the mace down.
.he mark on her forehead was gone. Falca whispered her name.

"Falca?" she said.

He nodded, holding her hands. Amala's eyes were fierce. "Is he
;one? Is it safe?" she said.

"It's all right now, Amala."

"Did he hurt you too? Are you all right?"

Falca squeezed her hands and smiled, finally. "I'm supposed to
sk you that."

She put a hand to her head, closed her eyes for a moment. "I don't
:now what happened, Falca. I was waiting for you, and that man, the

one you thought you'd killed, forced his way in. I fought him for as long as I could. . . ."

He brought her up gently. Her arms gathered around him, and they held each other tightly there on the floor. His hand stroked her head, and Ellele heard him whisper to her, "There's so much to tell you, Amala."

Ellele nodded to Hallys, and he and Ballast left the room. Ellele followed, looking back once to see Falca rocking her gently, telling her that he loved her.

She closed the door.

They passed the time in the drawing room. Ballast told Ellele and Hallys about the Ebony Isles, the first night they met Frikko. When Falca came out, they all stood. "She said she wanted to rest. I'll be back tomorrow, after Amala has a chance to tell her mother and father about Alatheus. Just so you know, she plans to tell them that he died bringing her back, and when Ballast and I appear tomorrow, we will be his friends who helped him. She says her mother and father will want her to stay, but she's still determined to go with us to the Rough Bounds. The Timberlimbs may not need or want our help, but the least we can do is tell them about Frikko. There is an old Limb in the settlement house named Gurrus, who Amala thinks might be able to tell us where her village was.

"You and Hallys, Ellele, were hired to take care of Amala, and when she goes, both of you will, too, probably." Ballast handed Falca a heavy leather pouch. He smiled. "This is for you." He tried to give it to Hallys, but he wouldn't take it. Nor would Ellele.

Falca plunked the bulging pouch down on a table. "Well, if you won't take it, keep it for Amala and me, if and when we return to Draica."

Hallys and Ellele looked at each other. Hallys nodded. "Only if you promise to return."

"And you, Ballast," Ellele said.

The stoneskin shook his head. "I'll be in the High Vales. But if there were ever any roakings who could make me come down from the Vales again, they're all in this house. Until tomorrow, then."

"I'll open the gate," Hallys said. As they headed for the hallway, Falca turned to Ellele: "She won't know who you are. Or Hallys. I'm sorry about that. It's been my pleasure to know you both, if only for a short time."

"It's been ours as well, Falca," Ellele said.

They left, Falca carrying the mace. Ellele went back to the room, peek in, expecting to find Amala sleeping.

She was looking out the window, her back to the door. She held a ngth of the knotted rope in one hand, working it through her 1gers, pausing at each knot. Falca must have seen her and waved, r she waved back, the rope tapping the windowpanes.

Ellele felt a little sadness that Amala would be going away, that 1e wouldn't get to know this tall woman. She knew that Falca was a)od man, that he would take care of her, and she him, but still . . . it as like her own last child moving away.

Ellele was about to go, to leave Amala with her thoughts of the 1an who'd returned and maybe the brother she'd lost. Amala must 1ve sensed her presence, for she turned.

Falca was right, but not entirely. Amala's smile broadened with a armth not given to a stranger. "You're Ellele," she said.

"Yes, I've taken care of you for a while," Ellele said, smiling, :o, at the silver brush Amala held in her other hand, the one Ellele 1d used so often as they sat together by the hearth.